# THE HUNGRY BLADE

# THE HUNGRY BLADE

## LAWRENCE DUDLEY

A ROY HAWKINS THRILLER

**BLACK STONE**

PUBLISHING

Printed in the United States of America

First edition: 2020
ISBN 978-1-5385-5701-3
Fiction / Thrillers / Espionage

1 3 5 7 9 10 8 6 4 2

CIP data for this book is available
from the Library of Congress

Blackstone Publishing
31 Mistletoe Rd.
Ashland, OR 97520

www.BlackstonePublishing.com

# -1-

*Sixteen months before the bombing of Pearl Harbor*

It was rather unnerving, the way the wires vibrated. It wasn't merely the loud twanging noise they made. No, you could actually see the wires snapping back and forth in a blur, slightly flexing the canvas around the attachments on the flying boat's big biplane wings, ready to shred the fabric away.

The pilot looked back. If there was danger he didn't seem particularly concerned, and Roy Hawkins didn't give a damn. A single thought occupied his mind: *Get there. Now. Before the bastards give up and sail off.*

Hawkins smiled, shook his head and clamped his hands over his ears. The pilot, Flying Officer Matthew Finster, grinned back, took a deep breath and shouted over the thunder of the twin engines overhead, even though Hawkins was only on the jump seat at the back of the cabin a yard away. "Now you know why we call it the flying birdcage, sir!"

Hawkins grinned back and shrugged. That was fine, he wasn't about to insult the young pilot's first command, even though he probably was only three or four years younger than Hawkins. But at twenty-five, like Hawkins, you could easily be the "old man" in a unit today, the way the services were all exploding in size.

1

The deferential "sir" felt strange, but then it was all rather strange anyway. As an undercover agent of the British Secret Intelligence Service, Roy Hawkins was an experienced practitioner of all the espionage black arts: deception, camouflage, insinuating yourself into the unwitting trust of others, frequent betrayal, theft, every form of sabotage from planting fake information to blowing things up, and finally, killing those who trusted you, if—and when—duty called for it, as it occasionally did.

Only this time Hawkins was infiltrating his own country's air force. That's what it felt like. Hawkins had never worn any kind of uniform in his entire life until about five hours ago. Now he was kitted out in the full day uniform of an RAF officer, and a high-ranking one, a group captain. It was quite the promotion. But security was paramount. He could not let on who he really was, other than to a few authorized persons.

*Shouldn't be such a big deal*, Hawkins thought. *But that's the thing*, he realized. *This lacks the clarity of knowing who I'm fighting, having people around who are enemies. The Nazis, Hitler, are my Polaris, the dark star that keeps me on track, that I navigate by.*

*When the car dropped me off on the pier at the base in Bermuda*, Hawkins recalled, *Finster and his crew had leapt to attention, snapping off sharp salutes, holding them for a long awkward moment. Only realized I had to return them when the liaison officer called out a brisk "at ease." I should've done that*, he thought. There had been brief introductions, more *sir*-ing, and odd expressions in the eyes of the men. Surprise. A touch of envy—*he's a group captain already?*—and possibly a touch of resentment. Also Hawkins was Royal Air Force and they were Royal *Canadian* Air Force, and there were some inevitable tensions at being under what was in truth another nation's command, however close the Commonwealth was.

Outside the plane's window sky and sea merged into an indistinct blue haze, shadows under the few brilliantly white fluffy clouds the only indication you were right side up. Then a black speck appeared, not an object but a distortion revealing the real line between blue sea and blue sky.

The Supermarine Stranraer of 5 Squadron, RCAF, banked and turned. Out the port-side window Hawkins could finally see their destination in the distance—two ships idling a hundred fifty miles off Bermuda:

the corvette HMS *Dendrobium* and her—and Hawkins's—quarry, the Chilean freighter *Santa Lopez*. Finster expertly throttled down, lining his flying patrol boat to land right between the two ships.

Now the seriously nerve-racking part: landing on the water, not in the *slightly* safer confines of a harbor, but in the rough of the open ocean. Finster said he had done it. A few times. Well, maybe once or twice. Back at Coastal Command HQ in Bermuda the CO had antagonistically demanded to know if it was really all *that* important. "We don't make a habit of this," he'd added. Hawkins had barely heard him. His answer had been a hard and flinty *yes*, Hawkins's word rushing hard on the CO's, hurriedly cutting him off, without elaboration, in a tone that said *don't dare think about asking*. Finster quickly volunteered. He was eager to go, *do something*. They all were.

The ocean rushed up, the smooth felty look opening into a menacing three- to four-foot chop, dusted with slight edges of white. Finster glanced back then again, now slightly uneasy, but also concerned.

"Aren't you going to take those off, sir?" pointing at Hawkins's sunglasses. "Safety?" *Damn*, Hawkins thought. *That's something else I'm supposed to know. No matter, I'll be off this thing and on the ship in a few minutes.* He quickly pocketed the sunglasses, tightening his belt and shoulder harness.

Moments later the keel caught the top of the first wave, suddenly decelerating hard, throwing them painfully forward against the straps, and then bounced up like a ball thrown against a hard floor. It slammed down again, into a trough, jamming them down into the seats, jaws and teeth clacking together, and bounded back up at a jarring angle, the starboard float plowing through the wave, disappearing for a split second, the wingtip nearly touching the water. The plane sailed up in a sickening roller-coaster climb and back down at an angle, snapping their heads side to side from the jolt. Finster expertly throttled one engine, straightening it out, the plane slowing, then evenly catching the top of the next wave, slowing the plane more. A couple more wrenching, vision-blurring, teeth-chattering bounces and the Stranraer settled into the water, the plane climbing only the waves now, water cresting over the bow.

Finster turned and headed for the *Dendrobium* and its catch. Amazingly enough, it was only a football pitch away. He glanced back at Hawkins, took a deep, relaxed breath and mouthed the words "made it." Hawkins loosened his safety harness, leaned forward and patted Finster on the shoulder. The pilot smiled back. Then Hawkins noticed the starboard window by his shoulder. It now had a long diagonal crack. He pointed it out to Finster, then leaned back.

"Now that we're down, you do understand we don't *land* these things on the ocean. It's more of a controlled crash."

"Right."

The HMS *Dendrobium* already had a boat in the water. Finster let his copilot taxi over, turning back to Hawkins, hesitating. The motors were quiet now.

"Group Captain, sir. If I may—" he hesitated. "Are you Canadian?" Hawkins shook his head. It was a common question. His transatlantic accent—half American, half English—threw people off. Americans assumed he was British and the British took him for a Yank. Now the Canadians thought he was one of them.

"No. English mother, American father."

"Oh, I see." Finster looked confused, then disappointed. "I was hoping for some pointers, you know, to advance. Our RCAF ranks are more limited than yours. But you didn't transfer over?"

"No. Sorry. No advice to give."

*If I wasn't in MI6 I'd probably be asking you for pointers*, Hawkins thought. *Have to start at the beginning, qualify for flight school if I wanted that, like anyone else.*

The launch pulled alongside. Hawkins shook hands with Finster and his crew and stepped into the small boat, slipping his sunglasses back on, nodding at the CPO over the noise of the Stranraer's idling engines. The chief snapped off a quick salute. After a hesitant second Hawkins remembered he was supposed to salute back. Hawkins leaned in to the chief's ear.

"Where's your skipper?"

# -2-

Minutes later Hawkins clambered up the ladder of the *Santa Lopez*. It was an old steamer, probably dating from one of the Allied shipbuilding programs of the last war. Irregular splotches of rust marring her hull had been carelessly painted over with already bubbling black paint, giving the impression you could easily punch your fist through in a cloud of dust. At the top Lieutenant Commander Trevor Blake and several of his crew watched as Hawkins quickly reached the deck and barely remembered to salute again. They all had the usual slightly surprised looks. Hawkins counted the three stripes on Blake's sleeve and stuck out his hand.

"Commander, thank you for waiting. Anything since your last report?"

Blake gaped at him a second. "Nothing—I—see here! Are you actually an air force officer?" He scowled and pointed down. "Is that your uniform? Those pants don't fit! And when's the last time you had a haircut?"

Hawkins felt his temper start to rise, then thought, *No, no, not now, not him.* But he'd half expected it. The uniform was hastily borrowed, the pants were tailored for a much shorter man, the cuffs six inches above his ankles. His hair, always stylishly Left Bank long, now reached his shirt collar and a tad more.

Hawkins ignored Blake's finger, squinting at him in the intense sunlight, casually slipping glasses and hands into his pockets. He looked around the deck a moment at the other men, then nodded his head toward the rail, out of hearing. Blake reluctantly followed.

"Yes. You have probably guessed I am with the SIS—you must keep that strictly confidential."

Blake's face was winding up in an irritably quizzical expression. "Are you a Yank?"

"No. Well, actually, I have dual nationality. I mostly grew up in London. As an undercover SIS officer I mainly travel on my American passport."

"Oh."

"You may not be aware we all have reserve ranks. As a senior agent I am a reserve colonel, captain or group captain. I happened to choose RAF." That was a bluff. The rank was undefined, more theoretical than anything else. Like the coat, it'd been borrowed from the base commander back at Darrell's Island. But he had to live up to it now. It did mean he was two grades higher than a naval lieutenant commander. *Just as well,* Hawkins thought, *have to assert myself here.*

Blake looked like he was practically gagging. He was old enough to comfortably be Hawkins's father, yet another reservist with experience in the last war called back to service. *Go easy,* Hawkins thought. *This must be galling.*

Hawkins was currently assigned to British Security Coordination in New York, a new umbrella organization set up to fight Nazi espionage and subversion in the Western Hemisphere and stand ready as a fallback head-quarters for British Intelligence if Britain fell. Which, for all they knew, could be imminent.

Early that morning his boss, William Stephenson, code-named W, had warned him. *Remember to look at it through his eyes. First, an intelligence operation, always irregular. An RAF officer on his ship. And not only are you in charge, you may outrank him. Don't throw your weight around.*

Blake's eyes kept flicking back and forth, from Hawkins's face to the four blue stripes of an RAF group captain on his jacket sleeve. That did fit, the base commander and Hawkins were the same size. The pants belonged to a flying officer who was in fact rather short. The naval base had been too far away, on the other end of the island, and they'd been in a hurry so Hawkins was now committed to the RAF.

"How could you possibly have earned that rank by now?"

*Earned?* Hawkins thought. *Fine.*

"Four days ago in upstate New York I confiscated—no, that's not the right word—I *stole* forty *million* dollars' worth of Swiss bearer bonds from an Abwehr agent."

"Million?"

"Million."

"Wait—wait. You were where? New York?"

"One hundred and eighty miles north of New York City. Halfway to Montreal."

Blake looked increasingly stunned. The idea of covering such a distance in so little time seemed to throw him, too.

"Four days ago?"

"Righto. And the bonds. Do you know where they are now?" Blake shook his head. "In the subterranean vault of the First National City Bank of New York in Manhattan. That deposit increased Britain's reserves of foreign exchange on hand by about forty percent. Because of the nature of the assets, they've already been mortgaged for about a hundred million dollars in Yank war material."

"What were they doing?"

*Damn,* Hawkins thought, *that's not going to help, this is going to come off as confrontational.* "I can't tell you that. I can say the Germans are bringing more money in to finance their covert operations, possibly substantially more. We want to either stop it from going through or seize what they have. What have you found?"

The HMS *Dendrobium* passed behind Hawkins, continuously circling and zigzagging around and around the slowly drifting *Santa Lopez* and the RCAF Stranraer bobbing in the water between them. Blake looked up, distracted, shook his head as if he still hardly believed it all, watching his own ship circle around them.

"Look, we have to get out of here. It's goddamn dangerous sitting dead in the water. In this clear air a U-boat can see the smoke from the stacks twenty or twenty-five miles away. We're sitting ducks. We've ransacked this ship from one end to the other. There's not a suspicious thing on it—a load of French Michelin tires bound for Veracruz and then Valparaiso via Panama. We've gone through the cabins, the engine rooms, the hold, the food lockers, everything—nothing."

"The bunkers?" That really pissed Blake off.

"It's been converted to oil!" he half shouted at Hawkins. Blake started to turn away.

*Damn. Dumb*, Hawkins thought. *Ignorant. I'm losing him. He's too busy worrying about his ship.*

"Ah. I see. Skipper, I'm not supposed to do this, it's strictly against orders, we all could be shot, but I know I can trust a man with your years of command experience with this information. We have a hard communications intercept from the same source as those bonds. There's something here."

That instantly settled Blake down. His attention snapped back from his ship.

"Bloody hell." Blake fumbled in his jacket pocket for a worn meerschaum pipe and pouch and started filling it. He sighed heavily, obviously thinking hard, eyes flicking from the *Santa Lopez's* bridge castle, its derricks to the bow. "Still, I—"

# -3-

"Captain! If you please!"

It was the captain of the *Santa Lopez*. He'd broken free from the crowd of men held in the bow. A CPO reached for his elbow to haul him back. Blake casually waved the chief away with the now lit pipe.

"Captain, I apologize, but we are going to have to detain you a bit more."

"You have no right. This is piracy."

"I do apologize. This is Group Captain Hawkins of the Royal Air Force—Group Captain Hawkins, Captain Perez." The captain shook Hawkins's hand in a very courtly way, very slightly nodding and bowing. He was a very thin, older man, pushing seventy, with thick white hair peeking from under his white officer's cap and a thin grayish mustache. "The group captain has generously flown out to get this over for you as fast as possible. We're waiting for his clearance."

*Smooth*, Hawkins thought, also tossing responsibility for a potentially bad international incident onto someone other than the Royal Navy. Institutionally quite smart. He'd probably done this a good bit, in two wars, now. Perez spoke English fairly well, which made sense, the Anglophilic way he was dressed, in a blue blazer, white duck pants and a silk ascot around his neck. He might have been out for a day at Henley, except his shirt collar was rather grimy and black. And group captain. *I guess it's official, now*, Hawkins thought.

Blake continued, "Captain, are you absolutely sure no unauthorized personnel boarded your ship?"

"No. And what does it matter. We are a neutral ship. You have no right to board us or hold us." Perez paused a long moment, working hard to stay calm and hold his temper. "I assure you there is nothing on my ship. This is piracy."

Blake briskly walked back to his waiting sailors.

"Men, I want you all to think about anything you might have overlooked. This is most serious. We have it on the best authority there's something on this ship, and—"

Hawkins interrupted. "Skipper—what you just said."

"What?"

"Also Captain Perez. You both said *on*."

"Of course. It—"

"Wait." Hawkins reached into his jacket pocket for his copy of the intercept, checking it. "Yes." He held it up so Blake alone could see. "They abbreviate something awful in these things. You see? They only used the letter *n*. We thought conventionally. Cargo *N* ship. On."

"Right. On board."

"No. Not on. In. It's not *on* the ship. It's *in* the ship itself."

"Good god. Perhaps, but where?"

"Sir?"

A very young sailor, couldn't have been more than seventeen, his red blotchy face an illustration from a dermatology textbook, was holding up his hand. It was black from crawling around in the tires. One of the chiefs barked at him, "Davies!"

"'S all right, Chief. What is it, lad?" Blake said.

"Beggin' your pardon, sir." He quickly glanced at the angry chief glaring at him and shot off a salute. "I saw something strange down there."

"Go on."

"Bulkhead in the bow covered with fresh paint. There's not another speck of fresh paint anywhere on this ugly old tub. I think I ought to know fresh paint when I see it, sir. I've been chippin' and paintin' ever since I landed in the navy and—" Blake stilled him with another wave of the pipe.

"Lead the way, son." He and Hawkins quickly followed.

"Don't get your hopes up. Probably nothing," Blake whispered to Hawkins. "The chiefs tend to be overprotective of the captain. Important to be reasonably accessible, though. The men need to know that." He clamped his pipe into his teeth and agilely followed Davies down the ladder into the hold, Hawkins right above. They followed to the bow, carefully stepping from one wobbling stack of tires to another, holding on to the deck supports above. Davies held his light up to the gray wall.

"See, sir?"

Blake pulled a key from his pocket and scratched the paint. It was still slightly soft, only a few weeks old, and clean. He began tapping across the bulkhead with the bottom of his pipe. It rang hollow. He put the pipe back in his mouth, puffed deliberately a moment and then turned and bellowed with surprising force toward the hatch. "Chief McCullum!" His head instantly swung down into the opening, halfway upside down. "Clear a pathway through these tires and have Machinist Mate Humphries and his acetylene torch brought over."

# -4-

Hawkins impatiently waited as Humphries and Davies slowly lowered the steel plate, ready to grab it from them and fling it aside, his anticipation and frustration rising by the second. *What's there?* Hawkins thought. *Can't see, damn it.* The sailor turned to his skipper first, of course, blocking Hawkins's view. Hawkins craned up on his toes, trying to see over Blake's shoulder, holding back, barely, although he happily would've shoved him aside. Blake peered in, then leaned back to let Hawkins look.

"Doubt this is your money, Hawkins." The space was filled with tall oblong wood packing cases. They were fresh, custom built, the plywood clean and white, barely a scuff on them. "This looks like smuggled guns."

*Ah hell*, Hawkins thought. Probably not money. Exactly the size of guns. His stomach began to sink. *Bugger it all, anyway*, he thought. Another wild goose chase. *All this for what, a load of rifles? Who cares?*

Blake pointed at one. The chiefs pulled it out. A lock dangled from one side.

*A lock?* Hawkins relaxed, then smiled, reaching out.

"I'll take it from here." He pulled his little leather lockpick set out and began working the keyhole. Blake watched, one eyebrow raised, puffing on his pipe.

"My, my. That's an interesting talent."

"Comes in handy in my line of work."

"No doubt. Keep you off my ship."

Hawkins smiled, slapped the lock on top of the case and lowered the door. Inside, nestled between wooden dividers, was a row of canvases on frames.

*Now what*, Hawkins thought. *Damn. Paintings? Paintings! What in the name of holy god on high?* He pulled one out. It was a cubist still life, a good one. He flipped it over. There was a large gallery label on the back. LE DÉJEUNER—GEORGES BRAQUE. Hawkins read off the inscription and the address in French.

The sense of surprise was actual shock, even after all these years in the Secret Service, where one was often surprised—it was that unexpected. *Paintings?* He looked over and down into the secret compartment. Maybe ten cases. *Goddamn. What's this all worth?* he thought. *A bloody fortune, that's what. What could they possibly be up to they'd need so much money? Could be millions here*, he thought. Actually, tens of millions. The mind reeled at it, simply staggering. For a second he almost wished the Nazis were running guns, although god only knows why they'd want to do that, either.

Blake studied the painting a second.

"Modern art, I assume?"

"Yes. An important one."

The commander peered inside the compartment, then motioned for the flashlight and shined it in. ECKHARDT had been crudely painted on the side of several cases.

"An artist?"

"Not that I ever heard. Probably the consignor or consignee."

"Oh, look there." Blake pointed to the back, flashing the light on another inscription:

**EILVERSAND NACH VERACRUZ FÜR ECKHARDT. HANDGRIFF SORGFÄLTIG. DIESE SEITE OBEN. HALTEN SIE TROCKEN.**

"What's that?"

"Express shipment to Veracruz for Eckhardt. Handle with care. This side up. Keep dry."

"You read German? And French?"

"Yes, my father was an executive for Western Union based in London, we also spent time in Paris and Zurich. Went to school in both places."

"I see"—Blake glanced warily at his men—"why they want you where they have you."

"Yes. After that I came back to the States for a while. Then when my father died—he was gassed in the last one—I went back to Europe as the sales representative of an American valve manufacturer. Went all over, great practice."

Blake absorbed that, carefully gazing at Hawkins over a long puff on his pipe, then grunted slightly.

"So sorry about your father. That's a hard thing. I lost my younger brother—Passchendaele. He was eighteen. You were in Germany, then?"

"Thanks. Yes. Saw altogether too much for comfort."

"How so?"

"One bright day like this I went into a factory in East Prussia to sell some valves and discovered they were making poison gas."

"Which one? The gas, I mean."

"Phosgene. Couldn't miss it. Mixing carbon dioxide with chlorine. That's why, or how, I got into all this."

"Ah, I see. That was personal."

"In part."

"You didn't go to the Yanks?"

"No. They don't have an intelligence service."

Blake frowned. "That's a bad joke. Seriously, why—"

"No, really, they don't!"

For nearly a minute he blankly stared at Hawkins, struck dumb before finally whispering, "Good heavens." He mulled the thought another long moment, shook that appalling tidbit off with a roll of his head and pulled another painting from its slot.

"Now this is more to my taste, look at these cheery sunflowers."

"That's a Van Gogh."

"How do you know that? You haven't seen the back."

"I don't have to. He's famous." Blake very carefully slid it back in.

"And I suppose it's quite valuable."

"Extremely. There's millions here."

"I can see it's time to set course back to Bermuda."

"Yes. I need to get a haircut."

Blake burst out laughing. "We'll hurry, then."

# -5-

The HMS *Dendrobium* turned and disappeared off the stern, seemingly back on the hunt for U-boats. Finster had lifted off earlier. He was going to set back down, tie up to the *Dendrobium* and wait with Blake once the *Santa Lopez* was out of sight.

Hawkins walked around the superstructure to the *Santa Lopez's* foredeck, inspecting the cargo derricks, checking the hatches. He turned and looked up. Davies saluted from the flying bridge, obviously enjoying himself, his Lee-Enfield casually dangling over his shoulder. *Ah, well,* Hawkins thought. The young sailor had volunteered to help escort the *Santa Lopez* back to Bermuda. Originally Blake was only going to assign a pair of chiefs to the prize crew, but since the boy'd spotted the painted bulkhead it seemed a nice reward to let him come along, too. Hawkins headed back up to the bridge—*there'll be a better view from up there,* Hawkins thought. *If I'm right. Only one way to find out quickly and we're running out of time.*

It started three hours later, four hours out of Bermuda. *About right,* Hawkins thought, *they can't chance getting closer to the harbor and the rest of the Royal Navy. Too bad I didn't coax Blake into a bet—he was skeptical.* A small puff of smoke from one of the ventilators and a couple of deck crew began shouting "¡Fuego, fuego!" running around, flipping open hatches and hose lockers.

Jollying around with Finster and Blake—infiltrating the Royal Air Force, as it were—had felt like a lark. But it still put Hawkins in his usual undercover mode: feelings and emotions battened down, locked away behind a carefully constructed facade. Now, despite the warm sun bearing down, he still felt a fresh hot flush of heat. *Nazis! Here*, he thought. *Under my feet. Trying to set this ship on fire and destroy the evidence.* The composed mode, the careful, calculated facade of the undercover agent blew off with a gust of sea breeze, the languor of an ocean cruise gone, too. Hitler himself might as well have been down there. *No more damn waiting*, Hawkins thought. *Time to fight.*

Martindale, one of the chiefs, an older burly man with a white crew cut and a nose professionally flattened by a boxer, started for the starboard ladder. "I'll check, sir!"

There was a loud rush of steam escaping followed by a thudding sound and vibration as the engine abruptly stopped. *That means there's at least two Nazi agents aboard*, Hawkins thought. *Predictable. Didn't think they'd send millions in loot off unguarded. Need to catch at least one of them, find out what they know, if we can. Bloody buggers. Not this time.*

"No! Go down in the hull," Hawkins said to Martindale, "take the upper tween deck, get forward, guard that hidden compartment." Hawkins stepped out onto the flying bridge. "Davies, you, too!" Hawkins opened his coat, pulled a long cardboard tube from his waistband, held it over his head with both hands and carefully fired the rocket flare straight up. The red streak hissed up a few hundred feet, popped and dangled a flare on a little parachute. Then he tossed his hat into the bridge, drew his Browning Hi-Power from his shoulder holster and started down an inside ladder. He turned into a narrow passageway, reflexively checking the clip—all twelve rounds, good—running to the back to the engine room. An alarm bell ringing, followed by a klaxon. Men began pouring out of the cabins.

"Get back!" Shouting, pointing the Hi-Power, holding it out with both hands. They leapt back, latching the doors with loud slams. Hawkins reached the end and headed down another ladder to the engine room.

He edged around the corner, looking down. One greasy-looking man in blue work clothes and a black leather cap had six members of the engine crew cornered with a revolver. A couple were wide-eyed and scared, but the others were talking and gesturing, not taking it seriously at all, pointing off at something, obviously trying to talk him out of it. One of the hostages saw Hawkins from the corner of his eye and turned his head, gaping. Locking eyes with Hawkins, he nodded his head so very slightly toward the gunman, as if the man in the air force uniform needed telling. The gunman caught that gesture and instantly swung up and around and fired, too fast, before ducking behind a large steam pipe. The engine crew scattered, jumping down through service grates and clambering down another ladder. The bullet struck the wall a foot above Hawkins's head, ricocheting harmlessly away.

Mind running on instinct now, in the moment, Hawkins stuck his gun hand out, first high, then low, a quick darting motion. Two more shots rang, two more clanging, zinging ricochets rattling around inside the steel walls, slowing down, the ring lowering in pitch with each bounce. Hawkins laid on the floor and edged forward, peering through the grated floor. The man saw him, stepped out and fired another two rounds. *Very good*, Hawkins thought. He slid back, fumbled in his pocket, found a big American silver dollar and tossed it out the entrance. The heavy coin made a deep ringing noise as it bounced. The man appeared from behind the pipe and wildly fired again.

Hawkins stepped out on the open grating over the engine, racing around to get the angle, aiming down. The man had barely managed to snap the revolver shut after reloading.

"No! Drop it!" Nothing. *Probably doesn't speak English*, Hawkins thought. *Maybe German?* "Nein! Lassen Sie es fallen!" The man looked up. Still nothing. *French?* "Relâchez le pistolet!" The man started to swing up. Hawkins instantly fired, putting a round right through the middle of his neck. A steady, hard, fast stream of blood squirted from the severed artery, tracing a dripping, zigzagging course across the pipe and the smooth, white asbestos-covered boiler. Hawkins stared a second—enraged, disgusted and horrified all at once, the rush of his mind demanding action momentarily paused—then stepped back, instinctively looking away, a slightly sick feeling in his stomach. The shut-down professional mode instantly returned. He could hear the man dropping his pistol with a loud, rattling clang. Hawkins stepped up again, coolly looking down. The man seized his neck, making a low gurgling sound, then a loud *uh-uh-uh* from down in his belly, a deep sound of panic and terror, frantically running around behind the boiler, blood shooting in hard pulses between his fingers, fumbling in his pocket for a rag. He'd barely gotten it to his throat when he passed out, collapsing on the deck in a rapidly growing pool of blood.

Hawkins ran down to check, gingerly plucking the revolver from the blood, needing to see but trying not to look at the same time. One of the engine crew popped his head up.

"¡Inglés! ¿Por qué? You kill?" the sailor said, staring at the dead man. His face scrunched in from the effort of assembling enough English. "He say they only want stop ship, get off." For all the world Hawkins wanted to say, *I'd rather not have*, but he now thought and felt nothing but *hurry*.

"Where's the sea cock?"

"We bunked and ate! Together!"

Hawkins poked him hard with the Hi-Power, shouting, "Where's the intake, damn it!"

The sailor pointed down a ladder. "There."

Hawkins motioned him ahead. "Hurry! Hurry!" They almost slid down the ladder like firemen on a station house pole. The man started to point, then hesitated and ran over to a large pipe, peering at something. On top of the pipe a life preserver had been carefully wedged between the intake valve and the side of the ship.

"Don't touch that," Hawkins said. He took his lighter out and flicked it on, checking. A large slit had been cut into the side of one of the jacket's bolsters. He carefully pulled the sides of the cut open. Red sticks of dynamite and a pull-type detonator were inside. A thin wire and a small wooden handle dangled from the slit. The sailor gasped very softly, slightly shaking his head. His whole body seemed to curl in horror, the way leaves do in front of fires.

"They would've killed you all first," Hawkins said. He carefully lifted the life jacket and started back up the ladder.

# -6-

The life jacket was heavy from the dynamite. *Have to hurry*, Hawkins thought. He climbed back up the ladder, holding it carefully, and ran forward through the passageway, then up another ladder, climbing high until he reached the top of the bridge castle and the radio shack. He gently put the life jacket on the deck and quietly edged up to the door, peering in, pressing the Hi-Power against the wall behind the door casing, watching for several seconds. The radio operator was lying on the floor, turned to one side, breathing shallowly, his eyes rolled up into his bloody head. It looked like he'd been badly bludgeoned. Another sailor was standing over him, straddling the body with his legs as he snapped out one drawer after another, flinging the contents about, rummaging around for something. The transmitter, dangling wires, had been pulled out, its top open, revealing the rows of glass vacuum tubes inside. All were dark. Next to it lay a tube chart.

The man suddenly saw Hawkins.

"Looking for something?" Hawkins reached into his pocket and held up the missing vacuum tube, smiling slightly, gently waving it back and forth in his fingers. The man cursed and jammed a fumbling hand into his pocket.

"Don't do it!" Not stopping. *Fine by me*, Hawkins thought, *get a taste of what you deserve, too.* He stepped from behind the door and methodically and easily put a slug into each shoulder. The man silently fell back from the impact. He tried to reach up and grab his right shoulder, then the pain suddenly hit him, a series of quick breathless gasps. In between short pants the man stuttered, first in Spanish, then pidgin English. "¡Por favor! ¡Favor! Please! No me dead! ¡En nombre de dios! Maria and José! Favor! No me dead!"

"Eckhardt?" Hawkins said. "Du bist Eckhardt?" The man stared uncomprehendingly. *He's not German*, Hawkins thought. *The other one I shot didn't speak German, either. Odd ... that's very odd*, he vaguely realized. "Êtes-vous Eckhardt?" The man started shivering, then softly whined in pain. *Damn it*, Hawkins thought, *he doesn't speak much English and I don't speak Spanish.* But Hawkins kept pressing. "The other man, below, is he Eckhardt? Eckhardt?" Nothing, still.

Hawkins ripped the microphone cable out, seized one of the man's trembling hands and then the other, quickly lashing them together and then to the table leg. He ripped open the man's pocket, partially lifting him off the deck. Another pistol, a small Colt auto, a .30 caliber. Hawkins started to angrily fling it hard against the wall behind the radio sets, then caught himself and pocketed the pistol. Pulling up on the cable, provoking another crying gasp, he leaned into the man's face.

"Hold that thought." The man seemed to understand. He nodded. *Yes, you get it*, Hawkins thought. *We'll get something out of you later.* He tossed the vacuum tube aside, breaking it, swung back out of the shack and down the ladder, gingerly picking up the loaded life jacket on the way, holding his breath, his attention now all on that business. *Got to get rid of this*, Hawkins thought, *get rid of it fast.*

As Hawkins came out onto the deck, swinging the vest back to throw, a man leapt from behind a cabinet and tackled him, slamming him against the rail. It was one of the hostages from the engine room, a tall but paunchy man with a droopy burnside mustache curling around his chin. Sweat ran down his face and bulbous nose, streaking over oddly white skin that obviously never saw the deck and sun. *Damn it—damn it—damn it all!* Hawkins thought. *There's another one? Hiding in the hostages? What in hell? Why? Something's wrong.* He knew it instantly, at the bottom of his gut: this was very dangerous.

Hawkins tried to pull up the Hi-Power and shoot him but the man blocked his arm, pushing him back through the hatch into the passageway. Hawkins got his footing again, tightly clutching the life jacket bomb to his chest, turned and managed to slam the man's head against a pipe, then stepped back and slammed him back against it again, leaving a small bloody mark on the pipe. The man cursed, crying in pain, then with a huge primal grunt spun Hawkins out and around and through the hatch onto the deck again. Hawkins planted a foot on the raised lintel of the hatchway and shoved them both forward against the rail. They turned and spun around against it, rolling along the deck, eye to eye, cursing. There was rage but also fear in the man's eyes.

"Don't!" Hawkins shouted. "You can't get away!" No reaction. They spun again. *Bloody fool*, Hawkins thought, anger surging again. "You can't get away!" *Bastard. Fool! Is he a Nazi agent?* Hawkins wondered. He repeated in German, "Anschlag! Sie können nicht weg erhalten!" Nothing. "Vous ne pouvez pas partir!" Nothing. *Might as well be barking like a dog.* The man grunted and hurled them through another turn, both men locked in a tight embrace around the life jacket, trying to rip it away from the other.

"Du bist Eckhardt?" Again, like the man in the radio shack, no reaction. "Ihr name? Eckhardt—" *Ah, this is ridiculous*, Hawkins thought, *he doesn't understand. Who cares, anyway, going to get yours, too.*

A bullet zinged past their heads. The man looked up, startled. *Didn't expect that, did you?* Hawkins thought. *But—who's shooting? There's a fourth? Two? Sure. Three? Maybe. But four! What! Why? Ah, bugger it all.* The shot was high, it must've come from one of the forward cargo gantries. With a tremendous heave the man shoved them forward against the bulkhead and out of the line of fire. Hawkins spun him around again and onto the edge of a deck cabinet, banging the man's head against it, and again, as if sense could be pounded into it.

"See," Hawkins shouted, "they don't give a damn about you! Let go!" Instead, the man heaved back, spinning them around again, and tried kicking Hawkins, missing and hitting the bulkhead between his legs. "Why are you doing this? Warum? Warum?" Total incomprehension in his eyes. "Pourquoi? Pourquoi faites-vous ceci?" *Damn it! If I only knew some Spanish* … "Eckhardt? Eckhardt?" Still no reaction. Hawkins tried kicking back, tripping them both. They fell to the deck with a painful, jolting crash. The fall broke both men's grasp. The man jumped up, then looked out, startled, into the distance, as Hawkins struggled to get back to his feet and aim.

The man grabbed the life jacket and flung himself under the chain in the gangway opening in the rail, sliding over the side. Hawkins barely had time to roll and catch the little wood handle before it slipped away, getting his chin over the side in the nick of time to see the man going down, clutching the life jacket to his chest, a smile on his face. The man was looking sideways at the empty lifeboat he'd already dropped, laughing, thinking he'd gotten away, until a split second later when he finally saw the gleam of the wire, a flicking look of alarm in his eyes.

*He doesn't know the bomb's there*, Hawkins thought, *knew*, in a split-second flash. Then the lanyard played out, the slightest tug on the handle.

The life jacket instantly exploded, a quick white spark, a flashbulb going off, then a big pink cloud, a bright cherry-blossom pink, the lovely color of a cheery spring dress on a young woman waiting to be taken somewhere sunny on a nice date. Hawkins blinked and felt droplets of blood and spoor stinging his face. He blinked again, his eyes red with blood, wiping them with his sleeve. There was something in the depth of his mind—or his gut—that went, very quickly, as fast as a flashbulb—*don't feel. Don't feel*, he felt more than thought, so quick. *Batten down that hatch. Feel nothing. Be fast. Think fast. Go cold. Keeping fighting. No anger. No disgust. Stay alive.*

Another bullet rang out from the gantry and he hurled himself away behind the bulkhead, thoughts ricocheting like bullets in the engine room, only speeding up and rising in a frantic pitch instead of slowing down.

*He didn't know the charge was there*, Hawkins thought, sorting it all in a frenzy. *So he was a hostage. Or—they weren't working together? Or was he a plant. Then who—what's next?* In the distance he saw what had startled the man: a large approaching biplane. *Finster, thank god we have the plane, bloody goddamn foul-up. Flushing them out? Necessary. Using ourselves as bait? Mistake. Three?* Another shot rang out from above and forward. *No—four! Wasn't aiming at the man with the droopy mustache. Aiming at me,* he thought. *Only need one or two to guard the shipment, maybe three. Why four? All biting each other in a circle, angry dogs going wild in a yard.* His fury suddenly, unexpectedly rose again, now at himself. *Damn, damn, damn ... shouldn't have assumed they would only guard it, wouldn't lay a trap, too. Damn it! Damn it!*

# -7-

Finster's Stranraer was gingerly floating down for a landing, coming at the *Santa Lopez* at a steep oblique angle, nose slightly up. It was getting late in the afternoon and a stiff wind had picked up, blowing a good rolling six-foot chop, at least two feet higher than before. The plane settled down and caught evenly across the first wave, a shuddering deceleration, Hawkins could see Finster and his flight crew painfully snap forward in their safety harnesses. It went up, the nose lifting, and hit the next wave at an angle. Hawkins inhaled and held his breath as the plane wrenched up again at a high climb for a heart-stopping second, nearly vertical, then tipped over and belly flopped onto the next with a huge splash that almost hid it for a moment. It bounded up again, twisting at an angle, starboard wingtip slicing the waves, the outrigger float plowing deep in, then rebounded again, digging in the port side. A couple of slamming, twisting bounces and it began cutting through the waves like a race boat, throwing up huge V-shaped waves, washing the lower wings. *A controlled crash, indeed*, Hawkins thought. Finster and his copilot revved one motor, almost standing on the rudder, and aimed the nose of the plane straight at the accommodation ladder on the side of the ship. It missed it, softly butting nose-first into the *Santa Lopez* with a dull thud.

Down below Lieutenant Commander Blake—he'd clearly taken command of the boarding party—flipped open the hatch on the flying boat's forward gun station, climbing up, standing on the bow, his men boiling out behind him, all slapping shut the bolts on their .303s. More sailors began climbing out the rear gun station and the cockpit hatch. Finster killed the motors. Blake threw a rope and a grappling hook over the rail and his men began hauling up a rope net with surprising speed. The skipper pulled a big Webley .455 from his uniform blazer—he still very properly had his white officer's cap on, too—seized the rope ladder with one hand and without looking back shouted, "Follow me!" and began scrambling up the net. Several sailors, shouldering their Lee-Enfields, followed him, the ones behind the cockpit running across the wings, the heavily painted and varnished canvas cracking and breaking under their shoes.

Finster popped his head out. "Not on the wings! Not on the wings!" Another shot rang out from the gantry. Finster ducked. The men on the wings looked up, saw something and fired a ragged volley as Blake reached the top. Finster and his aircrew gave up on the wings—it was too late, anyway, there were rips, pockmarks and indentations all along them now—lashed the Stranraer to the net, drew their pistols and followed Blake and the sailors up the ladder. Blake waved a hand behind him, checking his sailors and the airmen back, and carefully peered over the rail.

Hawkins was edging to the corner of the bridge castle, looking up for the sniper. As the navy men fired, he spotted a man in overalls hastily climbing down the back of one of the cranes. The sailors fired and hit him, several times, halfway down. The man jerked back, his head flipping around in a circle, one foot catching and wedging in the steel rungs, swinging him around and upside down at an angle. His rifle fell and clattered to the deck, followed first by a splattering of blood, then a messy *plop* as his shattered brains slid out of his open skull.

Hawkins waved at Blake and pointed at the sniper hanging down.

"There! Come—" But another pair of shots crackled out, this time directly above, from the bridge overhead. Both rounds missed, one going over the lieutenant commander's head, another ricocheting off the inside of the steel railing. Blake ducked back down.

*Goddam it all,* Hawkins thought, *more? More! How many can there be?*

One dead in the engine room, one lying on the floor of the radio shack, the pink cloud, the dead sniper on the gantry, there had to be at least one below setting the fire and—given the speed of those shots, two men firing from the bridge. *Six? Maybe seven? Eight? Makes no sense. Why would they send that many? Too many mouths to flap. And how could they spare that many agents? Insane. Every bit.*

The men standing on the wings caught the shots and began firing at the bridge. Hawkins angled around the corner and looked up. The muzzle of a rifle pointed out, barely a puff of smoke, then jerked back at a hard angle. Forward, some smoke was starting to rise from an open hatch. Broken glass tinkled down as the men on the wings shot out the bridge windows trying to hit the shooters, pinning them down. Blake poked his head up, followed by his men. Hawkins waved. With a huge heave Blake clambered over the rail and flung himself against the bulkhead next to Hawkins. More shots rang out overhead followed by another volley from the rail and the wings. Hawkins began loading more bullets into the Hi-Power as Blake checked his Webley.

"Where's your cutlass?" Hawkins said. It was the tense banter of men trying to distance themselves from an ugly world whirling around them. Both eyed the other, thinking the other man was grimacing and breathing very hard.

"They don't issue us cutlasses anymore."

"Pity. I suppose they got rid of grog, too?"

"They're trying. Today's navy has the soul of an accountant."

"It's the way of the world."

"Was that pink cloud what I think it was?"

"It was."

"That must've smarted."

"I would imagine."

"What's going on? You were right they'd guard it—but—"

"There are more men than I thought. Sorry. I've fouled up here."

"How many?"

"Six, seven, maybe eight. I'm not sure."

"What? What the hell for!"

"I know. Makes no sense at all. Crazy. Simply crazy."

"Bugger. Glad I have a ship with a cannon and a crew."

"Yes. I've got to get below. Do you need me?"

"Young man, the Royal Navy has been boarding ships for four hundred years. We don't need any help from the air force." In the distance HMS *Dendrobium* was rapidly bearing down on them at full throttle, smoke billowing from its funnel. More shots from the men on the wings.

"Ah, yes. I happily stand corrected. There's two wounded men in the shack, one of whom will talk. He needs attention right away before he bleeds out. We want him alive."

"Righto. We'll retake the bridge, then get the wounded over to my ship." He gestured Hawkins off. He saluted with his Hi-Power, took a deep breath as Blake waved his men up and bolted back into the hatch and down the passageway. Another volley of shots rang out behind him.

# -8-

Hawkins exited a hatch onto the upper tween deck. Massive flat rows of tires were stacked to the ceiling. Somewhere tires were burning, filling the hold with growing, billowing clouds of acrid, choking smoke. Hawkins began carefully crawling on hands and knees along the top of the stacked tires, staying low, trying to avoid coughing and giving himself away. He stopped and tied his handkerchief over his mouth. It didn't help much. His eyes started watering. Overhead he could hear the sharp *ping!* of bullets hitting the deck, then here and there the quick thud of footsteps as Blake's sailors began running from derrick to raised hatch and on to another derrick, seeking cover, followed by the muffled cracks of their .303s.

Nearly impossible to see, a row of lightbulbs stretched toward the bow, dim stars in a cloudy, dirty sky. Hawkins began crawling from one wobbly stack to another, edging toward a deep long well that ran through the center of the hold from the engine room to the bow. He leaned over the edge, peering down. There was another tween deck below the one he was on, giant balconies stuffed with tires, the bottom of the hold obscured in total darkness.

Whoever set the fire had to be down here—but where? And how far down was it? One way to find that out. He pushed a tire off the stack in front and listened, counting. *One thousand one, one thousand two ...* A soft *thunk* and then a springy bouncing sound. *Thirty-two feet per second, around sixty feet,* he thought. *Won't try jumping that …*

He began moving forward again, carefully staying away from the swaying tires on the edge of the well. He stood, holding on to a steel rafter, peering forward. One of the dim stars broke from its constellation and began moving, swaying slightly, abruptly growing larger, accompanied by a rolling, whirling sound. It was a large ball of burning tires. As it zoomed closer he could see it suspended by a chain on a traveling crane overhead, coming straight at him. He tried to step aside and duck—it followed him. A man must be behind it, pushing it.

Hawkins instantly fired three shots into the burning mass, sparks and shards of rubber flying off. No effect. Too many tires! It half-passed him in the dark and swung back around, a blast of fiery air and smoke as it passed. Hawkins holstered the Hi-Power and grabbed the steel rafter overhead with both hands. As the burning ball rushed in, he heaved up and kicked the chain with both feet, slamming it back around. A man's cry, faint, behind the tires. Another push, the tires flaming in toward Hawkins, another kick back. Then another swing and pass straight at him, another kick back.

*He can't see, either,* Hawkins thought. His own eyes were watering madly now. As the flames receded for a second he stretched down, felt with his feet, and dropped straight into a stack of tires, catching himself with his arms and elbows, ducking his head. Eyes closed tight, he felt the intense heat waft overhead, opened one watery lid and saw a foot and ankle. He reached out and grabbed the ankle, pulling hard, yanking the man off balance, tripping him forward. The ball of burning tires swung back and slammed right into the man. A loud scream—*"Ah! Ah!"*

Hawkins scrambled up, feet climbing tires like rungs on a ladder, standing atop the stack again. With no one pushing them, the burning tires aimlessly spun around, slowing. Still impossible to see. Something lightly grazed his head. He reached up and touched it. A steel pipe, a handle. He seized it. Now he had the tires! The man scrambled to his feet, still grunting and crying in pain. Hawkins shoved forward, toward the sound. A jolt and cry as it connected again. He shoved the tires away, down the trolley. The man was barely visible for a split second, an outline of glowing sparks and tiny flames of burning bits of tires and clothes. He saw Hawkins, too, and reached into his pocket. *A gun!* Hawkins drew his Hi-Power first, blasting away at the general direction of the fading silhouette. Most missed, uselessly ricocheting off the rafters or the opposite tween deck. But one had hit true. The man cried out, slightly stumbling and tripping, falling, pushing the swaying tires. He started to go down, grabbing at the edge, then slipped and fell all the way to the bilge, a loud receding cry.

All the tires now started tumbling. Hawkins barely caught a rafter overhead with one hand, swinging crazily, holstered the Hi-Power, then grabbed with his free hand as all the tires began a rumbling avalanche into the well. Swinging hand over hand, he inched back to a still-standing stack, and finally got one shaky foot on it, then another, onto safety.

A blast of light. One of the Royal Navy sailors had thrown open a hatch over the well, sunshine pouring through the venting smoke. Several .303s poked over the edge.

"I got him," Hawkins shouted. A hand waved.

Hawkins made his way back to the hatch and then forward. A single thought struck him—*The paintings, are they all right?* As he reached the hidden compartment Chief Martindale and Davies were peering out, coughing lightly, pointing their rifles. They'd climbed inside, picked up the steel plate that'd been cut free and wedged it in front of them for armor.

"Did you get him?" Martindale said. "We knew he was there but we couldn't see him."

"Yes. You can come out."

Martindale nodded and he and Davies began angling the plate away.

Hawkins headed back to the deck. When he got outside the fresh air triggered a paroxysm of coughing. Blake ran up, still waving his Webley.

"You all right?" It took a second for Hawkins to wheeze yes. Blake took him by the arm and guided him to a seat on a hatch. After a minute the coughs started tapering off. Blake wordlessly began picking small pieces of bone from Hawkins's hair. He reached up and felt them too.

"Ah, god, the pink cloud."

"'Fraid so. I think you owe someone a new uniform. I don't think a dry cleaner's going to be able to do much with that. You're absolutely covered with blood."

"I'll have to put a voucher in," followed by another rack of coughs.

Davies popped out beside them, a huge smile on his pimply face, almost jumping up and down, saluting. He burst out, full of excitement, unable to restrain himself.

"That was bloody marvelous, sir! Bloody marvelous! I'm ready for that anytime, sir!"

Hawkins looked at him, expressionless. Then he felt his stomach start to heave. He bolted for the rail and vomited over the side, hard, several times. Wiping his mouth on his dirty sleeve, he tiredly slunk back to Blake, sitting heavily on the hatch.

"Must be the smoke," Hawkins said.

"Of course," Blake said. Davies was staring at Hawkins, his mouth open. Blake waved him away.

The *Dendrobium* had pulled alongside and the crew was throwing lines over, tying up. Captain Perez suddenly appeared on the bridge, gaping out the smashed window of his ship, his mouth open. Hawkins coughed again and gestured at him.

Blake leapt up, pointing and shouting, "Throw that son of a bitch in irons!"

# -9-

General Houghton's big mahogany Hacker speedboat sliced through the waves pushing forty knots. They reached the far end of the Great Sound, the wide expanse of water Bermuda wrapped around like a giant fishhook, then slowed and turned into the Royal Naval Dockyard. *Ah well,* Hawkins thought. The air whipping through his hair never felt so good. Even with deep draughts of the fresh sea breeze he still couldn't get the stench of burning rubber—and the coppery tang of blood—out of his mouth and nostrils. *Hard to believe that was only a few hours ago,* he thought.

Hawkins was back in mufti—who would loan him a uniform now anyway?—after a quick trip to the Princess Hotel in Hamilton and a long hot shower. It'd taken most of the ride back in the launch to brief the general on what had happened on the *Santa Lopez,* which was now tied up at the dockyard next to HMS *Dendrobium.* As the commander of the Imperial Posts and Telegraph Censorship Station on Bermuda, General Houghton was now officially in charge of any intelligence investigation. At the same time he wasn't exactly Hawkins's superior officer, which lent a note of ambiguity to the proceedings. But they'd met each other on Hawkins's recent trip back from Europe, enough that they trusted each other.

Sailors and officers were milling around the old freighter. Bullet holes and ricochet marks all over the bridge castle were visible from the water.

*Look at them all*, Hawkins thought. *Survived that. Great god. What a bloody hell of a mess.*

The numb feeling, deliberate or otherwise, however it came to him, was starting to slip away in little epiphanal waves, his mood bumping up bit by bit, aiming toward an almost giddy high.

Hawkins realized the general—a big, bluff man in khaki shorts, over tanned hairy knees—was looking at him strangely, his gaze sharp, penetrating and concerned. *Oh. I know*, Hawkins thought. *I'm smiling, laughing, that's what it is. Must look damn strange. Got through another bad scrape in one piece, pretty much. I am alive. They are dead. Not going to get me this time. Joke's on you instead.*

Houghton frowned ever so slightly and mouthed his name, watching him carefully. Hawkins shouted over the motors, "I'm fine. Just glad to be here." The general nodded. Yes. He was a veteran of the trenches. He knew.

*I fouled up*, Hawkins thought. *Or did I? Was there any other way to find out if there were hidden agents on that damn ship other than drawing a bull's-eye on my chest? Hauling them in, interrogating the crew of a neutral ship one by one? Impossible. Not quick enough. And a dangerous violation of neutral rights, too far to push. No. No other way. Risky, but I pulled it off anyway.*

When a bullet goes by your head, there's reaction—reflex, actually—and a moment of fear. Then indignation—*how dare they!* Following that was a sense of being thoroughly pissed off and wanting to get even. If you were lucky, or had the jump, there came an end, presumably satisfactory, followed by the shaky letdown, a light-headed, giddy feeling. That was where Hawkins was now, on an emotional high. The adrenaline was still roaring, the danger, the crisis, now an afterglow of excitement, rolling around and around the mind, like wine in the mouth, reliving it.

Lieutenant Commander Blake was waiting at the dock as they tied up. When Hawkins and the general climbed the ladder there was a quick exchange of salutes.

"Commander, a pleasure," General Houghton said. "How's that man Hawkins shot?"

"He'll live. We patched him up, gave him a transfusion, then transferred him to King Edward hospital. Doctor says he needs emergency surgery on one shoulder."

"I see. And where's our captain?"

Blake led them into the old brick complex and a large room overlooking the pier. The glowing sun was setting through the windows, filling the room with a reddish-orange light. A sailor with white spats and a matching belt and holster was guarding the door, cap tipped at a jaunty angle, standing at parade rest, watching the prisoner intently. Captain Perez was sitting at the end of a long blond-wood table. He looked badly frightened. Houghton pulled out a chair on the same side of the table and sat facing him, one ankle up on a bare knee.

"I swear, I had no idea they—" he checked himself, "those men were there!" Perez's voice quavered slightly. Houghton took off his hat, carefully set it on the table and hooked his thumbs across his ample stomach, impassively eyeing the captain. The captain swallowed. "I swear."

"You realize we could treat you as an enemy combatant out of uniform," Houghton said. Captain Perez didn't seem to understand, a confused look on his face. "A spy! We shoot spies, do you understand that!"

"I was out on the open ocean! I am a neutral ship—"

"That open ocean is a war zone!" Houghton thundered.

Hawkins leaned in, elbows on the table. "Captain, please. Don't insult our intelligence by telling us you didn't know about that compartment. It took time to do that. You had to know. Commander Blake, how long do you think it took to create that hideaway?"

"I should say no less than two days, and probably three. Moving enough tires alone could take a good day," Blake said.

"I am not a spy," Perez said, "I am a captain."

"And you carry cargo," Houghton said, his voice very quiet, "do you not?"

"What?"

"Carry cargo."

"Yes."

"I suggest you help yourself here."

"I—I—have mercy, please, I did not know about those men."

"Fine. The men. You didn't know about them. Let's stick to the cargo for now."

"Cargo? I am the captain of a ship. I am in the shipping business. That is all." More confusion. Then a noticeable hardening in Perez's face as General Houghton pressed on. *Something's wrong here*, Hawkins thought. *That's a shift, he's backing off now. Making him shit his chair wasn't working. What is it anyway? I know, the ascot. And the blazer with the fake yacht club patch. What's with that?* Hawkins nosily cleared his throat.

"Captain, your English is very good. Where did you learn it?"

"At home. In Valparaiso."

"Why?"

"I wanted to go to sea. British ships, all over the world."

"You sail on one?"

"Yes, to learn, get my master's license. Many men from many nations do this. British merchant marine, biggest, best in the world."

"Well, yes, that's right. British ships everywhere. Britain rules the waves! Even now. Germany may have the Continent, but Britain rules the waves. Isn't that right?" Captain Perez nodded. General Houghton impatiently glanced at Hawkins, waiting for this interruption to end. Hawkins ignored him, still on the edge of his giddy high mood. "How's the song go? 'Rule Britannia' ..." Hawkins start to sing a bit, "*Rule Britannia* ..." He looked at the others. The general's face froze, obviously pissed at this seeming distraction. Behind the general, Blake started to laugh a little, then came in halfway through. "*Britannia, rule the waves, Britons never, never, never shall be slaves—*" Hawkins looked back at the sailor guarding the door. He smirked a bit, joining in with a deep bass voice after Blake started, "*Rule, Britannia! Britannia, rule the waves. Britons never, never, never shall be slaves.*" Hawkins dug in for another chorus, gesturing with both hands at Perez. After a split second he shook his head, half smiled and ingratiatingly started to sing along, too, "*Rule, Britannia! Britannia, rule the waves.*" Several sailors on the walkway heard them through the windows and started singing too.

At that General Houghton rolled his eyes and head at the ludicrous spectacle, face reddening with anger, before finally, grudgingly, joining in when Perez kept signing, *"Britons never, never, never shall be slaves."* Hawkins began slapping his hand on the table, Houghton couldn't help himself, laughing now, too, Perez starting to smile and laugh. They kept on going until the end of the next stanza, *"… shalt flourish great and free, The dread and e-e-e-nvy of them all,"* breaking up in more laughter at the absurdity of it.

But Perez knew the lyrics.

"With that we should have some tea," Hawkins said. "You would like some?"

"Please," Perez said. General Houghton watched, head bobbing back and forth, unsure whether to be angry at being upstaged, uncertain whether his authority and position were being challenged, or intrigued.

"Commander, could we get some?" Hawkins could hear Blake chuckle ever so slightly behind him. Probably a little army-navy rivalry there.

"Well of course. This is a Royal Navy base. Biscuits, too." He ordered the sailor at the door to go get it.

"We were talking about the shipping business and cargo," Hawkins said. "We understand all that. Business. We do it, too. Maybe we can do business together. Even make you a nice offer."

"An offer?"

"I have to check with my superiors, I am making no promises, understand?" Perez nodded. "But I should think so."

"I see," Perez said. They were in a different place, now. The fear was gone. Houghton watched, surprised, his mouth opening a bit, still quite annoyed, but hardly objecting, quickly looking back and forth.

"With whom were you doing this business?" Hawkins said.

"I'm not sure. They gave me names, but …"

"Yes, I know. There was money involved?"

"Of course."

"Cash?"

"Yes."

"I thought so," Hawkins said. He glanced over at the general. "That's the way they do these things. It's a dead end. We won't want to be bothered with that." Houghton nodded at Hawkins, now in the swing of this new game.

"How much money?" Houghton said.

"Five thousand dollars. In American twenties."

The rest of the story unfolded over ninety minutes and two cups of tea and a plate of cucumber sandwiches that was produced unbidden, much to Captain Perez's pleasure.

It had started two weeks earlier when they made a landing at the port of Constanta in Romania. Perez was approached onshore by a man who identified himself as a Mr. Demetriou, a Greek name. However, he clearly was not Greek. He spoke English, and although Perez spoke English reasonably well, he still didn't have a native's ear for accents. Demetriou seemed to know that the *Santa Lopez* delivered tires under contract for Michelin, mostly to Latin America. Mexico, of course, because of its size and proximity to the United States and its vast car industry, was the biggest market for tires in Latin America. Would Perez be interested in a profitable arrangement? A certain amount of smuggling was always in the background of the international shipping business, so this was nothing particularly new or unusual. Even for a ship captain, five thousand dollars was a great sum. Half in advance, half on delivery. Perez agreed, adding hastily, he now truly regretted the whole affair—never, never, never again, rhythmically echoing the never never-nevers in "Rule Britannia."

Once the tires bound for Romania were off-loaded Perez gave the crew two days' leave. Demetriou and a team of men came that night and installed the hidden compartment. Not all of the crew returned—which was somewhat routine. They were still drunk, they'd hopped another ship, one never knew. His engineer had been approached by three sailors who were looking to sign on, so they were hired. They promptly sailed for Marseilles and another load of tires.

Once they'd landed at the Port of Veracruz Perez was to give the crew another overnight leave. He was to wait for two men, and he had the names: Horst Eckhardt and Werner von Falkenberg.

"Eckhardt?" Hawkins said, asking him to spell it out to be sure, glancing at Blake, who leaned forward, too. He did. It was the same name as on the boxes. They nodded at each other, then the general. "Go on."

"They were to come aboard with a welder," Perez said, "pay the second installment and take away whatever was in the hidden compartment." A fairly straightforward transaction. "But I swear on my mother's and father's graves, I knew nothing about those men."

Houghton started to bristle at that, but Hawkins gently waved him off. The general harrumphed, obviously unhappy, but went along for the moment. Hawkins guessed Houghton was probably restrained more by Hawkins's personal relationship with their boss, William Stephenson, than any formal institutional considerations.

Hawkins was assigned to British Security Coordination in New York, a new umbrella agency encompassing all intelligence operations hemispherically, including the Bermuda Imperial Posts and Telegraph Censorship Station. Stephenson was now their superior. And it was Stephenson who'd enlisted Hawkins in the British Secret Service several years back. Hawkins had been casting about trying to figure out what to do after he accidentally saw Hitler and the Nazis making poison gas at that plant in East Prussia. Stephenson, who was in close contact with Winston Churchill, caught wind of Hawkins and followed through. They'd become good friends, with the older man as Hawkins's mentor, too.

"That's enough for now. Thank you, Captain."

Outside Houghton finally confronted Hawkins. Blake watched warily.

"You really believe he's telling the truth, that he didn't know?" Houghton said.

"I wouldn't tell him. He could get the rest of the crew to throw those three over the side, one at a time. They're badly outnumbered and they have to sleep sometime. And Perez is the captain. There was safety in anonymity," Hawkins said. Houghton mulled that a long moment, an exasperated sigh finally venting his pique like a locomotive letting off steam.

"Very well. I have to admit that makes sense."

"Yes. The sailors they replaced are probably floating facedown in the Black Sea."

"Did this Eckhardt and Falkenberg do that, too?"

"Maybe, maybe not. It could've been compartmentalized. Exactly like Captain Perez not being told they were on board."

"But if only three came aboard in Romania, what about the other gunmen? Where'd they come from? I think we should interrogate them right away."

Hawkins thought a moment.

"I think we start with the man in the radio room as soon as he sufficiently recovers. He wants to talk. Begged for his life. Told me he'd do anything. That's interesting. I can tell you that's not the voice of a true-blue Nazi talking, they're not like that."

"I see. Right. Makes sense, too. He must be one of the three who came aboard—"

"Precisely. He was trying to send a transmission back, or call a U-boat, whatever, that was his job. He's the only one left who knows the whole story, who the other men were. We box the others in first."

"Sensible. I agree." Houghton turned to Blake. "Commander, let the captain go back to his cabin, but keep the ship under guard and make sure that transmitter isn't working. And keep the two crew who fought on the bridge in the jail for now."

"I'm starving. Can we get something to eat here?" Hawkins said.

"O-club is closed," Blake said. "Gentlemen, join me on the *Dendrobium*. You could say I know someone in the galley."

# -10-

The ship's mess had emptied out, the galley crew busy cleaning, filling the tin-ceilinged compartment with the clanging of pots and pans. A few sailors readying for the night watch lingered in the back over mugs of black tea. Hawkins, Houghton and Blake sat down in silence. Not much else being available, plates of tough leftover corned beef, mashed potatoes and soggy peas were quickly ordered. Houghton left for the head while they were waiting.

"You take chances, Hawkins," Blake said.

"It's a dangerous line of—"

"No, I mean with the general. Those of us who come up in the Services learn very early on to fear the men with big shoulder boards." He spoke in an almost fatherly tone, respectful, concerned, perhaps coaching a bit, a quizzical expression on his face. Hawkins recalled what Blake had said about the chiefs and being accessible. He could see what made Blake a good captain, or what made a good captain.

As Houghton came through the door Hawkins reflected he had in fact thrown his weight around a bit, after all.

"I'm sure I need to mind that. And haircuts."

Blake smiled, then laughed just a bit again. "Yes, and haircuts."

Radio broadcasts were piped into the mess. The operator up in the *Dendrobium*'s radio room started tuning in the BBC on the shortwave bands, but the program distantly wavered in and out of a howl of vibrating noise, only snippets distinguishable. Blake rose to a nearby phone, clicked the receiver and said something, then returned to the table.

"We try to get London, hear from home, does wonders for morale, despite the news. Unfortunately, the jamming's rather bad tonight," Blake said.

"That noise?" Hawkins said. "That's new."

"Yes. They started that recently, I assume they don't want people in Occupied Europe to hear any real news, just their propaganda."

"I'm sure," Hawkins said. "Hitler and Goebbels call the BBC fake news."

"Yes. We jam them, too, now," Blake said. "Retaliation. Out here we usually end up listening to CBS or NBC from New York. They've powerful transmitters, quite clear over the sea at night." With a swooping chirp the operator quickly caught the signal. The mess instantly quieted, the galley crew carefully setting things down, listening, too.

*... with the great air raids of yesterday and last night only a few hours past, it is reported this morning that German bombers and fighting planes are again over southeast British coastal towns. Berlin says the renewal of attacks only awaits the clearing of mists over the Channel.*

"I'm sorry if I stepped on your toes back there, General," Hawkins said. Houghton's temper seemed to have settled.

"It's fine. I'm not a man to argue with results." He looked and gestured at Blake. "I spent three years in the trenches trying to butt through. I think like a soldier. Guile doesn't come naturally."

"Same here," Blake said. "You saw Perez quite differently, Hawkins."

*... now a report of Larry Lesseur from the British capital.*

A new voice spoke, this one higher pitched, less clear.

*This is London. I am speaking from a crowded air-raid shelter two floors underground. This morning large forces of German bombers are continuing their unprecedented attempt to bomb England. We do not know yet how many more planes the Royal Air Force have added to their record score of yesterday when the Air Ministry announced that the RAF had destroyed one hundred forty-four out of a German armada of one thousand planes for a loss of only twenty-seven fighters of their own.*

A cheer went up from the men working in the kitchen and finishing their tea, clapping and slamming their hands and mugs on the tabletops, voices bouncing off the shiny metal ceiling, magnifying into an ear-piercing din. A few other sailors drifted in to listen, keeping a respectful distance from their skipper and his guests.

"You were looking at the crime, not the man," Hawkins said.

"He is a criminal," Houghton said, "even in peacetime. Smuggling's against the law."

"You go on the Continent these days, it's full of people who only want to get along and go along. That's Captain Perez. Looking for a few quick quid, get by, nothing more to it than that."

"Damn it, Hawkins. Those kind of people make it all possible!"

*… during last night the Midlands area of England was heavily bombed. One raid lasted three hours. Naturally, there were casualties, as yet undetermined. Two nurses were seriously hurt when their sanatorium in the Midlands was hit, but the three hundred thirty patients were taken safely to air-raid shelters.*

The mess crew and the sailors in back let off an angry howl, standing and shouting, "Bastards!" and "Bloody huns! A hospital!" and "We'll make them pay!"

"Yes. They do," Hawkins said, "I know that. But that means they aren't necessarily *against* us, per se, or *for* Hitler, either. We have to get those people turned around, make them get along and go along with *us* if we're going to win."

"That makes them less culpable? I'd as soon take him out and shoot him," the general said.

The cook came out with a mess boy carrying their plates, tarrying a second, listening too.

*Yesterday the German Air Force launched eleven attacks along a five-hundred-mile front. When the sirens sounded in London I watched all traffic stop for a moment. Buses unloaded their passengers at air-raid shelters. But before the all-clear signal sounded the buses were running again and people stood in little knots on street corners watching the skies ...*

"We will, won't we, sir? Make them pay?" the cook asked.

Blake sat up slightly, glancing back, speaking loudly so all could hear, "You can count on it, men! We're going to hit them hard, very hard!" All the men cheered. The cook and the mess boy went back to the galley. Blake and his guests immediately began wrestling with the corned beef.

"We can't shoot him," Hawkins said, "you know that. We may need him."

"Oh, I know. But do we have to pay him?" Houghton said.

"Surely you admit that's a rather obnoxious prospect," Blake said, "rewarding him for what he was doing."

"Well, of course. What of it?" Hawkins said.

"It's just expediency?" Blake said.

"Spying is nothing but expediency."

"Aren't you angry? It makes me angry," Houghton said.

*I was astonished by the number of people who walked around wearing a neat white bandage on their heads like a skullcap. The reason was apparent—the ones nearest the field had their shingle roofs holed by falling bricks ...*

More howls of anger from the galley and the back of the mess room.

"You happen to know I did kill three of them this afternoon ... and several more back in New York last week," Hawkins said. "And before that a couple in Portugal, or at least I assume they were Nazis."

"I'm sure they were," Houghton said. He stopped sawing at the meat.

"I'm sorry, Hawkins. Don't mean to criticize. You've killed more of them than most of us will probably ever see."

*... if they figured they could break the morale of the London populace, they have just as obviously failed, for even those people wearing the skullcaps, the white bandages, managed to grin very often ...*

And yet, the air raid—*it does seem rather remote, doesn't it?* Hawkins thought. Almost an entertainment, another diversion on the radio you might casually listen to in the evening, sitting in your easy chair, thinking tough luck for those people over there. To the general and the commander, it did seem more personal. Their homes, their towns, burning. They, the *Dendrobium's* crew, they were simply mad as hell. No doubt they'd be happy to lynch Captain Perez and anyone like him and all the people who went along and got along.

Hawkins closed his eyes, trying to see in his mind. Walking up the street to their family home on Ridgway Place in Wimbledon. The tidy old Victorian houses. Overhead, planes crossing above the trees, hundreds of planes, darkening the sky. Bombs falling, smoke rising, the street, the houses all vanish into the cloud. Only screams now.

*My mother,* Hawkins thought. *She still lives on Ridgway. Where is she now? In a shelter at this moment? My aunts and her people, my cousins? In one, too? Or under a pile of rubble? Do I not care? How can I not care?* He began to feel the anger the others felt, at least a little. *Bastards.*

"That man in the radio shack begging for his life, you said that's not the way a real Nazi talks," Blake said.

"No, it isn't," Hawkins said.

"You've spent a fair amount of time with these people? Do you know many Nazis?" Blake said.

"Sure. Go undercover for any length of time, of course you get to know them. You have to, to understand them, find their weaknesses, see any opportunities. They're people like people in any other place, there's good and bad in them, even if the bad ones are running the show now."

"Don't you get angry at them?" Blake said.

"You can't *allow* yourself to feel anger at them, ever, you have to guard against it all the time. Anger is the emotion that's hardest to hide, one flash of it, and you're done. You can't give in to it. It's a form of mental hygiene."

"It all sounds rather … risky," Blake said, "if you know what I mean … Spend too much time around them, start to think like them … Sorry."

"Oh, I know that all too well," Hawkins said. "It can be insidious, like a tiny spot of mold on a peach, and suddenly it's all rotten, taken over."

"So, not you?" Blake said.

"I'm not worried. There are dangers in my line of work, of course. But it's easy when you have an enemy like Hitler. Know what you're fighting, you can handle anything."

*No—not the real danger,* Hawkins thought. *Yes, you have to numb up to chum up, not let your feelings about them give yourself away. But not giving in to anger, being numb to things gets to be a habit, that's the real problem. I let—or make—myself go dead inside, a lot,* Hawkins thought. *But you have to present the facade that you want, or rather, must have merely to stay safe and alive. I don't want to feel numb, though.* But he hardly wanted to admit any of that to Houghton and Blake.

*Now for news of the German capital …*

*The roundup of yesterday's daylight operations has been given out by the German High Command. In large-scale fighting virtually over all of England, the Germans claimed they shot down ninety-eight British planes and destroyed eight others on the ground, at the same time the Germans say they lost only twenty-nine planes. Also, the Germans say that five more balloons were knocked down in their attacks on the barrage at Dover yesterday.*

There was a terrible silence in the mess and galley. A sailor in the back flatly said, "Liars."

The broadcast, the others' reactions, still felt quite distant. *But I know what I'm fighting as clear as anything could be,* Hawkins thought. He pictured in his mind the last time he saw Hitler. The Führer had been standing in the front of a black Mercedes parade car, his hand on the windshield at the head of a long convoy of gleaming cars. It was cold that day in Vienna, in early March. The crowd was enormous, excited, raising a huge roar far up the street as the car approached. Hitler's cheeks were ruddy from the cold and he had the smirking expression of a man who knew he'd gotten away with something.

But that wasn't as disturbing as the first time Hawkins had seen him, at a business conference a year earlier, before Hawkins joined the SIS. Hitler had an unsettling quality. It was hard to describe, or define, but he seemed to react to those he met not as a person, but a *representation* of that person, looking at them, or perhaps through them, as if they were mere things. Wax dummies in Madame Tussauds. Or lifelike carnival automatons that shook hands. Not beings that had hearts or feelings. But there was also a blankness to the man in idle moments that allowed others to write onto his face whatever they wanted to see. The evil came as no surprise when it showed itself, like the day after seeing him parade into Vienna, when the SS rounded up prominent Jewish businessmen and made them scrub the sidewalks while they watched and laughed.

*I know who and what I'm fighting better than almost any man*, Hawkins thought. He found comfort and certainty in that. *Knowing so well what I am against keeps me safe, keeps me from straying, from losing myself.*

They'd finished up. The mess boy came and took their plates. All sat quietly listening.

> *... the German paper for Occupied Holland reports that Joseph Simon, who is the German civil administrator for the tiny duchy of Luxembourg, has decreed that there is to be no longer, quote, a Grand Duchy of Luxembourg, unquote. The constitution of Luxembourg is no longer valid, he states in his decree, because the government has fled. The oath of public officials in the former government is canceled out and they are all to transfer their loyalty to the new German administration ...*

That brought another long, brooding silence.

"We're next," the general finally said. "If we let them."

Hawkins and General Houghton thanked Blake and headed ashore, walking past the *Santa Lopez*. Hawkins stopped, gazing up at it. Houghton paused, looking back.

"General, I never asked. How did you know this was the ship?"

# -11-

"We were intercepting peculiar and irregular messages to and from the old Abwehr drop boxes in Lisbon," Houghton said. "Didn't make any sense. Mainly a series of complaints coming one way and excuses going back. But it was clear the Germans were having difficulty selling something in New York because of the American Neutrality Acts. Could've been machine parts, bottles of aspirin, books about Hitler, who the hell knew, no details at all. Then this came in and all the pieces snapped together."

It was now very late and Hawkins had been continuously on the move for over twenty hours, flying into Bermuda in the wee hours of the morning. Exhausted, his body wanted nothing more in the world than to collapse face-first into bed the way logged trees fell. But his mind had insisted on rushing back to the general's center at the Princess Hotel to see what had tipped them off about the *Santa Lopez*. He knew he'd never sleep if he didn't see Houghton's answer first.

General Houghton clicked on the sloping light table, the glow in the dark basement room flooding their faces from below, then fumbled in his folder for the right transparency. Hawkins turned impatiently, tiredly waiting, uneasily watching the frenzied activity behind them. The room ran nearly the entire length of the big hotel, filled to overflowing with long rows of metal work tables staffed by a large force of young women—girls, really, barely out of their teens, mostly from Canada. At each table were several workstations composed of a steaming kettle, gooseneck lamps, tools, wire baskets and piles of letters fresh off the latest plane from Europe. The women were steaming open all the envelopes to inspect their contents, reading and puzzling over them, holding them up to the lamps for any markings. Occasionally they'd set one down and carefully scan it with a magnifier or douse it with chemicals in search of invisible ink. Then they'd seal it up without a trace, lightly toss it in the OUT basket and move on to the next. The mail had to be processed quickly. They needed to get it back on the plane and not interrupt its layover. Failure could tip Britain's hand to both friend and foe as to what it was doing.

Thanks to Britain's blockade of the Continent and the parallel German U-boat war against Britain and the Commonwealth, the Atlantic was now partly closed. That meant virtually all of the mail between Europe and the Western Hemisphere went by air from neutral Portugal through the British colony of Bermuda, where all planes making the crossing had to land to refuel. When one did, the IPTCS covertly unloaded it, rushed it here and secretly opened it. Odd as it may have seemed, little Bermuda out on the edge of the tropics was Britain's window on Europe, all from letters, magazines and newspapers going back and forth. The photoed document Hawkins was waiting to see came from this operation. Britain was utterly dependent on it.

With the fall of France, the tardy Italian entrance into the war in June and the Nazi occupation of most of the Continent, the Secret Service's networks on the Continent were shattered. Virtually all its sources of information on what was going on inside Europe were torn away. That was the greatest intelligence disaster in the Secret Service's long history, all the way back to Elizabeth I and Walsingham. There were a few listening posts in places like Stockholm, Geneva or Istanbul, but they were small and closely watched—not only by the suspicious locals, who desperately wanted to stay out of the war, but also by the Germans and the Italians.

Hawkins knew all that. *And yet, what an appalling sight*, he thought, *the privacy and trust of so many so cheerfully violated. But ... what else are we to do?*

He thought back a couple of months. *The worst day of my life, the day*

*I was ordered out of Paris. Same day the Wehrmacht marched in. That was bad. Got stopped on the street by the Wehrmacht twice. That was frightening. Thank god for my American passport. I got out. But my friends …*

Thanks to the steaming kettles the room was as overheated as a Turkish bath, the women covered with sweat, their clothes sticking seductively to their bodies. But Hawkins felt chilled by the memory of leaving Paris. Several nearby girls were eyeing Hawkins curiously. Most of the men on the island were either old, overweight or had their skittish wives surgically attached. Hawkins was a catch. But he was so tired and preoccupied that he never noticed.

"Caused quite a flap when it came through, not that many celebrity letters. Or at least someone famous," Houghton shouted over the din, gesturing at the large blowup of a letter in Russian, of all things.

"Who?" Hawkins said.

"Leon Trotsky." The general laughed a little, as if to say, *Can you believe it?*

"What? The Bolshevik leader? From the Russian Revolution?"

"Yes, him."

"What the hell is he doing in Mexico City?"

"On the run from Stalin. The Soviet Great Leader wants him dead."

"I know he got pushed out."

"Right. But he still has friends and supporters back in Russia—the USSR, I should say. What you could call a holy war is going on inside Communism. What's the true faith? Socialism in a single state—that's Stalin—or wait for world revolution—that's Trotsky. Absurd, the whole lot. Mexico's a safe haven for people fleeing Stalin. Also the losing side in the Spanish Civil War."

"So this letter?" Hawkins said.

"He apparently still has some surviving friends in the Red Army."

"I thought Stalin purged that."

"He did, but Trotsky created the Red Army," the general said. "Whatever you think of his politics, the man's a genius, won the civil war, saved their revolution. As a soldier, I have to tell you that was an amazing feat, maybe the greatest of the century. We have to conclude he still has friends tipping him off. Could be coming out through a military attaché, an agent in Istanbul, we have no idea."

"What's it say?"

"The sender is warning Trotsky the Nazis may have made a deal with Stalin to go after him—that a strange German shipment went through Russia to Romania and is covertly bound for Mexico."

"Probably right. If Stalin is doing Hitler a favor, he's getting something valuable in return."

"Count on that."

"Going east through Russia makes sense, though. More secure than getting ten locked boxes through Hungarian or Romanian customs," Hawkins said. "It wouldn't have to leave the port to enter customs and be inspected, it could go from one ship to another."

"Exactly."

"But we're the only ones that know the Germans want to sell something in New York."

"That's it. The sender assumes it's about Trotsky because it's going to Mexico."

"But it's actually merely being transshipped through Mexico to New York."

"Right. Objects of great value, it says. Mentions a ship, so it all falls into place. This letter to Trotsky is where the excerpt you had came from."

"I assume you omitted the rest on the copy I had for security reasons."

"Not letting that out of the office! This is so sensitive we couldn't share it with the local navy men—no need-to-know—gave you only enough that they'd cooperate. We arrived at the *Santa Lopez* through a process of elimination. It couldn't be any other."

"That fits, too. I can tell you if they're routing artworks through Mexico to New York it's because that's where the real money is," Hawkins said.

"Exactly." An attaché came up and handed the general a telex. He gave it a quick glance. "W is flying in this morning."

## -12-

A slim silver plane emerged from behind another pristine Bermuda cloud. Moments later a Lockheed Electra, the same fast model Amelia Earhart piloted, zoomed in for a fast touchdown on the small strip. It belonged to the Royal Canadian Air Force but it was kept in civilian livery for covert purposes. After flying Hawkins in the previous day it'd repeated the early morning trip, flying in from an airbase near Ottawa, briefly stopping for an early morning pickup at the Teterboro Airport across the Hudson from Manhattan.

Despite being the head of British Security Coordination in New York, the top man, W opened the door himself before the plane had stopped taxiing, flipping the three steps down, almost jumping over them, hands sliding on the handrails. W ignored protocol and seized Hawkins's hand first, blond hair flying in the sea breeze, heavily lidded eyes squinting in the sun.

"Hawkins, damn good, damn good! Knew I could count on you," pumping it in his usual athletic way, then the general's, striding forward, pulling him along to the waiting car, plucking Hawkins's sleeve with his other hand. Stephenson was a short man, both Hawkins and Houghton towered over him, but Stephenson seemed to spin the other two around him the way circus rides spun little cars. "General, a pleasure again. How many have we got?"

"Forty. Counted them this morning," Hawkins said.

"Forty paintings! Extraordinary."

After a fast drive through town to the Princess Hotel they followed W into the large penthouse suite where the Royal Navy had overnight moved all the cases from the *Santa Lopez*. The wooden boxes now filled the sunny room. First thing that morning Hawkins had picked all the locks, so now the doors on the cases were hanging open. A stenographer and a photographer, both women from General Houghton's staff, were waiting on the sofa, nearly hidden behind the cases, peeking over at them.

"Any papers or manifests inside?" W asked.

"Not that I saw," Hawkins said.

W pondered the cases for a second, saw one was marked #1, and pulled the first painting on the end out, a rather dour picture of a gaunt man holding a book down at an angle, as if it was too heavy or he was too tired to read. It was all in shades of blue, except for the cadaverous bright green of the man's lips.

"That's rather a gloomy thing," Houghton said.

"Yes. It's Blue Period Picasso," Hawkins said. "It's a really good one." W set aside the case and pulled another out. "That's another Picass— er—no, it's a Braque. There's the signature. Picasso's and Braque's cubist paintings are often hard to tell apart. That's a swell painting, too."

The general gestured to the women. They bounced up and strode over, one of them unlimbering her steno pad, the other lifting a Rolleiflex on a wood tripod. Alice, the steno, began talking notes in shorthand as Hawkins described the paintings. Lilly, the photographer, began photoing them.

Hawkins had a limited arts experience. Even before he had joined the Secret Service, back when he was traveling around Europe selling industrial valves, he'd had idle hours. Instead of hitting a bar for drinks or a cinema for diversion like most commercial travelers his age, he moonlighted by rummaging through the local antiques shops and galleries looking for small treasures he could easily ship back to Manhattan. It turned into a profitable sideline, one he especially needed when he came into the Service because His Majesty's government didn't pay anywhere near what the industrial valve business did. There were, after all, no sales commissions in spying. Unlike many of the men in the SIS, Hawkins had no personal, family money. He needed the extra cash merely to stay even. But it was a useful education, doubly fortunate now. The fact he had no formal training in modern art wasn't much of an impediment because where would you go to study something brand new like that anyway? You had to be there.

"Is there any organization to these?" W said.

"Let's see," Hawkins said. He went halfway down the row of cases and pulled another work out. It was a vibrant, lush scene of the tropics, with a dark-skinned woman in a grass skirt picking improbably large fruit. To one side a tiger peeked out from under a cluster of enormous flowers.

"That's a Rousseau! Look at the colors …"

"So different, I don't see how they have anything in common," W said.

Hawkins leaned the Rousseau against the box and drew another. It was blue, like the Picasso, but the effect was entirely different, full of rosy hues and sunny yellows, a couple embracing in the center, a traditional Jewish marriage canopy to one side with a rabbi flying overhead on the back of a large white bird.

"In a way they do, yes, everything," Hawkins said. "I know this one. A Chagall. A Jewish artist. These are all works the Nazis banned. Degenerate art, they call it, they despise it. To them this stuff is disposable. That's why it's here."

"If they hate it so much why didn't they destroy them?" Houghton said.

"Because they're greedy and corrupt," W said. "It's worth money." He pointed at the Chagall. "Even if they don't understand *this*, they understand *that*."

"Where'd the Nazis get them, then?"

"They stole them," Hawkins said. "Before I left Paris one of France's leading art and antiquities dealers told me the Nazis had already looted the major Jewish collections in the countries they'd occupied. She was certain they'd do the same thing in France."

"What happened to the people who owned them?"

"They're probably facedown in the water, too, so to speak."

They all contemplated that for a long moment.

"They've gone to a great deal of trouble," W finally said.

"Yes. But there's great value locked up in these paintings, as much as real estate or securities. They're worth it," Hawkins said.

"But won't it take a long time to get the money?" the general said.

"No," Hawkins said. "As you know, I've dealt with these big New York auction halls before." Houghton and W both chuckled. *Yes*, Hawkins irritably thought, *you intercepted my invoices, didn't you? Bastards.* But he ignored their amused, knowing reaction. "If you go in with one or two items, it can take forever to get paid. You know that joke: you owe the bank money, they own you? You owe them *a lot* of money, you own the bank? It's like that. If it's big enough and valuable enough, they'll advance you the cash right away. A hoard like this? Hell, they'll practically spin on their heads and sing 'The Star-Spangled Banner' for you to land a big, season-opening sale like this."

"How much money?" the general said.

"I'm not sure," Hawkins said. "Many millions, maybe tens of millions. We need to get an expert in here from London, from the National Gallery."

W cut him off. "We don't have time. We've got to hurry or they'll catch on."

"Why—what the bloody hell are they up to?" Houghton said.

"That's what's worrying me," Hawkins said. "It's big, whatever it is."

"Absolutely," W said. "This is more than you'd need for a usual spy ring. This could fund their operations across the hemisphere, well beyond the US or Canada."

"But what for, specifically, what operation," Hawkins said, "that's the thing."

"Perhaps we'll get another intercept," the general said.

"No. Only one way to go—put it back and follow it," Hawkins said. "It's the only way we can find out."

"I agree," W said. "Again, no time."

# -13-

"Wait—you said this is all *looted* property?" Houghton said. Hawkins and W both nodded.

"Why, yes," W said. Houghton's ample face started to redden. Two worlds suddenly collided, one that lived by rules, order and procedure, and a contingent, opportunistic and spectral one that did not.

"We can't do that. Under the Geneva and Hague Conventions we have an obligation to return looted property to its rightful owners. We should impound these," Houghton said. "Send the empty cases."

"That won't work," Hawkins said. "The weight alone—"

"What? My god—"

"What choice do we have? We have to learn what's going on," Hawkins said.

"And we can't risk blowing our intercepts," W said.

"Isn't there another way?" the general said.

"No," W said. "If we seize these paintings they'll probably try it again, and we may not get a lead the next time."

"They could send something by U-boat, who knows?" Hawkins said.

"We have to get at the people behind it," W said.

"Ah, Christ." The general's indignation and sense of rightful order began to wind down with a slow shake of his head. "I suppose they could. But—this is dreadful. If we keep it, it's like we're complicit."

"We'll have to try and return them when this is all over," Hawkins said.

"But they'll be out of our hands, in Mexico," the general said.

"We control them until they reach Veracruz, and once they get to the US," W said, "the FBI will impound them after we tip them off."

"But what if we lose them—"

"Why would that be risky? Wouldn't the Mexicans seize them, too, if they knew?" Hawkins said. W shook his head, eyes closing to a slit again, grimacing slightly.

"Mexico? Cárdenas? His party? *Don't* count on it. Bunch of bandits," W said. "Have you been paying attention to what they've been doing?"

"Sorry, no. Who's this Cárdenas?" Hawkins said. "You know how it is, one skips over stories about Latin America in the papers. I do recall we broke diplomatic relations with them a while back."

"That's Lázaro Cárdenas, president of Mexico. Head of the Revolutionary Party. Two years ago he started expropriating foreign-owned companies, first cotton plantations, then oil, then railroads. Pulled the rug right from underneath the people who owned them, built them, mostly in Britain and the US. That's when we, the Commonwealth, broke relations. Nationalized them, that was the word he cooked up, *nationalized* them," his voice raising sarcastically. "Also stole half the properties of the big landowners, gave it all away to other people. Another flavor of Communist, that's all. Little wonder he likes Trotsky, or all those other Reds who ran like rats out of Spain. As far as I'm concerned, not a penny's worth of distance between them, or Stalin and Hitler, for that matter. Another dictator, taking things they don't own. Rule of law? Bad joke. Watch, they had an election in July. He'll find an excuse not to hand over power. Cárdenas created an entirely new force of popular militias, supposedly committed to their revolution. He's got the means, he'll be thug-for-life soon enough. So no, don't count on him for a damn thing. Once you steal an oilfield, a pretty little picture isn't a very big deal, is it?"

"Bloody wogs," Houghton said. "What do you expect? When President Wilson sent General Pershing and the US Army in after Pancho Villa in '16, they didn't finish the job like they should've! Had a chance to clean the goddamn place right out, they did! Make it another Philippines. Softheaded, the Yanks."

"And it's even worse now because oil is in such short supply because of the war. He's got the whole world in a corner," W said. "When the war started, the Yanks asked Cárdenas for bases to help defend the Panama Canal. Had the gall to turn them down flat. Can you imagine that!"

"I had no idea," Hawkins said. "Very well. Got that."

"Back to your original question—there is some risk there with the paintings. You'll have to handle it, Roy."

"What about Captain Perez?" Hawkins said.

"Do you trust him?" Houghton said.

"Not a question of that. He was smuggling, he's no saint as you were saying. He's with us now but what if he runs into someone else down the line, flips back? Not because he cares about our side or theirs, but because someone makes him a better offer? And what do we really know about him? We have to plan for that. You can't be sure about people, there are gray areas, and info—like about him—more often than not isn't fully complete or reliable, and it's sometimes contradictory. Half the time we're groping around in the dark, can't see what's going on at all. That's why espionage work is so dangerous."

"What we'll do then is replace his sailors with Royal Navy men," W said. "Keep an eye on him, the ship."

"But we don't want Perez to know that," Hawkins said. W pondered that a moment.

"Then we'll let him hire off the docks in Hamilton harbor, we'll make sure the only men there are ours. Pay him off once you get there, if he sticks with us. You'll have to go on your US passport, of course, since we have no relations with the Mexicans."

"You're going into a hostile country," Houghton said.

"Nothing new there," Hawkins said.

A sergeant came and rapped his knuckles on the doorframe.

"Sir? Your prisoner is awake."

# -14-

"You asked me not to kill you. Said you'd do anything," Hawkins said.

The translator, a round-faced and well-tanned young woman with curly hair, a member of General Houghton's small army of mail cover clerks, quickly began a running translation. They'd already determined from his papers he was Romanian. The man grimaced as the nurse cranked the head of his bed up slightly, checking his IV. The man's right arm and shoulder were canted up at an angle, supported by a brace, encased in a thick cast. The left was packed in a large bandage. They'd tapered down his morphine so he could talk. He obviously was in considerable discomfort.

"Yes," the man said.

"What's your story, then?" Hawkins said.

"I suppose you'll shoot me if I don't talk."

"I shot you twice already, why wouldn't I do it again?" Hawkins drew his Browning Hi-Power from his shoulder holster and gently set it on the stand. "You better understand I have the authority if I need to."

"Hawkins, put that away," W said. He acted cross, but Hawkins knew he wasn't. He reholstered the gun.

"Very well," Hawkins said.

"We don't have to shoot you," W said. "If you don't fully cooperate with us we'll have no choice but to turn you over to the civil or maritime authorities. That man you bludgeoned?"

"Yes."

"He's in a coma here in the hospital, likely to die. If *or when* he does, you could be charged with murder and piracy."

"A pirate?"

"You tried to hijack the ship. That's piracy under maritime law. I assure you, you'll hang," W said.

"We're your only hope," Hawkins said.

"What's your name?" W said.

"Constantin Marinescu."

"You're a Romanian citizen," Hawkins said.

"Yes."

"How did you get into this?" W said.

"I was in the Green Shirts—"

"The Iron Guard?" Hawkins said, referring to Romania's native Fascists. He was sitting across the bed from the young woman translator. Her face froze, lips tight. She'd originally come down from Toronto. *She's probably Jewish, a refugee*, Hawkins thought. The Iron Guard were worse anti-Semites than Hitler and the Nazis, ultraorthodox Christian nationalists. They'd launched pogroms before the Depression had hit or Hitler had come to power. Her English was perfect, she'd clearly been in Canada for quite a while.

"That's right," Marinescu said.

"Why'd you join the Guard?" Hawkins said.

"When I got out of university I discovered the Jews had all the jobs." Hawkins noticed W slightly touching the girl's elbow … *steady*. "Imagine that! No job. I had to go to sea, off and on."

"Keep going," Hawkins said.

"But then I got a position, a good position, as a paid officer in our party. I was marked for a ministry position when we came to power."

"I still don't see what that has to do with all of this, other than that you spent some time as a merchant sailor," W said.

"Our German friends were helping us financially. Of this we were deeply appreciative."

"They were paying your salary," Hawkins said.

"That is correct. And we got to know them. They invited me to Berlin for a fraternal party conference. They put me up in the Kaiserhof! Like heaven. When Reichsmarschall Göring shook my hand he told me he was married there!" He smiled slightly and nodded his head in pride and satisfaction at the happy memory.

"And ..."

"They asked for a small favor. Of course we were more than happy to help. And they were going to pay me for my time."

"How much?" W said.

"Twenty-five hundred reichsmarks before we left, then twenty-five hundred later."

"The others, too?"

"No, the others got seven hundred and fifty."

"Continue."

"There was this ship that was going to France and then Mexico. They knew I had been in the merchant marine."

"You were to be the radio operator," Hawkins said. The man nodded. "What was that message you were trying to send out?"

"That we'd been stopped—if we were stopped. The only thing they were concerned about was the captain. They didn't trust him. They were afraid he'd steal whatever was on the ship. If he didn't go straight from France to Veracruz we were to sink the ship, or set it on fire, and alert them. I was only to contact them if something went wrong or when we landed in Veracruz."

"Were you to contact anyone ashore in Veracruz?" Hawkins said.

"No. We were told nothing about that."

"Did you know what was on the ship?" W asked.

"We thought—guessed—it was a shipment of weapons for Mexican supporters. We never thought it was objects of great value. That's when all the trouble started."

"How so?" Hawkins said.

"Petru and Leonte, after the navy stopped us, when they realized something valuable like that was on the ship, they began talking. They went mad. They decided that since the shipment wasn't going to get to Mexico, anyway, that we might as well take advantage of the opportunity and help ourselves."

"Steal the cases," W said.

"Yes. I thought it was crazy, but they were greedy. Where will we sell these things, I asked. But they would not listen. When I didn't want to go along—I swear!—they began talking and then, without asking me, they tried to enlist the other crew members. They all went mad with greed, they all thought they were going to get rich." He sniffed in contempt. "They were not university men like I was. They did not think. Idiots. Ask them! I will talk to them if they will not tell you the truth."

"I'm afraid that's not possible," W said.

"Why?"

"The ones in the engine room?" Hawkins said. Marinescu nodded. "I shot them."

"They're dead? I see." He soberly thought that over a minute. "Then they got what they deserved."

"I want to make sure we get this very clear: Captain Perez did not know you were aboard and as far as you know the people receiving the shipment in Veracruz did not know you were aboard," W said.

"That is right. We were not to contact anyone ashore."

"Then what?" Hawkins said.

"We were to go home, or go to Panama with the ship and get off there, if we wanted to."

"When you sent one of these two radio messages, were there code words to be sent?" Marinescu rather feebly nodded in assent. He seemed to be wearing out from the interrogation, his face now drawn and gray. The nurse began hovering at the door, arms folded, looking annoyed.

"Are you willing to send one of these messages on our command?" W said.

Marinescu hesitated, then tried to shrug and grimaced instead, his breath a tiny gasp. "Sure. What does it matter now?"

"I don't think there's any need for the civil or maritime authorities to be involved in this affair, do you?" Hawkins said.

"I should think not. I must warn you, however, we may intern you until the end of war," W said.

Marinescu suddenly roused and grinned. "Oh! Fine. That won't be long."

"Anything else we can think of?" W said.

"Yes," Hawkins said. "Where'd the cases come from, do you know?"

"No. Only that they came off a Russian ship. In Constanta."

"You mean the Soviet Union?" Hawkins said.

"Yes. From Odessa." His eyes rolled slightly, he put his hand over his stomach. "I feel a little sick—" His face turning vaguely green. The nurse stepped back into the room and sharply ordered them out.

"We're done anyway," W said. Hawkins drew out his Hi-Power again, snapping up a stricken, frightened expression on Marinescu's face. Hawkins pulled the slide back, ejected a round, set it on the stand, and nodded. Marinescu hastily nodded back.

# -15-

The waiters cleared away the plates of grouper poached in coconut milk. General Houghton snagged a piece of johnny bread from the basket and then waved that off, too.

"How's it coming?" W said.

They'd been working hard and fast, Hawkins dictating to Alice, while Lilly, the other mail censor Houghton pulled off the floor, hung each painting on a wall and photoed them with the Rolleiflex. They all came down for dinner together. Alice and Lilly were Hawkins's age, Canadians in their early twenties. They rose to go.

"Lilly, stay a moment," General Houghton said. He checked the corridor and shut the door, picking up a dossier from the side table.

She stepped back, slipped back into her seat, wary, slightly confused, "General, if I did some—"

"No, no, you're fine." She visibly relaxed. Lilly was a fit-looking girl of average height, not much of a tan—she must be spending more time in that basement than the beach—with startlingly green eyes. There was a curious, searching quality to her expression that bespoke an intelligence that was measured, holding back, sussing it all up. And a soigné polish, thoughtfully put together, very urban. Unlike many of the censorship clerks, she didn't say the hell with it because there were no men around. That pointed to a sense or vision of self, who she thought she was.

*Interesting*, Hawkins thought. There also was a gold wedding band on her finger. Good guess her husband was in one of the Canadian services.

The general paused a long moment, flipping through the dossier.

"I understand you are trained on the Typex cipher machine," the general said.

"Yes, I was—am."

"Have you ever used the portable one, with the crank?"

"Some. We have to be ready to use them if the power goes out."

"Right. I see a valid driver's license, two years at Royal Victoria College, volunteered from there."

"Yes—"

"Bilingual family, French Canadian father, English mother, secondary school in Saint-Laurent, Quebec—"

"Where is that?" W said.

"Suburb of Montreal," she said, "by Mont-Royal."

*Ah, yes*, Hawkins thought, *a Montrealer.*

"A year of Spanish," Houghton said. "Married to Hector Billedoux. He's in the army—where?"

"Yes—somewhere in England. First Canadian Division."

"Very good." He slapped the folder shut and lightly threw it aside. "I am temporarily seconding you to the Secret Intelligence Service."

"Oh. I thought we already, well, here—"

"The censorship station? Not exactly. We need a cipher clerk in Mexico."

"Excuse me?"

Houghton nodded her over to W.

"Mr. Hawkins here has to go into the country covertly," W said. "Although he will carry a radio for emergencies, given the situation, it won't be practical for him to take a cipher machine, too suspicious. We'll need secure high-level communications. The problem is, we and the other Commonwealth countries no longer have embassies in Mexico, and the one man who is there is too exposed. We are going to covertly insert you into the country separately with a portable Typex. Hawkins has to leave immediately, you'll follow and catch up."

"What—I'm a clerk, I've never been out of the office—"

Lilly seemed absolutely flabbergasted, now badly rattled, her eyes damn near rolling back in her head. Hawkins sympathetically watched her nervous reaction. This surely was not what she had signed up for. Nice girl. Sheltered, middle-class life in a prosperous suburb. Thought she'd serve her country and have a nice adventure in Bermuda. Like being at a women's college, down here, in the Princess Hotel, in loco parentis and all that, watching over you. Now she was being told she had to be a Mata Hari, only without the dance and revealing costume. On her own in a foreign country she'd never visited. It was, in truth, like learning to swim by being thrown off a bridge.

She started to protest. "I—no, I didn't sign up for this."

"I gather you didn't read the papers you signed," the general said. No response, an open-mouth stare. *Obviously not*, Hawkins thought. "We can transfer you at any time to a regular enlistment," Houghton said. "You are now in the British SIS. Like everyone there you now have a reserve rank. Umm … probably second lieutenant."

"I outrank my husband? I can't outrank Hector!"

"I'm afraid you'll both have to carry on."

"But I've never been to Mexico. Been to Toronto once, Ottawa a couple of times, Quebec City, upstate New York, Vermont, now here, I—" Her eyes glancing at the door and then again and again gave it all away. Out. She wanted out—*where's the door*, that was all she could think of, pure instinct screaming, like running from a burning building, breathing slightly hard now. "How would I do that?"

"We're going to give you an American passport and fly you down to a remote section of the Texas border," W said. "We'll give you a certified check. You are to buy a *new* car. Reliable. You'll take your things, of course, and the portable Typex. Also a radio, although taking the encrypted messages to Western Union should not be a problem, businesses do that regularly."

"I'm not meeting Hawkins?"

"No. We won't come into contact at all, only remotely, probably by phone," Hawkins said.

"I drive in?"

"We'll give you a map," W said. "You'll go out of town into the desert, around the customs stations, then drive across the desert and get back on the main highway to Mexico City. You are to take the main roads, drive straight through, if possible. The highways there are generally quite safe, but we don't want to take chances."

"Mexico City!"

"We'll arrange a good hotel in a top neighborhood." She grabbed hard on a thought. You could tell from her expression, getting indignant.

"Isn't there a man? This is a man's job!"

"There isn't a man," General Houghton said. "And there is not going to be a man. You know the machine, you have a driver's license and you studied some Spanish, which is very helpful. We don't have time to do the background checks, the training, the clearances on anyone else. Many girls are stepping forward today to do new things, and they are succeeding. Like this operation here. I wouldn't be sending you if I didn't think we could rely on you."

Hawkins watched, wondering if a stiff drink wasn't in order right about now. Lilly stared at the general, then slowly shifted her gaze to W and then to Hawkins and back. Her head started to shake a bit.

"You're from Saint-Laurent, outside Montreal?" W said. She nodded. "I grew up in Winnipeg."

"Oh." Quietly, "Never been out west."

"Practically on the frontier. Wanted to get out. The war came along, duty called, I volunteered. Best decision I ever made. Wouldn't be here now."

"I see. Yes," she said, beginning to settle down, "I've heard that sort of thing. Hector seems rather excited from his letters. I hear from—" There was a long pause. Hawkins thought he detected a sigh. "From time to time," she added. Her chin, then her head, sank toward her chest. She obviously wasn't hearing as often as she'd like.

At first Hawkins had been vaguely amused, her distress a bit distant— *she'd signed those papers rather casually, hadn't she?* But now, without warning, he felt a tremendous connection and sympathy, as images and memories of a woman he'd met on his last mission, a woman he had fallen for hard in a way that didn't feel like a fleeting crush: Daisy van Schenck.

The scion of an old New York Knickerbocker family now down on her luck, she'd played a pivotal role in cracking that case. He thought back again to the morning they'd spent over tea and coffee at the Saratoga Race Course, watching the horses work out in the morning light, talking about galleries in Manhattan and marchés in Paris, followed by an incredible night at a lavish racing ball. Tough and resourceful, ruthless, too, in her own way, they had so much in common.

The flash of Lilly's gold wedding band caught his eye. *Why didn't I ask?* he thought. *What was the matter with me, what was I thinking—or not?* For a moment he felt almost stricken by the idea. But … but. It would've been so soon. Too soon. *Had to leave so fast*, he thought, *had to get here. Like Hector, had a war to fight, only right now, today.*

*And if war is dangerous, espionage in wartime is doubly or triply so*, he thought. *What are my chances of seeing this through to the very end? Marriage at the bare minimum is a promise, but what kind of promise can I make with the tread of hobnailed Nazi boots echoing in all corners of the globe? I can't even write back and tell her how much I still care unless I'm in New York or Bermuda—too big a security risk. People were almost getting married on train station platforms, that was true, but at least they could send a letter home. I can't have a home. For her, each and every day watching the mailman walk by would be a moment of pain, longing … and fear. No, wouldn't be right to dump that on her, not in a world as chaotic as this one, who knows where or how we'll all end up.*

*Lilly is lucky*, Hawkins realized. "Let's have a toast," he said.

"To opportunity?" W said. He smiled, jumping to a bar by the side for a bottle of Crown Royal, quickly pouring a set of drinks.

"To the ones we leave behind?" Hawkins said.

"To king and country!" General Houghton said.

"Yes." A small wry smile from W, a glance at Hawkins. The general didn't quite get W's drift, but he wasn't wrong. "And Canada!" W added.

Lilly held her glass up near her lips, thinking hard, then her eyes snapped back into focus very suddenly, mind now organized by a single thought.

"To doing our duty," she said. "Like Hector." The glass raised, "My husband." She added, "Get this over and get him home," then popped it back.

"To duty!" they echoed.

Hawkins slammed his back feeling the numbing warmth slide down his throat, seeing Daisy in mind. *And love*, he thought.

# -16-

*Pick your poison, indeed,* Hawkins thought. *What's worse? Swimming in your own sweat on the deck in the sun? Or choking in the heat and humidity in the forecastle?* He decided sitting in the shade made more sense, for the moment. Then he heard footsteps.

"Launch's coming, sir." It was Chief Petty Officer Farley. He and six other Royal Navy sailors were aboard in civilian clothes, all with carefully concealed pistols—no chances this time. Hawkins stepped out to the rail, made the mistake of touching it, bounced his fingers back the way you would off a hot stove and squinted into the steamy haze. HMS *Dendrobium* was visible about a mile astern, rippling like a waving flag in the Caribbean heat waves. Blake had tailed them all the way from Bermuda. They now were about twenty miles out of Veracruz, getting close. The launch meant only one thing: Blake had gotten an important radiogram. Farley and his navy men quickly lowered the accommodation ladder over the side. One went down and rushed back up with a single sheet of paper and handed it to Hawkins. He started to read, saw nothing but white glare and stepped back into the shade.

Flash from HMS *Malabar* Bermuda: Today received telex from W at British Security Coordination in NYC. States he is in contact with British national employed Parke-Bernet Gallery in

New York. Confirmed PBG received feelers from individuals in Mexico re: sale of valuable artworks including Matisse, Picasso, Chagall, Braque and others. PBG wary as to identity of individuals, sources, legitimacy, possible fencing of stolen merchandise due to contacts being unwilling to appear in person in NYC, high quality of items as stated, unusually large number of items & requested financial arrangements specifically wire transfers to Mexican banks. W states he believes it is certain involves objects under our investigation. Due to apparent difficulties to arrange sales in NYC, possible US impoundment, ascertain danger of Mexico City sales. W states no further information, otherwise continue on as planned. Good luck, Blake.

Hawkins carefully tore it in tiny pieces, scattering them over the rail. Of course, they'd go to Parke-Bernet. *Hell, I'd go to Parke-Bernet,* he thought. Sure, there were other galleries, but none matched the prestige and clout of the big auction house on the south end of the Bergdorf Goodman block, kitty-corner across the street from Tiffany's main branch. He'd been there a few times over the years trying to get them to take on the small valuables he'd picked up in Europe to supplement his income. The fresh smell of money usually overpowered the aroma of roasted chestnuts and pretzels from the street carts.

*Could they fence the works in Mexico?* he wondered again. It was a real concern. *Risky at auction,* he thought. *Have to take less, presumably, but … could that bring in enough for whatever the hell it was they were doing?* Maybe, maybe not, but in either case they probably wanted every dollar they could get, if not for whatever operation was at hand, then for the next.

Hawkins checked back. *Dendrobium* was winching up the launch. The ship turned and disappeared into the August heat as planned, back into the Gulf of Campeche. *Dendrobium* was going to meet the *Santa Lopez* in Colón, on the Caribbean side of the Panama Canal, and take its sailors off. They didn't want the Royal Navy too close, lest they be spotted from the shore.

An hour and a half later Veracruz slowly rose out of the sea, a big city of white-and-dun buildings with red tile roofs, punctuated by undulating church domes and spires, sprawling along the shore. Outside the city center the curving white beaches were packed with people. A few minutes later the ship turned by a long stone fortress, approached the port and took the harbor pilot aboard. As the ship slowed, the oppressive temperature, a thick, wet, claustrophobic casket of heat, rapidly mounted, the steel deck now burning through the shoes to the soles of the feet. A tug slowly began nudging the *Santa Lopez* into a berth.

Hawkins climbed to the bridge. Captain Lopez brightened when he saw him. With a small gesture he invited Hawkins back to his cabin.

"Been a pleasure, Captain Perez." Hawkins handed him a small, white, slightly sweaty envelope. The captain looked in, to see, without counting. There were ten one-hundred-dollar US banknotes. He smiled.

"Thank you. Rule Britannia."

"Yes. Rule Britannia." Big smile. "And those men?"

"Yes, when they come aboard I will hang a light in the window on the port-side bridge."

They shook hands and Hawkins left. *So far ... so good. We'll see,* he thought. *A very lucky man, and he knows it. Maybe General Houghton slapped some sense into him. Maybe he remembers how he went to sea in the first place. Must be the "Rule Britannia." I hope he doesn't fuck this up. I do rather like the old coot.*

It would be several hours before the tires were unloaded. Hawkins quickly collected his things, disembarked and passed through a cursory and efficient customs, the agent quickly stamping his American passport. The only delay came as the agent inspected Hawkins's suitcase radio, humming softly in curiosity and admiration. The set was in fact a considerable technical achievement, packing that kind of power into something as small as a suitcase, the best any secret service could produce anywhere in the world.

"Many stations?" he said.

"Yes. Very many." Hawkins had a fiver in his pocket, just in case, for the bribe he'd heard was routinely expected in Latin America. In conversations about foreign travel in Britain and America you always heard sighs about the corruption of South American officialdom. It went like a well-rehearsed litany: *What can you do … or … What do you expect?* Sad expressions, head-shaking reflections on the ethically lazy Latin character. The hand was supposedly always out, one needed to expect a sneering, hostile demand of largess from *gringos*. And sometimes the refrain was, *You have to make allowances!* And finally, the patronizing *a simple, sleepy people, you know?*

But clearly, not only was no bribe expected, the sense of crisp professionalism the agent conveyed—despite the withering heat—was such that the mere suggestion of a bribe would constitute a gross affront, and probably very serious legal trouble. The man smiled and carefully closed it.

"¡Recepción a México!" the agent said, adding, "Enjoy your stay." The efficiency did have its limits. The agent missed the double bottom in the case hiding his Browning Hi-Power, ammo, lockpick set and other tools. But then, customs in the US had never spotted it, either.

He hailed a waiting taxi outside, quickly checking his phrase book for the words for "good hotel" and "bath." *Really want that bath*, he thought.

"¿Un buen hotel? ¿Un baño?" The driver nodded, took him a short distance along a large seaside esplanade, the Avenida Malecón, and around a corner to the nearest decent hotel with a bath, a fairly new facility on a wide, long modern boulevard lined with palm trees, their trunks painted white partway up.

"Estacion?" Hawkins said, pointing to a large building with high windows at the end of boulevard.

"Sí," the driver said. "Ésa es la estación de tren."

Hawkins knew he was going to need transport. He checked the phrase book again.

"¿Vuelve? Come back? ¿Aquí? Here? ¿Noventa minutos?"

"Sí. Pick up. One hour and one half." Better, he spoke some English.

"Hire you for the night?"

"Sí. For night, yes? Tourist?"

"No. Business. ¿Cuánto?" The man looked confused. *Maybe I'm not pronouncing it right*, Hawkins thought. "How much?"

"Well—"

"Twenty?"

"Sí. Twenty. Bueno."

Hawkins promptly gave him a ten. "Your name?"

"Raul. One hour and one half."

"Roy." They shook hands. "Gracias."

Hawkins quickly checked in, changing some dollars for pesos at the desk, then hurried up to the room. It had a high ceiling and was painted an odd bright blue enamel, but very clean and neat. He unpacked, pausing to take the small photo Daisy sent in her last letter, rested it against the lamp on the nightstand, and gazed at it for a long moment, then quickly settled into the cool water of the tub, happy with relief from the heat.

# -17-

Ninety minutes later he emerged from the hotel, thoroughly refreshed, and found Raul waiting. It was getting dark. A cooling breeze was coming in from the ocean and people were coming out onto the streets and into the cafés and shops. Raul quickly whisked him to the head of the street, waiting and idling outside.

The train station was an impressive Spanish colonial style building, with pinkish red walls, white stone columns and tall arched windows. Very traditional. If it'd been built by British or American railroad companies, it certainly didn't look it—no Georgian brick or Greco-Roman marble. Inside was more of the same Spanish colonial style, with a large portrait several feet high of a very determined-looking man with a high collar and forehead, a full mustache and a double chin coming on—El Presidente Lázaro Cárdenas del Río.

All over Europe today one saw portraits of the Dictator: Hitler, Mussolini, Stalin, Franco. Stern miens all, often angry and belligerent, harshly glaring *down* at you. He studied the photo a moment. So this was W's nemesis. In contrast to all the others, this Cárdenas fellow didn't seem very menacing. The image had a different feel—softer, dreamier, in some way, Hawkins thought, gazing up and off, to the horizon, perhaps.

He checked the board. The last train for the day had left half an hour earlier, the next, for Mexico City, first thing in the morning. *Good.*

Raul quickly whisked him to the harbor. Longshoremen were still lifting bales of tires from the hold, piling them in a small hill on the pier. Hawkins had him park up the street, after a while sending him for some *agua mineral*s from one of the ubiquitous push carts. Hawkins got in the front seat, gesturing at the ship. They sat quietly watching, sipping the cool, sweaty bottles.

Occasionally a tattered beggar, face heavily lined and tired, would come up to the car, cupped hand held out. Raul would reach into the ashtray and toss them two or three centavos—Mexican pennies—and the man or woman would shuffle and scrape and bow away. Raul seemed to do this in a rather automatic way, not paying much attention, apparently very routine.

Sitting in silence was a trifle awkward, the language barrier making small talk impossible. Then Hawkins noticed Raul's mustache. It was exactly the same shape and size as Presidente Cárdenas's. Hawkins brushed his empty upper lip, pointed at Raul's and said, "Mustache. El Presidente."

Raul warmly smiled. "Sí. Presidente Cárdenas." He put his palm over his chest, then made a fist, lightly tapping his chest like a heartbeat. "Mi presidente. Mi corazón. Umm ... heert?"

"Ah. Sí. In your heart." He checked the phrase book. "Entiendo." The word for "understand."

*Hard to know what to make of that*, Hawkins thought. As Blake and Houghton had observed in Bermuda, Hawkins knew quite a few Nazis and Fascists in Germany and Italy. None of them ever put their hands over their hearts like that in reference to Hitler or Mussolini, nor would such a sentiment probably ever occur to them. *But ... now I'm in Mexico*, he thought. *Maybe dictators have a friendlier face here.*

An hour later the longshoremen were done with the Mexican part of the shipment. They and most of the *Santa Lopez*'s crew headed for the usual nearby bars and brothels. Hawkins saw Chief Farley on the deck, slowly and carefully coiling a rope, killing time.

Lieutenant Commander Blake had carefully chosen and briefed this contingent of sailors. What was often overlooked about the Royal Navy was that it was also an imperial navy, with men from all over the vast expanse of the Empire. One of the sailors was from Trinidad, another Gibraltar, a third Malaya. These were men who would not arouse suspicion. Farley himself was from Belfast and aptly managed a powerful Irish brogue. Most were fairly seasoned and reliable. On orders none had gone ashore.

A pair of men in white suits arrived and climbed the gangway, then two more men in work clothes arrived at the dock with a cutting torch on a dolly. A light appeared in the port window of the bridge. Eckhardt and Falkenberg, if those were their names, were aboard. A large box truck with big gold letters F DE M on the side—he'd seen that at the train station, short for Ferrocarriles Nacionales de México, the Mexican national railway—arrived and pulled up to the gangway. *Good,* Hawkins thought. *And predictable, sending that much by rail. Really the only safe way to do it.*

Some time later Chief Farley and three of his men emerged on deck, carefully carrying the first of the cases. Hawkins stared in disbelief as they made their way down to the pier. *Dear god, the Royal Navy is offloading the Nazis' loot,* he thought. Then it overtook him, he couldn't help it, he began laughing so hard he had to lean on the dash to steady himself. *Oh, too rich ... dare I put that in a report?* He imagined Blake's face when he heard, then W's and General Houghton's. *Incredible.*

Raul looked up from his newspaper, watching him laughing, puzzled. "Roy?"

But there was no explaining, or letting him in on the joke, either. Instead Hawkins held his palms up to the heavens. Raul smiled, shrugged and returned to his paper.

A customs inspector arrived, checking the cases, opening them and looking inside, then pasting them with stickers, waving at the men to load them on the truck. One ... two ... three ... it took about an hour and the trucks were full. The sailors were loitering around. Then one of the men in white suits, presumably one of the Germans, went over, took out his wallet and tipped them. That brought on another laughing jag for Hawkins. *The Nazis tipped the Royal Navy! Oh, too, too much!*

The trucks shortly left. Captain Perez and the two men in white suits came back down the gangway, all smiles, and shook hands again. The pair in white briskly walked away, probably heading for a nearby bar. When they were out of sight Farley came down the gangplank, jogging along the pier. He'd spotted Hawkins at the far end of the ship, watching. Hawkins met him partway, circling around the mound of tires. Farley instinctively started to salute, then caught himself, instead jerkily reaching into his pocket for four 100,000-peso notes, excited, laughing too.

"Group Captain! They tipped us! What's this worth?"

"About two pounds."

"Oh." His face fell, disappointed, then brightened. "Oh well, draughts on the Führer!"

"They didn't suspect anything."

"No. All we Irishmen hate the English, don't you know?" in a perfect Galway lilt.

"Righto. Hear any names? Eckhardt or Falkenberg?"

"Yes. Both of them."

"They tip, so to speak, that customs agent?"

"No. No duties on artworks, it seems."

*Oh. Another surprise*, Hawkins thought. He reflected a second, then realized, *Well, no … Of course not. I never paid duties on the old things I carried around. No one collects customs duties on art and antiquities. Why on earth did I—no, we—we automatically, unthinkingly assume the Nazis would be bribing Mexican officials?* The hidden compartment was for the Royal Navy, nothing more. Once they made it to Mexico they were fine. No need to bribe anyone. *Why did we assume that?*

No time to be thinking that over, he knew, mentally brushing it away.

"Get the address?"

"Yes." Farley handed Hawkins a small scrap of paper. Wilhelm Aust, Calle Matamoros 81, San Ángel, Ciudad de México, Distrito Federal. Which made sense.

"Perfect. You better get back. Enjoy those drinks."

"What? These lads aren't going anywhere until we get to Panama!"

"Of course. In Panama."

But who was this Aust? A cover? Or a real name? Either was possible. Or were Eckhardt and Falkenberg themselves merely cutouts? *Not in the know? Time will tell*, Hawkins thought. He ran back to the cab.

"La estación—"

"¿Los carros? Ummm—trucks?" Raul said, pointing at the F de M van. Hawkins pointed, too.

"Sí. Los carros."

"Understand."

When they got to the main entrance, instead of dropping Hawkins at the door, Raul gestured around the back. Hawkins nodded in assent. Raul quickly sped around to the side of the station. The van was parked next to a set of tracks. Railroad workers were lifting the cases into the baggage car of a train.

"Ah-ha!" Raul pointed. "El Jarocho Expreso. A Ciudad de México!" Hawkins had seen that on the board on his first trip to the station: an express train leaving for the capital at 8:00 a.m. They watched for a few minutes, then the men closed the back of the truck and drove off. Moments later, the yard workers closed and locked the doors to the baggage car. While they waited, Hawkins gave Raul the second ten, and then another five as a tip, holding a finger up to his lips for silence.

"Raul, gracias."

Raul winked back. "Mi placer."

# -18-

As they drove past to the hotel entrance Farley was waiting at the near corner. When Raul was out of sight Hawkins walked around and past him, gesturing for Farley to follow. He wordlessly handed Hawkins a note. There was an address on the front and a message on the back.

*Wir wurden vor Bermuda gestoppt. Sie werden von einem Mann gefolgt, der Hawkins benannt wird. Treffen um acht Uhr? Viel Glueck! Heil Hitler.*

"What's it say, sir?"

"We were stopped off Bermuda. We're being followed by a man named Hawkins. Meet at eight? Good luck. Heil Hitler."

Farley repeated the last in a soft whisper, "Heil Hitler."

Hawkins silently read it again, then a third time, a sense of disgust and disappointment rising. *Heil Hitler? Heil Hitler! So the goddamn bugger waited until he thought we weren't looking, then made his move. Damn fool, to think we weren't watching. I was right, though, he flipped back.*

"Aw fuck. Did you take this from Captain Perez?"

"No. One of the original sailors. Perez sent him."

"Does Perez know you nicked his man?"

"I don't think so."

"Where is he?"

"Down on the dock."

"What's his name?"

"Jorge."

Hawkins's mind, moments ago ready for rest, was now racing over what happened, assessing the possibilities. *The note isn't signed,* Hawkins realized, *and Farley didn't see Perez. Bloody hell. That's a serious problem.* Perez could've sent it. Or, the sailor could be lying, blaming the captain. Then Hawkins realized there was still another possibility: that Marinescu was lying and there was yet another man on the ship. All were dangerous— once they got to Panama a simple telegram could blow the cover on the entire operation. *Got to find out,* Hawkins thought.

After a hurried walk back to the dock, Farley led Hawkins behind a large stack of tires. Two of Farley's men were standing over a sailor sitting on the ground, their hands on pistols in their pockets. The seated man looked scared, breathing hard.

"Jorge. Is this yours? Tell me the truth." He looked back in complete incomprehension. *Is he German?* Hawkins wondered. He repeated himself in German, "Dieses ist Ihr? Sagen sie mir die wahrheit," Hawkins waved the note, pointing at it, "Dieses," and then the man, "Ihr? Sprechen!" Jorge finally got it.

"No. No. El capitan—"

"Francaise?" Another head shake. He tried to remember the phrase book. "¿Hable inglés?"

"No."

*Still have to be sure,* Hawkins thought. Then another realization— someone could be pressuring Perez, or blackmailing him, another possibility, a fourth. Have to get him off the ship in that case, alone, away from the others. He looked around. The was a truck emblazoned HERMANOS DE GONZÁLEZ parked right on the edge of the dock, the tail almost over the water. At night the harbor was desolate, not a soul around, no passing cars or trucks, no streetlights. Only the moonlight and a few lights on some distant ships.

Hawkins wrote a quick message on the back of the note, *Treffen sie uns in der halben stunde an den González-Bruder-Packwagen* and handed it back to Jorge.

"Al capitán. ¿Entiendes?" He nodded. Hawkins stepped away with Farley. "Take him and make sure he gives that to Perez, then get out of sight. After Perez leaves, launch a boat and come down behind the Lopez brothers truck here. I told him to meet me in half an hour."

"Right." With a few gestures Farley sent Jorge back, following at a discreet distance.

Half an hour later Captain Perez came around into the dark on the far side of the Hermanos de González truck. Hawkins coughed slightly to disguise his voice and said, half in a whisper, "Guten Abend."

"Ach! Guten Abend," Perez said. It was dark but the uplifting tone of voice said he was smiling. *Aw bloody hell*, Hawkins thought, anger and annoyance rising now. *Goddamn son of a bitch! Make me have to do this. Bloody idiot, walk into a trap and … smile. No questions now. I know what I have to do. Steel yourself, go cold. You can do this*, he told himself, *you can do what you have to do.* He had his Hi-Power, but a gunshot on this deserted quay wouldn't do.

A deep breath and Hawkins swung hard and hit the older man over the head with a steel bailing hook he'd found among the stacks of tires. Perez went down without a cry, he didn't weigh much, only a soft *thump*. Hawkins grabbed his hand and started to drag him. Perez roused, raising one hand up. Hawkins swung down again. Perez caught the hook, pulling and holding it for a second. Hawkins ripped it free, slammed it down again on his head. Perez slumped, a bare moan, then a shudder again. Hawkins pulled the captain's blazer around his head as he started to stir, wrapping his head up, and then began pounding away, just to be sure, or so he told himself, all semblance of control slipping away, a released fury rising with each blow, harder and harder until he could feel the skull bones giving and crunching, the unexpected explosion of a dormant volcano, a one-man Vesuvius. Everything he had to hold down, all the numbed-out feelings, what was safely deeply buried under the careful facade of the confidential agent blew out in one mad eruption.

*Bastard.* Bastard! *Son of a bitch! Lie to me, lie to us, will you? Damn fool.*

*Made me have to kill you. And to think I liked him. Rule Britannia, my ass. Blazer with fake yacht club patch. British merchant marine, the best. Hide the fact you speak German? Lie to me? Take our money? Kick me out of Paris? Send planes over London? Bomb my mother's house? Kill my relatives, my schoolmates? Fucking Nazi bastard. Think you'll get the jump on me? Leave me lying facedown in a pool of blood, will you? Bastardbastardbastard*—hitting and hitting and hitting. Then he flipped the hook around in his fingers and slammed it back down again. It easily punched through the broken skull. Hawkins pulled to yank it out and hit him again. Instead it plunged in and caught, the hook poking out through the captain's eye socket. He pulled him forward by it, dragging Perez's limp body over to the edge of the dock. Finally, he gasped to catch his breath, fell back against a bale, wiggled and worked the hook out and threw it as hard as he could off into the water.

"Hey, watch out," came a voice from below. It was Farley. *Good,* Hawkins thought. He took another deep breath, hands on his knees for a second catching up. He searched Perez's pockets, then shoved the body off the dock by its feet. It landed facedown, half in the water, half on the mud. The sailors quickly hauled him in. Hawkins looked over. It was a long drop. He couldn't see any ladders.

"Back at the ship," he whispered.

"Righto." They quickly rowed off.

A few minutes later Hawkins was waiting at the top of the accommodation ladder as they carried the body up onto the ship, wrapped in a piece of dirty canvas.

"Now what, sir?"

"The engine room." Hawkins grabbed one corner of the canvas and they carried the body inside, through the passageway, hauling him down the ladder and into the engine room. The ship was due to sail on the tide, before dawn, so the boiler was already fired, building up pressure. Hawkins opened up one of the old fire doors left over from the ship's early days when a black gang shoveled in the coal, squinting in at the white-hot heat.

"That'll do it." He pointed in. They all wordlessly picked up the body by the canvas, swung it back and gave it the heave-ho through the fire door into the center of the boiler, pushing with a poker that came out steaming hot. Hawkins slammed it shut with a hard *bang*. *Good enough for you, you bloody, lying bastard*, he thought. Then he kicked the door again.

"Can you get this thing out of the harbor yourself?"

"Of course," Farley said.

"Good. Cast off and get out of here as soon as you can. Keep the rest of the crew under armed guard down below. Once you're on the open sea radio Commander Blake, rendezvous with *Dendrobium, then* let him know what's happened. Don't use the radio for that. There's also a thousand American dollars in a white envelope somewhere in that bastard's cabin, plus whatever those two Germans gave him. Give that to the skipper."

"Right." They all stared at the fire door a long moment, then wordlessly left.

Hawkins walked back up the Avenida Malecón and around the corner to his hotel, feeling nothing but exhaustion. Inside he unpacked the suitcase radio, strung the aerial around the room, and began searching the dial for news, one eye on the photo of Daisy by the lamp. It was CBS again, this time a station out of Houston. The radio reporter was midstory, but the first thing Hawkins heard was an air-raid siren in the background. The reporter's voice was tense and urgent—whatever was going on over there clearly wasn't good. Massive air battle over the Channel. London burning. He listened a few minutes then sharply clicked it off.

He sat back in the chair. *That numb feeling's back*, he thought. Or perhaps there was nothing left inside after that outburst, the steam in the boiler gone. He cradled Daisy's photo in his hand for a moment. Still nothing. A burst of lively music floated for a second through the window. It was still early. He was tired but at the same time felt an agitation or restlessness. He went out and began aimlessly walking the streets and under several lovely old arcades, not with any purpose in mind, not running from the radio and news, instead aimlessly exploring the unknown, perhaps seeking distraction, scratching an itch he couldn't find. He paused by a crowded café. Inside a small band was playing a lively, jumping tune. A waiter brought him a cold beer. He tarried at an outside rail, listening. They played with great feeling, a tremendous happy energy. He could sense what they felt, without feeling it himself. *How nice*, he thought, *to let yourself feel, to be happy like that.*

# -19-

Hawkins walked down the aisle of the train, brushing his hand along the red plush seats, looking for the two men he saw with Captain Perez yesterday. *They're government men, too,* he thought, *on an expense account. Almost certainly in the first-class section.* Hawkins had already made another quick check of the baggage cars—a tip to the handler was required for that, although in no way was there anything illegal about it—confirmed the ten cases brought from the ship were still there, and double-checked the address, Wilhelm Aust, Calle Matamoros 81, San Ángel, Ciudad de México, Distrito Federal. He'd also checked the harbor—the *Santa Lopez* was gone. Leaving was far easier and faster than entering.

El Jarocho Expreso jarred slightly with a series of tapping noises as the locomotive pulled the couplers tight, ready to roll. Hawkins spotted the men in the second car. He sat a couple of seats away and caught a snippet of German.

One of them, maybe ten years older than the other, was quite fleshy in a muscular way, red faced and sweaty—all that mass trapped the heat. He was wearing a plain white shirt, not necessarily a bad idea—the day, as well as the locomotive, was already building up a head of steam. He had a tight crew cut, almost a shaved head, hard to tell if it was very blond or white, and an exasperated, tight-lipped expression that seemed to say he didn't approve of anything he saw, an unreflective agitated quality.

There was something odd about the man's eyes. White all around the iris, giving them a staring quality, resembling those dog breeds—a husky or pointer, perhaps—that never blink or take their gazes off their quarry for a second of introspection or reflection. The cropped stubble on the left side revealed a long scar, and the tip of his ear was missing, as if it'd been sliced or shot off. *Could that be a bullet crease on his scalp?* Hawkins wondered. With the scar and the missing part of the ear, he absolutely had the look of a tough old veteran.

The younger one, lithe and very fit looking, was wearing an expensive linen suit with a fine woven panama hat, fresh, crisp despite the heat, everything in place, handkerchief points precisely poking from his pocket. He exuded a sense of composure and self-possession, an aristocratic confidence or an ordered Apollonian quality, his gestures as smooth as his face. He had a hardcover book in one hand with torn notes sticking out the top. He was trying to read, but there was a touch of polite frustration in his glances at the other man, controlled annoyance at an unwelcome distraction. But he also had a tight-on-the-sides army haircut that didn't quite fit with the rest. Accordingly, both looked to be military types, the older one, who nonetheless acted in charge, gave the feel of a tough old master sergeant confronted with a young new lieutenant. Hawkins got the unmistakable impression they both resented the arrangement.

Veracruz's *estación* had the usual newsstand found in train stations all over the world, large and decently varied. There were, of course, many Spanish-language newspapers and magazines, and quite a few English-language ones, including papers from the States, but also local foreign-language papers. Like the US, Mexico had a significant immigrant community. One stood out to Hawkins immediately: *Deutsche Zeitung von Mexiko. Perfect*, Hawkins thought, *tailor-made*. He'd eagerly plucked it up. *I'm ready.*

The car was less than half full. Hawkins sat a few seats away from his targets, unfolded the *Zeitung* and started reading. He'd positioned himself between them and the lavatory. The train was going to make a few stops along the way, it was several hours' ride, they were bound to get up and go by at some point. *Sit back and see if they take the bait*, he thought. *Not go to them, not look like I'm aware of them or thinking about them or anyone else.*

A whistle blew and the train powerfully pulled from the station, rapidly accelerating, the end of the platform a blur as they whipped by. A few minutes later they were out of the city center into the suburbs. Hawkins looked out expecting to see the usual suburban landscape one saw in Europe or North America: industrial parks, suburban housing developments, countryside, trees. Instead the express passed through a vast and barren encampment, for lack of a better word, stretching into the distance, covered by a miasmal haze.

In the US one from time to time saw "Hoovervilles," shantytowns named after the president who presided over the start of the Great Depression, built from cast-off lumber, salvaged windows and mismatched roofs with sheet metal stovepipes sticking through. Often salvaged car seats were perched on blocks outside, holding an old man smoking.

These shacks looked nothing like that. A stove? Windows? Obviously, unimaginable luxuries. A car seat—what an absurdity. Instead, dirty smoke from small fires poured directly through the low open doorways, past the rags covering the few raw openings, if there were any, that passed for windows. The roofs were made from every kind of scrap imaginable: flattened tin cans, cut-up pieces of tire, broken halves of tiles, the walls bits of wood and cloth and mud, whatever the builder could scavenge from a dump, or the earth itself. The train slowly passed around a turn toward a switch. Indescribably filthy, mostly naked children played in the garbage-strewn mud outside the hovels.

As he stared the train slowly passed by a doorway, offering a flashing glance inside at a disheveled woman sitting on blocks of dirt. His eyes caught hers for a second, dead despair in hers, and he looked away, feeling in a vague and undefined way that looking was a guilty act of violation. *Dear god…*

Hawkins was well traveled. He'd been everywhere from Chicago to Moscow and down to Rome. The Crash and Depression had hit hard everywhere. Poverty was never difficult to find. But this was different, this shocked the senses.

A shadow crossed his paper. He looked up. The older crew-cutted man was standing over him, head at an angle looking at his paper.

"Sprechen zie deutsch?"

"Ja. Sie auch?"

Then man nodded, leaned over a bit, frowning, and said in German, "You should close that window until we get out into the countryside. These dirty animals burn dried human manure for fuel. You'll get the ashes on you. It's not safe." When he'd sat down Hawkins had opened the window in the station to get some air. He glanced around. No one else had their window open. Hawkins replied in German, "Oh god, I had no idea. Thanks!" leaping up to close it.

The man nodded again. "Enjoy your paper," looking out, shaking his head in disgust, walking back to his seat.

*Disconcerting*, Hawkins thought, felt. *Although … exactly what was disturbing?* he wondered. Getting distracted? The sight out the window? Not seeing him move? Or was it this known Nazi agent doing something decent? *Of course, only if what he's saying is true … is it?* He only needed to ponder that a second. Yes, shit, once dried, would probably burn. Dirty, like peat. *Oh god … that brown cloud. I guess all of it is true*, he decided. He turned back to his paper, now keeping an eye on them. *Letting myself get distracted*, Hawkins felt that more than he thought it, *need that numb feeling: stay on the beam.* About fifteen minutes later they were deep into the country passing cornfields. The crew-cutted man rose and opened their window, letting in a fresh and welcome breeze. He turned and caught Hawkins's eye and nodded again as Hawkins rose to open his, too.

The two men rode along like—well, two friends or acquaintances quietly talking, reading a bit, nothing seemingly going on. Hawkins kept discreetly watching but not actually looking, going through the *Zeitung* from front to back. After two or three hours a white-jacketed steward came through softly tapping a tune on a set of boxed chimes. The dining car was open for this section. The two men rose, the older man getting his jacket. Hawkins followed along.

# -20-

As they passed through the cars, the younger man held the door behind him and nodded slightly in greeting. Hawkins asked in German, "Do you know anything about the menu? I'm new here. You know how you get warnings about the food and the water." Hawkins was now fully back in undercover mode, cool and coldly sizing them up.

Both turned, open, friendly, looking at each other in a manner that said *why not?* Then the younger man said, "Yes. Come join us."

"Thanks. You been here long?"

The dining car was clean, bright and modern, maybe ten or fifteen years old, a round white enamel ceiling, mahogany trim, blue plush seats. The white-jacketed waiters were quickly setting out fresh, crisp white tablecloths. The men sat.

"A while. It's not hard, just make sure it's all cooked and only drink bottled water," the older man said.

"How do you speak German?" the younger one said.

*My accent must be off,* Hawkins realized. But it didn't matter. "My parents immigrated to the US after the last war. We spoke German at home." And in fact many had. "I kept it up, it was too useful to lose."

"A smart move these days!" the older one said.

"Yes. Germany is on the rise," Hawkins said.

"That it surely is."

"Where was that?" the younger one said.

"New York. It was easy. There are many associations, schools, the Bund, of course."

"You're a friend of Germany?"

"Of course. What brings you here?" Hawkins said.

"Business. We represent a consortium of aircraft manufacturers. And you?"

"I represent an art and antiques gallery in Manhattan. I've come looking for some Spanish colonial things we can sell at a good price, also silver. You can buy things very cheap here, get a good markup. With the crazy rents in Manhattan today, you have to have that." Hawkins handed them a pair of fake business cards they'd quickly made up in Bermuda—Alpert Gallery, Broadway and Eleventh Street. They in turn gave him a pair of theirs. To Hawkins's mild surprise, they indeed read Horst Eckhardt and Werner von Falkenberg, representing Norddeutsche Luftfahrtpartner, with an address in Mexico City.

*The name on the cases and the names the Germans gave Captain Perez,* Hawkins thought, probably real. *Von* was the key. The *von* probably meant old Prussian nobility, and Falkenberg had that to-the-manor-born air about him with a precise Hochdeutsche, or High German, accent. Eckhardt, by comparison, had traces of a Plattdeutsch, or Low German, accent, a tendency toward a hard *k* sound, a bit-off, *maken* instead of *machen* or *dag* instead of the more drawled out *tag.* Slight, but noticeable. Working class, for sure, probably from one of the north German coastal cities.

The waiter arrived for their orders. To Hawkins's additional surprise both seemed to speak decent Spanish, fluidly telling the waiter what they wanted. The waiter hesitated a second, smiling.

"¿De España?" apparently asking if they were from Spain. No was the answer. But they obviously weren't speaking the kind of Spanish spoken here in Mexico, something must've given them away, too. Then Hawkins noticed Falkenberg's tattered old book: *Spanisch Für den Hochentwickelten Kursteilnehmer—Spanish for the Advanced Student.* He'd brought his old university textbook. Perhaps he was working on his accent, Hawkins thought.

"You studied Spanish at university?"

"Yes. In Berlin, then the Kriegsakademie." There it was, the prestigious Prussian military academy, the German Sandhurst or West Point. And a member of the officer class. That seemed to make Eckhardt uneasy. Obviously, not a university man. And defensive.

"But you've been in Spain?" Hawkins said. *That was a key thing to know*, he thought. The vast and savage civil war in Spain had ended only sixteen months earlier. At Hitler and Mussolini's incitement, pro-Fascist Spanish Army units under General Francisco Franco had mutinied against the democratically elected government. The major powers, thinking they could appease Hitler and Mussolini, proclaimed their neutrality and did nothing. The two dictators at first covertly and then openly sent "volunteers" to crush the Spanish Republic and support Generalissimo Franco's coup, and get their own countries ready for war. It proved to be a dress rehearsal for the new world war.

"Yes, some years now," Eckhardt said, "that's where I learned. On the job!" He apparently realized he had divulged something he shouldn't have, quickly changing the subject, "Ah, feel that." The train was leaving the lowlands and steadily climbing into the Sierra Madre Oriental, a long range of very high mountains, the temperature dropping, a huge relief. The tracks began running along a high series of cliffs cut into the forested hillsides, a vertiginous drop below. As they rose their ears began popping, all of them working their jaws.

Eckhardt peered down. "I hope these animals don't jump the tracks."

"I didn't bring my parachute," Falkenberg said.

"Yes. These fools have no business running a railroad. Or anything else."

Hawkins was about to say, *The Mexicans seem to be doing perfectly fine*—what was there to criticize, actually? Nothing—but bit his tongue. *Better agree*, he thought. What was it people said?

"A simple people," Hawkins said.

"Exactly."

"You jump?" Hawkins said to Falkenberg.

"No. I'm a pilot. We don't plan for that! It would get expensive."

A pilot. That meant Luftwaffe, not army, Hawkins thought. And these men have both been in Spain. Did Falkenberg fly with Göring's Condor Legion on Franco's side, for the Fascists? If so, why wasn't he with the Luftwaffe now?

# -21-

"Lots of Englishmen in parachutes these days," Hawkins said, picking up his paper, setting it on the tablecloth. On the front cover was a news report about the air battle over Britain that'd been taken verbatim from Germany's Trans-Ocean News Service, which Nazi Propaganda Minister Goebbels had taken over. 150 BRITISH PLANES SHOT DOWN OVER CHANNEL, it said.

"I doubt it's that many," Falkenberg said.

"What? Of course," Eckhardt said.

"No, no, that's simply not possible. We never got kill ratios like that and the Soviet-built planes and pilots we were flying against were nowhere near as capable as the British ones." *Yes*, Hawkins thought, *the Condor Legion*, the German "volunteers" Hitler sent. That seemed to really annoy Eckhardt.

"What are you saying?"

"A big air battle, you're not going to knock down a quarter of their force, especially when you're escorting bombers. Chasing after a fighter is not your job. You can't abandon them. And you have to get to where they are, the sky is a big place, you're always chasing specks on the horizon. You have to think about the closing speeds, the arithmetic of that, how long it takes to climb to a high altitude if you're low. If you're on the deck it can take as much as fifteen minutes." He seemed to sense he was treading somewhere dangerous. "Someone's giving them bad information."

Lunch arrived, the conversation suspended by food and cold beers. Hawkins took a long sip, ending with a genuine *ah*.

"That's good."

"Yes. Made by German settlers."

"Oh, my ears. You can tell we're getting higher."

"Yes, every now and again, getting higher!" They all laughed, working their jaws as their ears popped, followed by another raising of the glasses.

Eckhardt had ordered a steak, very rare. As the waiter set it down he removed a small folding leather case from his jacket pocket. When he flipped it open there was a row of curved jet-black knives. He saw Hawkins's quizzical expression.

"Have you ever seen one of these?" Hawkins shook his head. "It's an obsidian blade, a copy I made from an Aztec original. I collect them. These are the kinds of things you should put in your gallery. Other Aztec artifacts also. I tell you, they have the most wonderful things here."

"Maybe. Can't say I know anything about them."

"Archeology is a passion of mine." Eckhardt picked one up and held it in the light for Hawkins to see. "This one's an original." It was about three inches long, with a smooth curved blade, the color an absolute black. "This is too valuable to use." He put it back. "I learned to chip my own so I would have ones to use." He took the other and went to work on his steak. Falkenberg watched with some amusement, glancing at Hawkins, then ever so briefly rolling his eyes.

"These knives seem perfectly nice," Hawkins said, picking up his own cutlery.

"No," Eckhardt said, "the Aztecs were the best flint chippers of any civilization. Didn't have metal tools, didn't need them. An obsidian blade—"

"What's obsidian?"

"Volcanic glass, formed in the intense heat and pressure of the earth. No foundry can forge material with such power. They're twelve times sharper than any metal object, by far the sharpest blades humans have ever made. The best Solingen swords are no better than butter knives in comparison." To illustrate he sliced his bloody steak with incredible ease and finesse, wavy undulations of precisely cut meat. "Here." He smiled and handed it to Hawkins. "You realize that's iguana you're eating, not chicken? Right?"

"Uh—no."

"That's what they do here. It looks and tastes like chicken but you're actually eating lizard."

Falkenberg laughed slightly, "It might be pollo."

"Is it tough?" Eckhardt said.

Hawkins sawed away at it.

"Maybe." It was a bit rubbery.

"Could be a tough old farmyard hen," Falkenberg said.

"Try it! But be careful, it's very sharp." Eckhardt held the knife out again. Hawkins looked down at his plate. *Could this white meat be from a big reptile?* he thought. It was slightly unnerving … but then, Eckhardt was probably right about the fly ash. Iguana. Maybe. Did it matter anyway? *Naw*—Hawkins took Eckhardt's blade and pressed it slightly against the meat. It was indeed astonishingly sharp, if "sharp" was an adequate word to describe it. It cut—no, *floated*—through the tough stringy meat, whatever it was, with an eerie effortlessness, as easily as a fresh meringue, hardly anything there but air. Further, the cut was even and smooth like polished stone, shining and clean looking. He turned the meat, looking at it in some awe.

"That's perfection."

"Yes! They are the most perfect things ever made," Eckhardt said. "Black is the color of nothingness, the color of death. They're a portal to another world, the world of the dead. The Aztecs used just such blades for their human sacrifices—they could cut a man's heart out in a second or two, one slice across, then around inside." He twirled his wrist. "Pull out the heart so fast they could hold it beating in front of the conscious victim's eyes for him to observe as part of the ritual. Did you know that in 1487, when the Aztecs dedicated their new temple to their hummingbird god Huitzilopochtli, they sacrificed eighty thousand victims in four days to consecrate it? The lines up the front of the pyramids must have stretched for miles, the captives bound between a pair of warriors caparisoned with rich feathered headdresses on their helmets, wild colors, their helmets sculptures of eagles, jaguars, serpents, with great feathered fans behind, towering over their heads and down their backs." He stopped for a moment, happily gazing at it in his imagination. "Can you imagine the magnificence of it!"

"Quite a sight I'm sure," Falkenberg dryly said. From his expression he looked like he couldn't decide whether to be amused or alarmed.

"They needed so many sacrifices they had what they called 'flower wars,'" Eckhardt said. "The chiefs of vassal tribes they'd conquered were forced to periodically send their armies into battles where they were hopelessly outnumbered so that the Aztecs could take captives. It was a form of tribute. The chiefs were then compelled to come to the capital, Tenochtitlan. As their men were sacrificed they would sit behind a screen of roses, anonymous and unseen by the victims, joining the Aztec rulers in a sumptuous feast, including eating the meat of their own men. When they were done the Aztecs saved all the skulls in a rack the size of a huge building next to the temple so that Huitzilopochtli could gaze on them. There were over a hundred thousand skulls in it. The Spanish counted them."

Eckhardt had that unfocused gaze again, staring off and presumably seeing it all, gently waving a piece of steak around on the tip of his obsidian knife. Hawkins's eyes carefully followed the meat and blade.

*Damn glad I have my gun,* Hawkins thought. *Damn glad. That damned thing is too close to my nose.*

Falkenberg warily watched, one eyebrow raised. "Did you know der Führer is a vegetarian?"

"I did not know that," Hawkins said. Eckhardt paid no attention.

"The Aztecs understood the transcendent power of death," Eckhardt said, "the power of death made their empire great. The Führer is right, Christianity made us weak, we lost that power. They have, too. If death returns to Mexico it will again be great. You will see!"

By now Falkenberg had completely stopped eating, resting his cutlery on his plate, fingers of one hand curled on his chin, carefully observing Eckhardt's growing excitement, an expression of deep unease on his face.

*Does he think Eckhardt is somewhat nuts?* Hawkins wondered. *That'd be my guess.*

"They worshipped a hummingbird god? When I see hummingbirds I don't think of killing people," Hawkins said.

"Huitzilopochtli was also the god of war and the sun. Blood sacrifice was required every day to ensure the sun's return. It makes sense. They had to go to war, had to! To get the sacrifices they needed. To make the sun come back. It was a jealous god."

*What to say to that?* Hawkins thought. "I can see you're quite the expert. You've been here a long time, then?"

"Only a year now last May." That meant he'd come right after the fall of the Spanish Republic.

"I came four months ago," Falkenberg said.

"It must be frustrating to miss out on the big show," Hawkins said. He sensed the beer was starting to loosen everyone up.

"Yes. It is. They didn't think they needed me. They were wrong." He frowned. "This thing with the British is taking too long. We thought they were finished. They should be finished." A wave of unease flowed across Falkenberg's face, his lips now tight, looking down, shaking his head slightly. Eckhardt's mouth was full but he looked irritated.

*There's a surprise*, Hawkins thought. *Actually, a big surprise. Falkenberg's worried? He looks it. That's a Luftwaffe officer's perspective? What's he hearing? Need to get that back to W as soon as Lilly gets here with her cypher machine. Got to play up to this.*

"Surely you're not worried," Hawkins said. "I mean, look what Germany did. You can go back a thousand years—" Falkenberg took a deep breath. He and Eckhardt both began nodding vigorously.

"Well, yes, yes, that is all so true," Falkenberg said. "I initially feared a drawn-out affair, like the last war, but"—he began laughing and smiling—"he pulled it off. It's amazing, simply amazing. You have to give Herr Hitler credit, truly—he saw something no one else did. Starting with going into the Rhineland, then Spain, Czechoslovakia, then Poland, and everything from Norway to France. You wake up in the morning, thinking it all must be a dream, then you rub your eyes and realize it's not, and you lay there laughing. It's delightful. Everyone feels it."

The train came around another bend. In the distance was a snowcapped mountain, maybe seventeen or eighteen thousand feet high, a volcano with a wisp of smoke or steam rising from the caldera. Hawkins turned to look.

"Popocatépetl," Falkenberg said.

"You worry too much," Eckhardt said.

"Perhaps so. It's in the breed, you know, it's drilled into us, to keep the eyes open. As long as the Americans leave us alone we'll be fine. This air battle? It's little more than a mop-up operation at this point, even if it is taking longer than expected."

"Yes, what about the Americans?" Eckhardt said.

*Be careful,* Hawkins sensed, *don't show how you feel, let that dead feeling work for you.*

"No one there wants the US to get in this time," Hawkins said. "After the last war, there were such misgivings, so much disillusionment. All those lives. What did it accomplish? Whose fight was it? Many questions."
*Parrot back the rhetoric,* Hawkins thought, what was Goebbels saying? "Except for the arms merchants, who want to profit, the banks, the Jews, Roosevelt and his English-loving friends, everyone wants to stay out of it. Not America's fight."

*Ja, ja,* they both heartily agreed, the US should stay out.

"Not America's fight," Eckhardt said. "Here, let's have a toast."

"To what?" Falkenberg said. "The Führer?"

"To another victory. Like Spain! ¡Viva la Muerte!"

Hawkins knew what that was: Long Live Death, the slogan of the Fascist troops in Spain, a salute to nihilism, death and destruction of the old order. *Ah yes,* Hawkins thought, *you spent some time there. And not well.*

Falkenberg raised his glass, looking at Hawkins, smiling slightly. "Let's stick with Heil Hitler."

# -22-

As the train climbed through and into the mountains you could actually feel the incline pressing you back into the seat, like a plane taking off, ears periodically popping from the altitude. After a couple more hours they came through passes over seven thousand feet high, past towering snowcapped mountains in the distance. Then around a bend and before them lay the Valle de México, stretching fifty miles across, a verdant, brilliant-green bowl hemmed by the mountains, classic volcanic cones five thousand feet higher. In the center sprawled La Capital.

Hawkins checked their business cards again. Clear addresses, phones, even a telex number. That made things much, much easier, no question of what to do next or whom to follow. He could easily pick up Eckhardt and Falkenberg's trail later—they weren't going to sell many airplanes if people couldn't find them. That meant he was free to follow the cases. A good guess was that another trucking company would pick them up and deliver them to whoever this Aust was, that Eckhardt and Falkenberg would keep the same distance and deniability.

El Jarocho Expreso plummeted down the mountainside into the city, picking up speed—a tremendous rushing, rattling, accelerating feeling, wind blasting through the windows. The people on the train began stirring in excitement, murmuring "La Capital! La Capital!" Into the city, the impoverished suburbs a blur, then the city center, domes of churches and monuments in the distance, finally a dark braking into the station that had them all leaning forward on the seats.

Hawkins checked his map against the business cards, then skimmed his guidebook for a good hotel near Eckhardt and Falkenberg's offices in the downtown off the Paseo de la Reforma. The Hotel Imperial seemed the logical choice, a top-class hotel, near the main government offices and embassies. Car agencies were nearby, too. It'd be good to rent one, if he could.

The station was another Spanish colonial like Veracruz, taxis waiting outside. As he hit the street with his bags he saw Eckhardt and Falkenberg several cabs down. *Good*, he thought, *I'm right on following the trucking company.* He gave them a big cheery wave. Waves and a smiling *Auf Wiedersehen!* came back.

A few minutes later Hawkins was tipping the Imperial's bellboy. The view out the corner window was spectacular, looking down the Paseo de la Reforma at a monument to what appeared to be Columbus. The avenue was vast, lined with trees and beaux arts mansions, all obviously inspired by Baron Haussmann's reconstruction of Paris, including the Hotel Imperial itself, surrounded by verdant topiaries. The concierge—first-rate man, anywhere—had a car, a black '32 Ford Model A coupe, fetched from an agency across the street by the time Hawkins had gotten back downstairs. And he was deeply apologetic.

"It's old, so very sorry, the best we could do on such short notice."

But it was perfect, nothing fancy that would stand out here, an anonymous car that would blend in. He had to hurry. The day was getting long, the light wasn't going to hold, and who knew if he could find the address in the dark? He turned down the grand avenue, passing by the leafy medians. The Champs-Élysées had nothing on it for scale, it was bigger, wider, cutting through the city, busy with cars, sprinkled with statues. The streets were crowded with people passing by the elegant old houses and smart, modern-looking shops. It was slow going, light to light past uniformed traffic cops with white gloves, along the pleasant-looking, crowded cafés. As he drove he could see more big beaux arts–style monuments in the distance.

The sun was setting when Hawkins finally found his way to the address in San Ángel, an old Spanish colonial town, now a rather nice-looking suburb about nine or ten miles south of the city center and the hotel. He drove by once, then twice, checking the numbers. All the houses in the neighborhood had high stone or adobe walls around them, hiding the homes, only red tile roofs, greenery and trees peeking over the top. A few had Spanish-style windows with curlicue iron grates over them and heavy, elaborate doors. All had large gates, big enough to drive a car or carriage inside. Few cars were on the street. He parked, waiting. Some people walked by, eyeing him suspiciously. Not good, he realized, too conspicuous. He drove back to a pretty square near a church and a café, parked and walked back up. After circling the house again, he looked carefully up and down the street, then slipped behind a large broad-leaved tree, toed his shoes off, checked the bottoms for filth, pocketed them and shimmied up the tree, climbing into the branches, pulling himself up with a heave.

As he teetered on the limb for a few seconds he felt dizzy and queasy. *What's wrong?* Then he realized: it was the 7,400-foot altitude, like going up the Alps, a pinched feeling in the head that'd been there all day. *Careful ... You were warned. Take it easy.* It passed after a few seconds and a couple of deep breaths.

He turned and sat and heard odd noises, a clucking sound. There were several chickens roosting in the branches, presumably waiting to sleep. They started making noises, alarmed at the intrusion. Hawkins froze. *Damn it*, he thought. *Going to be given away by a bunch of bloody birds? What the hell are they doing up here?* For a second he wondered if he could grab one, wring its neck and stuff it in the branches. But the light wasn't good, they seemed pretty agile and how many were there? Hard to tell. Would they fight back? Roosters do fight. He came here to fight Nazis, not chickens, they had no creed or cause, and they already had their freedom, what with being up here in the tree instead of a coop. But the damn birds were going to give him away if they didn't shut the hell up. He began making a clucking noise, trying to calm them down, moving as slowly as a sloth, not looking at them. They obligingly moved farther out on the branches, giving him some room.

He checked the big limb he was perched on. Not too clean. He spread a handkerchief and sat on it. The chickens warily watched him and when they decided he wasn't about to grab their necks they finally settled down. *Good. This'll work*, he thought. But what a contrast, to have the countryside intrude into the edge of a metropolis like this. Despite the boulevard and elegant mansions, this was a place not far from its rural past. Or perhaps to travel outward from the center was to travel back in time, to that rural past. How far back could one go? San Ángel looked very Spanish, very quaint, lovely. Were Eckhardt's Indians here, too? The people in the shantytowns, who were they? Where did they come from? The country, probably. And that past.

A man walked by, then a pair of women wrapped in shawls—it was starting to get cool and fresh. No one saw him. It was dark now and the chickens were asleep.

About half an hour later a large truck came up the street, slowed, hunting for the address, then stopped. One man got out and knocked. A light went on. There was nodding and agreement at the door. A man came out to watch. The moving crew opened the truck and began setting the cases on the sidewalk. Then with nary a glance around they began whisking the cases inside the compound.

Hawkins stood, trying to see over the wall, but the tree was too far out on the opposite side of the street. All he could see was a solid mass of broken glass bottles cemented all along the top of the parapet. He looked back at the wall behind him. It, too, was lined with long shards of broken glass, pointing upward, ready to impale him or any other intruder. *Not going to be sneaking over these walls*, Hawkins thought. *No way of telling who's inside, either. Damn.*

It took forty minutes to unload the truck and move the cases inside. The first man who came out returned and signed a clipboard, then the truck charged up and left. Hawkins waited about five minutes, then he surrendered the tree to the chickens.

# -23-

When he awoke Hawkins found a small note had been slipped under his door. It had a phone number and a time: *9:10 a.m.* That was prearranged. Public phone booth to public phone booth, untraceable, move them regularly, no room phones where the desk clerk, or the police, or who knew who, could listen in. The phones in the booths had numbers on them, they were easy to call.

At 9:10 precisely he sat in a booth off the Imperial lobby, dropped some pesos in the slot and dialed. It rang once. Lilly's lightly accented but unmistakable voice came over the line.

"Mr. Hawkins?"

"Everyone calls me Roy. Or Hawkins."

Hawkins was still waking up, hadn't had his morning cup. But Lilly was flying, high and bright, talking incredibly, almost inaudibly fast.

"Ah, Hawkins! There you are! Hello again! It's me, Lilly Billedoux! Reporting in! To you! I have my machine set up! Ready to go!"

"Ah … yes. And where would you be?"

"At the Reforma. Or, you mean right now? In a booth. In the lobby. At the Reforma."

"Lilly, slow down, my god—"

"Oh. Oh! Oh! Oh! Am I talking fast? I'm sorry. I'm talking fast. I haven't been to bed in two days, I think? They told me to drive straight through. So I got some Benzedrine inhalers. Asthmatics use them. To open the bronchial passages."

"Yes, I know, pilots sometimes use them to stay awake on long flights. I gather you broke the tube open and swallowed the little paper strip?"

"Yes. In Mexico. Twice. I got in late last night, set everything up, cleaned the room again. Ha ha! Isn't it funny I did that? These things are great, like twenty cups of the best coffee!"

"How did it go? Other than not sleeping?"

"I bought a car! Never bought a car before."

He chuckled. "You're one up on me. I only *expropriate* them. What did you get?"

"Ford V-8. With an automatic. Not such a big selection on the border."

"Nice. Then what?"

"Drove down the road at dawn, counted off the miles, turned into a field, crossed a dry riverbed, got back on the main highway. First hour or two I was scared to death I was going to get caught."

"Then?"

"Bored to death. It's a long ways!"

"It's not Denmark, to be sure."

"Late in the day, maybe eight o'clock, broke open the first inhaler. Swallowed that little strip. That was quite a kick! Zing! Drove all night I did!"

"I better get my report to you before that stuff wears off."

"Why?"

"You're going to go beddy-bye when it does. Don't make a habit of those things, you're not going to like the comedown."

"Oh. I see. Of course. I have my pad, fire away."

Hawkins quickly began dictating the report: The trip to Veracruz. Eckhardt and Falkenberg were their real names. The unloading, them tipping the Royal Navy men. She interrupted with a brilliant high giggle, suddenly slam-shifting back and forth between French and English.

"Ah, mon dieu, c'est hysterique! Le funniest thing."

Then he added killing Perez. There was a huge sucking gasp.

"What! You killed a man?"

"Um. Sure. Had it coming, you know? Bastard tried to double-cross us."

"That's awful."

"Not the first time, won't be the last, if I'm lucky."

"How could that be lucky?"

"They didn't kill me first."

"Oh. Sorry. Oui oui."

"Take a deep breath, Lilly."

"Righto. Encore pardon. I'm new to all this."

"Don't apologize, it's fine."

He finished up with Falkenberg's odd worry about the progress of the air battle over England. That finally slowed her down.

"Whoa. That is peculiar."

"Yes. One last thing. Have W immediately send a telegram via Western Union telling me to check with Trotsky, my address at the Hotel Imperial. Better go! Let me know when you wake up."

"Talk to you later!"

"Ah, it'll be tomorrow, or probably the day after, if you're lucky."

"Right. Tomorrow. Or the day after."

# -24-

Hawkins walked around the corner of the Avenida Viena craning his neck up. Crude red-brick pillboxes with narrow gun slits had been erected on the corners of the gray-green plastered walls and balusters. There were, presumably, armed guards in them, although in the bright sun it was impossible to tell. The towers were obviously needed. Fairly fresh bullet holes pockmarked the walls and the bricked-up windows. He pounded on the gray steel door of the garage, the only apparent entrance. A man holding a pistol suspiciously looked out. Hawkins handed him his fake New York business card.

"I wonder if it would be possible to talk to Mr. Trotsky."

"'Bout what?"

"Art in the Soviet Union." The man looked at the card, stared at him.

"Wait," and slammed the door. About five minutes later he returned with another man, both with revolvers pointed at his chest and gestured for Hawkins to step forward, quickly and thoroughly frisking him, including the inside of his hat. Hawkins assumed that would happen—he'd left his Hi-Power in the hidden compartment in his luggage.

"He's very busy, don't presume on his time," the guard said, although what Trotsky had to do these days that was so important seemed rather vague. Hawkins followed the guard through a nice walled garden, up a low set of stairs, through a baroque-style door and into the house, the other man close behind, holding his gun in his pocket. They turned a corner, past a kitchen, a small, plain dining room and around to Trotsky's study. He was waiting at a table covered with books and papers.

The place seemed a rather seedy setting for a man who once was one of the triumvirate ruling the largest country on earth, second in command of the Bolshevik Revolution, and created and led the world's biggest army to total victory in a civil war. Cheap furniture, cracked plaster walls, wood floors painted bloodred, like the decks of ships of the line in the age of sail. Was that supposed to be the color of revolution? *And to think he was going to lead a new rebellion against Stalin from here. Sad.*

Trotsky glanced at his card again and rose to offer his hand, speaking a heavily accented English, but well.

"Art in the service of revolution has long interested me. In the Middle Ages the Christian myth employed monumental art in the service of the Church, investing powerful meaning in stone and glass. In so doing they created a new man, the Christian man, from the pagan. We must do the same to create a new Soviet man from the capitalist one. What about art in the Soviet Union do you want to know?"

"Was modern art part of that project? Was it needed or wanted?"

"Specify, please."

"Abstract painters, the impressionists, the cubi—"

"Of course not. That art is evidence of the crack-up of a decadent and declining bourgeoisie. Why are you asking about those kinds of works?"

That was distressingly like the things the Nazis said, Hawkins thought.

"The Bolshevik Revolution confiscated the imperial estates along with the houses and possessions of many wealthy people. There were, presumably, works from the last forty or fifty years or so of, this, well, decadent art you are referring to. My employer has received some mysterious offers of artworks that seem to be transiting here. Some of them also seem to have been on ships that have transited Soviet ports. We're wondering where they actually came from, if they could be from these confiscated properties, or from somewhere else in Europe."

"Nothing was brought into Russia after the last world war started. I am doubtful there was anything more recent. What do you care if the Soviet state is selling them? The state had the right to seize them in the name of the Revolution, and if it is selling them, it has the right to do so, too."

"I suppose, but our problem is that many of the original owners fled abroad. We are worried these people could sue us to get them back."

"I see. Yes, yes, of course, the international bourgeoisie will close ranks to protect its own and its privileges."

"Are you aware of any current sales by the Soviet Union? Anything you can tell us?"

Trotsky leaned over the table, curiously studying Hawkins for a quick second.

"Who are you actually working for?"

"Excuse me?"

"The British SIS?"

"What? No!"

"Moscow would have no interest in asking such questions. If these things came from there, they would know. So, too, Berlin, Rome. They would know, also. France, Holland are now occupied. The Americans have turned in on their isolation. That leaves London."

*Good lord*, Hawkins thought. He suddenly began to wonder about the man with the gun behind him.

"No. I'll confess, I am a sort of investigator. My employers have an interest in this question." Hawkins took the telegram from his pocket and handed it to Trotsky. It had taken only an hour and a half for Lilly to send the report and the request and for them to respond, incidentally confirming she got the transmission out before she crashed. Trotsky read it in a glance.

"Sent this morning. From New York. Very impressive." Trotsky leaned back, smiled indulgently and adjusted his little round glasses. "Of course, I agree the artworks probably could not originate from Soviet sources. But there are many strange things going on in the world today."

"Stalin helping Hitler?"

"Stalin and the bureaucracy will do anything to hold on to power and prevent the creation of a workers' state, including helping Hitler. But that doesn't matter, it will backfire."

"How so?"

"Hitler will eventually attack the Soviet Union." He said it with a smile.

"You act like that's a good thing."

"From the wreckage will come a world revolution and the final realization of a true socialism."

*The Great War killed twenty million,* Hawkins thought. *How many would another?* Trotsky was discussing death and suffering on an unimaginable scale as calmly as the virtues of various laundry detergents. Hawkins thought back to his father, gassed in the trenches of Flanders, his eventual decline, the final months gasping in an oxygen tent when the hydrochloric acid formed from the chlorine gas he'd inhaled rotted his lungs out. The circle of pain and suffering from that one death alone. Multiplied by millions. *Imagine it—no, you can't imagine it,* he thought. *Impossible. My god. This man is stark raving mad,* Hawkins realized with an almost neck-snapping start.

Hawkins also sensed an overwhelming feeling, one he tamped down like all his other reactions: he intensely disliked this little man, his inhumanity in the purported interest of a purely abstract humanity, his intellectual pretentiousness—Christian myth, indeed—the crumbs on his lapels, the garlic on his breath, the arrogant manner. But if Trotsky knew something, he needed him. And after that unsettling exchange, there was certainly no doubting his genius.

"If you say so. In the meanwhile—why are these things coming here? Could the Soviet government—Stalin—be doing Hitler a favor, moving art objects stolen in Occupied Europe past the British blockade into neutral countries?"

"That is a dangerous matter, if it is true." He stared hard at Hawkins. "*Why* is the question." Another pause, then ponderously, "What would Stalin demand in return? *Hmm.* He has no interest in the goodwill of others. This expands the picture here greatly. Very serious. As you may imagine I have a considerable interest in helping you, whoever you're working for."

"The Alpert Gallery—"

"You may have noticed my guards and the towers on my house. Stalin has tried to kill me several times. The last was only a few months ago, his agents machine-gunned the building. You may have noticed the bullet holes in the walls. He thinks the death of a man will mean the death of the Revolution. He is wrong—it is inevitable. Nonetheless, I do not calmly accept my own destruction. I also have an interest in what is going on, who is involved, and I will try and find out more. I will make inquiries. Come back in a day or two. In the meanwhile, if these things are coming here, there are members of the artistic community, *real* Communists, that is, the anti-Fascist vanguard, who may see something here or be able to find out." Trotsky began writing a short note, "A truly revolutionary art is still emerging, but they are making great progress here in Mexico," then wrote a pair of names and addresses on the back and handed it to Hawkins. "Start here. Madame Kahlo and Mr. Rivera are good friends of mine, with many contacts. I owe my asylum here to Mr. Rivera. He intervened with President Cárdenas on my behalf. The president is not a true revolutionary, but he is the most honest politician in the world. Go down Viena to Allende, around the corner to Londres. The blue house, you can't miss it."

# -25-

Trotsky was right, the blazing azure building, which wrapped around a long corner, was impossible to miss. No brick guard towers, either, and surely no guns. Hawkins had walked over, his head having adjusted to the altitude, reflecting on what a brilliant day it was, the sky a perfect cerulean blue. The eye seemed to penetrate deeper into the air at this high altitude, the sun somehow more direct and near, intensifying the lush greenery all around, an early morning shower washing the pavements and air. The Valle de México had the most amazingly weirdly wonderfully perfect climate. Because cooling high altitude and tropical location balanced each other off, temperatures never varied much from season to season. Winters dry, summers it rained. Evenings cool and refreshing. In this clear morning, it was a heady feeling.

Hawkins rang a bell at the gate, tipped his hat to the maid and handed her the letter. She took it and gestured for him to wait, quickly returning. She led him through a house filled with Mexican folk art to a ground floor studio. A beautiful but severe-looking woman was sitting in front of a large easel next to a table littered with paint and brushes, wearing a loose white dress embroidered across the top with roses, her hair in braids. She was reading the note again, a big smear of paint on the paper. She looked up.

"What a wonderful place for an artist," Hawkins said.

"Yes?"

"I walked over thinking how incredible the light is here. It must be the altitude."

"Yes." She looked out. "An artist must have light. It's good today, but not always."

Hawkins properly introduced himself and she gently took his hand between her fingers.

"This is such a shocking message from my friend Leon. I truly love him and I will do anything to help. Every artist would be horrified to think their work has been stolen from those who love it. And by the Fascists! These are modern works?"

"Yes. What the Nazis regard as decadent works. They'd like to erase them but they're worth too much money, at least at the moment, to discard."

"By who?"

"Braque, Picasso, Matisse, Chagall—"

"Pablo! You are sure?"

"Yes. I'm absolutely certain of it. You know him?"

"Of course I know him. He became a good friend at my exhibition in Paris. This is terrible. He will be enraged. He has such a temper. He is a passionate man."

"I'm sure. These works may be here now, and in the hands of a German named Wilhelm Aust. He lives in San Ángel."

"I will ask Papa. If there is an Aust here, he will know him. Papa was born in Germany. He knows all the German people. It's not so large a community."

"He's from Germany?" Concern was obviously in his voice.

"You must not worry, he is part Jewish. He is no friend to the Nazis! Unfortunately, there are too many. Papa is the finest photographer in Mexico. All the people go to him, especially the Germans." She pointed at a portrait of herself on the wall. "That is his work."

Hawkins stepped over to look, a clear and serene image of her taken from below silhouetted against the sky and clouds.

"That is wonderful. He is very good."

"Thank you. Wait here." She got a cane and swung on it into the hallway, grunting and crying softly in pain, holding her stomach in. Hawkins noticed a withered leg and a bandaged foot. Polio, probably. He could hear her distant voice, then a knock of her cane.

"Papa? Meine Liebe? Es tut mir leid Sie aufwecken. Wie war dein Nickerchen? Sólo un poco de dolor. Sí, es difícil envejecer." They chatted on for few minutes, swirling from one language to another. Then she asked about Wilhelm Aust, that she had an interested guest. And of course he knew him. They talked for a few more minutes while Hawkins looked around at her paintings, including the self-portrait with a pair of black cats she was working on. Then he heard the cane tapping up the hall.

"Papa says Aust is a former Imperial German naval officer. He settled here after the last war. He owns an insurance agency, Seguro del Capitolio, representing a Swiss company. Highly respected. His office is near the Zocalo. Papa has taken many photographs for him, pictures of wrecked cars and burned houses. Eh, when you have a photography studio you must oblige paying customers."

*Insurance? That makes all kinds of sense*, Hawkins thought. *And offers all kinds of possibilities. Actually, that's half the equation.*

"Thank you, that's marvelous. What about galleries, are there any dealers here who are, well, on the shady side? Or are Nazi sympathizers?"

"Sympathizers? I would say no, and I think I know them all, but shady? Heads can be turned. Money ruins everything."

"I'd like to meet some of those. The ruined ones, that is."

"I cannot help you myself, but I have a friend, a young protégé, a talented artist, who can show you around. Come back tomorrow. And I will speak with Diego. He knows every—" The maid was at the door, mouth open on the edge of a shriek.

"Es camarada Trotsky! Ha habido otro ataque! Algo terrible ha sucedido!"

"What?" Hawkins said.

"Stalin! That monster! He's tried to kill Leon again." She started off without her cane, almost fell, reached back as Hawkins grabbed it for her and hobbled to the phone. "I must call Diego. Go. See what they have done. Return tomorrow."

Hawkins raced out of the house and began running. As he turned into the Avenida Viena he could see a crowd at the end of the street. He sprinted down hard, holding his hat, had to stop halfway, bend over, hands on knees and catch his breath, his head suddenly buzzing—*damn, the altitude*—started again and pushed his way into the crowd. Police were running in and out of the house, guns drawn. The people's voices were rumbling in an angry, excited way, some shouting, mostly in Spanish, here and there he could hear the words "Trotsky" and "Stalin" and the question "Muerto? Muerto?" *Dead? Dead?*

An ambulance arrived pulling up to the gate, opening its back doors. The gate opened. The guards carried Trotsky out, his head wrapped in bloody cloths. He waved slightly with one hand. They cheered, a burst of applause, then one man began singing "The Internationale" in Spanish— "*Arriba, parias de la Tierra*"—others joined in, in several languages, loudly, as the ambulance drove off.

Then another commotion at the door. Several police officers and plainclothes detectives emerged surrounding a man with a bandaged head. The crowd surged forward to get at him, cries of "¡Asesino!" and "Assassin!" and "¡Justicia ahora!" rending the air. The officers began swinging with their nightsticks, thudding against arms and shoulders and heads, forcing the mob back, jostling violently, pushing their way through. After a minute of two of struggle they got the man in a police van and sped off, siren wailing, the crowd running and screaming in pursuit, shouting curses and insults.

Hawkins drifted back down the street, his head feeling in a vise from the air or something. He found the old Ford and heavily sat in it until he recovered a bit. *So they finally got him*, he thought. He queasily remembered the almost flip casualness with which Trotsky proposed the death of millions, and implicitly his father's own suffering. *Maybe it's a good thing*, Hawkins thought, *maybe he got what he deserved, the millions who died in Russia. What a horrible place he helped create. And his opinion of Cárdenas. An honest man who seizes other people's property. There's a novel idea.*

But his head began to clear some more as he rested. *Wait ...*

*Waitwaitwait—what if he doesn't recover? What am I thinking? No—don't think that. Damn*, he thought. *This is damn bad.* Trotsky's messages started all this. What could he find out? Damn.

Then he realized, *I probably need to eat something. Find a café.* His hand touched a newspaper—*Deutsche Zeitung von Mexiko.* He opened it and began scanning the ads. There it was: Seguro del Capitolio. Tarifas Justas. Servicio confiable.

*Something odd*, he thought. *What is it?* He puzzled over it a long moment. *What? Maybe it's the thin air, brain still adjusting. Then ... No, wait ...* He fumbled in his wallet for Eckhardt and Falkenberg's business cards, then checked the *Zeitung*, holding the cards to the paper. *Damn. There it is*: Norddeutsche Luftfahrtpartner, 37 Calle de Tacuba.

# -26-

"Guten Tag." Hawkins shut the frosted glass door labeled SEGURO DEL CAPITOLIO in arched letters and handed his fake Alpert Gallery card to the clerk at the desk. He'd checked the building register in the lobby, then quickly scanned the corridor. Seguro del Capitolio was at number four, number six, Norddeutsche Luftfahrtpartner's door—dark with no name—was down the hallway. In German he asked if Herr Aust was in? Aust heard German being spoken from his office a few feet away and quickly came, hand outstretched in welcome. The usual introduction, the reference from the Kahlos, and they were sitting in Aust's office.

Aust was a tall well-tanned man with large brown freckles across the top of his balding scalp. He was pushing sixty, but seemed uncommonly fit, no paunch, a flat stomach, exuding a relaxed athletic vigor, small frameless glasses perched on top of his head.

"Are you newly arrived from the Fatherland?" Aust asked.

"No, I'm American," following up with the same explanation about his parents coming to New York after the war that he gave to Eckhardt and Falkenberg, growing up in Manhattan, keeping his German, and all the rest.

"I came here right after the Great War, too," Aust said. "Once the Revolution ended here the prospects seemed better than under the Weimar regime. Those were terrible times back home."

"Ever return?"

"No. Never felt the need to. I do like it here. Wonderful climate. It's a nice way of life."

*Yes,* Hawkins thought, *that I believe.* Aust's casual, easygoing manner was diametrically opposite the stiff formality one normally expected in a German office, or anywhere on the Continent, his coat off, sleeves casually rolled up, a colorful bow tie. Life here in the sun of Mexico had obviously relaxed and mellowed him.

"Lately we've been wondering—my family and I—if we made a mistake leaving when we did. Considering …" Hawkins said.

"Yes, I know what you mean. Extraordinary events, there, eh? I do stay in touch. Amazing. And England soon."

"A battle all in the air," Hawkins said, as neutral and numb inside as possible, keeping it cool, although a twinge in his stomach threatened a roll.

"Yes. I was in the navy, but who could've imagined such a thing. You have to feel pride in it all. Despite the propaganda."

"What propaganda?"

"The papers from El Notre. You'd think Hitler has horns and a tail, from what you read."

"You read English?"

"Oh, of course. I initially worked for an American oil company when I came over. I handled shipping—naturally, I had experience from the *Kriegsmarine*—including dealing with the insurers. Became expert. I wanted to get off on my own, move up to La Capital, get out of Tampico. You can't believe a thing you read. Same lies about Germany as the last war."

"Like what?"

"That Kristallnacht business? Lies. Like the posters of soldiers in the last war with babies on their bayonets. All lies. The Jewish shops? Didn't happen. I have it on good authority that it was a put-up job."

There were lies told for sure during the last war, Hawkins thought. The posters with babies on bayonets were a disgrace Britain had yet to live down. But the real danger was they'd blinded people—like the fable of the boy who cried wolf—to the things the Kaiser and his government actually did do: the unprovoked invasion of neutral Belgium, the mass looting of Belgian industries, the forced deportation of the laborers, starting the gas attacks, bombing civilian cities with zeppelins, all true. And now those old lies about babies and bayonets were immunizing people against the truth of what Hitler was doing now, even to Germans themselves. *I saw the broken windows and looted shops myself,* Hawkins thought, it was all true.

Aust was understandably proud of the new German victories, but was he that naïve about Hitler and his regime? Possibly, Hawkins thought. If he was getting his news from state-controlled services like Trans-Ocean and the *Zeitung von Mexiko,* and had never been back, it was quite likely he was entirely ignorant of the current scene in Germany.

"Coffee?" He checked the fake card again. "And you work for the Alpert Gallery?"

"Yes. We're looking for art and antiques here. Interesting, colorful things, amazing prices. Really interesting. But then there's shipping or, rather, shipping losses. Duties. It's more complicated than I thought. It's got me worried."

"That it'll be destroyed or lost."

"Or stolen. Or get hit with costs we didn't anticipate."

"Ever do any international shipping?"

"No."

"There are issues. And you know, you'll want—no, excuse me—*need* insurance. I can help with all of that. Also the shipping. Who to go to, who's reliable. Crating and trucking. Oh! Storage and warehousing. That's always a major concern. All the way around and out. We're a full-service shop."

"Say, that's a relief. Yes, thanks!"

That exchange provoked Hawkins to wonder something else: Did Aust know what was going on with those cases of paintings? Hawkins did not believe in coincidences, in his gut his inclination was to take it for granted Aust was complicit in whatever the hell Eckhardt and Falkenberg were doing—solely because he was German.

But logically, his mind told him it could be risky to take anything for granted, you could blow things up for nothing, accidentally expose yourself. There was no guarantee Aust had any inkling there was a covert operation underway, or that Eckhardt and Falkenberg were spies, or anything else. Just because he was German? Maybe he was one of those malleable people who only wanted to get along and go along, whatever General Houghton thought of them.

Aust could think Eckhardt and Falkenberg were on the level, and for their part they could've thrown the business to a friendly and sympathetic local face, a purely commercial transaction. In effect, using him, or employing him, however you wanted to look at it. A full-service shop? Help with shipping, insurance and storage? Why wouldn't they find that attractive, too? And Aust seemed, well … rather credulous. Or perhaps, faithful to something that didn't exist anymore.

Aust checked his watch. "I'm expecting another client shortly. Would you like to come for dinner?"

# -27-

A gentle sprinkle began falling. Hawkins, Aust and his wife, Elise, moved their chairs back under the colonnade. The pink bougainvillea trained along the arches began dancing from the droplets as a maid hurried to clear the table in the center of the brick tiled courtyard. They'd had a leisurely dinner, a whole roasted chicken that obviously was not an iguana. Plump, too, unlike the scrawny birds in the tree up the street. The Austs were a couple from two civilizations now, Hawkins thought. A delicious avocado soup started the meal which ended with a Black Forest cake made with kirsch.

The rambling house had been built in 1719, Elise told him, the country manor of a minor Spanish nobleman in the old government of New Spain. It was large, with a second story above the colonnade. The ten cases probably filled a room or two somewhere in here, there was more than enough space, although that wasn't guaranteed, Hawkins thought. One major thing Hawkins had learned was that the Austs had live-in servants: a cook, a maid and a gardener. That ruled out waiting for them to leave, picking the locks and searching the place. Someone was always around.

"He's a vulgarian," Elise said, setting her drink down, pulling her shawl over her shoulders.

"He's just another politician," Aust said. The conversation had turned to the German victories. "What do you expect?" She still acted disgusted. Both were annoyed with each other, in the slight, smiling way married couples often had. They'd obviously had this conversation before. However, Aust wasn't exactly admiring Hitler himself.

*You are right, lady*, Hawkins thought. *Hitler's not just another politician.* But Hawkins was careful not to join in. Every part of the evening seemed to confirm the impression Hawkins got in Aust's office: He was no Nazi. He knew little about them or their policies and understood far more about the political situation in Mexico than Germany. In fact, he was remarkably ill-informed about things in the Vaterland today, and, frankly, rather naïve. Elise seemed to know more about it.

"If the boys go back and join the army, I'm disowning you all," she said, then looked at Hawkins and defiantly smiled, as if to say, *So there!* Elise was a tall, attractive woman, very little tan, unlike Aust, with an immaculate bob of perfect white hair. *If only more people trusted their gut like her*, Hawkins thought.

"Drop out of college? No, they're not going to do that," Aust said.

"Where are they?" Hawkins asked.

"One is here at the National Autonomous University, the other at the University of Texas. Premedicine and petroleum engineering, the two of them."

A doorbell rang.

"Good. *They're* at the door again. Excuse me, Hawkins. A pleasure."

"But aren't you worried they'll expropriate your company the way they nationalized the railroads, the oil companies, the plantations, the—"

"Naw." He waved his hand dismissively.

"I don't understand, where's the difference? If they can do it for one, why can't they do it for another?"

"No. They won't—"

"You came from the Vaterland, why can't they see you as another foreigner?"

"It's too diverse a country. Indian in origin, then the Spanish, waves of new immigration."

"Perhaps, but simply taking things from others—"

"They didn't do anything illegal. They have a constitution, courts, a parliament. Mexico belongs to Mexico the same way Germany belongs to Germans." His tone turned contemptuous. "The oil companies? They asked for it. They refused to negotiate with the unions, they gave nothing back. I saw it all in Tampico. In Texas, one wage. Across the border, a few hundred kilometers away, same oil terminal jobs, another, very low wage. *Very* low. Why? If they were asking for parity, well, maybe, it's a poor country, wages are lower, but no. Pennies on the dollar. Stupid *and* greedy. Then they were offered compensation and turned it down—demanded to be paid for oil in the ground they never owned in the first place—all while extravagantly guessing how much there was. Words can't describe it."

The most startling comment was that Aust agreed with Trotsky about Cárdenas. An amazingly honest man, Aust thought, although Hawkins hardly let on about how he'd heard that before. It certainly wasn't a view W and General Houghton shared.

"I hate to see El Presidente go. Big improvement in business conditions with him. Instead of the usual collection of political cronies that you normally get in this part of the world, including the US, he filled the government posts with a whole new class of educated technicians."

Hawkins heard footsteps and looked back expecting to see Elise returning. Instead Eckhardt and Falkenberg were walking across the courtyard. *It's late*, Hawkins thought. *They're staying with Aust? What the bloody hell?* Was this good? Or bad? Hawkins wondered. *Careful*—

When they saw him a flickering reaction crossed their faces: surprise, a touch of confusion, some alarm. Then Eckhardt went blank, Falkenberg coolly managed a small controlled smile, all while greeting them—Herr Aust! Herr Hawkins!

"Herren! Kommen Sie vorbei!" Aust cheerily waved them over, adding in German, "You know each other?"

"Yes, we dined on the Jorocho," Falkenberg said. "Fancy meeting you here!" all smooth and graceful.

"Yes, what are you doing here?" Eckhardt blurted out, face still blank.

"Our friend Roy needs insurance and help with his shipments," Aust said. They thought about that a second, then their faces went *oh, of course*, and relaxed. "Join us for a drink. A Dos Equis? Negra?"

"Thank you, Wilhelm, but no, we have to be up early," Eckhardt said.

"Oh, you work too hard," Aust said.

"Ach, no—" Eckhardt said.

"Work, work, work. Have a beer, it's a lovely evening. Enjoy it." *Work, work, work? After living in Mexico all these years Aust very much has absorbed the more easygoing Mexican way of life,* Hawkins thought, *you don't hear that in the Reich.* Eckhardt kept shaking his head. But not Falkenberg, much to Eckhardt's obvious annoyance.

"Well, all right then." Aust whistled for the maid. But they both sat and relaxed for a moment.

"Finding things for your gallery?" Falkenberg said.

"Making progress," Hawkins said. "Stumbling across Wilhelm was a lucky break."

"What kinds of things are you buying?" Eckhardt said.

"Still mainly Spanish colonial," Hawkins said.

"No, no, here, let me show you some *real* things," Eckhardt said.

# -28-

Eckhardt led them carrying their drinks to his second-floor room overlooking the courtyard, laying a large padded folder or binder on the table, opening it. Inside, like a photo album, were an array of flat flint and obsidian objects: more knives, spear points and small flat sculptures. He took a greenish-whitish one out and laid it in Hawkins's hand.

"I probably shouldn't show you these." Eckhardt laughed. "I don't need the competition. It's a votive statue." Hawkins held it under the light. The partly translucent stone had been worked as carefully as a small cameo, a spectacularly detailed Aztec god in profile holding a club or snake.

"That is awesome," Hawkins said, the others murmuring along. More of the remarkable obsidian blades followed, straight, slightly or highly curved, some more like saws. The final example was a ceremonial sacrificial knife, a perfect oval blade with an elaborate decorated handle. With a few slashes and swirls Eckhardt demonstrated how Aztec priests used it to slaughter their victims on top of the pyramids.

"And here's who used it," Eckhardt said. He opened the doors on a case standing on the dresser the way you'd open a small altarpiece. A full-sized mask was inside, perfectly carved and assembled from matching pieces of jade. The mouth parted as if about to speak, the pupils were drilled through to see, an elaborate headpiece rolling up and forward, large ears pierced with contrasting colored rings. It was slightly abstracted, smoothly finished, but clearly the portrait of an actual individual.

"Do you know who it is?" Hawkins said.

"Not exactly. A priest or king."

"It's as much a true likeness as the best Greco-Roman bronzes."

"Yes! Exactly! You see that!" Eckhardt almost cooed at the delight of having someone who appreciated what he had, more so than the Austs or Falkenberg, eager to impress. His excitement building, he drew a small box from under the bed, setting it in the center of the table. He spread out a black velvet cloth, then carefully set the contents in the center and stepped back.

"This is my most valuable piece."

Hawkins leaned over to look and actually gasped slightly. It was a skull, jet black, carved from an iridescent obsidian, obviously of great antiquity and value. The mastery of the artist was more astonishing than the mask, the exposed teeth and bones of the nose precisely articulated, the wavy plates in the skull delineated with complete precision, including the seemingly detachable jawbone.

Hawkins stared at it, for a moment mesmerized. It was stunning in its morbid magnetism and perfection, the impact on the senses almost magical. Like the Mexico City sky, the eyes could penetrate deep into a seemingly infinite vanishing point.

"So easy," Hawkins said, "to imagine the supernatural. It's a powerful object. It isn't a portal to another world. It's from another world."

"Yes," Eckhardt said, "you understand! The power of death, the underworld, is in it."

Hawkins looked back at Aust and Falkenberg. Aust looked concerned, not interested. He took a sip of his drink and set it down.

"Horst, how can you afford all this?" Aust said. For a split second Hawkins thought he saw an expression of worry or defensiveness in Eckhardt's face.

"I had a little bit of family money," Eckhardt said, "and I find good buys in the markets."

"Oh. I see." Aust looked skeptical and sounded skeptical. But then he laughingly waved it off. "I'm a good Lutheran," he said, "this stuff is too morbid for me. I like to collect colonial figures of saints, retablos." He emptied his glass. "Elise hates it, too. Werner, another beer?"

"Please, I need one after that." They headed back down, shaking their heads.

"It's good they're gone," Eckhardt said. He put the skull away. "This is the most valuable, but I want to show you my favorite thing. I know you will appreciate it." He opened an armoire and removed a long object wrapped in white flannel and carefully tied with ribbons. He unwrapped it on the bed and stood back for Hawkins to admire.

It was a wood club-like object, over a yard long, like a thin cricket bat, with a round knob on the handle, decorated with painted diamonds, only lined on the thin edges with continuous tight rows of gleaming obsidian blades. Eckhardt handed Hawkins a pair of white cotton gloves. He put them on and picked it up, looking carefully at the rows of blades. They were shaped with incredible precision, fitted together on the sides so tightly light couldn't pass through, the sharp edges almost a perfect straight line, only the tiniest undulation, effectively a single wicked blade.

"What?"

"It's an original Aztec sword called a macuahuitl. They and the warriors of the other Indian nations carried these in battle, tens of thousands of them. Be very careful, it's incredibly sharp."

"I can actually see that."

"Yes. During the Spanish conquest of Mexico it was written that Aztec warriors decapitated some of the Spaniards' horses with a single blow using one of these," Eckhardt said, "right clean through."

"That must've shocked them."

"It did. The Conquistadors didn't really defeat the Aztecs, the diseases the Spanish brought did most of the killing. Do you know what 'macuahuitl' means? The hungry blade."

"Hungry—for blood?"

"Yes. Look closely." On the edge of the wood, between the diamond decorations and blades was a wavy stain. Blood. It'd been used.

"It was hungry," Hawkins said.

"Yes. It is always hungry."

"Where'd you get it?"

"In Spain. When we retook the castle of the Conde de Altavista from the Commies and anarchists. They looted it, of course, and tried to burn it, the bastards, but they missed this. I knew it would be lost, so I kept it."

"It's slightly loose."

"Yes, it's too fragile to use. Over four hundred years old! I'm making a copy, I want to see if that claim is true." He wrapped it back up and then pulled another bundle from under the bed, quickly and alarmingly flipping the cloth away.

"The horse's head, you mean?" Hawkins said.

Eckhardt held up his copy, bright new wood gleaming, remarkably similar blades lining one side, and handed it to Hawkins.

"Yes. Others have failed to re-create one, but I've discovered the ancient secret: The wooden part has to be soaked in water. The wood swells and expands. That locks the blades in very tightly, like a single piece of steel, and it strengthens the blades, keeps them from breaking. However, you have to find the right kind of wood. That was their great secret—my secret. I've been experimenting. Very close to perfection, to what they had."

There was a bright, thrilled look in Eckhardt's eyes, a pair of headlights shining through. He was breathing deeply and rapidly, an almost sexual excitement.

*Merely crazy isn't the word*, Hawkins instantly thought. *Obsessed and compulsive. And he saved it from the Conde's castle? Sure …*

Hawkins handed it back.

"It's fascinating you've figured that out. If you manage to chop off any horse heads let me know."

"I will."

Hawkins checked his watch. He had to get going soon, too.

"Thank you, this was very informative. I'll keep my eyes open."

"Yes," Eckhardt said, his eyes still fixed on his macuahuitl.

# -29-

It was only minutes after dawn, the sun breaking through the high snowcapped mountains to the east, lighting their sides with a golden glow. The merchants had already been out for hours, setting up in the dark, eager for business, eyes following the gringo as he hurried past their stalls, smiling and cheerfully gesturing him in. The feel of tremendous hustling energy so early in the morning was startling—*no wonder these people take siestas in the afternoon*, Hawkins thought.

"¿Sombreros? ¿Sombreros?" he called out. One man pointed around an already busy corner, past a cloud of piñatas bright as neon. Beyond them an avalanche of straw hats of every description. *Perfect*, Hawkins thought. The owner's smile lit up brilliantly the instant he saw Hawkins— this presumably rich gringo would surely want the best hat he had. Lightly touching Hawkins's sleeve he tried directing Hawkins to the back corner where he guarded the expensive ones. Instead Hawkins stopped and began rummaging through the pile of cheap ones just inside. He plucked one out, a coarse straw weave with a wide brim and a high black band.

"¿Cuánto? How much?" Hawkins said. The man looked confused, then nonplussed. He held up two fingers for dollars. That was probably a good shot, a high tourist price, but Hawkins was in too much of a hurry to bargain. He quickly handed over the bills and raced out.

Several minutes later he was several blocks away, sitting in the car, watching the entrance to Aust's house through a good-sized hole he'd punched in the hat band with a key, arms folded as if he were taking a siesta after the early market, the hat covering his face. Now that he knew where Eckhardt and Falkenberg were, he was going to find out where they went. When he had left Aust's office the previous afternoon he'd walked by Norddeutsche Luftfahrtpartner's office. The frosted glass door was dark, a paper leaned against it, and it was the only office on the floor that didn't have a business name painted on the glass.

The Austs' gate opened and Eckhardt and Falkenberg drove out in a gleaming wood-bodied Oldsmobile station wagon and turned south, out of town. *Exactly as I expected*, Hawkins thought. *They're not going to work downtown.* He started up and followed at a careful distance.

The road outside San Ángel was lined with the same disturbing sprawl of improvised hovels—one wouldn't dignify them with the word "shanty"—that were visible from the train window outside Veracruz. Again, low and desperate, built—if "built" was also the right word—from any sort of cast-off material the luckless inhabitants could find: cardboard, scrapped cans flattened out, mud and wattle, bundles of straw, cut up tires, here and there a jagged piece of car body or salvaged roofing. The same filthy children aimlessly wandering through indescribably disgusting puddles, the same revolting brown haze from dully burning little fires. And also the same sense of horror and the sense there was something indecent about merely looking, that witnessing it somehow confirmed it or made it real, completing the degradation and humiliation these people suffered. Hawkins drove along, trying to avoid eye contact. The desperation of so many people in one place was unnerving. In some men the sight might evoke a sense of satisfied superiority, they'd motor by and think, *Ha! Losers! I got you beat!* But it made Hawkins uneasily squirm—a sense of shame, possibly.

After a distance that was presumably too far to walk, the traffic flowed out of town into an open green plain and simple farm plots. Ahead Hawkins could see an airplane rising. Then a side road and an airfield. He could see the wood-sided station wagon turning in.

Hawkins pulled over by the side and watched the field for a few minutes. Either Eckhardt or Falkenberg drove up to a low building behind the tower and then went in. *Was this part of Norddeutsche Luftfahrtpartner, too?* Hawkins wondered. Off to one side an old trimotor airliner was parked. At first Hawkins thought it might be a Ford, but decided after a mechanic walked by that it had to be a fairly new Junkers, in a similar corrugated bare metal.

He drove into the access road and around the parking lot behind the tower, keeping a safe distance. A sign read CUAUHTÉMOC ACADEMIA DE VUELO with an image of an eagle landing. Cuauhtémoc, according to one of Hawkins's guidebooks, was the last Aztec emperor, who'd tried to expel the Spanish. The name meant "descending eagle." *Is Eckhardt's hand in that choice?* Hawkins thought. It did seem to signal his Aztec preoccupations. Hawkins drove back, watching again from the road, assessing it all.

It was plain to see the main activity at the field was training. There was a long row of open cockpit biplane trainers, mostly Focke-Wulfs or Bückers, a pair of old American Jennys, and what looked like two or three Focke-Wulf advanced trainers.

A plane took off, circled the field and came around, almost overhead. He idly watched, then startled. *That's not a trainer*, Hawkins realized. It looks like an Ar 68, the pointed nose, the fixed gear with the teardrop wheel fairings, very distinctive. It banked and turned, coming almost a few hundred yards away, fast. Yes, there they were: ports for the twin machine guns atop the fuselage.

The Luftwaffe's last fighter before the Messerschmitt, and their last biplane fighter. To the casual eye, an Arado Ar 68 might look like a trainer, but it was a fighter, nonetheless. The higher pitched, powerful snarl of the engine alone gave it away—a high-performance aircraft. The Germans had shipped large numbers to Franco's fascists in the Spanish Civil War, also supplied them to Hitler's Condor Legion. Had Falkenberg flown one then? Hawkins wondered. Was he flying it now? With its power that plane called for an experienced pilot.

Except for the two American Jennys—antiques, these days—all the planes seemed be German: Junkers, Arado, Messerschmitt, Focke-Wulf.

Hawkins didn't believe in coincidences, not on that scale. There was a powerful connection to the Reich there, in some way.

At the same time, the Cárdenas government had implicitly backed the Republican side in Spain, and then taken in tens of thousands of refugees fleeing Franco. Would Cárdenas really be buying planes from Berlin? Hawkins thought back to the sprawling shantytown he'd drove through earlier. *No,* he thought, *the real question is could Mexico afford this in the first place?* Did it even have an air force? He'd never heard about it. *Get Lilly going on that question when I get back,* he thought.

*So what's going on here,* he wondered. One could say … so what? Mexico no doubt wanted trained pilots to develop its aviation. Nothing wrong with that. But even if the Germans were doing this for nonpolitical reasons, that still brought them influence. *Who are the instructors? That's a key question,* Hawkins decided.

Were Eckhardt and Falkenberg involved in some way? Hitler had intervened in Spain. Was it possible the Nazis were trying to foster Fascism in yet another country? Sure, Hawkins thought. They were doing that all over Europe. No doubt they had their sights on Latin America, too. But did they need a flight school for that?

The kind of money the sale of so many major works of art would generate surely far exceeded what it would cost to run a school like this, particularly here in Mexico. *Could it be a conduit?* Hawkins thought. *What are they intending to do with those paintings, anyway? A cutout to move money around?* That was always a possibility, create a seemingly legitimate business as a front to finance what you wanted, but at a distance. But then there was quite a load of overhead they didn't need. The Nazis were well funded, but they weren't that wasteful.

*Should I simply go into the office and mosey around?* he wondered. *Ask questions? Maybe go right up to Eckhardt and Falkenberg, query them about air-freight rates?* He mulled that a moment. No, he decided, that's stalking them too closely, that might rattle them. Have to get more inside with them first.

He turned and headed back into the city.

# =30-

"Oh, Natalya, ella debe estar devastada!" Frida was sitting in a wheelchair, a handkerchief to one eye. The maid had just ushered Hawkins into her studio. He sat over to the side, next to a skinny teenage boy with close-cropped dark-brown hair, watching and waiting. The boy was wearing a traditional white guayabera, the Mexican man's baggy shirt, loosely hanging above the knees of his white cotton pants, speckled with paint. *This must be the artist friend*, Hawkins thought. The boy nodded, leaned over and whispered in English in Hawkins's ear, keeping a running translation going in a low, raspy tone of voice.

"Natalya, that's Trotsky's wife. Frida says she must be devastated."

An enormous, tall man with a huge potbelly was sitting near her, filling his chair to overflowing the way a baked muffin overflows its cup. He wasn't just fat—his arms, legs, head, all were massive and powerful, stuffing his three-piece suit like a string of sausages. He looked equally upset, but without her tears, his double chin quavering in distress.

"Perhaps I should go to her," Kahlo said.

"Frida! You slept with her husband." The teen grimaced but translated that, too.

"I don't care, I refuse to be shamed!" she shouted. The man rolled his eyes. Kahlo finally noticed Hawkins.

"Hola," with a quiet wave of the handkerchief.

"Perhaps I should go," Hawkins said.

"No," she said in English. "Señor Hawkins, this is Riley Echevarria. Riley has come to help you. You *must* find out now. He wanted you to find out. What the Fascists are doing. It was last thing he did—" She started crying again. The boy stood and extended his hand for a shake, then sat down. "And this is my Diego." Hawkins walked over and shook his hand, too.

"Roy Hawkins. I gather something bad has happened."

"I spoke this morning with El Presidente. Leon is in a coma. He has only hours left," Rivera said.

*Ah bloody hell!* Hawkins thought. *He's going to die? Stalin succeeded. That means those sources of information Trotsky had will scatter forever. If we could find them—a very big* IF—*and connect with them, they'd still be too terrified to say a peep now. Bugger. Bugger it all.*

"I'm so sorry," Hawkins said.

The phone rang. Rivera heaved himself to his feet with surprising force to answer it. He listened a moment, nodded, said "gracias," then slammed it down.

"That's my house. The police are in San Ángel looking for me. Unfortunately, Presidente Cárdenas says he cannot interfere with a police investigation. I have to go. Señor Hawkins, we will talk later." He thudded out.

"They'll probably be here next," Kahlo said. "You two better go."

"Why would they come here?" Hawkins said.

"We both knew the killer, Jacson. No one suspected him."

*Makes sense*, Hawkins thought. *Sleeper agent, slowly works his way in.* There was careful, long-term planning behind this. That made it all worse still. Not only would Stalin kill Trotsky, but spread terror all around him—no one would know whom to trust. Corrode every relationship with suspicion, old friends included, spread confusion, discredit people, disrupt every organization. And so she is a suspect, too, now. Brilliant, in its way.

"Riley is also an artist," she said, "knows the galleries, the dealers, the other artists." There was a pounding on the door outside. A distant voice could be heard, loud—"¡Policía!"

"Oh no! They're here already!" Riley said.

"Hurry! Go! Find out what the Nazis are doing."

"Follow me," Riley said. They flew out, Hawkins close behind, into the courtyard. Another pounding at the front door. "This way!" They ran back across the garden to a door on the street. Riley motioned with a hand for Hawkins to wait, crept up to the door and peeked through a crack, flinched back, making a shushing gesture, whispering, "Oh no, they're there, too!"

"Well—why? What would they want with us?"

"It's what they do, round up all the people they can find. We were in her house. That makes us suspects. It's their way of doing things."

*Not something I can afford,* Hawkins thought, knew instantly, alarm mounting second by second. *Ignore the danger of exposure—just the length of time off the street and off the case. Could be disastrous. But what? If I was on the Continent I'd shoot my way out ... can't do that here,* he thought. *These coppers may be my problem but they're not my enemy. But what?* He quickly scanned the courtyard.

"This way!"

In a second he sprinted across the courtyard, Riley now in close pursuit, to a volcanic stone staircase across from the studio. It had a high wide stone wall or railing going down the side, at least a foot wide. At the top was a low portico roof over the stairs and door, that in turn was below another roof. They climbed up the railing, then pulled themselves up another three or four feet to the portico, then took a few steps to the upper roof. In seconds they were on top of the house.

"Keep down," Hawkins said. They crouched along low, almost on hands and knees, to the roof of the next house. Hawkins checked the street. Cops and cars were outside.

"Back! Away from the street." At the far side they rolled over the parapet onto the neighbor's roof, keeping down, then raced along that to the next house, swinging out, hanging over and dropping down onto that roof, then racing to the back of the house to a tree. They reached out and caught a branch, swung out and climbed down into the courtyard. Hugging the wall, they sprinted around to the back gate, watching the windows behind them. No one saw. The gate was latched from the inside. Hawkins lightly opened it with a finger and looked out. Nothing. He straightened his tie and hat and motioned to Riley. A café was down at the corner. Hawkins gestured to it.

"Walk slow. No cares." They lightly sauntered down to the café as a police car sped by, went in the side door, looked around a moment, then walked out around the front.

They wordlessly doubled around the corner, peering down the street. Two uniformed policemen were waiting outside Kahlo's house with a car and van, their backs to the door.

"The bastards! They'll have to take her in her wheelchair!"

"My car's down there."

"They could be outside for hours." Another police car went by. It slowed, the officers looking back.

"They had people watching the house! This way!" Riley sprinted back up the street, led him into a narrow alleyway filled with trash, out onto another street. A siren sounded nearby. They went around another corner, then another and then made a straight line across the street to a slummy-looking garage built of stained adobe. Riley unlocked the big door and pulled Hawkins in. Seconds later they heard the sound of a car and siren speeding by.

# -31-

The garage had been converted into a small studio with skylights made from a pair of discarded glass doors crudely cut into the ceiling, the white porcelain knobs staring down. Riley had painted a pair of unblinking eyes on them. Over some scanty-looking rafters was the underside of a corrugated tin roof painted sky blue, matching the high Mexico City sky outside, with a few white clouds, giving the room an airy, bright quality. A pair of spindly, whitewashed saplings partially held the roof up, little knickknacks and mirrors hanging from the stumps of lopped-off branches. Canvases and masks were scattered about. A bed with a rumpled blanket was folded against the back.

"You live here?" Hawkins said.

"No. I rent a small room nearby where I share a kitchen. Sometimes I sleep here, though." There were a pair of kerosene lanterns and some candles around. No electricity.

"You rely on sunlight?"

"Plenty of light here in Mexico!"

"Yes. Wonderful light here. Your English is very good." *But there's an interesting trace of an accent*, Hawkins thought. He began looking around at the paintings. Most were unfinished. The siren sounded in the distance again. *Interesting paintings.*

"My mother and her family came from Ireland." *Ah, yes. Irish along with the Spanish*, Hawkins thought. "Who did these paintings the Fascists want to sell?" Riley said.

Hawkins went down the list of works he'd seen in Bermuda: Braque, Matisse, Rousseau, Picasso and more.

"We don't see many works by those artists here. That will cause a sensation because they are famous and foreign. People will think they have to be important."

"A sensation? Good. I don't think the Nazis will want that."

"Yes!" Riley started to laugh. "I like disturbances. Too many people are so set in their ways. We must shake them up."

"Have you been exhibited?"

"A few, but not like Frida or Diego. Not yet."

These paintings … unusual, Hawkins thought, a mixture of techniques and styles, surrealist, but not the frozen nightmare quality of a Dali, a folkloric, mythic element, perhaps.

"Abstract works? Surrealist?"

"Modern works. But Mexican! We must work from our own traditions, not ape foreign examples to create a revolutionary art for Mexico. We are not the States. We are an ancient country, you should go to the Olmec gallery in the anthropological museum, great art, three thousand years ago." Riley pointed at a small bowl-shaped object, a reclining man wearing a headdress, looking to the side. "Like that Chacmool, it was for offerings to the rain god Tlaloc." Hawkins walked around, studying it.

"How old is it?"

Riley laughed. "Two weeks."

"What? It looks ancient."

"No," A big grin. "It's a copy. I made it to order."

"That's remarkable. For who?"

"A dealer. He has a gringo customer who wants one. He will never know. All the artists here, except the big names, make things to get by. We have to."

"My, my, Riley, I won't judge, though."

"They took half our country—we take their money."

"I suppose that's sort of fair. You're very talented."

"Thank you. I make masks, too. Heads and masks, they inspire me."

"Masks?"

"Yes." Riley pulled several more from a box, hanging them on the wall. "I am trying to get these exhibited. We all wear masks. It's in our nature. What are the masks we wear? We do not ask this question. We should be aware of the masks we make. But mostly we are not."

"Quite a thought. Yes, we all wear masks." *I surely do*, Hawkins thought. *Depends on who I'm talking to, what mask I wear: Secret agent. Art dealer. American, British. Group captain. Valve salesman. A man sickened by violence. A man who regularly kills people … and surely will again. I wear a great many masks*, he suddenly reflected. *My job is … wearing masks, after a fashion. This Riley is interesting.*

"Yes!" A brilliant smile lit Riley's face, then the rasp broke into a helpless and melodic giggle, voice rising and falling. As Hawkins looked over he realized something with a great start.

"What masks do you wear, Riley?" Now it was Riley's turn to look startled. *Yes, that confirms it*, Hawkins thought. He'd thought Riley was a late teenage boy, maybe eighteen or nineteen. But no. Riley was a young woman.

"Yes?"

"I think I know—"

"This is another mask I wear."

"Why this one?"

"The mask of a man?"

"Yes, why that one?"

"I cannot stand the strictures our society places on women. Mexico is such a conservative country. Cárdenas tried to give women the vote. He failed. It was terrible. Many of us felt crushed. Mexico was not ready. Then, of course, the Church. Always the Church."

"Does Frida know? About your mask, I mean?"

"Yes. She approves, but then does not. She has great difficulty as a woman, to be an artist, she fights all the time, you have no idea how hard it is to get exhibited. There are terrible newspaper articles—*oh, how amusing the wife of a famous artist dabbles in paint.* But then she is a feminist, her life, her womanhood, her femininity is her art. She refuses to agree to efface herself."

"Do people know? About you, I mean."

"It's none of their business." She handed him a mask, a jaguar, then another, tiled with small mirrors.

*Perhaps*, Hawkins thought, *but still—I think have more experience with wearing masks.*

"A dangerous business, these masks," he said. "Can you can keep track of which mask you're wearing?"

"They are all acts of creation. What does it matter?"

"But can you get lost, lose who you are? Have too many masks?" *I sometimes wonder, too*, he thought. *It can get confusing … all the masks I wear.*

"No, all of life is a mask—death, too." She handed him a mask in the form of a bleached skull, with rouged cheeks and ringlets of hair. "This is the mask of death."

"Who wears the mask of death? The giver of death? When it comes for you?" *Who wears that mask? That's the thing. A mask I wear all too often*, Hawkins thought. *Hasn't come for me. Not yet. Perhaps, I wore it first, or better, or maybe simply luckier to find that mask first.* "Many men are wearing that mask today."

"No, that mask *is* death, death itself."

"No, death is not a mask, or if it is, it's a mask you will never take off."

"Yes, you do lose yourself, at that moment, under the mask of death. The world, too."

Something struck Hawkins with great force: *We wear masks all the time, all through life.* Then he thought of his girlfriend, Daisy van Schenck, back in New York. *Not with Daisy*, he thought. *That's what's so different— being with her. There were no masks, it was liberating, in a way, to totally be oneself. Can we—she and I—get that truth back? After I had to put my masks back on, after I had to leave?* He brushed that thought aside.

"Can you wear a mask with one you love?"

"Yes. The mask of love!" She began sorting through the box, looking for one.

"No. I think it's the nature of love, to let the masks all fall. That's its blessing." *Or at least what I get out of it,* Hawkins thought. *It's a moment without the masks—where all of my life is real again, I never have that numb feeling, be numb myself, feel nothing. With her, I feel again.* But Riley seemed troubled by the idea.

"I don't know …"

"Because if they're in love with a mask—are they in love with you? What happens if the mask falls? What are they in love with?"

Instead of answering she rose and checked the window in the garage door.

"We should go."

# -32-

Hawkins was driving along the Via del Centenario, another wide boulevard, wet and shiny from an early morning shower. A brilliant sun broke through the dark clouds. The lush green of the trees lining the wide boulevard and the Parque Hundido seemed to glow from within, as though made of living neon tubes. He was heading toward the distant city center but Hawkins was watching Riley, fascinated. There was an *I-don't-give-a-damn* quality to her, she'd stuck her head and arm out of the window, the way dogs and children do, breeze whipping her hair, not caring at all who saw or how silly it might look, holding her straw hat in her lap, a few stray drops from the sprinkle dotting her forehead.

"I rarely ride in a car," she shouted. "We will go to the Zocalo. Around there we'll find the galleries where all the rich people go." She glanced over, adding sourly, "With their cars." She sat back in, levelly gazing now at Hawkins, then took a deep breath. "This gallery in New York that you work for. Could it exhibit my works?"

*Ah, well ...* Hawkins thought. "Possibly. But the owner likes old things, antiques, artists long established. Nothing risky. He'd probably like that bowl."

"That can be arranged!"

"Thank you, but no! I will take your own works up with him, though."

"Good! When we go to these galleries, could you say you are interested in my art?"

"Why, yes. The least I can do."

"¡Maravilloso! If they thought a New York gallery was interested, that might do it for me. We'll start with Galería de Arte Mexicano. Frida and Diego exhibited there. It is very prestigious. Rich gringos go there first because they also exhibit foreign artists, like your stolen Nazi paintings."

Hawkins stopped by the Hotel Imperial, collecting from the concierge a waiting three-day-old copy of the *New York Times* that'd arrived that morning. He checked in back. There it was. *Perfect*, he thought. The BSC staff in Manhattan had adroitly created a fake photo of the Alpert Gallery and placed it in a small display ad in the back of the paper. It was, needless to say, an extremely convincing fake, as good or better than Riley's Chacmool. *A casual mention*, he thought, *Then—oh, perhaps it's here. Ah yes. See there? That's us.* Only a slightly ironic touch there—*that's us! Busy at our work* … Probably convincing to someone from uptown for a few days, to say nothing of someone two thousand miles away.

He heard voices behind him.

"¡Oye! ¡Tú! ¡Largarse! ¡Este lugar no es para campesinos!"

It was one of the hotel clerks, irritably gesturing at Riley to leave, catching her sleeve to push, handing out a few centavos with the other. Riley slapped his hand away, hard, angry, face red, sending the pennies scattering across the marble floor, answering in English, waving a fist under his nose.

"I am not a beggar. I have every right to be here!" That startled the man, hearing what appeared to be a poor campesino speak *inglés*.

"Señor Riley is not a campesino, he is with me!" Hawkins said.

The clerk froze for a split second, a horrified look on his face, said, "Pardon me!" then bowed and shuffled away, "Pardon me!" picking up the centavos as he went.

Riley began coolly moseying around, inspecting the elegant lobby.

"This is where you're staying?"

"I know what you're thinking. For rich people. I have an expense account. What the hell was that about?"

"He thought I was a beggar because I am wearing a straw hat and a guayabera. He shouted at me, told me to scram. They think they are too good for the people. These little bowls of pennies one sees at all the businesses? They pay the poor to go away."

"I see."

They got back in the car and headed east in an awkward silence. Hawkins turned a corner, ready to cross to the Zocalo, but down at the far end, near the square, a large crowd could be seen, blocking access across.

"Oh! A demonstration," Riley said, mood suddenly lifting. "We should get out and see."

Hawkins parked and they walked up, pushing and angling through the throng in the street. The massive square in the center of the city, once the site of the Aztec temples razed by the conquistadors, was now flanked on one side by the immense cathedral and the equally immense Palacio Nacional, a long ancient-looking edifice built with the same dark, reddish stone one saw all across the city. It was filling with a surging crowd of people, many waving Mexican flags or red banners covered with slogans. The tone of the crowd was energized, militant, perhaps, but enthusiastic and not unfriendly.

"What's going on?"

The crowd began chanting, "¡Ningunas bases! ¡Ningunos concesiones! ¡Ningunos fascistas!"

"No bases, no concessions, no to the Fascists. President Cárdenas made it clear we will never allow foreign bases on our soil or give out any more oil concessions."

"Who organized this?" Hawkins said.

"No one."

"What? Someone had to call it."

"No. When something exciting happens people rush here."

"What happened?"

"The government announced today that the first foreign oil company accepted compensation. People are excited because we all helped."

"How?"

"After the oil nationalization, the US government stopped buying silver for coinage from Mexico—it was pressure, to break us. Presidente Cárdenas made an appeal to the people. The square—"

"This square, the Zocalo?"

"Yes, here, two hundred thousand people came here to donate their valuables. People gave their wedding rings, their silver. I have a neighbor who brought his last chicken."

"I … don't understand. Why?"

"To pay the companies back for what they invested here. That was only right."

Hawkins tried to imagine the scene, the people surging in, tossing pieces of jewelry and silver onto the mounting heaps—no, impossible, he thought. Tens of thousands of people taking their wedding rings and tossing them in a pile? Because this man asked them to? Who could believe it? But here these people were …

He'd seen big rallies in Europe: the precise goose-stepping at Nuremberg, marches in Moscow carrying giant banners and portraits of the leaders, even protests in Paris marching in loose ranks behind their union banners. Nothing like this. Those were carefully organized. Riley was right. These people organized *themselves*. You could tell from the happy but casually chaotic quality of it: clearly no one was in charge. The crowd shifted to another chant.

"¡Viva la Revolución! Viva México!"

Hawkins and Riley pushed farther into the crowd, the people were cheering now, for something or someone.

"Look!" Riley said. She pointed at the center of the long Palacio Nacional. A tall man in a white suit appeared on the balcony. An incredibly excited *whoooo* went rocketing from one side of the square to the other, people waving their arms, flags and banners. Riley started waving her hat, then grabbed Hawkins's sleeve, shouting in his ear before snatching his hat off his head, waving both hats overhead, jumping up and down.

"It's Cárdenas! It's Cárdenas!"

Hawkins watched her for a long, surprised moment, amused, starting to feel the contagious emotion of the crowd himself. There were tears in Riley's eyes. He looked around at the others. There were tears in their eyes, sad, but smiling at the same time, and celebratory. *I know that look,* Hawkins thought. *The masks have fallen. There's love in their eyes. That's what that is.* Unselfconscious. Unforced. Spontaneous. They love this man. It was impossible not to feel it, to feel their emotion, to be caught up in it too. Cárdenas would leave office in December. That was sad for them, but there was joyousness, too, a joy that had vanished from Europe, and from much of the world. Who wouldn't want to share in that joy? Hawkins felt it powerfully, too, and soon was smiling happily with Riley, applauding along, watching.

The crowd quieted down. El Presidente was speaking. But he was too far away. After a few minutes he finished, waved and went back inside to thunderous cheers. The crowd was breaking up. Riley began eagerly asking people coming back, "What did he say? What did he say?" She caught one man's sleeve, quickly repeating to Hawkins, "A government that gives natural resources to foreign companies betrays the motherland."

Another man passing by heard and called back, clapping his hands over head, "He affirmed the permanent abolition of the death penalty! There will be no more killing in Mexico."

# -33-

They began easily walking through the crowd and flowing along with it toward the car. Hawkins followed behind Riley trying to sort out what he thought and felt about the afternoon. Mexico was still seized with a revolutionary fervor. That was plain to see. The anti-Fascist atmosphere was fascinating, thrilling. *¡Ningunos fascistas! Wonderful to hear*, Hawkins thought. *Wonderful! These people are against what I'm against. We share the same cause.* For a long happy moment he felt at one with them, a fulfilled feeling.

But, then—*No, not exactly*, he realized. On reflection it felt confusing and awkward—Britain was a great imperial power, ruled a quarter of the globe, and all this was very anti-imperialist. No bases, no oil company concessions. W, General Houghton, would be enraged. This revolution seized British assets at a terrible time and got away with it because of the international crisis. *These people are against what I'm against*, Hawkins thought, *but are we for the same things?*

The cab driver in Veracruz, Hawkins remembered, putting his hand over his heart. *Mi presidente. Mi corazón.* Someone obviously liked him—they gave up their jewelry for him. Abolished the death penalty permanently? To Hawkins, that was the most disturbing news, and provoked the deepest reflections. It was a great good thing, of course, abolishing the death penalty. What dictator since Caesar had done that?

Never. None. They all wanted that power, that fear—every last one of them wanted to wear the mask of death.

But this man did not. Perhaps Cárdenas wanted to wear the mask of life? But, no, Hawkins thought, that was not it. The faces in the crowd had to be reflecting his, the masks fallen, each self unguarded—love for him, his for them, for the country, for Mexico. Dizzying, almost, the idea of it.

But not all were admirers of El Presidente. At the far end of the Zocalo, loud voices, men shouting, people started running toward the noise, then a few police officers began sprinting through the crowd trying to catch up. People began racing away, crashing into each other, pushing and shoving, crying out. *What? Impossible to see*, Hawkins thought. He ran to a fountain and climbed on the rim, stretching up. There was a line of scrimmage, of sorts, at the inlet of one of the avenues, a jousting of different flags, a few black, from a line of men pushing, grabbing and punching below them, indecipherable insults flying. Then a pair of gunshots, then another rang out, and another. The screaming and yelling rose.

"This way, out of here!" Hawkins jumped off and they began running away, toward the street they came in on and Hawkins's rented Ford. As they bounded around the corner, rushing along with the tumbling crowd, people began screaming and turning back, a crush of bodies again, looking for a way out, fear and panic in their eyes. Then Hawkins and Riley saw them: a group of counterprotesters marching up the street, mainly young men, waving flags, too, and banners similar to the Nazi swastika—blood red with a white circle, except in the round field was a green outline of Mexico. Some were swinging sticks and clubs. About half the men were wearing gold shirts, along with black pants and boots. *Each nation has its own Fascist color*, Hawkins thought, *like sports teams: brown in Germany, black in Italy, gold here.* He grabbed Riley and pulled her back.

"Who are they?" he shouted above the crowd.

"It's the Fascists and Sinarquistas. Unión Nacional Sinarquista! Acción Revolucionaria, they call them the Camisas Doradas, the Gold Shirts," Riley shouted over the din. The surging, boiling crowd began running back, frantically trying to escape. The counterprotesters reached the edge of the protesters. Loud shouting. Then in seconds came the thud of clubs and cries of pain, people were falling, the rest struggling to stay on their feet, bodies and hands slamming into one another, the faces frightened, fighting to get away. The line of Fascists wasn't that large, though—a row of young toughs maybe only two or three deep at most, but well organized, armed and ready to fight.

More men began running and pushing their way back through the crowd, toward the Gold Shirts and Sinarquistas, hurling things at them, trying to hit or stab them with flag poles or whatever came to hand. A shot rang out, then another. *Damn! Someone has a gun*, Hawkins thought. A man in front of him fell back, blood on his face. Through the blur of tumbling, swirling heads he spotted a pair of men in gold shirts with bolt action rifles. One ejected a shell, ready to shoot again.

Then in the middle of their rank he spotted it. A pair of swastika flags. That did it. Undercover he might be, Hawkins wasn't turning away, nothing confusing, nothing ambiguous about anything now, he was struck by a sudden and overwhelming clarity, totally focused. These were the people he *lived* to fight, the *reason* he lived, this was the one thing he knew above all—*this was what he was against.* He knew the risk. He didn't care. He didn't think, reason it out. He knew it in the marrow of his bones. At the sight his own mask fell, the carefully constructed neutral facade of the secret agent. He turned and pushed Riley, shouting, "Go!"

The crowd swirled back, leaving him momentarily close to the edge of the front row. Hawkins looked quick. Riley was nowhere behind him. Hawkins squatted down, half prostrate, as if he had been shot, drew his Browning Hi-Power, holding it low under him, hiding it, the sides of his coat falling down. Firing almost prone, one hand on the pavement, he aimed a pair of shots at the man snapping the bolt shut, into the gut, to wound. The men in front and to the sides moved. He lost sight of the gunmen for a split second then, shooting between a man's legs in front of him, he put a third round into the second man. They both crumpled and started going down. The Gold Shirts' heads spun around, looking up, scanning the windows and rooftops, not down, confused where the echoing shots were coming from in the enclosed street, shocked, angry. In the crazed tumult no one saw him shoot. The Gold Shirts paused, several looking behind them.

*That face,* Hawkins thought, *is that ...* He reholstered the gun, and partially rose, grabbing another man's shoulders in the ricocheting bodies, glancing from behind his head and neck. *It's Eckhardt,* he realized. *Eckhardt! Can I shoot—no—should I shoot? Damn—damn! No. No. Can't. Need to know what they're doing—bloody hell! What's he doing here now?*

Eckhardt jerked his head back and vanished into the opposing crowd. The men in front seized their wounded and began running out of the street, carrying them by the arms and legs. Realizing the Camisas Doradas were retreating, the crowd began racing after them with a roar, screaming threats and insults. Hawkins turned and began running in the opposite direction. A few dozen yards into the square he spotted Riley, straightened up and began strolling calmly toward her, hands in his pockets. A phalanx of what Hawkins guessed were members of Cárdenas's new militia wearing armbands ran into the street, carrying a mixed assortment of old rifles and pistols.

"We need to get back to the car," he said.

"What happened?"

"Nothing. They decided to run away."

"¡Bastardos! This way." They doubled back up to the corner of the Zocalo, around to another avenue, cutting across to the car. Within minutes they were driving out of the area. They stopped at a sidewalk café, waiting for the streets to clear and the nervous shopkeepers to raise and stow their shutters. The waiter, in a black jacket and bow tie with a white apron around his waist, slowly set the coffee and empanadas down, glancing at Riley, then Hawkins, then back, obviously uncomfortable seeing Riley in his café.

*Probably wonders if she's a rioter,* Hawkins realized. *If I wasn't here they'd never seat her. This isn't going to work,* he decided. When they were finished he gestured across the street at a haberdasher's.

"Come, on, Riley. A man needs a proper suit. On me. It's the least I can do."

"No, we must be one with the people, our traditions, to make our art. Many artists here dress like this, it is part of our art, to be what we are." She realized that might seem a rebuke, although Hawkins didn't mind, quickly adding, "But I am very appreciative."

"Would you rather have a dress? Something floral?"

"No."

*Time for a white lie,* he thought. "Then when you show at the Alpert Gallery in Manhattan, you will need a suit. All the major artists wear suits. And shoes. Besides, do you want to keep slapping pennies away?" It took a second or two to absorb that, then she was on her feet, ready to run.

"A suit now. Maybe a dress later."

# -34-

It was a wrenching shift, going on to the galleries. From the joyous crowd. From the lives of the average people in the square. From the exhilaration of a real living revolution still underway, the fresh possibilities of a world made new. And then the riot and shooting, and seeing Eckhardt—it was wrenching, indeed, to end up in the peaceful enclaves of the rich and comfortable, people who not only could afford it, but had the leisure time to collect art. Jarring, all in one day.

They descended from the most prestigious galleries in wealthy neighborhoods that could've been in Belgravia, Sutton Place or Le Faubourg Saint-Germain. And ended at dealers in *artes y antigüedades* next to grimy, noisome bars on narrow streets, shops that clearly specialized in the wares of considerably less-talented fakers than Riley.

The drill was the same at all of them. First, the introduction, then the card. *Perhaps you are familiar with us?* Some enthusiastically replied, "*The famous Alpert Galley? Of course, honored to have you!*" Or in some there'd be a blank look, maybe a tiny shrug. A simple response to that: "*Oh no? Hmm. Oh, wait, I have my copy of the* Times." A look of surprise at seeing the ad for the Alpert Galley, then "*Thank you for coming! How can I help?*" And so on. There were, Hawkins reflected, interesting similarities between the art business and espionage.

Then the focus would drift to Riley. It often took a minute or two to recognize her. She looked good in her suit. Dark, double breasted, narrow chalk stripes—her pick. Hawkins selected the tie: striped regimental, very British, his little joke. With her hair pomaded, and the white straw fedora tipped at a rakish angle, she looked only a touch androgynous, rather tough with her hands in her pockets. It helped she was on the tall side.

"Yes, we are considering a showing of *Señor* Riley's work at our gallery in Manhattan," Hawkins said. "Most interesting paintings, the Mexican Movement." The surprised mental recalculation—augmented by a good suit—was then interrupted by Hawkins's query, "We're also interested in modern European works. We are aware that refugees from the fighting in Europe are on occasion bringing works by modern masters with them to Mexico and—well, it's a sad reality—many of them are now financially embarrassed and looking to sell. We would be interested in helping them. Would you be interested in helping us help them?" *Help.* "Of course we want to help … them. Help … Oh yes. Of course." So earnest.

*Ah, yes, many similarities between the spy business and the art business,* Hawkins thought. They would definitely keep an eye out and make discreet inquiries where possible. *It'd be an honor.* Of course.

But no one had seen anything. *Not particularly surprising,* Hawkins thought. *Eckhardt and Falkenberg are probably still looking to get those cases to New York somehow, and the big American not-at-war money.*

It wasn't a completely unproductive day, however. Riley certainly benefited from it. One private collector who'd taken a painting to see if "it worked" in their home suddenly managed to produce a check, telling Riley how much they now loved it. They were riding back to Riley's garage studio in Coyoacán after stopping at a bank. She was re-counting the cash, an exultant expression on her face.

"Maybe I should open a collection agency," Hawkins said.

"Go around and stick them up!"

*Well …* he thought, *there's two pounds of warm steel in my armpit that explains why I didn't go into the bank with you.*

"If only I spoke Spanish."

"I will teach you." She started right in: "*¿Dónde está el baño?* Where is the toilet?"

After checking with Kahlo's maid—"Madame is still in custody," they were told—he dropped her off at her studio and returned to the Hotel Imperial. The desk clerk waved him over. A small note.

# -35-

"And I lost four pounds!" Lilly said. "Eh, bien, didn't eat for two days. Didn't feel like it."

"That can't be good for you."

"Likely not. I ached all over. Probably from lying like a log for fourteen maybe fifteen hours. I was so groggy when I woke, I wasn't sure."

"Ah, no doubt. What do you have?"

"A flash last night from BSC New York. Here …" She began slowly reading:

To: 48700
From: 48100
2030 hours EDT

Postal airmail interception received today IPTCS Bermuda. References Gen. Miguel Corrialles, identified by us, commander of military district southeastern Mexico between capital city and Veracruz. Artworks under investigation to be sold sequentially through MXC dealer Galería Esteban and others to Corrialles. Purpose, create record of ownership, paper trail, prior to sale, meeting requirements of PB Gallery, others, in NYC. Nature Corrialles Nazi ties or if only sympathizer, unknown at this time.

Proceed with your investigation, include Corrialles, determine his role, interest, possible political security orientation, affiliation, galleries used, etc. —48100

"Not sure what all that is," she said.

"IPTCS is General Houghton's Imperial Posts and Telegraph Censorship Station. 48100 is W's code number. Mine is 48700. You've heard what we call the States? In the SIS?"

"No, what?"

"Forty-eight land—"

"From the forty-eight American states! Oh, that's funny-clever."

"Righto, forty-eight plus one hundred is the top listing."

"What's that about a paper trail?"

"The big New York galleries and auction halls won't accept the paintings for sale unless they can show where they came from. The US Neutrality Laws are quite strict—"

"Oh, them and their precious neutrality!"

"Ah, but those laws are working for us now. Eckhardt, Falkenberg, this Corrialles fellow, they have to prove these things aren't looted, which is quite the problem because they are. To be fair, good for the Yanks, they don't want to be fencing stolen merchandise. What the Nazis are doing makes sense. No record of ownership? Create one! Drop the works in a gallery, maybe run them through another gallery, maybe more—"

"Oh, I get it. Voila! Sales receipts! Records!"

"Exactly, the collector—Corrialles—comes in and buys the paintings, he ships them to Manhattan, there's now a paper trail, everyone is happy."

"Except us! They get the money—"

"Not really. Good news, actually. Eckhardt and Falkenberg can't do this in a day or two. It buys us time. Ready for the report back?"

"I'm dying to hear."

"Don't use that word!" She quietly laughed. He listed it off quickly: Meeting Trotsky. His assassination. Rivera and Kahlo. Her father, from Germany. Knew Aust. Another small knowing laugh.

"In like Flynn, Hawkins!"

"Yes. Unexpected, that was nice." He added Aust. Dinner in San Ángel. Another encounter with Eckhardt and Falkenberg. Eckhardt's collection. The Cuauhtémoc Academia flight school. The Focke-Wulf and Bücker trainers, the Ar 68 fighter—she needed to check on the Mexican Air Force. Riley and the riot. He left out his shooting.

"That's a big mess of Nazi agents."

"It's possible, but we can't assume that. Most of these people—especially General Corrialles and the galleries—don't have to be Nazis, or sympathizers, or have any notion of what's going on, including Aust. He could easily be a contractor looking for a nice commission. Aust seems quite deferential to Eckhardt, more like the way you'd talk to a client. A spy? With a kid in college in Texas? Well, maybe. And spies who know what they're doing start getting worried any time money or spending questions come up. He could be a dupe, we'll have to wait and see. I am sure Eckhardt's in charge of whatever is going on."

"Does Aust understand how dangerous all this could be?"

"I doubt it. You should see the house—"

"To die for?"

Now Hawkins laughed.

"Righto. It's awesome, gorgeous. The kind of life he has here could go away in a second. And that's assuming he and Elise would have a chance to make an escape. Imagine starting over in Germany at his age. And that's not to mention it's altogether possible to end up facedown in a ditch in the countryside. Powerful incentives not to get involved. I'm wondering if he could be turned, if he knew how he and his family were being used."

"I'd be angry."

"Yes. I'd be too. If we turn him, that'll be ice cream with the cake."

"This'll be an interesting report."

"Hear from your fella in the army?"

"A little. He's in Sussex. Bored to death and tremendous tension at the same time."

"Why?"

"The First Canadian was the only division in the BEF to get out of France with all their equipment. If the Germans land, they'll catch the brunt of it. Meanwhile, they sit and wait. And wait. It's got to be unnerving, waiting for them to come."

"They won't. The RAF will hold."

"I hope so." There was a small waver in her voice.

"Have you told him you now outrank him?"

"Umm—no. It'll wait."

"Where are you?"

"I found a Sanborns up the street. I was nervous about using the same phone bank."

"My, you are getting into the swing of this! But don't worry, you can call from the Reforma. That'll be fine. I'll see you in a minute."

Five minutes later he was in front of the Imperial waiting for the car when she walked by. Elegant, chic, a dark-red silk dress, small hat with some netting, rakish angle, white gloves, big white sunglasses. She walked on, face straight ahead, only the slightest turn of her head to the side as she passed, a little smile. Hawkins made a long, low whistle. She laughed, almost doubling over for a second, firmly marching along.

# -36-

"Corrialles? Yes, I know who he is," Rivera said. "He is a reactionary pig." Hawkins, Riley and Rivera were sitting around Frida's bed. She was pale, plainly not well. A trip through police custody and sleeping in a jail cell had drained her badly. They'd been released that morning.

She nodded, then said, almost a whisper, "He is not interested in the kind of revolutionary work Diego does, but he bought one of mine last winter, once it was exhibited. At Galería de Arte Mexicano."

"He's a collector, then?" Hawkins said.

"Of sorts," Rivera said. "He has pretensions, seeks prestige. *That* is his concern. But he traffics antiquities, which he illegally loots off his land. There are many ancient sites there. He has an old conquistador family. They were immensely wealthy. Much land was lost to the land reform."

"Antiquities? How so?"

"He has his men dig them up on his lands. He sells them in a gallery he owns," Rivera said.

*That's my in*, Hawkins thought.

"Which one?"

"La Galería del Tlaloc."

"And this is illegal?"

"Yes, antiquities in the ground belong to the nation. It is a crime. But this is a huge country. There are so many ancient sites, no one truly knows how many or where they are, new ones are constantly being found. The law is impossible to enforce."

"Gentlemen, Diego, I am sorry, I must rest," Frida said.

"I have go, too," Hawkins said. "¡Mucho gracias!" They left Rivera gently holding his lover's hand, worry in his face. He clearly hated to leave. She closed her eyes and began drifting off to sleep.

Forty-five minutes later Hawkins was back downtown at La Galería Esteban, one of the galleries he and Riley had visited the previous day. Within seconds after entering Hawkins spotted a painting in the back. *And there we are*, he thought. One of the Braques he'd seen in Bermuda. The gallery was decidedly on the small side for such a major work, and yet there it was. But as he approached he saw a red sticker hanging down emblazoned with VENDIDO in black.

"Mr. Hawkins, I'm sorry." It was the manager, Mr. Garcia, nervously rushing out to intercept him. "It's already spoken for. We sent a message to the Imperial when it came in, but a buyer arrived only moments later. Extraordinary."

*Not an accident at all*, Hawkins thought, *but it hardly matters, we know now exactly where it's going. They neatly choreographed that one.*

"Well, doggone. We would've been interested." Mr. Garcia assured him they would make every effort to contact him if another came in. Was Garcia in on the game? Hawkins wondered. Maybe, maybe not, but that probably didn't matter very much, either.

La Galería del Tlaloc was next to a French restaurant on Avenida Parras, a pleasant tree-lined street in the tony La Condesa neighborhood. Nothing about the gallery signaled shady. The space was modern and spare, large plate glass windows and doors, small letters at the top of the window, barely clearing the head of a large and ancient statue of, presumably, Tlaloc. The god of rain and thunder was colorfully painted green and blue with hollow red goggle eyes openly staring out, seemingly to terrify passersby. What were either streams of blood or bloody tendrils flowed from its mouth.

There was the usual introduction, the card, and the presentation of the copy of the *Times*. A waiter in a gray jacket immediately appeared and asked him if he wanted an espresso. Ancient-looking objects rested on immaculate white plinths. All in all, impressive. If this was General Corrialles's doing, he was no fool. A man of some taste and discernment, or if he wasn't, he knew to hire those who were.

But there was a discordant note. The manager followed him carefully from piece to piece, overeager, tipping his hand badly. No doubt the man wanted a commission, but he simply was too eager to sell. The prices were low, that was the problem. Hawkins had a good sense of what primitive or historic art sold for in London, Paris or New York, at least before the war, and these seemed very low. It was possible a combination of the fighting Europe and, as Rivera said, there were so many sites, so many things, coming both out of the ground and into the country, that prices had been driven down. What collector wouldn't want a discount Picasso?

The manager stiffened up and smiled. A man was coming from the back of the gallery, his hand outstretched, Hawkins's card in the other, a broad easy smile on his face.

"Mr. Hawkins. I'm the proprietor, Miguel Corrialles. Welcome to La Galería del Tlaloc." He spoke English comfortably, with a slight accent. The manager quickly bowed out. Corrialles was a very big and powerful man, over six feet tall, very fit, with a salt-and-pepper mustache and full head of jet-black hair. He firmly shook Hawkins's hand, touching his elbow just so slightly, leaning in, quizzical eyes giving the impression the only thought in his mind was the guest in front of him.

*Now that's a switch,* Hawkins thought, *not introducing himself as an army general?* No sense of evasion. *This is a man who's very secure in who he is, knows who he is, feels no need to impress. And cultured. I can see him getting along with Falkenberg, but Eckhardt? Hardly.*

They were standing in front of a stone statue of a big cat, presumably a jaguar, round eyes fixed on its prey, powerfully crouching as if ready to spring across the centuries. There was a hollow space in its back.

"I'm guessing it's not a planter," Hawkins said, raising an eyebrow, smiling slightly.

"No," Corrialles said, in on the joke. "It's called a cuauhxicalli. It held the severed hearts of sacrificed victims."

"That's quite an image. I'm not sure the wives of my customers would want it in the house."

Corrialles laughed. "I've encountered that. Mine, either. Perhaps I should put some flowers in it. Are you looking for things for your gallery?"

"I came down looking more for Spanish colonial. Well, at the very least, we know we can get that and sell those kinds of things. But I also wanted to find out if modern works were coming out from Europe because of the war. We'd be very interested in that, the market in New York is very strong in that area. Yet I find myself increasingly interested in these ancient things. There's a—what would one say, between modern and ancient or primitive art—"

"A resonance?"

"Yes! An acquaintance got me interested. That's a remarkable, powerful object. But I need to know more."

"You know more about modern art?"

"Yes. I'm more interested in that personally. That's where the real excitement is."

"Yes, very exciting! I'm thinking of displaying modern works alongside these ancient things, for that resonance. Perhaps we could work together."

A van had arrived outside. While they talked a pair of uniformed movers brought in a carefully wrapped and padded painting. The manager followed them, nodding to Corrialles, pointing to the rear. He nodded, also gesturing slightly to the back. The Braque he'd bought that morning was being delivered.

Hawkins had gone in thinking he would have to hustle Corrialles, but over the next half hour it became clear the reverse was going to happen. Corrialles was smoother than the manager, but he also wanted to deal. And he could get modern works. Whether those modern works were imported or by Mexican artists was unclear. And the origins of his ancient pieces were unimpeachable. If he was digging them up on his land they couldn't be Riley's fakes. Then came a surprise.

"I have a private museum at my little finca outside Tlaxcala. I am going tomorrow. Come and be my guest."

# -37-

A small hissing. The old car was overheating. Hawkins pulled over to the side to let the radiator cool. He'd just reached Río Frío de Juárez, at the top of the pass through the mountains, on the road from Mexico City to Tlaxcala, through mountains covered with immense pine forests. He checked the map. Three thousand meters, almost ten thousand feet high. No wonder the climb was straining it.

He got out to stretch, working his jaw, his popping ears hurting from the changes in elevation. In the distance giant volcanoes loomed on all sides, seventeen, eighteen thousand feet high, snow and shining glaciers trimming the tops. Río Frío had the mood of an alpine mountain resort, Bavarian style chalets dotted the hillside. But poverty, like poverty everywhere in Mexico, was never far away, and here impossible to hide in the narrow defile. A row of tattered, smoky huts clung to the edge of the road, beneath the chalets. He walked on a few dozen yards to a construction site. From an official sign—EL MINISTERIO DE EDUCACIÓN— he made out they were building a new school for the village, a white, modern-looking building with large windows. At the bottom of the sign was EL PRESIDENTE LÁZARO CÁRDENAS. Hawkins thought of Riley, the crowd in the square, the taxi driver with his hand over his heart. *Good thing someone is trying to do something for these people,* he thought.

A few minutes later he was finally heading down the mountain divide, ears painfully popping again as he descended. An hour later he was speeding across a sunny plateau. The landscape around Tlaxcala looked eerily like the old Spain he'd seen from the train when he had left Europe a few weeks earlier, the intense, blinding sun, brilliant blue skies, the golden, sere fields sparsely dotted with trees. At a gas station in the middle of nowhere he pulled in to refuel. As the attendant cranked the pump Hawkins began watching an old farmer on the other side of the road. The man was behind a wooden plow pulled by a donkey, feebly pushing it through the hard-looking soil, a bent-over question mark.

Both man and donkey trudged forward, heads down, stoic. They hit a rock. The man stopped, pulled it up and tumbled it to the side of the road, grunting. As he turned back to his plow Hawkins realized he wasn't grunting from the effort. It was a barely stifled cry of pain, or anguish. Who could tell?

Hawkins turned away, the guilty feeling welling up again, at … looking? At not wanting to look or seeing? Or was it a misdirected empathy, that if it wasn't seen it wouldn't exist? But that wasn't so. His eyes fell on two men sitting knees up against the wall of the gas station, heads down, worn hats covering their faces.

It was the classic image of old Mexico, lazy men sleeping away the day. Hawkins had a manual, *Guide to Mexico for the Motorist*, full of paintings of precisely this sort of thing, Indian women in serapes, men in sombreros, cactuses. As he paid the attendant one of the men raised his head, eyes a dull stare into the distance.

The eyes told the story. The man wasn't lazy, Hawkins realized. The very opposite was true. The man was utterly, to the bone exhausted, simply spent. The artist or publisher who commissioned those cartoon images missed entirely what was before his eyes.

A few miles farther along Hawkins slowed through a village of white adobe buildings and a brilliantly painted church. A pair of elderly women were pulling carts with big wooden wheels, pain from the exertion in their faces. They looked so worn and tired it seemed they, too, no longer had the energy to cry. Outside the village a row of men with hoes were bent over, tilling a field by hand. He felt the same urge he'd felt on the train, looking at the slums, or on the way to the airfield, a cringing desire to look away. Perhaps it was a form of shame, that wealthy gringos like himself, so wrapped in the comfort of their lives, in the things they took for granted, were unable to see things right in front of their eyes.

The images in that guidebook—well, they were illustrations, not art, he thought, because they were a form of propaganda, like the official art the Soviets and Nazis approved of—the heroic worker, the noble Aryan. Their intention, the intention of all propaganda, was precisely to keep people *from* seeing things, and, like the guidebook, even anesthetize their vision, to prevent them from seeing things they did not want to see.

Then ahead, the entrance. He turned under a large white adobe archway under the words HACIENDA CUAUHTLATZACUILLOTL: PUERTA DEL ÁGUILA—Eagle's Gate. There were a pair of armed sentries: a corporal and a sergeant in a guardhouse. The sergeant bent down, glancing in the window.

"Señor Hawkins?" waving him through after he nodded.

It was a full fifteen minutes following the dusty road without a building in sight before Corrialles's "little" finca emerged around a low bend, a brilliant white assembly of buildings with red tile roofs, a long columned arcade, and a decent sized baroque church with an elaborate facade and lantern tower capped by a dome. A small palace. Around it were tidy, white-fenced fields with herds of menacing-looking black bulls.

How beautiful, almost dreamlike, Hawkins thought, a fairy-tale vision of warm, inviting, aristocratic splendor, a mythic Mexico, only real.

Next to the road a group of men were gathered around a corral, some sitting on the fence, boot heels hooked on the rail, hats tipped back. Some of them were in guayaberas or overalls, but some of them were in khaki army uniforms. Inside two men on horseback with heavy leather chaps were riding around a bull. A man dressed in jeans jumped off the fence into the corral, a flat old straw hat tipped over his eyes. It was Corrialles. Out of his fine suit, his shirt open to his sternum, revealing a broad and hairy chest, General Corrialles exuded a sense of tremendous energy and athleticism. Hawkins pulled right over and got out to watch, joining the men on the fence.

"¡Hey, toro! ¡Hey, toro!" Corrialles shouted. He snapped a cloth at it the way a boy in a locker room would snap a towel. Instead of angry the bull looked intimidated, head down, obviously wide-eyed, watching the men on horseback, who would ride by and poke it with pointed poles. "¡Hey, toro! ¡Hey, toro!" But the bull wouldn't lower its horns and charge. Instead it wagged its tail. "¡Usted novilla!" Corrialles shouted. The men on the horses and the fence laughed. "¡Cobarde!" *That's coward*, Hawkins thought. The bull looked from man to man, as if pleading. The men on horseback poked it again. It tried to get out of the way, fleeing around the outside of the pen.

It trotted by Hawkins and the men, who slapped it on the back with their hats as it went by. Corrialles saw Hawkins, now sitting on the fence in his white suit, the only man wearing a tie. He lightly raised his hat and shook his head, returning his attention to the bull, bending over, hands on knees, shouting again.

"¡Cobarde! ¡Acto como un hombre! ¡Un hombre! ¡Un hombre!" Nothing. The bull simply stood in the center, staring at him. Act like a man? It obviously had no idea.

Corrialles shouted again, "¡Hey, toro!" and reached for a handful of dirt and threw it at the bull. It blinked and didn't budge.

Corrialles angrily turned away, an utterly disgusted look on his face. Then a jolt, and he almost ran to a man on the fence near Hawkins, plucked a rifle from him, turned and shot the bull through the heart. The bull made a slight moaning cry, mouth open, eyes wide, and fell over dead, one horn digging a long gouge in the dirt.

*Was it surprised?* Hawkins wondered. Was it thinking, *Why did you do that?* It felt that way.

Corrialles handed the gun back, stretching his arm out, then leaned over to shake Hawkins's hand.

"How about that, eh? We're having steak tonight."

# -38-

The white-jacketed servant took the plate away. It'd been an elegantly casual dinner, and the steak in fact was very good. Certainly fresh. They'd gotten around in a lazy way to politics.

"Half my family's land. Three hundred and fifty years we are here at Eagle's Gate. Two hundred and seventy years ago we built this house." Corrialles crushed a cigarette out in an ashtray. "It was the bulls that saved us."

"For the bullfights?"

"Yes. The corrida is such a part of our culture, and we raise some of the best bulls in Mexico, as good or better than those in Spain. They were afraid to interfere with that. But we lost so much. It was a sad thing for everyone."

"Weren't the tenants happy?"

"Yes, after a fashion. But they have been misled by Yankee consumer culture and movies—that false individualism." He made a disgusted, dismissive gesture, the same expression when he shot the bull who wouldn't fight. *Would he shoot them?* Hawkins thought. "You know what we say here in Mexico, Hawkins?" Hawkins shook his head. "So near the United States, so far from God." They both laughed. "They took half our country, and now they want bases on our soil."

"The other day I stumbled into a protest against that at the Zocalo. The people were very emotional."

"Yes, we are all enraged. I hate to say it but I must give Cárdenas credit even if he did steal half our lands—"

"You lost properties to the land reform?"

"Yes. It was costly. But as I was saying, Cárdenas did tell Washington to go to hell. Right away. Of course no true Mexican patriot would do otherwise, even a thief." He glanced at Hawkins, then caught himself, a baleful expression on his face. "I am sorry, please do not take offense."

"Not at all. My family, we are German immigrants in America. We often criticize. There is nothing wrong with honesty between friends."

"Then you understand. And now they take our culture. Coca-Cola everywhere. It is a symbol. We must resist. The humble people, they are simple, they need spiritual guidance and temporal care."

"Spiritual guidance?"

"Yes, we must restore Mexico to its true Catholic self. The attacks on the Church, the confiscations of its estates, this turned out to be a terrible thing, nothing but disorder has risen from it. That is why Generalissimo Franco is such a great man."

"You admire him?"

"Very much. He brought Spain back to Christ. We brought Christ, salvation to these people. They need someone to take care of them, that's the Church and the responsible elements of society."

"That was your role?"

"Yes, when the Communists who have seized the government—"

"Cárdenas?"

"Yes, when they shattered the estates they destroyed that, too—our caring, our guidance, men like myself. Yes, they lived on our lands, but we are responsible for the people, they are like children, we must hold them in our hands like birds fallen from the nest. Now they are abandoned, on their own. Hawkins, have you stopped to reflect on how quickly the conquistadors took over such a vast country, with tens of millions of people, and Christianized it in only a few short years? Because they brought a god who died *for them*, not a god *they* had to die for. The sacrifices ended, the blood no longer flooded down the steps of the temples. The temples took centuries to build but the people tore them down in a few months. How could that happen? I am telling you they were frantic to tear them down, they couldn't destroy them fast enough, even though many were sick from the new diseases, they wanted the temples gone as soon as possible so that no more hearts could be slashed out—their hearts. This we gave them. We brought salvation and the Church then, and they need salvation now."

*A striking insight*, Hawkins thought, and surely true. *A god who died for them.* A simple idea, but overwhelmingly powerful given Mexico's past, an idea probably more powerful here than any other country the Apostles confronted. Uncounted millions must have lived in constant terror, for millennia. Millions must have perished under those obsidian blades. Ending that was an extraordinary achievement. Only a true liberation could explain the zeal to tear the temples down.

But as Hawkins listened to him rambling along, in his mind's eye he couldn't help seeing the old man pushing the plow behind that sad donkey, and the fifteen-minute drive from the highway, merely to get to Corrialles's hacienda. Hawkins felt a gut instinct: *Corrialles might see himself as the epitome of noblesse oblige*, he thought, *but that poor farmer needs Corrialles's guidance a lot less than he needs a tractor.* Exactly how did Corrialles and his ancestors build this palace? No wonder they had a revolution, like the one that tore the pyramids down. No wonder they'd rushed to the Zocalo with their jewelry.

He might believe this self-serving drivel, but how to change the subject? *Ah, yes*, Hawkins thought. "They need to be led to higher things."

"Yes!"

"Art, too?" That did it.

"Yes! Let's take our drinks. I must show you my museum."

They exited the long, high wood-beamed dining room onto an arched colonnade that ran the length of the house and down a broad staircase onto the lawn. Corrialles stopped, pointing at Popocatépetl in the distance. A reddish orange glow crowned the volcano's peak, lighting an eerie trail of steam or smoke from underneath. The Milky Way and incredibly bright stars crossed the high, clear dark sky.

"The Aztecs called it the smoking mountain. They had many legends. Here, I must show you something." He led the way to the front door of the church, their path lit by fireflies in the air—the grass, the trees, another scene from a fairy tale. The ancient hacienda, Popocatepetl glowing in the distance, the fireflies dancing in the dark with the stars overhead, it had an intoxicating, enchanted quality, as if spirits from time immemorial still inhabited the high plateau.

Inside he flipped a switch. A brilliant, strong light now bathed the nave. But this was no fairy tale. The altar had been mostly removed, along with all the benches. The church had been fully converted into a modern art gallery, with paintings on white partitions and sculptures on the usual white plinths. *So much for Catholicism*, Hawkins thought. *He's turned his church into a gallery?*

Corrialles pointed to a large partition toward the front. Hanging on it was a large fresco of an ancient Mexican warrior or chieftain that'd been carefully removed and mounted. Hawkins found himself drawn forward by an incredible hidden gravity. The vividness of the colors, the deep blues and reds, the freshness of the image, the flowing, sure-but-crisp hand of the artist, recalled the best Athenian vase painters or Florentine muralists. The determined expression on the warrior's face, his towering and flowing bird headdress, the detail of his eagle feather cape, the tension of his arms and legs, standing on the feathered serpent god Quetzalcoatl … amazing, a masterpiece, equal to anything from ancient Egypt or Rome … *Breathtaking*. The drums and horns of ancient fanfares in the royal procession behind him resounded in the imagination as one looked at it. *Behold my greatness*, it proclaimed.

"Where did you get this?" Hawkins said.

"On my land. There's an ancient ruined palace over there. Buried a thousand years."

"It's not in the Gallery Tlaloc—you're keeping it."

"I could never part with it," almost a gush, he clearly loved it, his mask fallen, too, exposing his joy in it.

He gave Hawkins a careful and studied tour. Corrialles knew a great deal about this ancient art. But he also wanted to sell. Perhaps he needed the money because of the loss of his lands, Hawkins wondered. The hacienda had to be an expensive establishment to maintain. Was that why he was doing business with Eckhardt and Falkenberg? For the money?

Corrialles clearly was very conservative. And he freely talked about his career in the army. But he didn't seem a Nazi. The Nazis wouldn't talk about caring for people who were mostly Indians or mestizos, they were racial *Untermenschen,* people destined to be destroyed, who *needed* to be destroyed in the name of racial purity. The Nazis, like Eckhardt on the train, went insane at that kind of race mixing. Corrialles's conservatism might be a condescension but it didn't seem to be racist or genocidal in character. Rather, it felt paternalistic. And the Nazis surely weren't devout Catholics like Corrialles. Although … art seemed more important than religion to him, this place was no longer a church, was it? None of it fit. Money had to be the answer.

They turned a corner. Beneath what had been a Station of the Cross hung the Braque.

"You collect modern art, too?" Hawkins said. Corrialles was working hard to make a good impression.

"Somewhat. I am a patron of the arts, of course. It goes with connoisseurship. That is also the responsibility of men like me. But I am sadly forced to sell. That is why I have opened La Galleria del Tlaloc. But as you saw, the sums are small compared to what the modern masters go for elsewhere. I've been looking for a high-level contact in Manhattan and better prices for a long time. The Alpert Gallery … perhaps we can make you an offer. We—" He caught himself. "I could commit pieces on consignment. Perhaps even help finance an exhibit, a larger space."

"That's a very attractive offer. I am sure something can be done."

Hawkins extended his hand. They shook on it. It was done, their word given, no more confirmation needed. The butler arrived with another tray of drinks. They went outside and sat on the church steps, watching the big, dancing fireflies, the stars and the glow of Popocatepetl. It was eerily spectacular and achingly beautiful, a true midsummer night's dream. *It's no wonder he wants to hold on to the magic,* Hawkins thought, *the beauty of this place, the enchantment of it … blissful, in truth.* He felt it powerfully, too. It was more than a sense of aristocratic privilege or ease, it was as if they were dwelling for a moment in the sublime, an elevated state of consciousness, of life and beauty. Who wouldn't want that?

The red glow around the rim of Popocatepetl, eerie, beautiful, otherworldly and supernatural. The hacienda, the mountains, the magic of the fireflies, all drew like an undertow at the beach. *I need to get back to my radio,* Hawkins knew somewhere in the back of his mind, *listen to the reports of the war, the battle, the bombs raining down. I need that. I need to keep focused on what I'm fighting against, why I'm here, in the midst of this wonder.* He tried to think of Hitler's face, him standing in the car in Vienna. But, still … the beauty of it was enough to make your heart ache.

A brightening at the top of Popocatepetl. A big eruption, the glow of a very big bomb going off, the fireflies, the thrown sparks. Then, focus.

*We,* Hawkins suddenly thought. *He used the word "we."*

In the distance, headlights on the road.

# -39-

A wood-paneled Oldsmobile circled the fountain in front of the house and drove to a side entrance to the hacienda. Eckhardt and Falkenberg got out, stretching, talking inaudibly in the distance. Then Eckhardt opened the door and turned on a light. Falkenberg swung out the station wagon's back, revealing a pair of wood cases. Then they both vanished inside. Corrialles coolly, silently watched them for at least four or five minutes, sipping his drink occasionally. *He seems to be studying them*, Hawkins thought. *What gives?* Then Eckhardt and Falkenberg emerged into the courtyard and began carrying in one of the cases.

Corrialles shook his head, made a *bouf* noise with his cheeks and lips, the sound a very French sort of dismissal, then gently poked Hawkins's sleeve, as if to say, *Come along.*

Corrialles approached them in the dark, quietly circling around the fountain. They didn't see him until he was almost on top of them. A firefly flew by his face, illuminating it for a split second, a fleeting apparition. They were standing near the headlights, with Eckhardt holding the bottom of the case, Falkenberg the top.

"¿No usted tiene gusto de venir adentro para una bebida, primero?" Corrialles said. *Usted—you?—gusto—have?—bebida—drink?—and no is no*, Hawkins thought, *I think he said something like, don't you want to come in for a drink, first?* Corrialles's Spanish was tight, clipped, not the usual musical rhythm.

They set the case down. Eckhardt's expression said, *Oh, hey,* but Falkenberg seemed abashed, quickly looking at Eckhardt, then down, mouth tightening. *Is he irritated, maybe because he's embarrassed?* Hawkins thought. *Caught in the bad manners of opening the door and walking into someone else's home without knocking?* Eckhardt and Corrialles bantered in Spanish for a moment, then Falkenberg spotted Hawkins standing behind the general. He looked startled.

"Herr Hawkins—"

"Guten Abend, Werner, Horst, wie gehts! Ja kerle, willst du nicht zuerst etwas trinken gehen?" *Yeah guys, don't you want to come in for a drink first?* Hawkins spit it out, cheerful, convivial and fast, using the familiar German *kerle*—guys—rather than the formal *herren.* They were in Mexico, after all, and in the country.

Eckhardt looked surprised, maybe a touch shocked. Not happy. Falkenberg glanced at Eckhardt and started to laugh, but quickly choked it down. Corrialles gazed at Hawkins blankly, uncomprehendingly, perhaps wary, then blinked twice.

"Oh, of course, your family, you speak German?" he said in English. "And you know each other?"

"I'm sorry. Yes," Hawkins said in English. "We met on the train coming into Mexico City."

"We all have a mutual acquaintance," Falkenberg said in English, apparently the only language they all understood, "Señor Aust. We also met at his home."

Corrialles's face slightly relaxed, the guarded look lifting.

"Insurance! Of course. Yes, Aust is a good man, we can trust him. Hawkins agreed tonight to help us in New York."

"Wilhelm will be insuring my shipments," Hawkins said.

"Ah, natürlich," Eckhardt said. "Good. Keep it close, among friends."

"It's a lovely evening," Hawkins said. "We were watching the volcano. That drink? A toast to our enterprise?"

"I don't know, we have to get back tonight," Eckhardt said. He was caught, now uncertain. "It's a long drive. Maybe a little beer, if you have some?"

"Of course," Corrialles said, "this way." He whistled for one of the servants as Eckhardt and Falkenberg put the case back in the Oldsmobile. They settled in chairs under the long colonnade. Corrialles still seemed tense and remote. *Well, helping themselves to Corrialles's house was presumptuous,* Hawkins thought. Need to break the ice here.

"Werner, I have not seen the *Zeitung.* How's the air battle going? Hear anything?"

"Not much. But the news will be good. We are on the way to victory. I am sure of it." But he looked uneasy, the bravado a little forced.

"Too bad you're missing the fun."

"Ja, I wish I was there. These things take time, I will admit. The resistance is much stiffer than we expected, the estimates of surviving squadrons after France had to be off."

"Worried?"

"No. They'll settle soon, I'm sure. We will grind them down."

"The British are fools," Eckhardt said. "They don't know when they're beaten!"

"They're not fools, Horst, they're a worthy adversary."

"Bastards—"

"No. I wish they'd listen to reason. We—many of my friends, they're asking why we're flying against Britain. They're troubled by it. The Führer himself said the British are not our natural enemies. We'll need them, their empire, for the postwar order, to organize the world properly."

"The British Empire?" Corrialles said, his voice chilling again. "We kicked them, the French out of here. That's one thing I agree with that Commie on—our soil is sacred. The Yankees, too, demanding bases." *He's obviously talking about Cárdenas taking over the foreign-owned railroads, the oil,* Hawkins thought. It was a tense moment—the pregnant, implicit question hung heavily in the air: Where, exactly, did a predominantly brown nation like Mexico fit in to Hitler's New World Order? Under a German sphere of influence, or maybe an "Aryan" Anglo-Saxon one, via the USA? Is that the role the Führer imagines for the States? A regional overlord under Germany's dominion? Or as part of the sprawling British Empire Falkenberg said the Nazis want to enlist in their new scheme of things? A touchy matter. But Falkenberg handled it adroitly.

"General Corrialles, we are in agreement. The New Order is an order of men of stature, men and warriors like ourselves, a new version of the old Teutonic Knights, the German shield and sword that for centuries protected Europe from invasion and devastation from the barbarians to the east. Or the Knights Templar, the crusaders, a brotherhood of the soul. Men like us, who remember the past of meaning and high-minded virtue and long for the poetry of a better future, and are willing to selflessly fight for it."

"Poetry of a better future?" Eckhardt said, contemptuous, annoyed. "I agree with your boss. When I hear the word 'culture,' I reach for my gun." That would be Reichsmarschall Göring, Hawkins realized. *That was all a bit much, wasn't it?* Hawkins thought. *Maybe old Hermann has a point, or at least you could see what provoked that.*

But Corrialles, or his Catholic self, seemed earnestly mollified. He had said much the same over dinner.

"Yes, men with a mission, like ourselves."

Another brightening at the top of Popocatepetl. Eckhardt excitedly pointed with his glass.

"Did the natives throw sacrifices into it? Pretty maidens for their gods?"

"No, not Poco," Corrialles said, "it's too high, the air is thin, and it's always cold. They didn't like the cold. Perhaps you are thinking of the Mayans, it's known they threw sacrifices into their sacred cenotes."

"Yes. That would've been something to see. And to hear their cries as they fell!"

"God forbid," the general said. Half in the dark, Corrialles crossed himself. Then something surprising. Falkenberg, sitting slightly at an angle to Eckhardt and behind him in the semidarkness, crossed himself too.

"You're too fond of death, Horst," Falkenberg said. "Killing at most is a means to victory, not an end in itself."

"Oh, I suppose. We have a long drive back. We must leave your things and get going."

"Of course," Corrialles said. "And this other gallery you found will come get them tomorrow?" Both Eckhardt and Falkenberg nodded. "Then we can move them to Galería Tlaloc." He glanced at Hawkins a moment, then very slightly smiled and shrugged, "Then I will buy them."

*Other gallery?* Hawkins thought. *Exactly as we suspected, creating a paper trail.* They drop them in one gallery, Gallery Tlaloc buys them from there, then Corrialles buys them from his own gallery. Presto, the record of ownership the big galleries in New York want, no risk of them being seized as looted property by the Americans under the Neutrality Acts. Corrialles watched them leave, then turned up the stairs.

"Hawkins, no one has any manners anymore. Eckhardt, no class. Volcano maidens …" He made another contemptuous *bouf* sound with his lips. "But Falkenberg?" He shook his head and sighed slightly, as if to say, *Now that one knows better.* "Eckhardt was an executioner in Spain, did you know? He admitted it. Went through the hospitals."

"What do you mean?"

"He shot the wounded Republican soldiers."

"In their beds?"

"Yes." There was a moment of hesitation and a slight shrug in the semidarkness. "Perhaps it had to be done. But he followed orders and did his duty. That is his problem. Seen too much death, like the old Aztec priests, killing day after day, always more and more until it lost all meaning—a drug you get used to, a higher dose every time."

# -40-

Hawkins climbed the corral fence, sitting with the other men, hooking his heels over the rail, rapidly warming sun on his face. Only minutes earlier he'd joined Corrialles for huevos rancheros, warm tortillas and very good coffee—from Corrialles's own beans. The general was already dressed in his jeans and old shirt, eager to test the mettle or manliness of another bull. This one trotted out, nostrils flaring, pawing the ground, ready to charge. Corrialles turned, rubbing his hands in satisfaction.

"Ah-ha! ¡Hay un toro verdadero!" Then at Hawkins, "A real one!" After a few quick turns in the ring, the bull sent Corrialles skipping and vaulting over the fence with a practiced ease, laughing and smiling. A real one, indeed. The watching hands buzzed and cheered. The two men on horseback herded it back out and swung the gate open for another.

After a few minutes Hawkins waved goodbye, climbed down, shook hands over the fence with Corrialles and aimed the old Ford back up the mountains toward La Capital.

By nine that night the streets around the building on Calle de Tacuba, near the Zocalo, were emptying out. Hawkins casually unlocked the lobby door. When he got back into the city that afternoon he went straight to the manager of the building where Aust's insurance agency had its offices. *Any vacancies?* he wanted to know. The man was pleased to see him. Yes, there indeed was a small office on the fifth floor. The rent was cheap, and quoted in dollars, interestingly enough: $25 US or £5, plus the same as a deposit. Two keys came with the contract, one for his office, one for the front door, to be used if working late.

Inside—no elevator operator at this time of night, of course—Hawkins almost skipped up the steps to the fourth floor and the office of Seguro del Capitolio. The hallway and all the offices were dark. Holding a small flashlight in his teeth, he quickly had his lockpick set out and opened the door. Not hard. A fairly simple American-made, Yale machine key lock. Inside, he snapped it shut and turned on the lights. That was actually safer. The beam of a flashlight flying around the room was more suspicious than turning the lights on, that was the equivalent of an alarm bell going off, at least if anyone saw it. But lights? The owners or staff could be working late, it could be the janitor, no one would pay attention. And he already knew there was no alarm system, he'd carefully if discreetly watched for one on his first trip to visit Aust.

*That other gallery will come and get them tomorrow,* General Corrialles had said. *Be nice to know which one,* Hawkins thought, *although not critical.* He mainly wanted to know more about that airfield. Airplanes required insurance to get a registration. Hawkins was betting if Eckhardt and Falkenberg were involved in the flight school, they'd gone to Aust to get it. After all, they had an office down the corridor. Aust could've helped them with that, too, of course, purely business, but … *I trust my gut on this one. That is not a coincidence.*

A dozen desks, piled with folders and papers. He flipped open a couple. All in Spanish. How would Aust handle this? Aust spoke German, a good guess said most of the staff probably did not. A good bet also said Aust handled that account himself. Hawkins settled in behind Aust's desk.

Where to start, though? He began riffling through the fourteen folders in Aust's out basket, checking each for names, anything that might be a gallery, for Corrialles; Eckhardt and Falkenberg, for Norddeutsche Luftfahrtpartner, the Cuauhtémoc Academia flight school, anything art and aviation, for that matter, or any address associated with any of them. But nothing.

*Perhaps he'd been cautious,* Hawkins thought. *If it was sensitive, where would I put it? In the out basket, for someone else to file? Hell, no,* he thought.

He got up and carefully searched the office, in the closets, under tables and cabinets. No safe. He headed back into Aust's office and checked his desk drawers. They were locked. Out came the little leather lockpick set. In the large bottom drawer he found a thick file marked NDLF. Norddeutsche Luftfahrtpartner? Yes. Going through quickly he found a sheaf of copies of registration papers for airplanes, trainers, a couple of Junkers transports, nearly two dozen registrations in all, including the Arado fighter he'd seen at the field. Then a sheaf of the insurance papers required for the registrations, with Eckhardt's signature. That settled it, the flight school was Eckhardt and Falkenberg's operation. He carefully put it all back.

Now the other office, he thought. Outside Aust's private office, at the far end of the main room of Seguro del Capitolio, another door was half ajar. Inside was a conference table with a few stacks of papers down the middle and a single used white coffee cup with a line of lipstick on it. On the far side was another glass door. He tried the knob, expecting it to be locked, but it easily swung open. A small storeroom, full of oak file cabinets. He tried the outside door, checking the number from the corridor: *6*. Norddeutsche Luftfahrtpartner's office.

Of course, he thought. The registrations, now this—a mail drop. The Cuauhtémoc Academia de Vuelo, all those planes, was Eckhardt and Falkenberg's operation.

# -41-

For a city of a million and a half people it was as quiet as a village out on the Paseo de Reforma at this hour of the night—about two thirty, when Hawkins got back to the Imperial. He tuned across the nine-meter shortwave band, searching for a news broadcast. Finally he found it, weak, fluttering and popping in and out, but there, the end of the lilting tune of "Lilliburlero," bringing up an instant and comforting image of marching grenadiers in bearskin hats. It was morning now in Britain, the BBC was back on the air after the overnight hiatus.

> *This is London calling. You are listening to the Empire Service of the*
> *BBC. Here is the news …*

Empire. Hawkins found himself musing over that word. *Empire. Why that word, why now?* he thought. How would Riley, Corrialles, the Riveras, take that word? *We kicked the British, the French, out of here*, the general said. *Perhaps it was a good thing Trotsky died when he did*, Hawkins thought, *saw right through me, he did, died before he could pass his little insight along, that I'm an officer of His Majesty's Secret Service, and I suppose, His Majesty's Empire. Incredibly smart man, to spot that so easily, so quickly.*

For a moment Hawkins was so lost in thought he almost missed the first part of the news until another word, "Luftwaffe," burned through his rumination. A raid on Southampton. That meant the navy, shipyards, also the Supermarine works where they built the Spitfire. Casualties on both sides. There was no jolly tone to the announcer's voice, none of the uplift of a pep talk, straight facts, plainly presented. There was, Hawkins thought, no gloss that could be put on it. This was a battle for basic survival, and yet also no alarm or panic. Pure determination. And concentration. If there was disaster pending, it wasn't here yet. The fight went on.

Falkenberg's worried expression and particularly, Falkenberg's comment that his mates were confused at fighting Britain would earn a prominent mention in Hawkins's next report. Could that confusion, and a lack of zeal, be at least partly a reason for the lagging expectation of victory? Hearts not in the fight? Possibly. But Hawkins still felt the same old twisting, winding-up feeling in the stomach, no cheering like the mess room on the *Dendrobium*.

They switched to the coast, a live broadcast. What an extraordinary thing, he thought, a critical battle fought out and covered live on the radio.

*From our position we can see the vapor trails of the approaching German planes, and our planes going up to meet them ... One of our fighters has engaged a German plane on the left flank of the formation ... They are maneuvering around, twisting in circles on circles, diving down. We can get a better look at them, now. One of the planes is trailing smoke ... it's diving down steeply, either trying to escape or blow the fire out. It's ... a German plane, a Messerschmitt, we can tell from the squared-off wingtips. A Hurricane is following it down ... it's firing again. Now it's breaking away. The German pilot is bailing out ... The Messerschmitt is diving down very fast now, trailing flames ... the chute has opened ... the plane has crashed into the Channel just short of the shore ... a huge ball of flame ...*

*Maybe one of Falkenberg's friends?* Hawkins thought. *Bailed out. Probably survived.* Could Falkenberg be listening to similar broadcasts? See himself coming down under that parachute? Not an attractive prospect. *That's no victory parade.*

*The vapor trails are steadily moving inland. More fighters are attacking, turning round and round, tracing large circles in the sky. Another fighter is now trailing smoke … It's turning away from the battle and heading inland … It's … a Hurricane … a German fighter is coming after it … another Hurricane turns onto its tail, defending its mate … they both turn away towards the Channel … the Hurricane trailing smoke seems to be heading back to base …*

*But not a victory parade for us, either,* Hawkins thought. The BBC switched to other news—measures in Parliament, the work of normal government carried on under white circles in the clear blue sky. He turned the set off and slowly reeled the antenna back in the window, gazing out at the quiet of the Paseo, watching a late-night delivery truck passing by. War was all-consuming. That was its nature. But, nevertheless, normal life insisted on carrying on. A good thing or not? When so much was at risk? Life does go on.

*Might as well call it a good thing and call it a night,* he thought. Exhausted, he fitfully dreamed of flying, then airplanes, and white circles in the sky. It was almost eleven when a pounding on the door woke him.

# -42-

He rolled over and checked his watch. Pounding again. Jumping out and across the room to the door, he caught it in midknock.

"Hawkins! Another painting," Riley said.

"La Galería Esteban?"

"No. A different one."

"A new one? Just opened?"

"No. Montaña Verde. They opened, I think, two or three years ago. We were there."

"Come in."

Hawkins was shirtless, only his boxers on. He quickly began getting dressed as Riley watched.

"You always change your clothes in front of women?"

"The suit has me fooled. You always go up to men's hotel rooms?"

"Fair enough. I live with my choices." She began idly walking around him. "Interesting. You have several scars. And a good body. I want to paint you. Have you ever posed?"

"No. I'll have you know I'm not great at sitting still."

"Yes. I've noticed. Always in a hurry. I will supply the tequila. It will calm you down."

As he knotted his tie Hawkins noticed there were now flecks of fresh paint on Riley's suit, particularly the pants and shoes.

"Riley, you painted in your new suit! What the hell?"

She shrugged. "I am an artist. Not a plumber. I paint. It is what I am, not what I do." Then she noticed his Browning Hi-Power hanging in the shoulder holster on a chair next to the bed. She walked to it and leaned over, hands behind her back, inspecting it. *Damn it*, Hawkins thought, *half-asleep, forgot it was there.* "I don't think you need that here on the Paseo." Before he could reach her she pulled it out and sniffed the muzzle. "And it's been fired."

"For practice. And put that back, will you please?"

"You come to our country, here in our capital, you think you need a gun?"

"No. But the countryside—"

"Camarada Trotsky called Frida and told her he thought you were a spy."

*Ah, bloody hell*, Hawkins thought. All the negative and dangerous possibilities flashed through his mind in a second. *Bugger! Bugger it all! Trotsky must've called right after I left. What did he say? Now what—dare not ask—fuck all this is bad—but what to say? Don't stop getting dressed*, he thought, *watch your face, a poker face, need that now.*

Every instinct said bluff it through, act innocent, say nothing, play it cool, maybe be amused, ask questions instead …

"He said what?"

"A spy. She didn't believe him. Are you?"

"Apart from the gun, what do I look like?"

"The representative of a Manhattan gallery. But, still, Hawkins—"

"The Americans don't have spies."

"Answer my question."

"I don't know how I could disprove that. Isn't it enough that I want to stop the Nazis from stealing artworks, smuggling them into this country and profiting from it?"

She gazed at him, chewing slightly on her lower lip.

"I still want to paint you. And your interesting … scars. Agreed?"

"Very well." He whipped the shoulder holster around and on and grabbed his coat. "Let's go."

Montaña Verde was in a magnificent nineteenth-century beaux arts mansion on Colima, a shady, tree-lined street in the Roma Norte section of the city. In the second room, on a side wall, there it was, the Rousseau Hawkins had seen in the Princess Hotel back in Bermuda. The same vibrant scene of the tropics, the trees loaded with fruit, the dark-skinned woman in a grass skirt near a tiger peeking out from the flowers. On this lush, green street, it seemed to fit in, its natural habitat. He and Riley stood in front, admiring it.

He checked his watch. Noon. Where was General Corrialles? At La Galería Esteban Corrialles somehow managed to get there first and buy his Braque before it stopped swinging on its peg. The Rousseau had now been in Montaña Verde since nine. *Something's off,* Hawkins thought. The manager came, he discussed the price. It was low. Hawkins told him he would think about it.

They retreated to a restaurant across the street.

"What are you going to do?" Riley said.

"Enjoy lunch."

"Yes …"

"And watch."

"You're waiting for the general?"

"Actually, no. I think he would've been here already. I only want to be sure."

They waited over leisurely plates of beef enchiladas in a tangy red sauce with rice, washed down with a pair of Dos Equis, then coffee. Close to two, Riley, bored, left for her studio.

"Do change your clothes, will you?" he said.

She laughed. "I already have enough for the right effect."

"Everything a work of art?"

"Now you understand. An artist, not a businessman." A huge, mischievous smile. "Or a spy."

"I am not a spy."

Hawkins moved the old Ford down the street, waiting and watching. But neither Corrialles nor anyone else arrived to collect the Rousseau. They would not, or at least, should not, take a chance of losing it. But it was clear Corrialles was not coming. Eckhardt and Falkenberg were not channeling this work through the general. Or do they need some quick cash? *Wish I had the money*, Hawkins thought, *take it back to New York myself.* Of course, if it was looted ... *probably was looted. What would Houghton, W say? Let it go*, he decided.

Time to report in.

# -43-

It took Lilly only five minutes to get downstairs to the phone. This time he'd given her the number. Since he was the one calling, he came down the street to the Hotel Reforma. He waited in a booth at the end of the row, hoping for a glimpse of her. She must've run. On the first ring he plucked the phone from the handset. She was already talking, her voice excited and urgent. He held his breath and his report.

"Hawkins! There are flashes from W at BSC in New York and General Houghton in Bermuda. Several, actually. I'm still compiling these all together. Late yesterday the censorship station in Bermuda intercepted an outbound airmail letter to Toledo, Spain, from General Corrialles to his son, Carlos Corrialles. He's a student at Academia de Infanteria in Toledo— General Houghton says that's Spain's big military school. Corrialles told his son to return home immediately, that they need him for service with the army back in Mexico. Carlos is going to get his own company. Here's the extraordinary part: Corrialles told his son that funding for a military takeover is nearly in hand, as he says"—Hawkins heard a rustling of papers—"'thanks to our German friends.' W states that:

Now clear the purpose of the art smuggling operation is not the general funding of North American operations but specifically a coup establishing a military government in Mexico, to secure a foothold in Western Hemisphere, create conservative regime friendly to the Third Reich. Emphasize, Corrialles is not a conduit for the funding of operations in the US or Canada: they will need all of funds for operation. Information received from source Parke-Bernet Gallery in Manhattan indicates offers of major artworks from Mexico has resumed, funds to be returned to Mexico, presumably to Corrialles or some other front organization or company, and not banked or transferred within the States.

"My god, that's extraordinary," Hawkins said.

"Yes. It is. And there's more. Corrialles told his son he expects to get their lost lands back. Boasting about it. From some other references in the letter they think Corrialles has also made contact with various foreign business interests that had properties in Mexico that were expropriated and want to get them back. Those businesses will also support a coup. It's not clear if any money is involved in those cases, that may only represent support, for instance, international pressure to recognize the regime. W thinks the likely success of a coup is very high. Canadian Army intelligence in Ottawa concurs. They are apparently more aware of what goes on in the hemisphere than London, army officers exchange visits and the like. They report President Cárdenas has been steadily professionalizing the officer corps, but there are still many army officers, particularly in the senior ranks, who came from the landed classes and want the return of their big family estates that were lost to Cárdenas's land reforms. Let's see, what else ... Oh yes, Corrialles expects the blessing and support of the Catholic Church. W says that makes sense, it lost lands to the reform, too, and it's opposed to the new secular school system. It wants to control all education and reverse the Mexican Revolution's anticlericalism."

"They want to restore the old feudal society."

She thought a second. "I guess that's right, yes. All of them. You have orders. It goes on, 'A military coup and a military government would be highly conservative, though not necessarily explicitly Fascist.'"

"Similar to Franco in Spain."

"Exactly, very much like Franco."

"Corrialles admires Franco. That's in my coming report."

"Ah. Of course. W goes on:

Such a regime would be friendly to Nazi Germany and Fascist Italy, a base of covert operations in the Western Hemisphere and a threat to British and Commonwealth security. Mexico is also highly influential in Central and South America, leading to more military takeovers. Goal is creating Nazi sphere of influence in the Western Hemisphere. You are to take whatever measures necessary to break up plot at all cost. Seize contraband artworks if you can or destroy them completely to deny funding to the Nazis if you must."

"Destroy them?"

"Those are your orders."

"Destroy them? The things we saw in Bermuda?"

She hesitated, then a barely audible, "Yes."

"My god—they can't be serious."

"I know." There was a very long break, from both of them, as that sank in. "It's—it's—it's terrible … what you may have to do. But—Roy— what—" she sighed heavily. "But you must do your duty if you have to."

"Yes. There may be no alternative."

"I'm so sorry."

"Don't be. It may not come to that. One thing at a time."

"Yes. One at a time. Do you have a report?"

"Yes." He read it off quickly to her, pausing for the faint *um-hum* to go on: The trip to Tlaxcala. Corrialles, his estate, his church gallery. Obvious criminal looting of archaeological treasures. An assessment of Corrialles. Reaction about bases. The arrival of Eckhardt and Falkenberg. The tension between them. Another gallery. Falkenberg's worried comments on the air war over Britain. His raid on Aust's office. Eckhardt and Falkenberg were behind the flight school. Finally the weird appearance of the Rousseau.

"Fascinating, Roy. We're having quite the adventure, aren't we?"

"Join the navy, see the world."

"That's it. Only no water up here in the mountains."

"How's your fellow?"

"Still sitting and waiting for the Germans."

"No waiting for us."

"No."

They both hung up.

# -44-

Hawkins sat back, and it all began to sink in. He left the Hotel Reforma, walking back up the Paseo to the Hotel Imperial. Then a spark lit. Without warning.

*Corrialles,* Hawkins thought. *That bastard! He wants to overthrow the government? Him and his kind? Stage a coup? Bloody greedy bastard wants to risk another civil war here to get his lands back? His feudal privileges? Warped sense of "guiding" the little people? That's what this is all about? Play footsie with Nazi Germany to do that? Become an ally with them? And ... the people those bastards murdered back there to get their hands on those paintings? The people they probably have to kill here?*

Then he thought of the people in the square listening to Cárdenas, the tears in Riley's eyes, the cab driver with his hand over his heart. That bent-over farmer, the women pulling those carts. *What about them?* he thought. The people in those hovels outside the city, next to the tracks in Veracruz? *What about them?* The sign in front of the new school in Río Frío, El Presidente Cárdenas? *What about him?* Lying in a pool of blood. No doubt on how that would work out. If Corrialles shrank from it, Eckhardt would happily oblige. The fact Cárdenas abolished the death penalty would not spare him. It might even increase the passion to kill him, to justify their own bloodlust. The ease and speed Corrialles shot that bull. And what he said about the Aztecs and the corrida—more and more killing, an addictive drug, more and more blood.

*Corrialles wants to be the Mexican Franco. Admires him.* What would he do to win? How many people was he willing to kill? How far would he go? The civil war in Spain slaughtered half a million. That was only part of it. The tortures—whenever the "loyalists" captured a Republican-held town, they systematically raped every woman they could drag out and then marched through the town with their victims' underpants on their bayonets. Rule by terror.

He turned and instead of heading back to the hotel, headed for his car.

Rage. Sheer rage, building and building. Blood surging behind his eyes, his carefully controlled professional demeanor blasted to bits by the heat, forgotten, gone out of mind. It was too much. He couldn't sustain it a moment more. He didn't think rage, he suddenly was rage itself—hot, frenzied, ready to kill. He started jogging for the car, got in and revved it up, darting into traffic, cutting off a bus, horns blaring, racing out of town, toward the mountains, the passes and Tlaxcala and the Hacienda Cuauhtlatzacuillotl.

*Stop this madness right now,* he thought. *Do what someone should've done to Hitler, Mussolini, Franco, years ago. Bullet in the head, right between the eyes. Fine with killing? See how you like it.*

An hour out of town he began climbing into the mountains, the cool air rushing in the windows. He began settling, thinking how to do it, how to get to Corrialles. Then he realized, *There's no guarantee Corrialles is there. He might be back in the city.* Then he thought, *His men were all around. He's a general, he commands troops, lots of them.* A few more minutes on, Hawkins thought of the painting Riley found that morning. *What the hell is going on there?* he thought, and pulled over to the side of the road.

*The general can't do this alone. There are others who have to join him,* Hawkins thought, *have to be. How many conspirators are there? Are Eckhardt, all the other Nazis, not merely Falkenberg, but the armed Gold Shirts in the street outside the Zocalo, are they dependent on Corrialles? Or could Eckhardt and Falkenberg merely turn to the next would-be Franco? If*

*I kill Corrialles, what happens next? Other than possibly tipping them off?*
*I don't know enough,* he realized.

He turned the car around and hurried back down the mountain, the lights of Mexico City glistening before him.

# -45-

Since there was no commercial service at the airfield, the Cuauhtémoc Academia was dark and locked at night, the dark stretching for miles, only a simple padlock on the gate, which yielded to his picks in seconds. Hawkins drove around the buildings looking for cars or trucks—only tractors to tow the planes and refueling tankers. No people about. The biplane trainers were neatly parked in rows behind the Junkers trimotors, canvas covering their cockpits. The valuable high-performance planes were locked inside the hangars. *No bothering with that*, Hawkins thought, *nor the tower.* Instead he parked behind a tanker truck between a pair of hangars and slipped around to the back door.

Obviously there was no alarm system, no bells on the outside—who was around to hear, anyway?—and apparently no phone lines. A large connecting conduit was there, but a thick bundle of loose wires dangled from the top of the pole. Presumably the field was too far out of town for phone service, although there was electricity. Another easy lock to pick. Inside he walked down the corridor, looking in at what appeared to be fairly normal classrooms filled with desks and chairs. He glanced through one, quickly flashing his light. Elevation maps of Mexico and Central America. Nothing special.

Second room, quite normal too. Charts on climbing, banking, using the rudder with large arrows showing the results of control actions. But there was an odd cabinet in the back, quite large, covered with the crinkly black leatherette material used on scientific and industrial instruments. It was designed to open up down the center. He flipped the chrome latches back and swung out the doors. Inside was a complete airplane cockpit, with a seat that rolled back revealing instruments, a stick and rudders. He drew the seat back and sat down.

*No ordinary cockpit*, he thought. Jammed with dozens of gauges, switches, indicators … What the hell was all this? To one side was a big cylinder with a yellow hose out the top, on the other a wheel-like reel. In front a blizzard of controls, turn and bank indicators, a compass, a clock, an altimeter, the word "Achtung" in a couple of places—there, the word "liter," that must be fuel, two marked "C"—centigrade, temperature. Several things he couldn't figure out.

He looked up several inches. A piece of clear plate glass extended from a gray oblong box. He flicked a switch on the side. The glass plate lit from below. In the center was a circle and crosshairs. He stared at it, taking it in, before leaning in to peek through.

A gunsight.

He looked down at the stick. It had a button on the top and buttons on the side. For guns.

There, he thought, down on the floor, a paper folded like a map. He picked it up and opened it. It was a map of the cockpit, with everything annotated in Spanish. One at the end didn't need translation: *MG 151 Canon.*

*Cannon?* he thought. *Cannon?* One thing he knew, the old Arado fighter he saw had light machine guns, all the planes a few years ago did. A 20 mm cannon meant only one thing. This was not a simulator for any old plane, this was a mock-up of the latest thing, the new Messerschmitt, the Bf 109. The planes attacking over the Channel this morning.

He threw the chart back on the cockpit floor, climbed out and paced up and down, before slamming it shut. *What on earth, why on earth, was this damn thing here? What was the point of training a group of Mexican students on planes they were never likely to see?*

Were the Nazis making promises to Corrialles and his supporters?

Hawkins thought. Money, of course. That was where the artworks came in. They needed money to pay people off, reward allegiance, cover expenses. Even a coup presumably needed a budget. Perhaps they could also send some weapons, small arms, machine guns, explosives, smuggle them in the way the paintings were smuggled. But airplanes the size of the Messerschmitt? No, absurd, there was no smuggling things like that. They couldn't be flown. It was too far. They'd have to be crated, fuselage in one large box, wings in two others and then carefully reassembled here by skilled mechanics. No small or easy matter. And why a school? Why not send "volunteers" the way Hitler and Mussolini did in Spain? Corrialles was an experienced military commander, he would have to know that.

*Damn, anyway, I need to get pictures of all this*, Hawkins thought. He quickly went out to the car and returned with his Rolleiflex and a box of flashbulbs, popping off a couple of photos.

Hawkins moved to another pair of classrooms. Nothing much of interest, like the first, from the charts and wall posters, weather instruction seemed to be going on in this one. However, in the fourth room there were a series of low locked cabinets against the back wall.

Inside were two sets of manuals. One shelf held the original German set, the one below the Spanish language versions. He checked the volumes on each end: *Maschinenhandbuch Für den Bf 109* and *Manual del Motor Para el Bf 109*. They were thick and heavy. He skimmed through the German version: a complete engine repair manual with photos and diagrams, very detailed.

He snapped a picture of the title page, pushed that back in place, pulled another. Radio repair. Another, instruments. And so on. The cabinets held complete sets of service and repair manuals for the Messerschmitt. In the last classroom on the end he found the final piece: a massive engine sitting on a heavy steel frame, surrounded by towering tool cases. He counted the spark plugs. Twelve cylinders. On top in white were the letters: DB 601. *Daimler-Benz*, he realized. The engine for Bf 109. That rated another picture.

In short, the Cuauhtémoc Academia de Vuelo was a somewhat small but reasonably complete training program for military pilots and ground crew. Neat and clean, professional, most likely not very different than a classroom back in the Reich, or maybe in Spain, now that Franco ruled it. *That's probably how the Germans got started on translating those manuals,* Hawkins thought. They were able to get plenty of Messerschmitts through Italy to Spain and into the hands of the Condor Legion. Now Franco's Spanish Air Force had those planes.

He glanced around the classroom. On the wood rack under a chair. One of the students had left a magazine. He pulled it out. *Los Dorados* was on the cover. ACCIÓN REVOLUCIONARIA MEXICANISTA. The Gold Shirts, the violent gun-toting thugs in the street off the Zocalo.

*Is Eckhardt recruiting from the ranks of his local Fascist allies?* Hawkins thought. Why, was the question.

# -46-

There was a final room on the end. Hawkins glanced in, flashing his light around. Several large drafting tables. He started to move on. An inner instinct brought him back. He reached up, pulling the chain on the light over the near table. It lit a large half-finished diagram. He puzzled over it a moment. *It's an airport*, he realized. *Not this one, though, bigger.* Very detailed plan. Parallel runways. A compass point north. Intersecting taxiways and cross runways. Hangars. Tower. All carefully annotated in Spanish. Quite a few offices. A normal airport, more or less?

But there were many other buildings. Near the runway, a small building labeled *Cabaña del Piloto*—*all right, that obviously meant "pilot's building."* Along the runways, around the buildings there were long narrow structures indicated with dashes, all labeled *Foso*, with one on the end labeled *Foso del Ataque Aéreo.* Air-raid trenches?

Farther away an ascending series of buildings in rows, like a hierarchy: *Cubierta del Oficial, Cubierta del Suboficial, Cubierta Alistada,* and finally, off to one side, a much bigger house, *Comandante Bajo.* Okay, that was obvious: quarters for officers, noncoms and enlisted men, and the big house, *commandante* meant "base commander." Around the whole area were circles labeled *Artillería Antiaérea.* Artillery?

*This is not a civilian airport,* Hawkins realized. *It's a military one. And it's not merely a field, a landing strip, but a complete military airbase with all the latest features, not only for training, but a frontline facility like the RAF bases in southern England with trenches, AA emplacements, ammo bunkers, aid stations, the works, ready for war.* In the corner, under a paper clip and a note, he found a legend: FUERZA AÉREA MEXICANA, Mexican Air Force, the name of what he presumed was a city or town and *Nuevo León*, a Mexican state near Texas. An arrow pointing southeast was labeled *Monterrey*. Pinned around the edge of the drafting table were aerial photographs and a topographical map of the region.

Over to the side stood a huge map case with large flat and shallow drawers with a chain padlocked through the drawer handles. That was a joke, Hawkins had it off in seconds. He began checking the drawers. Some were labeled *Fuerza Aérea*, others *Armada*—navy. There didn't seem to be any drawers for the army—perhaps they had those already. He began pulling out the drawers and checking the contents.

As he went down through the drawers he counted plans for at least fifteen airbases circling the country, from Yucatán and Veracruz in the south, to Baja California and Sonora in the north then around to Michoacán in the southwest, with several around the capital.

Down at the bottom, the *Y*'s, he found a thick set of finished engineering blueprints and architectural drawings. He brought that back to the drafting table and settled in on the stool, going through them.

Under one of a general site plan, he found an engineering blueprint for a pair of doors mounted in a cliff face, designed to swing out. Another revealed an interior plan: a canal or channel dug into a cliff face and extending out into the ocean. Walkways lined the channel with service and supply tunnels to the side, connecting to workshops. Overhead a large traveling crane mounted on tracks was set into the side of the artificial cavern. Forward, toward land, was another for an underground reservoir, with a road and connected pumping station on the surface. He found an overhead plan of the complex. There was a series of dotted lines in the channel or well, in the shape of a submarine.

Hawkins had heard about things like this, of course. A giant revetment, or bunker, on the coast that a submarine or U-boat could sail into and shelter from attack, until it sallied out on a new mission. Very possible.

But also *very* expensive. An enormous excavation, immense amounts of concrete and steel. And a series of airbases to cover them would be required, and probably batteries of coastal guns. The major powers could afford such emplacements, but Mexico? Well, *maybe* it could. But as far as Hawkins knew, Mexico didn't have any submarines, at least not yet. He moved another light over to the drafting table, made it nice and bright, and took a series of pictures of the airbases and the submarine installation.

He turned out the lights and closed the door, looking down the corridor to the stairs. He was about to run up, when he realized there was a large door under the stairs.

# -47-

The door was unlocked. He went down, flashing his light. At the bottom of the stairs was a large switch panel. He yanked the lever down and stood taking it all in for a good minute or two, camera loosely hanging around his neck.

A basement. A long row of overhead lights. A very big room, the entire floor under the building. In the center, on a table, a giant topographic map of Mexico and the adjacent American states, probably forty feet long. To the sides, rows of tables under regional maps on the walls, all lit. Phones on all of them. Pads, pencils, filing cases, all at ready. Beyond the map, two rows of tables with radio transceivers. In front of him, a low balcony with a bench all the way across, dotted with more phones. He went down the rest of the stairs. Under the balcony, a huge telephone switchboard, big enough for a couple dozen operators.

But the forty-foot-long topographic map—all of Mexico from Tijuana in the north to Quintana Roo in the south—drew him over. Around the map were painted wooden markers with standard military symbols indicating regiments and divisions, field headquarters, fortifications, battle lines, along with air and army bases, waiting and ready. More symbols were stacked on a low shelf around the map. Pointers and hooks to move them all about the map were at ready, too. Mexican flags were dotted around the map, on the major bases, with American flags lined up on the US side of the border from Texas to California.

The map, the regional stations to the side, the phones, the switchboards, the banks of radio transceivers, the raised platforms for commanders— *incredible*, he thought. This was a military command center of the highest order. The defense of an entire nation could be run from a room like this. There was even a table to one side with coffee urns.

The whole setup was far too elaborate for training. Could they be building it as a fallback option, a hidden command center for the Mexican Army, Navy and Air Force? All they needed was to have the phone lines brought in.

His eye shifted to the southeast. He walked over to look carefully. There, around Yucatán, was a set of red, white and black Nazi swastika flags. The naval bases on the coast. Farther inland, airfields, with more swastika flags. He picked up one of the swastika flags and twirled it in his fingers before snapping it back down.

*Oh, I need a cup of coffee*, he thought. *What in hell … What the hell …* and then just, *What? What!*

He had an odd lack of reaction, he realized, or conviction, or something. *I should be horrified*, he thought, *or mad, or appalled, or astonished, or something. Alarmed. Above all, alarmed. But I don't feel alarmed. Not at all. Irritated, maybe. Why? Something's off*, he realized. A mental guard dog was faintly barking in the back of his mind or in his gut. But what shadow was it barking at?

He rested the Rolleiflex on the newel post of the staircase, took more pictures, then headed back upstairs.

# -48-

There was no missing Eckhardt's office: in between recruiting posters for the Camisas Dorades and a glaring Hitler labeled EIN VOLK, EIN REICH, EIN FÜHRER! were more copies of Eckhardt's ancient macuahuitl, along with various obsidian knives and blades hanging on hooks. In the center, on a console, was a painted beaker. Hawkins picked it up, curious. A bare-chested man was bent backward over an altar, hands bound, with a priest slashing his chest open, blood flying, the victim's head turned to the side, mouth wide open, eyes staring straight back at the onlooker, as if to say, *See.* He put it down with a shudder.

A long table occupied the center of the room, loaded with a large quantity of newsletters, magazines and pamphlets from the Camisas Doradas, the Unión Nacional Sinarquista, Acción Revolucionaria, ultra-Catholic groups, too—a fairly comprehensive survey of right-wing, right-wing-leaning, Nazi, Fascist or generally reactionary Mexican literature.

The desktop was clean and neat, not a paper on it, everything in its place, lined up in sharp right angles. More locked drawers, another rather easy challenge. In fact, this all felt a little too easy, but that was what it seemed to be.

In the top drawer was a smattering of business records from *Norddeutsche Luftfahrtpartner*, employee time sheets, miscellaneous bills. On the left side there was a large volume of letters, invitations, copies of notes, all to and from the Camisas Doradas, the Unión Nacional Sinarquista, Acción Revolucionaria—political type things.

When Hawkins opened the bottom right drawer he discovered several thick folders full of bank envelope after bank envelope stuffed with cashed checks, all signed by Eckhardt, from Norddeutsche Luftfahrtpartner. He began cross-checking from month to month. The same names kept appearing. Every two weeks. All with Spanish surnames. *Payroll checks*, he realized. He flipped through, checking the sums. There seemed to be two, maybe three pay scales. Then he noticed a note on one: *Lehrer*—instructor. Right. Higher pay. He began looking for a note on the lower ones. Finally, *Kadett*—cadet. Interesting. Not *Student*. Or *Lehrling*—apprentice. Kadett.

That aviation school—*the students are being paid*, Hawkins suddenly thought. *Why?* That meant the students couldn't be from the ranks of Corrialles's men, either the army or the air force. The government would be paying them.

*What the bloody hell?* Then, *Oh, wait … they were all in khaki … Not Corrialles's men? A private force? Why?* Those men in the street off the Zocalo were likely his students, Hawkins realized. Eckhardt probably brought them to the demonstration, gave them a taste of blood, to see what they're made of, how committed they were.

*But what the bloody hell? If Corrialles is serious about staging a coup, if he's almost there, how could he conceivably do it and not be using his own troops, men loyal to him? And his son was coming back to be with the army, command a company? Makes no sense to use anyone else.* The missing piece, the one Hawkins sensed was in the very center of the puzzle, wasn't here.

At the bottom of the drawer was a steel fireproof box, locked. His pick set made easy work of that, too. Inside was what looked like a leather mail sack. Under the usual Nazi eagle standing on the globe with a swastika were the words "Reich-Außenministerium" and "Diplomatische Post."

*Good god*, Hawkins thought, *a diplomatic pouch? Really?* He began shuffling through the papers and letters. But a set of professionally printed leather-bound documents drew his attention. He flipped back the cover to read, in German:

TREATY OF ALLIANCE AND MUTUAL ASSISTANCE BETWEEN
THE DEUTSCHES REICH AND THE UNITED STATES OF
MEXICO, SIGNED AT MEXICO CITY
4 September 1940

His Excellency, Adolf Hitler, Reichschancellor and Führer of the Deutsches Reich, and his Excellency General Miguel Corrialles, President of the United States of Mexico, desiring to confirm in a Treaty of Alliance between the Deutsches Reich and the United States of Mexico;

Convinced that such a Treaty will further the spirit of mutual understanding of all questions arising between the two countries;

Intend to strengthen the economic relations between the two countries to their mutual advantage and in the interest of prosperity;

Resolve to cooperate closely with one another in preserving world peace and resisting aggression;

Intend to resist in all ways the advance of the Commitern or Communist International and its atheistic and collectivist agenda;

Determine to collaborate in all measures of mutual assistance in the event of aggression against the two nations;

Have decided to conclude a Treaty of Alliance with these objectives …

*Crny Hill,*          *Gen. Miguel Corrialles,*

Führer                     Presidente

There were two copies, one in German, the other in Spanish, which appeared to be identical. Hawkins began hurriedly skipping through the attached letters. He stopped at what seemed to be a list labeled Appendix

A—actually, he realized, a shopping list, and quite abruptly, the flight
school made sense:

```
To be supplied by Reichsluftfahrtministerium:

    300 Bf 109 Fighters

    75 Bf 110 Attack Planes

    300 Arado Trainers

    200 Heinkel 111e Bombers

    Fuel Wagons

    Spare parts

    Training
```

```
To be supplied by Reichminister für Bewaffnung und
Munition:

    300,000 Mauser Rifles 98k

    10,000 Luger P.08

    50,000 Machine Pistols MP40

    15,000 Machine Guns MG34
```

It continued for two full pages, everything from Panzer tanks to
first-aid kits and helmets.

On the final page,

```
In consideration, the United States of Mexico agrees to:
```

- Supply the Deutsches Reich with 1.2 million metric tons
  unrefined petroleum annually;

- Grant to the Deutsches Reich military, naval, air
  rights as enumerated in Appendix and Map B.

Hawkins skimmed back through the document, then noticed an oddity:

There were multiple cover pages. The first was dated September 4, 1940. The second, September 18. The next, October 4, and so on, to the end of the year. He flipped to the back and glanced down at the signature line.

It was already signed by "President Corrialles"? This wasn't a draft, Hawkins thought, an option to be explored, or a proposal. This was an actual treaty. He dug around in Eckhardt's top drawer and found a magnifying glass. He held the sheet under the desk lamp, looking at both signatures at all angles. They weren't printed. They were real signatures, done with fountain pens in blue ink. Could the Führer himself have personally touched these papers at some point? *Extraordinary, if true,* Hawkins thought. *Simply mind-boggling to think Hitler may have held this damn thing.*

But what about General Corrialles? Both the German and Spanish copies were here. If he had signed it, why wouldn't he have taken his copy? What were they doing in Eckhardt's desk?

The mental guard dog was still barking. *But at what?* he thought. *The puzzle isn't complete,* Hawkins simply felt that in his gut. *Something's wrong. That Corrialles wants to overthrow the government, the coming election here? Sure. Corrialles and his rich friends want their land and status back,* Hawkins thought. *They want to be the grandees they once were. Selfish, conscienceless it may be, but it is an understandable reason. Hitler, Eckhardt, Falkenberg, all the Nazis here and abroad, they want to advance their system. Morally deprived, but logical. And if Corrialles successfully overthrows Cárdenas, the election, and takes over the government, he'll restore diplomatic relations with his Nazi friends that Cárdenas severed.*

*But this treaty doesn't make sense,* Hawkins thought. It was a sort of irritable shiver he felt. For one thing, how would Germany get this awesome pile of stuff and duff to Mexico, past not only the Royal Navy, but the American Navy? Then there was the command center in the basement. All too obvious someone was considering the possibility of a war with the United States. But even so … if they somehow got them here—a very big *if.* Of course, the Messerschmitts would no doubt be superior to the American P-38 and P-40. But in a dogfight with the superbly trained and professional US pilots the neophyte Mexican trainees would be cut to pieces in minutes.

*This is bullshit*, Hawkins realized. Suddenly he thought back to Cárdenas's speech. The vehement way he rejected foreign bases, what a cheer that brought from the crowd in the Zocalo, how they'd chanted, *Ningunas bases, ningunos concesiones ... Ningunas bases, ningunos fascistas ...*

That was the final touch that tipped him over. *This is bullshit and that signature is a forgery*, he thought, knew, with the cold certainty that two and two equaled four. Not even Corrialles would agree to foreign bases on Mexican soil. He'd made that clear over dinner. Oil? An alliance? Maybe. Bases? Never. *No one in this country*, Hawkins thought, *don't care who they are, left, right, up, down or sideways would ever agree to foreign bases on Mexican soil. Anyone who had any concept of this country, its sensitivities, how it lost half its territory to the United States a century ago, how they threw out the French seventy-five years ago, how they threw out the foreign-owned oil and railroad companies, how hundreds of thousands of people gave their wedding rings and last chicken for the independence of Mexico, how Latin Americans generally feel, no one who knew any of that would think this was remotely credible.*

*Except the Americans.*

*What were they doing right now? Demanding bases, that's what. They don't get it. And the Nazis are banking on that, playing on that, that was why the proposed U-boat bases were as close as possible to the Panama Canal, to touch the Yanks off.* This treaty, Hawkins realized, the blueprints, the command post downstairs, none of this was real. *It's for show, a form of theater, like a stage or film studio set.* That was why the phone lines weren't installed. That would expose too much to the wrong people.

*That's why all this is here*, Hawkins realized, *the Nazis are trying to start a war between Mexico and the United States. Coldly. Deliberately.*

But how would they get the audience into their little theater? *Something's still missing.*

Next to the desk was a table covered with a thick linen cloth. He'd ignored it until he turned and hit a glancing touch on it with his toe. A mental alarm went off: heavy. He looked down: the shape. Under the drape was a strongbox with one of the new circular-key type locks.

It took him a full half hour to pick the complex lock without scratching or damaging it, his back and knees aching from bending down to get at it. When he swung the door open there was surprisingly little in it—a petty cash box, which made sense, and a thin folder of grainy photos of various men on the streets of Mexico City. All were wearing business suits, the usual fedoras, often carrying briefcases. The photos were taken at various angles and had the look of being done covertly. Several showed the men exiting hotels, particularly the Reforma. Then Hawkins found one, and then farther on a second, showing those men leaving the same building. On one photo a plaque could be seen next to the door. It read EMBASSY OF THE UNITED STATES OF AMERICA. Safe assumption they were Americans, going from their hotel to the embassy.

At the end there was a single carbon copy sheet. It'd been folded several times. At the top was a letterhead:

EL MINISTERIO DEL INTERIOR

POLICÍA JUDICIAL FEDERAL

And a simple list of seven men's names and the hotels they were staying at, a few with addresses back in the United States. No indication of who they were, why these men were of interest, nothing. Hawkins quickly copied the names, closed it all up and headed out.

Hawkins hurried down the stairs, wondering how Eckhardt and Falkenberg had a contact at the Interior Ministry, how they got this thing.

*Get out of here,* he thought, *get back to Lilly. Rush order job. I think have what I need.*

# -49-

It was near dawn. He got an envelope from the desk clerk at the Reforma Hotel, put in the list of names, with a quick note, and had it placed in Lilly's box.

It was noon when the bellhop at the Imperial woke him. Fifteen minutes later he was waiting in a phone booth at the Reforma. Lilly walked by, glanced at him slightly with a small nod, stepped into an adjacent booth across the aisle and dialed his phone.

"I should be a secret agent. Then I could sleep as late as I want," she said.

"I wish I could say I was dancing till dawn."

"Maybe when we get back to Bermuda, but they've always turned in rather early there, or so I'm told. It's not Montreal, I'll have you know. Far better than Toronto, though. Anyplace is better than Toronto."

"What's the matter with Toronto?"

"Haven't you heard it called Toronto the Good? The bars close at ten. *Ten!* Worst blue laws in the world."

"Sounds like prison. What've you got?"

"New York was able to identify them. W made some calls, including to a Mr. Kelly, who I gather you know?"

"I do. He's a special agent at the Bureau."

"Kelly confirmed they're all with the FBI."

"I thought so."

"W says Mr. Hoover's trying to move into Mexico."

"No surprise."

"Why are the Mexican police following these men?"

"Because Hoover's trying to move into Mexico," she lightly laughed, a snorting sort of giggle, "and they're dumb enough to work out of the embassy."

"Kelly asked for a favor in return. He's concerned where this list came from, how the Policía Judicial Federal know who they are."

"I'll do what I can. Got your pad? Ready?"

"Fire away." He quickly began dictating his report. Only this time instead of *um-hum* to go ahead, she interjected with a soft, lilting "god" or "really?" And finally a breathless "mon Dieu."

"It's all fake?"

"Yes."

"To start a war between two other countries."

"That's it."

"General Corrialles?"

"He's a dupe being played for a sucker."

"And Mexico?"

"The next Belgium. They're expendable. Nothing in it for them."

"Seems like a great deal of effort."

"Compared to the potential cost of the US helping Britain? Maybe coming into the war someday? It's nothing. Petty cash. Right at this moment Roosevelt wants to trade fifty destroyers for British bases in the Caribbean. Stopping that alone is worth this. But triggering a war between Mexico and the US could tie the Americans up for years, keep the Yanks out of the war in Europe, keep them from helping Britain. It's absolutely worth it if they can pull it off."

It only took a split second for her to consider that, she breathlessly burst out, "Right. We don't have years." She hurriedly began reading it back to him when a man passed by their phone booths to one on the end. Hawkins leaned out checking. It was one of the men in the photos in Eckhardt's safe.

"Lilly," he whispered, "don't hang up."

"What?"

"That's one of the men in the photos."

He could hear the rustling of her pad.

"You said two of them were staying here? Which one?"

"Don't know the name, just the photo. I'll have to follow him, keep talking." He glanced down the aisle again and switched to French, to be safe, "Je suppose qu'il y a de bons clubs à Montréal?"

"Oui, nous avons de grandes boîtes de nuit à Montréal, we're half French you know, ooh la la, et tous!" The man went back out. Lilly saw him, too. "Bonne chance, Roy." Hawkins stepped out, looked down, winked at her and followed.

In the lobby the FBI man headed straight for the door. Another man abruptly stuck his folded copy of *La Prensa* under his arm, jumped up and made for the door, too, studiously not looking at the agent. Hawkins instinctively held back, giving man number two some room. Outside, on the Paseo, the second man quickly leaned in the window of a parked car without taking his eyes off the FBI agent. Another man got out and followed man number two. The car started and pulled into the traffic.

Hawkins walked along behind, no longer really needing to keep the Bureau man in sight at all. The Mexican cops, if the file in Eckhardt's safe was any indication, were almost certainly officers from the Policía Judicial Federal. The officers were executing a perfectly competent tail, switching back and forth between the two men on the sidewalk, alternating in the lead, occasionally changing places with the three officers in the car. Their target, and Hawkins's, clearly had no idea he was being followed, or that he ought to be taking the standard precautions from time to time to be sure he wasn't being tailed.

The odd parade proceeded down several blocks and around two corners whereupon it stopped. The FBI man stationed himself on a corner opposite a house with a crimson banner floating out front. Hawkins walked by all of them to a shoeshine stand on the far corner. He sat down, gave the bootblack several pesos and settled in to watch.

The house was the office of a Communist newspaper. The red flag was square with a large, blocky stylized hammer and sickle filling the center, not the crimson banner of the Soviet Union. Headlines about Trotsky's assassination were pasted up in the windows—¡CAMARADA TROTSKY MUERTO! ¿ERA STALIN?

Hawkins started to laugh. The shoeshine man looked up, startled.

"No, no usted," Hawkins said. "Not you." The man went back to snapping his rag on Hawkins's loafers. *Ludicrous,* Hawkins thought. He bent his head to his chin, trying not to laugh, or at least not be seen laughing. The British Secret Service watching the Mexican Policía Judicial Federal watching the American FBI watching a bunch of Commie writers. Like one of the silent comedies where a cop gets a cat out of an old lady's tree by shooting it and then handing it to her.

*What a monumental exercise in cluelessness,* he thought. In fairness, though, the PJF seemed rather good at what they were doing. One could hardly blame them for wanting to know what the hell was going on in their own capital city.

And the FBI. Did it not understand the implication of the headline right in front that man's eyes? ¿ERA STALIN?—Was it Stalin? That Communism was ripping itself apart? And Stalin was systematically murdering the losers? *J. Edgar Hoover and the FBI probably think Mexico is full of Communists, but Cárdenas had broken relations with the Soviet Union and … nothing happened.* Communism wasn't a threat here, and if it didn't have a future in Mexico, with the vast poverty-stricken slums surrounding its cities, it didn't have a future anywhere. The Bureau was chasing its own fevered imagination.

And meanwhile, the Nazis … they had to have a source in the Policía Judicial Federal. How else did Eckhardt get that list? Hawkins mulled that a minute. Could be a sympathizer. Also might be a mole they inserted long ago. Didn't have to be a field agent or supervisor. A government minister? Possible. Or might be someone small—a secretary or clerk. Eckhardt and Falkenberg could be bribing someone with them having no idea where the money came from. Maybe that's why they had to sell the second painting, to pay someone off.

*But does it matter?* Hawkins thought. Probably not, or at least not much. *What counted was that Eckhardt and Falkenberg had found a credulous conduit to Washington.* That was the missing piece Hawkins knew had to be there.

From the photos and list of agents' names in Eckhardt's safe, their plan was perfectly obvious. Once Corrialles was installed in power and restored relations with Berlin, Eckhardt and Falkenberg would leak, or drop, or expose the treaties, the command center, the Bf 109 trainer, all the kit and caboodle in the flight school to one or more of the FBI agents—maybe this man right in front of him surveilling a two-bit Trotskyite newspaper. They'd lap it up like hungry kittens, flash it back to Washington and then the real fun and games would start.

The bootblack finished, snapping his rag with a large flourish.

"Perfecto!" Hawkins said, and gave a him a big tip.

*Time to get back to work*, Hawkins thought. *At least I know who I ought to be fighting against even if the Americans, or last least some Americans, don't.*

# -50-

"I am not a spy."

"Of course, you would say this," Rivera said. He looked over at Kahlo, that magical look lovers had dancing between them as they both began to laugh.

"Comrade Trotsky did not agree," Kahlo said.

"I am not," Hawkins said.

"That's why you carry that expensive-looking gun," Riley said, "a mild-mannered art dealer," tapping her chest in the manner of a delicate lady with the vapors, going *oohhh*.

"The world's a dangerous place."

"Indeed, on that we can agree," Rivera said. "Real Nazis."

"Real Nazis."

"So is it the Yankees?" Kahlo said.

"No, I am not an employee of the US government."

"That would make sense. Camarada Trotsky thought you were working for the British," Rivera said.

"How could he know that? We barely met. Will you help or not?"

"Of course, Hawkins," Rivera said, suddenly serious. "No matter what that pig Corrialles is doing with the Germans, it will not be good for Mexico, for its people. We are through with caudillos, at least in this country."

"Good. And thank you. I want to tip Corrialles off about something, preferably by someone in the German community here."

"What do you want to tip him off about?" Riley said.

"I'd rather not say."

"You are a spy! A secret agent. With secrets," Kahlo said, a little exuberant, a big joke.

"Must I repeat myself?" Hawkins said.

"Never mind," Rivera said. "Frida, por favor?"

"I am thinking along the lines of a credible go-between who might know something about Eckhardt and Falkenberg. A person who would want to confidentially warn Corrialles about something."

"Not sure—" Kahlo said.

"Anyone in the Policía Judicial Federal?"

"Why them?" Rivera said.

"The American Federal Bureau of Investigations has officers here in Mexico City. The Policía Judicial are following them, watching every move."

"You might say we know the federales—they interrogated us only a few days ago, remember?" Kahlo said. "About Leon's death. It was quite unpleasant. I would not recommend such an encounter."

"I would not, either," Rivera said. "I think I know a man. He is German, but he is a comrade, a supporter of Trotsky's, not one of the Stalinists. He joined the International Brigades—the Thälmann Battalion—and fought in Spain under an assumed name, to protect his family in Berlin. When Spain fell he came here and kept quiet. Ah, well, he has been despondent for a long time. He cannot return home. And he took the fall of the Republic very hard. The German volunteers fighting the Fascists took terrible casualties, most of his friends died. Then Franco executed the wounded from the hospitals they captured."

"I think I may know who actually did the shooting."

"Who?"

"Eckhardt. Corrialles told me he was an executioner."

"Madre de dios ..." Kahlo said. She covered her mouth with her hands. "And he is here in Mexico?"

"Yes." He turned back to Rivera. "This man of yours?" Hawkins said.

"I think he will help," Rivera said. "Can you meet us later?"

"Yes. I was wondering also ... I need some film developed. Someone discreet. Can you recommend anyone?" Kahlo smiled and held her hand out. "What?"

"Give them to me. I used to develop Papa's film. Do you know how I got started as an artist? I retouched his photos. I am *very* good at that. Want a mole or cowlick removed? I will make it vanish."

Rivera looked at her then him and started to laugh. "This is why I love her. She surprises everyone."

Hawkins handed her the foil-wrapped film rolls and she slowly led them down the hall, carefully stepping along, swinging her skirt with one hand to hide her limp. Twenty minutes later she was spooling the first of the developed negatives into the printer as Hawkins and Rivera waited in the red light. She clicked on the printer. A crystal-clear image of the command center filled the platter. She and Rivera leaned over, gaping at it. She began winding the crank, slowly rolling the images over the plate. She stopped at the little Nazi flags on the bases in Yucatán and softly gasped, "Dios mío."

She and Diego leaned back, looking at him.

"I hope you have a plan," Rivera said.

"I do."

# -51-

Hawkins drove in, slowing past a row of light tanks—tankettes, actually, mounted with machine guns, little two-man jobs. On a battlefield they might be useful if properly supported by covering infantry, although the lightest shell would rip them inside out. But on a city street? *Well ... it depends*, Hawkins thought, *on what your intentions are.* Under buildings? In Mexico City's ancient, narrow streets? Nothing more than ovens for any two men unlucky enough to be caught inside. But on the big boulevards? They could sweep them clear with those machine guns, then fire down the side streets, clearing them. Deadly enough for Corrialles's purposes.

The armed guard at the warehouse wore a French-style steel helmet, the kind the Republican troops wore in the civil war in Spain, rather like the domed helmets steelworkers in Manhattan sometimes wore, only with a brass infantry arms medallion on the front. But underneath, the serious face of an Aztec warrior looked out. He sharply saluted, grounded his carbine and stepped aside. The general—now in uniform—unlocked the door and gestured in.

Corrialles wasn't taking any chances. The Campo Militar where he had his headquarters was at the far edge of the Valle de México, a good distance from the city, surrounded by truck farms. What's more, the warehouse was in the middle of the base. And he had this armed guard on duty. No, no chances here. Corrialles had finished buying up all the paintings Eckhardt and Falkenberg had dropped in various galleries around Mexico City—including, for the moment, his own gallery, and brought them here for safekeeping. The legal paper trail the people in New York were looking for was complete, the taint of looting washed away. It'd been a merry game of musical chairs. Now Aust needed to see them to know what he was insuring and Hawkins ostensibly needed to photo them for the Alpert Gallery, although he also had Lilly's photos from Bermuda if he needed them.

Hawkins motioned for Aust to follow Corrialles. *Can I flip him?* Hawkins thought. *Why not bet the daily double?* Hawkins looked down the aisle. There they were, ten wooden cases.

"How many paintings are there?" Hawkins said.

"Thirty-seven," Corrialles said.

*Thirty-seven?* Hawkins thought. *We counted forty in Bermuda. He doesn't know the Rousseau is missing? And two others? Does Aust?* There didn't seem to be any reaction in the insurance agent's face. *Maybe not. Maybe he never counted them. Or maybe they never let him.*

"Thirty-seven!" Hawkins said. "It's too bad we don't have that much space in the Alpert Gallery. I think what we'll do is have a wall with photos of the rest. We could rotate the paintings on request."

"I will need a copy of these pictures," Aust said.

"If you don't object, General, I'll make sets of prints," Hawkins said. He unlimbered his Rolleiflex, drew out the first painting, the Braque again. "Can I take them out in the light?"

"Of course." Corrialles ordered a pair of sergeants to begin carrying out the paintings and set them on a bench against a white wall. The setup was perfect. Hawkins was shooting with the new Agfachrome stock he'd bought from a camera shop downtown. It might be German made but it could be developed with prints made locally, not shipped to Rochester like Kodachrome. Plus he could have as many copies made as he wanted.

They made methodical work of it, a steady rhythm, the sergeants carefully bringing the paintings out, the general hovering around, checking on his soldiers, Hawkins snapping photos. Aust wrote a short description of each painting, checking the labels on the back.

They'd gone through thirty paintings when an adjutant, a wad of photo prints in hand, came up behind the general and touched Corrialles's elbow, whispering in his ear. Corrialles nodded, listened more. His eyes seemed to darken a moment, then a blank professional look. He took the papers, slowly flipping through them.

"Sí, aquí," he said. Hawkins had picked up enough Spanish to know that meant, *Yes, here.*

Two paintings later Rivera's contact, a man named Fischer—a tall balding German with a prematurely aged face arrived. His suit hung on him, he'd lost serious weight, his cheeks gaunt over a dark five-o'clock shadow that made them even more sunken. Corrialles led the adjutant and Fischer inside. Hawkins, Aust and the sergeants kept working. Off and on Hawkins could hear distant voices inside. Three more paintings later the adjutant emerged with Fischer following. They disappeared up the company street.

General Corrialles came and stood in the door a moment, arms folded, the papers in one hand, watching carefully. Then stepped out of the way and sat on a bench as Hawkins and Aust worked, looking at the papers occasionally. When they finished Corrialles rose and brushed Hawkins on the shoulder, gesturing for him to follow inside. He spread the papers on top of one of the cases, very serious.

"Señor Hawkins. That man you saw here brought me these papers, wanting a reward. He is a German refugee. As you probably know, there are quite a few in the capital today. Also he is probably a Communist, he admits he fought with the Reds in Spain, which is not good. I do not trust him. You speak German. Please look at these photos of papers for me."

Hawkins began going down the photos of the treaty he'd found in Eckhardt's desk, slowly, carefully reading as if he'd never seen them before. When he got to the end he stopped, then leaned over, looking carefully at the signature: *General Miguel Corrialles, Presidente.* Then he slowly leaned back and raised his eyebrows.

"You're getting a promotion ... should I congratulate you?"

Corrialles burst out laughing, a hard laugh driven by emotional tension. "No."

"Then—I'm not sure I understand. Why did you sign that?"

"I didn't. But does this look real to you otherwise?"

"Yes, it looks very authentic. A treat of alliance between Mexico and Germany."

"I agree."

"What's going on?"

"I don't know."

"You said that man's a Red?"

"He says he's not. It's possible. S-2—excuse, that's our military intelligence branch—says the majority of the foreign volunteers who went to Spain weren't Commies. Many—very many, actually—of the survivors came here. They were investigated, of course. We were also interested in their experiences. They learned many things of military, tactical importance during the civil war there. Naturally we want to draw on that." He set the rest of the folder on the case and opened it. "He says he got this from a photographer here in the city." Hawkins flipped through the photos, stopping at one of the outside of the Cuauhtémoc Academia de Vuelo.

"This is Eckhardt and Falkenberg's business—"

"It is? I thought they were in Centro, near the Zocalo."

"That's Aust's office." Hawkins was ready for that. He got his wallet, got both Eckhardt's and Aust's business cards and held them up together. "The real office is south of the city. There are no airplanes downtown. Didn't you know?" Corrialles tightly shook his head, eyes locked on the cards. "Ask Aust." Corrialles abruptly stepped outside.

"Señor Aust. Who owns the Cuauhtémoc Academia de Vuelo?"

Aust hesitated. *That's interesting*, Hawkins thought. *The German's on the spot. He doesn't know what General Corrialles knows.*

Aust carefully answered, "Eckhardt and Falkenberg."

The adjutant had returned. The general spun about and gave a quick, firm order, "Forme el regimiento para arriba. Consiga los carros. Marchamos." He turned back to Hawkins. The sound of shouted orders and men running came from outside. "You're coming with me. I need someone who speaks German I can trust."

# -52-

The sun was getting low in the sky. The column split going in the entrance road, encircling and enveloping the airfield, rushing along the far sides of the runways as the final few training flights of the day landed. More of Corrialles's men surrounded the flight school, then pressed in, guns drawn, and herded all the students, instructors and other personnel into the large hangar next to the school. As he got out of the car with the general, Hawkins could see them lined up against the hangar wall, hands raised, frightened expressions on their faces.

A lieutenant followed from a truck behind them, motioning to a shocked-looking Aust with a Colt Automatic. Aust hurried up to Hawkins, uncertain whether to raise his hands, too, head darting from the lieutenant to General Corrialles, who was now striding into the flight school, and around again to Hawkins.

"What's going on?" Aust whispered in German.

"I'm not sure but I think General Corrialles has received some upsetting information."

The lieutenant pointed at the hangar, gesturing at Aust to go in. Aust raised his hands slightly, going along, looking back at Hawkins.

"Don't worry," Hawkins said, "I'm going to talk to the general."

As Hawkins entered the corridor Corrialles was going down into the basement. Hawkins sprinted ahead and caught up, holding on to the camera he still had around his neck.

The general stopped on the commander's balcony, leaning over, fingertips pressed on the desk, taking it all in.

"Guau," he said, his voice barely a whisper. "Guau, guau, guau." His painful expression said it all: he'd had no idea this place existed. The general picked up the phone, put it to his ear, realized it didn't work, tossed it aside.

Then down the stairs he went, checking out the regional stations, the maps, the banks of radio transceivers, tapping his fingers on top of the radios as he passed. He stopped and clicked one on. The receiver lit with a soft glow. Hawkins thought he heard a low whistle from the general. The adjutant was right behind him. Corrialles turned.

"Estas cosas son costosas. Pila de discos las para arriba. Tenga cuidado, son frágiles." The adjutant ran back up, calling for a squad of men. They began gently unplugging and carrying away the expensive radio sets. Corrialles walked along the huge map, idly picking up the unit and line markers, looking at them, then tossing them back, rattling across the map until he got to Yucatán. He stood glaring at the little swastika flags, his head starting to slightly nod up and down, then increasingly side to side. Hawkins came up beside him.

"Do you want me to take pictures?" Hawkins said. That seemed to finally light the fuse, a very short fuse.

"No! No photos!" half shouting. Corrialles snapped one of the little Nazi flags off the map, turned and bounded up the stairs.

Hawkins followed as Corrialles began racing through the rooms, walking around the Bf 109 engine, into the next room glancing quickly at the Messerschmitt manuals his men were holding out, then into the next room. Several men had opened the training simulator and were standing in a circle gaping at it, murmuring away. They looked as surprised and shocked as Corrialles. The general pushed in. The power was on, the gauges lit. A major turned. The man looked stunned, like a professional boxer had punched him in the stomach knocking every bit of air out. He suddenly inhaled, a gasp. "Es para su nuevo luchador, el Messerschmitt 109." *Yes, they got it*, Hawkins thought, *the newest, latest German fighter plane.*

The general reached in, taking the stick lightly with his fingers, moving it around, watching the gauges. He didn't look shocked. He looked awed.

"¡Incredible!" he finally said.

A captain came and seized his elbow, "General—¡Usted necesita ver en esto!"

Corrialles followed him into the drafting room. They'd been going through the cases, pulling out drawings, blueprints and maps, spreading them across the tables.

Corrialles went from one to another, the swastika flag still tightly in his fist, methodically inspecting all of them. The general had his command face on, but Hawkins could see his knuckles whiten around the little Nazi flag and his hand begin to vibrate in anger ever so slightly, waving the flag. The airbases, the maps—he carefully looked them over, nodding as the captain pointed out one feature after another. Then he reached the final one, the blueprints of the fortified submarine bunker. Corrialles rustled through them with one hand, silent, his face darkening. Then a low sound started in his belly rising to a full-throated roar as he turned and raced up the stairs.

# -53-

A major was waiting in the door to Eckhardt's office. The man's face actually looked pale, a sickly cast. He was holding the copies of the treaty, the diplomatic pouch draped over his arm. Corrialles seized the hem of the pouch, glancing at the legends REICH-AUSSENMINISTERIUM and DIPLOMATISCHE POST, grunting. The major flipped through the copies of the treaty.

"Vaya al extremo," gesturing to the back of the treaty. Corrialles took it with thumb and forefinger. There it was. Hitler's signature. And his. In Eckhardt's desk. In Eckhardt's office. That they had seized by surprise.

Corrialles stared at the signatures. Now he knew. It was all real. And not a Commie plot. Tears welled up in his eyes for a second. He wiped them away with the hand holding the Nazi flag, not noticing it. *He thought these men were his friends*, Hawkins realized with a start. *This is personal.*

"Muy convincente," the general said. "Muy convincente."

"General—what? What is going on? What's convincing?" Hawkins said.

"Los bastardos." Very quiet, "They did it. It's not someone else's trick. They forged my signature to a fake treaty." He gulped hard, now calm, and turned to go into the office.

Whispering, Hawkins waved him back out, "General—General!"

Corrialles stepped away from the door, exasperated, "What!"

"I apologize for interrupting, but do you know President Roosevelt is starting to help Britain?"

"No. What of it?"

"He is proposing to Congress to give fifty destroyers to the British in exchange for bases in the Caribbean. That's only the beginning. Obviously, the Nazis don't want that, they probably want to draw the US into Mexico and—" Corrialles sharply waved the papers again, curtly cutting Hawkins off. He needed no explication.

"Oh yes, of course. I know that."

He strode into Eckhardt's office. Hawkins and the major followed him. Eckhardt and Falkenberg were standing at the far end of the room, hands held chest high, guarded by a sergeant with a Colt Automatic and a corporal with a rifle. Eckhardt seemed to be smiling slightly—*did he have no sense of the gravity of the moment?* Hawkins wondered. But alarm radiated from every pore of Falkenberg's face, breathing hard, the whites of his eyes clearly visible, darting about, scanning everything. Corrialles shook the treaty.

"Horst, Werner. Why?"

Eckhardt shrugged slightly, his light expression and demeanor unchanged. "We wanted everything to be ready."

*His tone—what was it?* Hawkins thought. Indifferent, was what it was, like he didn't care.

"Ah. Ready. Ready for what?" Eckhardt shrugged again, saying nothing. Falkenberg watched Eckhardt with the same expression Hawkins had seen on the train, waiting, deferring to his senior partner, expecting *something,* rapidly glancing back and forth, alarm growing. But there was nothing but more of Eckhardt's amused indifference. *Now Falkenberg truly knows Eckhardt is crazy,* Hawkins thought. Falkenberg lowered his hands a few degrees, turning them outward, gesturing dismissively.

"These are contingency plans," Falkenberg said, "for all possible circumstances. Also for—"

"There only seems to be one contingency here. A naval base? Surely you are aware Mexico does not have any submarines."

"Every nation creates these things. We wanted to have plans ready if we were called—"

"No, why are you doing this?"

"Only to help Mexico."

Corrialles waved the little swastika flag under their noses, pointing it accusingly. "This is help?"

"Why, of course," Falkenberg said, "all armies conduct war games. You have plans and conduct war games in case the Americans invade, don't you?"

"Yes."

"This is only a broad program of preparation, contingency plans, training, war gaming …" The little flag in General Corrialles's hand started descending. "General, sir! Sincerely, this is all being misrepresented, a misunderstanding. They sent a kit of these things so we set them out." Falkenberg raised his hands now, trying hard to smile. "General Corrialles! We're all brothers here, like the knights of old, men of mission and purpose."

Hawkins glanced over at Eckhardt. His head was turned away a bit, eyes on his shoes. Was there a slight smirk? *This is a man who doesn't give a damn*, Hawkins realized. *Bizarre.* Crazy.

Corrialles was too preoccupied to notice. Falkenberg rushed on.

"That includes these treaties. We knew in the event of moving forward, there would be action, we realized we might not be able to reach you."

*Is the general buying this rot?* Hawkins wondered. *Why take a chance?* he decided.

Corrialles turned back to Eckhardt and Falkenberg.

"Bastardos! Tell me the truth! Is it Germany's plan to provoke an American invasion of Mexico?"

"No! Of course not!" Falkenberg said.

"What kind of fool do you take me for?" Corrialles said. "You are setting up me and my country! Once the coup occurs and we take over, you expose this shit to the Yankees. If this is all preparation"—he waved his arms out—"why did you not inform *me*? No! It's a secret from *me*! Not the Yankees! At the prospect of bases, Messerschmitts, Panzers and the rest, the US will promptly invade—our denial will never be believed. Never! You think I don't have a realistic sense of Mexico's strength against the US, how the Yankees see their interests and how they will respond?

You would devastate my country for a temporary advantage? Like Belgium and Holland? Little countries that are expendable for your great German empire?"

"That's not so," Falkenberg protested. "An alliance is the best way to deter that attack—"

"No, they would invade. And strange as it may seem, I could hardly fault them for responding to such a turning maneuver. And when they did there would be an uprising of the people, not only the Mexican Army but all the new militias joining in. It would be total war, far more massive than the one between us and the US a century ago. Mexicans would never rest until the Americans were expelled and the Yankees are too proud and stiff-necked to accept defeat. It would be a bloodbath that would go on for years and swallow both countries."

Eckhardt finally spoke, an excited look on his face, "No, Germany will stand by you if you are attacked, you will win as we did—"

"They have six times our population! Steel mills! Car and airplane factories! Arsenals! Munitions plants—"

"No! War will purify and redeem Mexico, do not be afraid of war or death," Eckhardt said, "it is the only path to power and greatness, welcome it. War will make Mexico great."

Corrialles gaped at him a moment, as if he could scarcely believe what he was hearing. A horrified and shocked expression blasted across Falkenberg's face. He lowered and moved his barely shaking hands, swallowing hard, as if to reach over, grab Eckhardt by the neck and strangle him.

"General …" Falkenberg started to say.

Corrialles shook his head no, then crossed himself.

# -54-

One of the captains came up behind General Corrialles, gesturing to get his attention.

"Yes," Corrialles said.

"Sir, some of those men in the hangar are Spanish."

"How many?"

"Maybe half."

"Ah, of course."

The general threw the papers on the desk and followed the captain back down, out of the building and into the main hangar. At least eighty men were lined up against the far wall, hands held high. A rank of soldiers with drawn rifles and two trucks mounted with Hotchkiss machine guns were guarding them. To get a clear view the soldiers had pushed the Arado fighter outside, out of the way.

The general stood in the center of the floor, studying the men. Some of them were dressed in either civilian clothes or tan flight-school uniforms, very military looking. Around two dozen, though, were wearing the same outfits as the Gold Shirts, the Camisas Doradas, but missing the armband and belt across the chest.

Corrialles gestured to one. He stepped forward.

"Where are you from?"

"Guadalajara."

The general grabbed his sleeve and pushed him back into the line. He asked the next man.

"Tampico."

"What did your father do for a living?"

The man hesitated. "He owned a pharmacy."

"On what street?" A longer pause.

"Calle Juárez." A clever, safe guess, but not enough.

"You do not have a Mexican accent."

"I am Mexican. I swear."

"Keep talking, you betray yourself with every word. Who was the last emperor?"

The man hesitated again. "Maximilian."

"No! You fool! Cuauhtémoc! Maximilian was an invader, like you!"

"No, General—"

"You're a Falangist! A Fascist! From Spain! Admit it!" The man shook his head. Corrialles put his hand in the center of the man's chest and shoved him back against the crowd, glaring at them all. He turned back, then stopped by the door. The lieutenant had holstered his Colt, but he was still hovering over Aust, who cowered in a chair. Aust seemed badly frightened, holding on to the seat with both hands, like a drunk with a spinning head who's afraid he's going to fly off.

"What do you know about this?" Corrialles said.

"General, I had no idea—" Corrialles grabbed Aust by his jacket collar, yanking him to his feet, dragging him out of the hangar, into the flight school and down into the basement war room. He half flung Aust down the steps, shoving his back, throwing him forward and down. Aust barely caught himself on the handrail, legs splayed out behind him.

"What do you know about this," the general shouted.

"Nothing."

"You were doing business. Did you insure those airplanes?" gesturing up.

"Please, General, wait—"

"What kind of training do you think is going on here?" He grabbed one of the little swastika flags and flung it down on the table.

"I—I thought the flight school was for civil aviation. General, Mexico is my home! I only wanted to help out the old country when I was asked. I didn't think I was doing anything harmful."

"Then you are an idiot or a traitor."

The cries of men's voices came from above, angry, panicked, confused, a tumult of running, crashing footsteps, a pair of shots.

Corrialles looked up the stairs, eyes widening, "Dios maldito!" And swinging a fist he ran up.

# -55-

Hawkins grabbed Aust by the elbow.

"You really didn't know?"

"No!"

"For god's sakes, they were staying in your house."

"It was business. They were good customers!"

*Hard to tell*, Hawkins thought. Aust seemed sincere, for whatever that impression was worth—which was, in truth, not much. But Aust was shaking, badly rattled. *Still possibilities here.*

"Come with me. I'll protect you."

From the suddenly stunned expression on Aust's face, it was clear that despite everything he'd seen, he still didn't realize his life was on the line.

They raced back upstairs, Aust breathlessly thanking Hawkins, Hawkins dragging him by the arm, running behind the general into Eckhardt's office. Corrialles was standing over the sergeant and corporal who'd been guarding Eckhardt and Falkenberg. Both of the Germans were gone.

The two guards were sprawled on the floor, legs at odd angles. They may have searched Eckhardt and Falkenberg, but they either missed his obsidian blades, or he grabbed one from his display on the wall.

The sergeant had a neat oblong puncture wound to the side of his head, rhythmically spurting blood with each heartbeat, his eyes staring lifelessly at the ceiling, one leg tucked up and under the other. The corporal's head almost touched the sergeant's, but his back was arched, arms and legs trembling and shaking, in the midst of a full-blown seizure. The front of his skull had been cleanly sliced open, a quick blow straight across the forehead, creating a conic section, a perfect geometry class lesson cut in blood. The piece of skull and brain lay upside down a few feet away, ringed with black hair. Inside the whitish ovoid section of bone above the man's eyebrows was a flat smooth expanse of pink brain starting to ooze blood in dozens of little beads. Another tremendous spasm, a gurgling noise and the corporal stopped breathing.

A window was open, overlooking a porch roof. After getting the jump on the guards the two agents had gone out and climbed down. From the distance below came the sound of an airplane revving up, a high-pitched sound—the Arado fighter, Hawkins realized. General Corrialles cursed, ripped the Colt from the sergeant's lifeless fingers and threw himself back down the stairs.

# -56-

The Arado passed by the door, nearly a blur, tail starting to lift off. Corrialles ran out, shooting at the plane, followed by several of his men firing a ragged volley. *Should I draw the Hi-Power?* Hawkins thought. *Join in?* Then—*No, no, too many questions. And no need.*

The plane whipped by the main hangar, half blurred, but Hawkins could see Falkenberg at the controls and Eckhardt in back. Eckhardt seemed to be leaning forward in the cockpit, arms around Falkenberg's neck and shoulders the way motorcycle passengers ride behind—holding something to Falkenberg's throat?

Several more soldiers sprinted out, officers shouting orders, trying to get into position, aiming to fire. More shots rang out, missing. The plane was lifting off, the wheels maybe a foot in the air. It reached the second hangar. Something extraordinary—Falkenberg banked hard. The fighter teetered over at a crazy angle, almost a crash.

*My god—what? He's going to crack up*, Hawkins thought. Instead the starboard wheel touched down and caught the tarmac with a piercing screech, braking it hard. The plane pivoted on the contact with a snapping jerk, spinning on the point of the wheel, whipping around ninety degrees, the nose aiming straight into the hangar. Falkenberg expertly banked hard the other way, touching down briefly on the port-side wheel with another screech, revving the engine to the max, straightening out, then lifted off again and roared into the hangar a foot or two above the ground. He flew through the hangar, vanishing out of sight and out of firing range.

Corrialles and his troops ran to the rear door, guns raised. In the distance they could hear the plane, now barely visible, disappearing into the dark, banking and turning away toward the mountains. Corrialles and the others fired a few desultory shots, then gave up, watching the dim speck disappear into the night sky.

Hawkins held back, still tightly gripping Aust's arm. In a way, he marveled at what just happened. The exquisite skill, the commanding mastery of machine and air it took for Falkenberg to pull that little maneuver off, to improvise so quickly and adroitly on the spot. *Amazing*, he thought, one simply had to admire it.

It was a damn shame they got away, of course. But this operation was in the crapper anyway, Hawkins simply *knew* that instantly, it wasn't the kind of thing you needed to think over. Corrialles could try reconstructing his coup, but even if he did, there'd be no Nazi alliance, no fakery with treaties, no use for the plans for bases, the planes and simulators, or all the rest of the stage props upstairs in the flight school. Mexico and the States would not be conned into a war with each other, there'd be no distractions or diversions from helping Britain and resisting Hitler for Washington.

*And the paintings? I'll happily help*, Hawkins quickly thought—*and we'll see to it they get impounded the moment they arrive in New York. What will Corrialles do with those Spanish Francoists?* Hawkins wondered, *he can't trust them. This should be interesting.* He remembered Corrialles shooting the cowardly bull. *How far will he go?*

Corrialles ran past Hawkins and Aust, the same deep growl as before. He sprinted into the big hangar, pointing the pistol at the line of men against the wall, turning to face his soldiers. He made a short quick speech. Hawkins and Aust followed.

"What's he saying?" Hawkins said.

"These men—foreigners—invaders—trying to get Mexico in someone else's war—others—traitors, betraying Mexico—would destroy all—duty calls—must defend Mexico—freedom and independence—" Aust said, all quick bursts, breathless.

The men against the wall began crying out, louder and louder into a screaming cacophony—"¡No! ¡No! ¡Por favor! ¡En nombre de dios!"— pushing and squirming, mouths open, eyes white.

*He's going to go all the way,* Hawkins thought. *But let's not have him go too far.* He grabbed Aust by the lapels and pushed him back by the door. Corrialles's next words needed no translation.

"¡Fuego! ¡Mátalos todos! ¡Dios sabrá lo suyo!" *Kill them all! God will know his own!* Aust gasped as Corrialles emptied his Colt into the ranks of men against the wall. After a split second the Hotchkiss machine guns on the trucks opened fire, followed a split second later by the soldiers raising their rifles and firing in single volley. Shouts turned into a single continuous scream as the bullets struck. The men in front fell forward onto the pavement or back into the arms of or against the now blood-spattered men behind them, the machine guns sweeping in from the sides, rolling all the men down in a steady tumbling wave. A second volley slammed out, now blowing dozens of holes in the sheet-metal hangar wall, blood and brains flying against the inside of the tin and the rafters.

The machine gunners reached the middle, stopped to reload, then swept fire back outward through the ranks of the remaining men struggling to get around or past the bodies of their fallen comrades, pushing and throwing the bodies aside. Fighting and shoving each other, the survivors were frantically trying to escape, desperate to get out of the way, a mad scrimmage of flying, twisting arms, elbows and fists, heads banging, bloodying each other more, all the while ducking and wresting one another in front, trying to hide behind each other at the same time, the stronger pushing the weaker forward, if only for a few precious seconds. Four or five made it to the front of the hangar and began frantically running across the field and up the runway, desperately trying to escape. Six or seven of Corrialles's soldiers and one of his captains sprinted after them, the infantrymen quickly down on one knee, steadying, aiming, and carefully firing.

As the bullets struck, the doomed men were knocked forward like they'd been swatted in the back by an invisible hand, legs flying and stumbling as if they'd tripped, crashing hard on one foot, arms windmilling, another hard step, then another before diving and crashing facedown into the dirt or the concrete, legs and arms splayed out.

Inside the firing tapered off. The soldiers moved forward, aiming and shooting at men hiding under the bodies of others, lying silent but uninjured, trying to assume the pose of death. It was to no avail. With the general watching and pointing—"¡Aquí! ¡Allí!"—with the empty pistol, stepping into the gore, kicking a few bodies, the soldiers gave a quick *coup de grace* to the heads of the ones not obviously dead and torn apart by the fire. After several more shots, then a final pair and the jingling of ejected shells, the hangar fell eerily silent.

# -57-

A thick wave of blood rapidly flowed across the floor. As it approached his feet Hawkins felt a momentary urge to throw up, right into the puddle itself. *No … won't do*, he thought. *Can't. Don't.* He choked it down. *Yes, disgusting, horrifying to see so many men die, literally, not figuratively, under your nose and watch the terror in their eyes.* The sight of tumbling bodies, the shattering shake of bullets tearing them apart, the smell of blood so strong that you could stickily taste it in your mouth across the hangar, together produced a prickly tension, a pins and needles sensation across the skin that told you this was not normal, this was hell itself. These men were the enemy. But they were men like any other men, like him. What General Corrialles did wasn't necessarily unexpected. Hawkins had instinctively known—assumed—this was bound to end badly for someone once General Corrialles caught Eckhardt and Falkenberg. Hawkins earlier shot two of them in the street himself. But still …

Knowing something was about to happen, Hawkins expected himself to go cold, to shut down and not feel as usual. But he did not, the professional mood did not hold, and he felt a sense of relief that surprised him. *Thank god I can still be repulsed and repelled by the specter of so much death. I'm not Eckhardt, at least not yet.* There was something strangely comforting about his nausea. *I haven't lost myself.*

Corrialles seemed nonplussed, pointing around with the now empty pistol for his men to fetch the trucks. He gestured his officers in, issuing orders as he walked, "¡Fíjelo en el fuego! ¡Consiga ese carro de la gasolina! ¡Fíjelo en el fuego! ¡Consiga ese carro de la gasolina!"

"What?" Hawkins said to Aust.

"He's going to burn the building down."

"Go back to the car and stay there," Hawkins said. He ran into the flight school past men carrying the bodies inside and up the stairs to Eckhardt's office. *Corrialles may not want anything up there, but I do,* Hawkins thought. Inside he swept up all the fake treaty papers, threw them in a sack, then rifled the other drawers for all the papers on the Nazi sympathizers. On the way out the door he glanced across at the ancient painted tumbler. He grabbed it and stuck it in the sack, too.

As Hawkins came out the door Corrialles was across the tarmac, directing traffic, after a fashion. One of the sergeants was backing up a large tanker truck, angling it into position. It was marked GASOLINA DE LA AVIACIÓN in big red letters. The sergeant drove it forward, getting some distance, then gunned it into reverse, door open, shoving something into place on the floor with his foot, then stepped onto the running boards, swinging on the door, jumping off. The tanker lurched back, picking up speed, roaring across the tarmac and parking lot. With a tremendous smashing boom it crashed through the wall of the flight school, almost disappearing inside, only the grill and headlights visible. A pop. Flames started to appear. Then a grinding, rending noise and the headlights suddenly pivoted up to the sky as the weight of the tanker, loaded with several tons of petrol, broke through the floor. With a rippling, rumbling sound the headlights slid backward into the basement, almost vanishing before an explosion echoed from the cellar. A huge ball of fire blasted out the hole in the wall, then blew out the windows with a tinkling crash before blowing open the doors. Flames engulfed the entire building in seconds, sending Hawkins, Aust and all the soldiers running back and away to escape the searing heat.

Behind him some of the trainers were burning, too, the flames spreading from the open cockpits and engine compartments, licking along the canvas wings.

Corrialles turned and saw Aust by the car.

"¡Usted!"—*you*, he shouted. He ran up to Aust, pointing the big Colt at his head. He pulled the trigger. It clicked uselessly. Corrialles cursed, almost throwing it, looking to his men for another.

"General—no!" Hawkins shouted, pulling Aust behind him. "They lied to him, too! He didn't know, you saw his face." The general grimly glowered at Hawkins, lips tight, then tapped the empty pistol on Hawkins's chest.

"Why—or why wouldn't he? They were living with him."

"Eckhardt probably didn't trust him because he'd lived in Mexico for so long," Hawkins said. "We still need him to insure the paintings. Here—wait." Hawkins pulled Aust around, handing him the fake treaty papers. "Look at this. Have you seen any of this?"

Aust read the first few lines, TREATY OF ALLIANCE AND MUTUAL ASSISTANCE BETWEEN THE DEUTSCHES REICH AND THE UNITED STATES OF MEXICO, SIGNED

"September?— September, wha—" Aust was skimming quickly, "Adolf Hitler ... Miguel Corrialles, Presidente—mother of god, what is this?"

"A conspiracy," Corrialles said, "against Mexico."

"Please, I swear, I knew nothing about this," Aust said. "I am Mexican now, this is my country—"

"Very well. You get a chance to prove that." The general turned, now tapping Aust on the chest with the pistol. "If you are lying, if you are involved in this, by god, I will kill you with the rest of these traitors. Do you understand?" Aust nodded, unable to speak, gasping and wheezing in fear.

"What about Eckhardt and Falkenberg?" Hawkins said.

"You saw—" He waved a hand out the hangar.

"Maybe they'll go back for their things."

"Yes. It is possible." Corrialles mulled that a second, then gestured and handed off the pistol to one of his men. "Hawkins. You said we need Aust. You still want to do business?"

"Yes. Why not?"

"Indeed."

"What about Eckhardt and Falkenberg?" Hawkins said. "What they know, they could ruin everything. The paintings are safe on your base, but—"

"Yes. They are now very dangerous."

"And who knows what other friends they may have?"

"This is true. Take Aust. I'll send men with you to his house."

"Not too many—"

"Agreed, they might see. We will talk later."

It was a long drive back across the Valle de México to the Campo Militar. Then Hawkins drove Aust back to his house followed by a troop truck, making sure all was in order there before returning to his hotel. Aust was silent the whole way, slumping against the car door, apparently stunned. *The silence is good,* Hawkins thought. *Time to think.*

Eckhardt and Falkenberg. *Not going to draw the US into a stupid invasion,* he thought. *Points for that. They got away. Deduct some. We may be able to pick up their trail, though. That's a draw. They've lost the paintings, and their base. Points for that. Corrialles still has the paintings.* A new thought struck him. *My god, the paintings—I don't have to destroy them! They're safe!* That brought a huge wave of relief, physical, palpable. *When I ship to the legendary Alpert Gallery, or to Parke-Bernet, we'll have the FBI seize them, and eventually get them back to their rightful owners, hopefully they can be found and they're still alive. Goodly number of points for that. W, General Houghton, in particular, will be relieved.*

*The men killed—points or deductions?* he wondered. *Don't know. Do I care?* he thought. *No.* Those men were a threat to his country. What, exactly, was General Corrialles to do with them? *He could hardly arrest them … the plotter of the coup. Take eighty prisoners? Where? How? What would he do with them? He's a general, he's a veteran of the civil war here—maybe he realized what that entailed. And the dead were all, in the end, Franco's Falangists, Nazi sympathizers, local Fascists Eckhardt recruited, the enemies of freedom and democracy and Mexico. On the other side of the ocean we're shooting them every day and every night, or trying as hard as we can to shoot them or blow them up. Is it that different? No doubt it was the only thing to do. I can live with it,* Hawkins decided.

With that, the deeper meaning of the night really hit him.

*I came here to fight the Nazis,* he thought. *I have. And I won.*

# -58-

The sound of traffic on the Paseo de la Reforma slowly slipped a soft baby finger into his ear, gently rousing Hawkins from his sleep. He rolled over, watching the curtains blow in the open window. Almost eleven. *Best night of sleep in months,* he thought. *No worries, at least for the moment.* Yes, a good night's sleep was the best spoil of victory. No doubt about that.

*Should go down, send for Lilly,* he thought. *Nah*—he felt no urgency. The tension had rolled right off. Instead, he lazily stretched in bed, then hopped into a long, satisfying shower before drifting down to a leisurely brunch in the hotel café. Half an hour after that he was waiting in a booth at the Reforma. Lilly walked in and sat down in the booth across from him, smiling and winking, looking spectacular as always. She must've been getting some sun—sleeveless short summer dress, legs tanned, face a little bit of color under her wide straw hat. She shut the booth door as she dialed. *Oh well,* he thought.

It took half an hour to dictate every detail, with both of them dropping extra pesos into the coin phone. He'd worried she would be upset or horrified at the shooting, some sort of squishy response. Instead a breathy "good riddance" came over the handset. He finished.

"I'll be heading out to Aust's now," he said.

"Brilliant, Roy, simply brilliant." She started to giggle. "The paintings are safe! And he's going to ship them straight into our hands. I do hope you plan to be out of the way by then. He's likely to be very cross with you."

"Yes, cross! I should say so." They were both watching each other laugh at a distance through the closed glass doors, their voices on the handsets oddly intimate and hushed, as if they were lying side by side whispering in each other's ears.

"Especially considering all those men he shot."

"Yes. Tough break for them. Hear from your fella in the army?"

"No." She sounded irritated and frustrated. "Not in ages."

"Any news of the war?"

"Yes. I've been telexing back and forth with Beth in New York, also Jenny in the army office in Ottawa. We're holding in the air. But catching up on the ground."

"How so?"

"We're replacing our losses. At the beginning of the battle Fighter Command was short on planes. Now the air force is short on pilots. Jen thinks they must be getting more confident, they're refusing to rush officers through training."

"They don't want to throw them away."

"Righto. Remarkable story, though. The air force is collecting the wreckage of crashed Hurricanes and Spitfires and dumping them in hotel ballrooms and the like, and then turning civilians loose on them with hand tools."

"They're not trained airplane mechanics?"

"No. No experience whatsoever. Told them to do their best, put one together from the pieces."

"And?"

"They did."

Hawkins opened the booth door and leaned out, "You're making that up!"

She flipped her door open for a second, "No!" before pushing it shut. "It's all true. I swear. I was a Girl Scout. No lies here!"

"I've heard some incredible things lately, but that takes the cake."

"Same here."

"I better get back to the Imperial. Thank you, Lilly, things are looking up."

# -59-

*In bar*, the note said. Riley was wearing the suit and tie, on a stool, hair pomaded, sipping a beer.

"You know, this is most interesting," she said as he sat. "If I was wearing my guayabera and sandals, dressed as a campesino, they would throw me out."

"They tried to."

"Yes. And if I was dressed in a dress—"

"As a woman."

"Yes. They would assume I was a whore. They might call the police, have me arrested."

"That doesn't only happen in Mexico."

"As you say. It is quite illuminating, the world you live in as a man, as a rich gringo."

The bartender put Hawkins's beer down. He took a long drink. *What to say to that?* he thought. A natural instinct said, *Defend the world you live in, justify and protect it, because you're in it and you have a stake in it*—but that didn't seem right, either.

"I don't know."

"It is good you don't know."

"Oh, I don't think so."

"No, it is. Artists—real artists, that is—are revolutionaries, rule breakers. We are always troublemakers, upsetting things, dangerous people. Do you know why?"

"Hardly."

"Because an artist has to actually *look* at the world. When you do, you *see* things."

"As they are."

"Yes. Not the way you think they are supposed to be. Like Picasso and Braque twenty year ago, with fauvism and cubism."

"That ticked people off."

"It did! It was a new way of seeing the world. The world had already changed, only now people saw it."

*Seeing. Yes*, Hawkins thought. The images in the *Guide to Mexico*—that man was an illustrator, a sort of technician, not an artist, because he wasn't looking. He couldn't see what was all around him for what it was. Instead, he saw what he wanted to see.

*What am I seeing now?* Hawkins thought. *I know—Lilly, over at the Reforma. She started as a clerk, was handed cypher duties because there was no man to do it, now was, effectively, a clandestine agent after sneaking into a foreign country. And doing great. A year ago, utterly inconceivable. The very suggestion would've caused outrage. Imagine the indignation: Send a woman? Not up to it. Too delicate. We have to protect them. Natter-natter, blah-blah. A revolution, of sorts.*

"The war is shaking things up, changing things. I see that."

"We can shake things up without a war. That is the value of art."

They clinked glasses.

"Then here's to art, not war, help us see a better world."

"Yes. There's something you should see tonight."

"What?"

"An auction preview. Two more paintings have appeared."

"I'll need to get one of my cameras. Come on."

Upstairs Riley began wandering his room again. Hawkins got his Minox from the suitcase.

"That's a camera?" He nodded. "Interesting things you have here, Hawkins. Guns. Cameras that look like cigarette lighters." She noticed the beaker and excitedly ran over, plucking it up. "Where did you get my vase? I hope you didn't pay much for it!"

"I didn't pay anything for it. You owned it once?"

"No! I made it."

"What? You're joking—"

"No. Here." She turned it on the stand, pointing, then picked it up. "See? Inside this small glyph? My initials. *RE.* They are very stylized, but it is my little mark. I always do that, it is my way of being honest with our past, but it is my little joke, too. Only the top experts at the Museo Nacional de Antropología will know it is not a real Mayan glyph, and they will be amused at my cleverness."

"But it looks so old—"

"Yes, looks very old after you bury it in shit for a month." She gestured with it, trying to hand it to him. Hawkins shrank back a bit. "Oh, it's clean now! I won't ask how you got it for free, *Mr. Businessman.*"

"Good idea. Let's go."

A few blocks down to La Roma again and Subastas del águila, another elegant old Porfirian-era house converted into an auction hall. People were milling around, looking especially at the two-star attractions, a Picasso and another Braque from the hoard in Bermuda. That accounted for all the missing works from the original forty. The sale was set for Friday night. There was no trace of Eckhardt and Falkenberg, however.

Riley seemed to know half the people there. There were several more Mexican artists, all of whom seemed to be Riley's friends, lounging around, warily musing over the foreign competition. Also several plump-faced American writers, talking loudly in English in one corner about *the workers.* Hawkins heard one say, "When I get back to the Columbia campus …" as the others sagely nodded. Riley pointed out three wan, hungry-looking men with hollow eyes who had come to Mexico City after fighting in Spain. A suave Mexican film director and his cameraman. Wealthy collectors in suits, obvious American bohemians in blue overalls living on the cheap in Mexico. An interesting mix. A tapping on his shoulder. Hawkins turned. General Corrialles had quietly come up behind him. He looked very concerned, frowning slightly, leaning forward.

"Hawkins. Of course you would be here. Are you going to be bidding?"

"Not if you are."

Corrialles relaxed, his posture shifting. "I see. Thank you." A big smile. "You're considering the Picasso and the Braque?"

"Yes, naturally."

"They will end up in the Alpert Gallery anyway. I think it best you should add them to your collection, if you can, consign them to us all together."

"Agreed. It will be expensive but that is fair, and you're right, they will still go to your gallery," Corrialles said.

*And how else would we get them back to their rightful owners?* Hawkins thought. *Can't have these things scattered to the winds. Further, neither I nor the Service has the budget to buy them. And if the general buys them, he will lose that much more money. Yes, let's bankrupt the bastard,* Hawkins thought. *No money, no coup, no worries here and I can wrap this up and move on.*

"I'm curious about something. Where'd these paintings come from? Refugees? Could they have more?"

"A good question. I will ask. They will dare not refuse."

Corrialles left for the office. Only a brief moment later, he was back. He looked angry, shocked, upset, or something, you could easily see it in his eyes, the way they snapped back and forth between him to the Braque and Picasso, teeth clenched.

"A German gentleman named Bruno, whitish crew cut, the tip of his ear missing, that is all they know."

"Eckhardt."

"Yes."

"But not Falkenberg?"

"No."

"There were empty spaces in those crates."

"I am thinking that, also."

"No matter now, I guess. We need to think about getting all of them to New York. I am worried about the security of rail, trucking. Also, it's now August. The big autumn season in Manhattan is approaching very fast. Then there's the war. Suppose something happens? Ship sinkings, a torpedoed liner, the US gets in the war."

"I see your point completely. Yes, we want to sell in a peacetime marketplace. We must not waste time. What do you have in mind?"

"Are you open to flying them? I could charter a plane in California. I am thinking one of the new Douglas transports. A little pricey but well worth it."

"Agreed." The general uneasily glanced around at the crowd. "A stinking collection of scum, isn't it? We'll have our work cut out for us. Please start making your arrangements."

Hawkins and Riley loitered a bit, talking. Riley seemed bored.

"Don't you like looking at art?" Hawkins said.

"No, I'd rather make it. Let's go back to Coyoacán. I want to start painting you."

"All right. I'll meet you out there. I have to stop and check for messages first."

# -60-

*Most urgent*, it said.

Lilly was already waiting in a booth when he arrived at the Reforma. The phone rang the instant he settled in his seat—by now she'd memorized all the numbers in the bank of phone booths.

"Big flash in from W." She hesitated. He looked over. Through both glass doors he could see the concern on her face. She had something she knew he wasn't going to like, easy to tell.

"Go ahead."

"Your reports have gone all the way back to London. They are extremely pleased with your destruction of the Nazi plot to lure the United States into a Mexican invasion. Commendations are coming, all that. Who knows, you could get an OBE out of this." Her tone was bright, almost like she was buttering him up, and knew it, and knew he knew, trying to blunt what was coming next, dreading, postponing the coming moment, however briefly.

"That and a dime will get me a cup of coffee. If I live to drink it. And it'll be classified, anyway, so who cares? Go, on, what is it?"

"They want to help General Corrialles."

"Do what?"

"Overthrow the government."

"Excuse me?"

"Those are your orders. They like the idea of a coup. It isn't only London. Ottawa, too, and international business interests in the States they're in contact with. They all want their expropriated Mexican properties back, the oil fields, railroads, everything. If Corrialles was willing to return them, and apparently he was, or is, along with the lands that were taken, they're perfectly congenial with a military government here provided it's friendly to Britain, the Empire and Commonwealth, and not Germany."

"Well, hell, how are we supposed to do—"

"Corrialles has cleared the titles, at least superficially enough, so that they can arrange a real sale at Parke-Bernet."

"What! No—"

"The paintings will go through the Alpert Gallery to auction, then the money will go back from the Alpert Gallery to Corrialles's front company to fund the coup."

"We're not going to have them impounded?"

"No."

"Hold them for their owners? Return them after the war?"

"No."

"But the Geneva Convention—"

"They don't care. They want to get back the assets they lost here."

"My god, Lilly—we're refusing to deal with Hitler because of the nature of his regime, but now we're not only going to deal with Corrialles, another would-be Franco, another Fascist, but also a dictator friendly to Nazism—"

"I know, I know—"

"Help him seize power? It makes no sense."

"I suppose not. But, Roy—"

"Yes?"

"I think this is personal to W, too. Some of his companies were hit hard. Be careful."

"Has he forgotten? Only weeks ago, we risked all to defend these other countries—Norway, France, Belgium, Holland, nearly lost the whole damn army. But now, we're going to turn around and throw away Mexico? What about them, their independence, their freedom? How are they any different than the French or the Dutch? If we do this, what's the difference between us and the Germans?"

"We're fighting for our survival now. We weren't then, before France fell. I'm guessing the seized properties here will all be mortgaged to the hilt the moment we—the Allies—get them back. That'll buy more war material from the States. It's all quite serious, in that sense."

"I don't care—"

"It's all cash-and-carry with the Yanks. They're slowly picking us clean while they make up their minds. If that's what it is. Britain's losing everything it built up over three centuries."

"I thought we were holding."

"We are. Militarily. For the moment."

"What the bloody hell—"

"I—I—" She heavily sighed and stopped. He leaned up to the glass, watching her. She almost seemed on the edge of tears. "Yes, this is an amazing place. Being here, doing this, it's been a dream. This—it's terrible. There'll probably be fighting in the streets. It's going to be a mess."

"A mess? The civil war twenty years ago killed a million people, and they didn't have the new popular militias Cárdenas created. That's not a mess, that's a catastrophe. They have no idea what they could be unleashing. And that's not supposed to bother Washington? That there could be security issues for them if the country breaks up like the last time? Warlords all over? Another Villa raiding Texas? Just the chaos, the refugees spilling across the border—millions of people, any of that could bring the Americans in, tie up the US Army—"

"They want a response soon."

"Fine. Since there's no real station here, send them this …" She began writing on her pad as he slowly parsed it out. "Coup likely to result in civil war between Corrialles, his conservative loyalists and new popular militias. Army could fracture, as well. Previous civil war, revolution, killed one million people, devastated country. Effective breakup of Mexico into warlord-controlled zones likely, resulting in US intervention like Pershing mission to catch Pancho Villa. Breakup could—no—*would* create opportunities for further Nazi subversion. Hitler likely to start soliciting, aiding individual warlords, seeking another Franco, similar to recent Spanish Civil War. All would distract US from aid, support and resources for British and anti-Nazi cause, also tying up US naval, army and air assets, possibly for years—no strike that—with certainty for years to come. The Americans won't be able to come in and go out, they'll have to occupy the country! Mexico's mountainous—ideal conditions for guerrilla war. My assessment is risk of these eventualities is utterly unacceptable. Request reconsideration of these factors and reconfirm previous order."

"Oh! Good, good, this is very good, Roy, I'll get this right out."

Hawkins sat numbly in the booth, watching her fly down the aisle, almost running to the elevator. His head felt empty, sucked clean, nothing but the distant sound of traffic out on the Paseo.

# -61-

A man was in the aisle, irritably looking for an empty phone booth. Hawkins vacated his, leaving the hotel, back out onto the Paseo de la Reforma. He stood in the warm sun, gazing up and down the busy street, his inner motor idling, half-seeing and not seeing. Instead of turning back to the Imperial, an urge overtook him—perhaps to get away from that, or what it represented?—and he began rapidly walking westward along the Paseo, looking in the shops, the cafés and offices.

The people were busy, happy, walking along chattering away, or determinedly heading here and there on their business. They seemed so normal. *Little do they know what's coming*, Hawkins thought.

After a short distance he reached a large square. In the center was a statue of an Indian warrior or chief. Cuauhtémoc, he realized. When Corrialles had been interrogating the men in the hangar, he'd demanded to know who the last emperor was. The fool answered Maximilian. *Cuauhtémoc!* Corrialles shouted. *Maximilian was an invader!* And so he was. That man came to Mexico knowing little or nothing about it, like the artist of that dumb guidebook, who could not see what was right in front of him.

Cortés, the Spanish conqueror of Mexico, murdered Cuauhtémoc. Hawkins had had several idle days on the *Santa Lopez*, and he'd busied himself reading about the country before he arrived. As he gazed at the statue he suddenly remembered Cuauhtémoc's last words, carefully transcribed by one of Cortés's men, who was horrified by the crime.

*May God demand justice from you, as it was taken from me when I entrusted myself to you in my city of Mexico!*

Justice was denied. *So much injustice in this country's past*, Hawkins thought, *and there's about to be more.*

*What do I see here? A pleasant, sophisticated street. But …* he closed his eyes and imagined the scene, seeing with his mind's eye, not what was in front of him, the way Riley would have it, but what was to be. Corrialles's tanks would be useless against a real invader—well, that would've been the Americans—but on a broad avenue like this? The machine guns would rip up and down the Paseo, the tanks would roll along, firing into the side streets, clearing them, the people tumbling down, another bloody sacrifice.

A few more paces brought him to a small park. He sat on a bench watching the traffic swirl around the statue. *I'm still in that shut-down, professional mode*, he thought, *keeping myself safe.* Then, with a start, he realized, *Not only does that keep me safe from others. It keeps me safe from myself. Should I? Or at the minimum, should I now?* But what he mainly felt was confusion.

*I came here to fight Nazis … I won … I thought I won … What have I won …?*

A spark fired and he sprang up and turned the corner, briskly walking up an avenue away from Cuauhtémoc, head down.

*How did this happen? I only wanted …* Everything had seemed so clear, days, no an hour ago. Only an hour. *I knew what I wanted, what I was doing, because I knew who and what I was fighting. Hitler. The Nazis. All I wanted was to fight Hitler. Stop Eckhardt, Falkenberg. Beat them. But … now there'll be a war, more massacres here. Those rich fools, whatever they get back will be in ruins by the time this is all over.* Aust was right on that, the companies are greedy and stupid.

*What have I done ... what the hell happened ...* rumbling over and over in his mind.

He reached a large intersection. Several blocks down was a colossus, a large dome on massive arches, a good twenty stories high: the Monument to the Revolution. *They built this because that revolution mattered,* Hawkins thought. He walked up, going and going, then stopped at the edge of the plaza, staring at it. A tour of schoolchildren noisily passed him, heading toward it. He watched them go, more thoughts incoherently tumbling in his mind.

*What will happen to them? Blood on the streets. Blood on them?*

*May God demand justice from you ...*

*What now?*

*Riley. Riley's waiting for me,* he thought. *Do I dare tell her, what kind of picture will that paint?*

# -62-

There were several more large canvases around Riley's garage studio. Hawkins stood in front of one, trying to think of something to say, trying to think at all. Or maybe it was that he didn't want to think, or wanted to think of something, anything else. It was going to be an agonizing wait to hear back from W at his headquarters in New York, and London, he knew that, vaguely. Riley's paintings suddenly crowded everything out of mind.

"Don't you want to wait for better light?" he said.

"No, this is fine, I'll do the base now, work the color later." She was getting her palette ready, squeezing out oils. Riley's paintings were modern, in a slightly abstracted style. Yet, at the same time there was a strong sense of tradition, the subject matter all people, not things or abstract shapes. And they weren't types, either, like the socialist realist art of the Soviet Union or the racial archetypes favored by Hitler or Mussolini. A finished painting was crowded with people, a procession through history, a Mayan noblewoman, then a Joan of Arc perhaps, a crusader, all of them sitting in the back of a taxi with a woman cab driver smoking a cigar. A closer look. *No*, he thought, *they're all the same woman, and it's Riley.*

"This is a self-portrait?" he said. "Different versions of you?"

"We are all multiple beings, although women much more so than men."

"How so?"

"I think there are many different voices in our heads. For instance we are repelled by violence but often attracted to those men who practice it. Or what are we to be? That is a question. Madonna or whore? Also a trap. Men are simpler, they want what they want and they are what they want."

"Perhaps. We have our contradictions, too. But, yes, a man is what he does. I have always thought that."

*A man is what he does,* Hawkins thought, *that is what I have always believed. What I have done ... makes me what I am? What am I now, then? Now I'm supposed to do the very thing Eckhardt and Falkenberg were trying to do? What's the difference between me and them? I am the very thing I wanted to fight,* he realized. *I have become my enemy. How did this happen ...*

She set a box out and threw a sheet over it.

"Sit here." And so he sat down, still numbly looking around the studio. She picked up her brush, ready to go. "Well," she said expectantly.

"What?"

"Aren't you going to take off your clothes?"

"What!"

"You need to take your clothes off. I want to paint your scars too. They were interesting. I need to see them again."

"You didn't say anything about taking any clothes off!"

"Well, of course. Artists' models shed their clothes. They have done it for thousands of years. Have you looked at any of those paintings? Been in a museum?"

"I don't—" This was not what he expected, it seemed, well, *something ...*

"I saw you half naked when you were getting dressed. That's when I asked. You didn't seem very bothered then."

"I was in a hurry—I guess I was—didn't seem—you looked like a man, in your suit—it—"

"You forgot that I was a woman?"

"Of course not!"

"For the love of god, they're just clothes."

"Just?"

"What is the big deal?"

"Eh—"

"Here. Silly scaredy-cat." She stuck her tongue out and began unknotting her tie, whipping away the shirt, tossing it aside, naked to the waist underneath it. "Come on." She bent over, untying her shoes. She stood back up, kicking the shoes off, her breasts bobbling slightly. "See? Only clothes."

*Only … Well, hardly,* Hawkins thought. She was young and very pretty. Her attractiveness was no longer hidden or camouflaged under the baggy confines of a guayabera or a man's boxy suit with its padded shoulders emphasizing the manliness of its owner. All her femininity was now impossible to ignore or miss. Her pomaded hair, slicked down tight all these days, was also lifting off in the heat, fluffing out on its own, a dark corona around her head. Then she lightly tossed the pants aside as if they were not freighted with the weight of centuries of tradition and custom and endlessly rationalized censure and inhibition—an airy nothing. All was exposed, head to toe, including her pubic hair and the private space that waits. She picked up the palette again, gesturing with it. "Well, come on, are you such a big coward?"

That jogged Hawkins out of his momentary paralysis. It wasn't that he was offended—he was no prude. Or that he sought to defend and restore whatever standard of conduct he was brought up with, even if deep down he didn't believe in it. He wasn't given to the reflexive conformity to which so many people instinctively surrendered themselves. Nor was it a sense of inhibition.

No, it oddly echoed Corrialles's massacre at the airfield, her demand radically out of the normal routine of life. Things went along as expected. That was the normal, quotidian fabric of life, the security of predictability. Apples were now falling *up* from trees. Life suddenly seemed off-kilter, but also, freer. Restraints were broken. Liberated. The excitement of a dog unexpectedly off the leash, looking around with wide eyes. What's here? What's next?

He began quickly pulling it all off, unknotting tie and unbuttoning shirt at the same time, kicking off the loafers. The speed was instinct, not decision, the way when swimming you throw yourself into cold water rather that torturing yourself an inch at a time.

"No. And you know I'm not, that's not—"

"I'm sorry. I know. Unfair of me. Want some tequila anyway?"

"Sure." She fetched a bottle. He took a swig and sat down as she directed him into position. The liquor was warm and good. She returned to her palette.

He'd been naked with women, of course. But like most people they only saw each other that way in the gloaming of a bedroom or hallway. But now here the two of them were, in the light and apparently unafraid. He took another sip, sliding the smoky warmth over his tongue. She began happily painting away, limning out the outlines of what she wanted with broad strokes.

Sitting still—simply sitting—was something he wasn't used to doing. But it was good to have an enforced moment to rest and think. *I knew she was a woman,* he thought, *but the way I met her at Frida's Casa Azul, thinking she was a teenaged boy, seemed to have disarmed me, or perhaps inoculated me against seeing her as a woman, although I still knew it. That governed my expectations to come. Now I am seeing her anew, as if for the first time.*

Then he thought, *I now am like a real artist, like Riley, actually seeing, looking at the world, the people around me, actually seeing her anew, too. Is this a revolutionary act? Or her ordering me to undress? Men aren't used to having women order them to undress. We may want revolution, but are we comfortable with it when it occurs? I wasn't at first. Still—I seem comfortable now ...*

*There are so many things I did not see. I came here and saw what I wanted to see: the things or people I wanted to fight. Was it a form of tunnel vision? Maybe more like a pair of tinted lenses that colored all that I saw. I was closer to that artist who painted those oh-so-quaint images of sleepy men in sombreros than I would care to admit.*

"Which manifestation are you now?" he said. "Priestess? Cabbie? Revolutionary?"

"Yes."

"What?"

"Yes. All of those."

"Ah. All right. The priestess of art driving us to the revolution in a cab."

"You understand! Exactly! You see! You are thinking like an artist now."

"I'm flattered." She began humming softly as she painted. He had another swig of the warm liquor. *If seeing is a revolutionary act, what am I seeing?* he thought. "Am I part of the Revolution here, now?"

"If you fight for it, if you think it's worth a fight."

"Yes. It's worth a fight. The Nazis, they wanted a coup. That's why they came here. I think I was able to break that up."

"That does not surprise me."

"Righto. Why were they here, otherwise?"

"You have interesting hobbies, Mr. Art Dealer Businessman. Are you sure you're not a spy? I think Camarada Trotsky would know one when he saw one."

He chuckled. "Hobbies. Maybe I should take up painting."

"Don't unless you are serious about it."

"I don't have time."

"And General Corrialles?"

"He was in the thick of it."

"That does not surprise me, either."

"No, it's no surprise at all."

"You seem troubled, Hawkins. If I stopped a coup I would be happy."

"General Corrialles still has the paintings. I should've destroyed them."

She dropped her arms, the brush and palette smearing streaks of paint on her bare legs.

"My god! Hawkins! No!"

At that his numbness, the cool mood, the professional self-protection, finally and abruptly shattered, the way a piece of ancient porcelain explodes into a cloud of dust and fragments when it falls from a high shelf. Words he was thinking, or didn't want to think, or thought he alone was hearing, burst out, surprising himself.

"Riley, I've made a terrible mistake. They're going to do it, there's going to be—my god, what have I done! What have I become! I've become a monster!"

"What? What are you talking about?"

# -63-

"Some … *friends* of mine—"

"Friends? What kind of *friends!*"

"All right, certain powers that be. They can organize the sale for Corrialles so that he can stage a coup on his own. Without the Nazis."

"My god!"

"I should've destroyed the paintings—"

"I see—but, Hawkins, how would you do that?"

"I don't know. I should've found a way, or not gone down this road at all."

"But you stopped the Nazis—if you had not come to Mexico—"

"Yes. That's true. But I wasn't for this, I was against a coup."

"Against Mexico, the Revolution, you mean?"

"Yes." He took another swig, thinking that over. "I now know what's here is worth fighting *for*. I've seen that. The people in the streets, the need for justice, for a better life." Another tip of the bottle. "I may not be Mexican, but I'm glad to fight for it."

"For the love of Mexico, for the Revolution? Really?" She started painting again, watching him warily.

*Love,* Hawkins thought, as the tequila loosened both his mind and tongue, *love, that's what I've been missing since that day three years ago when I walked into that plant in East Prussia, hoping to sell some valves, and* discovered the Nazis were making poison gas, breaking all the post–World War I treaties. I have been against them ever since. I wanted nothing else except to fight them, against Hitler, that smug, smirking man in the car in Vienna. Because I knew what and who I was against, I thought that was enough.

But that was not enough, he realized. *I didn't know what I was for, because love is the most powerful way of being* for *something.*

*Love connects you to everything else.* He thought of Raul, in his cab down in Veracruz, tapping his fist on his chest, *mi corazón*—my heart. The people in the Zocalo, listening to Cárdenas, the love in their faces. Or the sailors in the mess room on the *Dendrobium*, or the pilots in the sky over England, they were enraged because they *felt* the horror of the reports in their hearts, and they *felt* it because they *loved* their families, their city, their country. *For unless you love something, why would you feel the horror? You don't think horror, you can't think horror, you feel it, you can only feel horror.*

*If you don't love something, it's a thing like any other thing. Or, if you can't feel love yourself, you can't* see *it in others.* He remembered the dead look in Hitler's eyes that time he had seen him back in Berlin, the way he'd looked at people, as if they were things. There was never love in those eyes.

Hitler, his people, they were insensitive to the horror they were unleashing because they couldn't feel or see the love others felt. In exactly the same way the people back in New York and London who wanted a coup were insensitive to the horror of what Corrialles's little counterrevolution was going to mean. Perhaps it was distance, but they couldn't *see* the love others felt.

Whatever happened—a proposed coup, blood in the streets, death, destruction—either way, it was just another thing that existed or that people did, an abstraction, an emotionless chess game, all soulless calculation. You don't feel the horror. The Germans dropping bombs on London? Merely another thing. A coup here? A thing. If you didn't sense or share a sense of what love brought to you or others, you couldn't feel the horror of anything, and you could talk yourself into *doing* damn near anything. And so they had.

*And I can see now why I couldn't feel the horror,* he realized. *Guarding against my anger, keeping myself safe from tipping my hand to others, even from myself. Yes, it cut me off from my anger but it also cut me off from love and, oddly but truly, horror.*

*But how … now what?*

A giggle broke him from his rumination. He glanced over at Riley.

"Hawkins! Come now!" It was a protest that was on the edge of a blush.

*Oh. Damn,* he realized.

"Ah, well, oops. It has a mind of its own."

He tried shifting his position, moving his hand and the bottle, trying to hide it.

"No, I'm trying to paint you that way! Stop!" Another blushing giggle. "You are distracting me!"

"I am horribly sorry. I am a total failure at this modeling business."

"No, no, not your hand there, you're changing your position again." She started laughing. He started laughing.

"Here, perhaps you're the one who needs the tequila …" He gestured out with the bottle, "I don't think this was a good idea, I'm a little *too* relaxed, now." He stepped over with the bottle. She took a good swig, holding on to his shoulder, lightly caressing it, then they wrapped their arms around each other, still laughing.

"What are you going to do, Hawkins?" Riley was far from what he had ever expected in a woman. There might have been something off-putting about it before, but now at the sight of her naked body all fears and doubts vanished. The sense of rebellion, her fierce freedom, it was irresistible—he was seeing, too, not only her, but the world anew. For the moment, all else was forgotten, lost in the immediacy of the turmoil he was feeling, lost in rebellion.

"The most revolutionary thing of all," he said. "An act of love."

# -64-

They were together on the old bed Riley kept in the corner of her studio. She was sound asleep. He could hear the soft whistling noise of her breathing, feel her chest slightly rising and falling, a comforting feeling. Hawkins tried to sleep, too, but every time he started to drift off the reality of what had happened jerked him awake. Corrialles. The paintings. The orders. *Send the paintings on.* Dear god ... first his stomach, then his jaw, then all his muscles would tighten up and the tension would snap him back awake. Then came fleeting pangs of guilt. *Days ago I was thinking I should've asked Daisy to marry me. Now here I am in bed with Riley. But ... I had to go. And she knew that. She understood. She told me to go.* It all seemed a long ways away now, anyway.

Finally, close to dawn, he fell restlessly asleep, and he began to see it all: Parke-Bernet. The auctioneer holding his little hammer high, snapping down, *Sold!* The uniformed attendants slipped a cover over a painting and started to carry it away. Only they weren't wearing Parke-Bernet's gray jackets, they were in tan, they were soldiers, Mexican Army soldiers, wearing helmets, Corrialles's men. They started carrying off the painting, marching away, to battle, saluting their general on the way. Corrialles was smiling, and why not? He'd gotten what he wanted.

They turned and marched off the stage, stamping their feet. Their legs, Hawkins realized, still dreaming, their feet, their legs, all red—covered with blood! Up to their knees, leaving bloody footsteps behind them.

The auctioneer ordered another piece brought up. A vase. Riley's vase! The one he rescued from the flight school, the one she'd made. Hawkins was laughing now in his dream—*ha ha, joke's on you!* The hammer came down again. Then the vase, on a desk at the museum. A man with a mustache, *looks like Cárdenas—no, it is Cárdenas!* He shakes his head, a small tolerant smile. *No.* The couple who bought it, a bald man in a gray suit and his wife in her mink stole, turn fire-engine red. The man pounds a fist on the table. Cárdenas points to Riley's signature inside the glyph. The man and woman disappear in flames.

Hawkins abruptly woke up.

"Riley! Riley!"

She woke with a gasp. "*Unh*—Hawkins! Are you all right?"

Hawkins leapt up. "Yes! Yes!"

"What the hell is the matter!"

"Riley, the beaker!"

"It's too early! In the name of god!"

"No, listen. The beaker. Do you have any more?" He began darting around the room, checking the paintings, the boxes.

"Why?"

"It's the answer. Don't you see?"

"No."

"Make fakes!"

"Of what?

"General Corrialles's paintings!"

"Wha—"

"You, your friends, people like the Riveras, you said there was a whole community of artists here who made money on the side."

"I don't know—"

"If you could fake that beaker so perfectly, you could fake anything." She lifted up on one elbow, now fully awake.

"I'm flattered you have such confidence in my talents, Hawkins. But why? What's the point? General Corrialles has all the paintings he needs."

"We'll make fakes and switch them. We can stop him!"

"Hawkins, maybe to most collectors, but not to the museums, the top galleries, you'll never fool them, you're going to get caught."

"You're not getting it. We want to get caught."

"You're talking crazy. Why would you want to get caught?"

He sat down on the bed with her, taking a hand, clasping it.

"Corrialles is going to have me ship the paintings. We make fakes. Then we switch them. All they have to do is fool Corrialles. Send the fakes on to New York. When they get there, exactly as you say, the real experts at Parke-Bernet will realize they're forgeries. Probably have a good laugh. Fakes go into the trash, Corrialles doesn't get his money. There's no coup. No civil war. No chaos. Peaceful transition of power from President Cárdenas to the new president. The US is free to concentrate on helping Britain, no distractions. You see?"

"Yes, I do, but how would we make these fakes? As you told me before, the paintings are in the middle of an army camp surrounded by soldiers!"

"I have good, really good photos of all the works, front and back. We get all your friends together, divvy them up. Make copies. Then switch them."

"Oh. I see. Yes …" The possibilities began dawning in her face, eyes darting from one imagined painting to another. "Yes! We can do this! With enough people!" Her expression rising to the heavens like an old retablo of a saint seized by an epiphany, throwing the covers aside, jumping up, excitement building. "Yes! We! Can!" Then she frowned, thinking hard, "What about the real ones?"

"I don't know. We'll talk to Diego and Frida. Maybe the government can take them into safekeeping." It was dawn outside now. "Wherever they go, this buys us time. Come. Let's get dressed. We'll go to the hotel first."

"Frida will be up later. Diego may be there. We'll invite ourselves to breakfast."

# -65-

Diego poured Frida's coffee. They'd arrived a few minutes earlier at Rivera's house in San Ángel. A phone call had located them there— the two artists had an intense but often tumultuous relationship, Riley had told Hawkins, and they kept separate houses. It was a startlingly modern structure, two pavilions joined by a flying bridge, one azure— Frida's studio, apparently—the other, white and rose, was Rivera's. The buildings presented flat angular planes, high square windows, flat roofs, curving outside staircases, every surface stripped of ornamentation, as avant-garde as anything in the world, a conscious architecture of the future. Breathtaking, in its way. There were a surprising number of these modern structures dotted around a city where people prided its cosmopolitan, revolutionary spirit. Riley was back in her suit. She and Hawkins both still had wet hair from a very friendly shower at the Imperial.

"What is it?" Rivera could sense the tremendous tension in their expressions.

Riley leaned out, the way an excited student would wave a hand in class—*choose me*—eager to tell.

"Go ahead," Hawkins said.

"Maybe you first, Hawkins, about Corrialles, then I'll handle the art part," Riley said.

When he heard the general's name Rivera nervously put his coffee back down, only a sip, clutching the arms of his chair.

"What's that bastard up to now?"

It took Hawkins fifteen minutes to fully cover the story of what was going on, with Rivera and Kahlo quietly interrupting from time to time with a terse question. However, Hawkins carefully evaded who had ordered the paintings shipped to New York and sold. Now it was undefined "outside interests." Except for Riley, they were lined with worry by the time he was finished. Riley had taken charge of the photos, passing them out, racing around, looking over their shoulders.

"It's terrifying," Kahlo said.

"I suppose so," Hawkins said. "The stakes are very high."

"So Camarada Trotsky was right," Rivera said. "You must be a spy."

"I am not. I am not spying on this country."

"Of course you would say that," Rivera said. "Señor Hawkins. In honesty. How would you know these things?"

"Tips get passed along to me by friends in New York. Business associates."

"Because you are a businessman," Kahlo said, slightly tense, smiling again.

"With a gun. And that funny little camera. Hawkins, show him your little camera, the one that looks like a cigarette lighter," Riley said, laughing and smiling.

"No—"

"Oh, go on, go on—" Rivera said.

"He has a big expensive camera, too," Riley said.

"Please," Hawkins said. "What does it matter? Do you want to help stop this or sit back and watch whatever happens?"

"Of course we don't want that," Rivera said. "We all must do what we can for our beloved country. That may sound pretentious, but it is true. Why did we become socialists? For the betterment of our country, for the people."

Hawkins started to ask a question, but Riley leapt in first, now filled with enthusiasm. "We can find enough artists to help us!" she said. "I know we can!"

"I'm not sure," Rivera said.

"We need to know right away," Hawkins said.

"Why the hurry?" Kahlo said.

"Because if we cannot do this, I may have to find a way to destroy them," Hawkins said.

Kahlo gasped, her voice rising in tone to a soft scream, "No! You would not do such a thing! These are treasures! The soul of civilization—"

"I will if I have to! They are not worth this country's future or the peace of the world. Think of all the people who would die. Please. Tell me what the alternative is?"

"Frida, it is up to us to make sure it doesn't come to that," Riley said. She held out another photo, this one of a Matisse. "Look. Do one, then do another."

Kahlo began soberly recounting the math of Hawkins's proposal.

"Forty paintings. That's quite a lot. How many days do we have?"

"Maybe three or four," Hawkins said.

"Please, four," Rivera said. "If we can get another half-dozen artists besides ourselves, that's less than one a day per person." He, Kahlo and Riley began passing the photos back and forth again.

"And they don't have to be perfect," Riley said.

"We don't want them to be *too* good," Hawkins said. "We want to be caught."

"Of course," Frida said. "That does help."

"And we have to swear everyone to secrecy."

"We better get going," Rivera said, "you've given us a big job." He paused. "Mr. Spy."

# -66-

Hawkins gave it a good sniff. *Yes. There's a touch of perfume on the envelope. What's that all about?* He smiled and slipped it open with a finger as the desk clerk at the Imperial turned to another guest.

*Report in. Lilly.*

Back at the Reforma, half an hour later, Lilly strolled by, glanced at Hawkins and winked, settling into another booth, dropping pesos into the phone with a white-gloved hand. She had another hat, although more like a visor, open on top with a spray of red leaves around one brim, a little work of art.

"Your report made quite a mark," she said. "They apparently are discussing the risks now, you certainly made that clearer, so much so it's all up in the air. But for now, they want you to proceed on the contingency the plan will go ahead. I say, wait and see."

"Very well. I guess that's a relief. Somewhat. I—"

"That's not the big thing ..."

"What?"

"There's been a new intercept out of Bermuda, a telex they caught off the cable, only a couple of hours ago. You may be hearing this before he does, depending on the delivery or how often he picks it up.

And it's bizarre. They don't quite know what to make of it."

"How so?"

"Falkenberg has been ordered to kill Eckhardt."

"What?"

She repeated it. "That's what it said. From an address in Lisbon, too. General Houghton thinks it was sent in a hurry, possibly out of regular channels so as not to alert Eckhardt. It's very unusual they are using telex. They have to know those wires pass through our controls. The message was obliquely split between two different cables an hour apart, and it was phrased in such a way one might miss it—obviously that's what they were hoping. Almost did, apparently. Used the phrase 'permanently conclude employment per your recommendation,' so it might seem businesslike and innocuous if you didn't know the players and context. The second said 'regrettable he has terminal illness, will perish soon,' so forth."

"Any reason given for the order?"

"No. That might have been separate, or the reason might be implicit from an earlier report we missed."

"A rather high price for failure, if that's what it is."

"Say, one less Nazi."

"Yes. Damn. Eckhardt is a little crazy, maybe they don't trust him anymore. Maybe they caught him stealing."

"Little? From your description—"

"Fine, he's barking mad. Risky business for Falkenberg. Eckhardt's no pushover. And Falkenberg's got to get away afterward, maybe leave the country."

She started to softly laugh. "Hey, one less Nazi ..."

"Ye-s-s ..." He started chuckling too. "God only knows. Be good to run him out. I wonder if I could get him to Texas, have him try and go out through New York. That has possibilities."

"W would be very interested in that one. Maybe our friends in the Mounties?"

"Yes. Tell them to start setting up the plane. The paintings should all fit in a Douglas if they take out the seats."

"Will do."

"That's it for today, then."

"I'll get that right out. Then I'm going shopping. I found this wonderful hat store near the park, the man's an artist. Great things here. Dress shops too. Amazing prices."

"Enjoy yourself. Watch out for the antiquities, though."

She winked across the aisle, hung up and walked back out, wiggling her fingers at him as she passed by his booth. *What a great way she has with hats*, Hawkins thought, watching her go. Duty brought her here, but there was a you-go-to-hell quality to the hat thing. She could not be a rebel, like Riley, but she could be rebel enough for herself with a wild hat, her way of saying, *so there!*

*All this is equally excellent*, he thought. *Whatever the case is, I am shipping something out. And Eckhardt and Falkenberg. What on earth …*

# -67-

The street in San Ángel was sunny, warm and deserted, with inviting pools of dark shadows beneath trees and against the walls. He rang the bell, then knocked. After a long wait he did it again, turning around, watching the street, waiting. Nothing. *Odd,* Hawkins thought. He hadn't checked on Aust in several days, what with the frenzy over the paintings and getting ready. They could've left, or be out, but still, *with all their servants, there ought to be someone here within a few rings.* Then a shadow passed over him and the wall. That felt alarming. An instinct, perhaps an atavistic one. He looked up, then back. In the tree where he'd perched with the chickens days earlier were three very large dull gray-black birds with tall red heads. They were dead silent, not happily chirping away like most birds, and hunched over, like worn out and elderly actuaries at a ghostly ledger. Hawkins walked across the street for a closer look. Vultures.

*Something's wrong.* He felt it in his gut. *Very wrong,* all instinct again now.

He carefully checked up and down the street—nothing but blank, windowless walls. In seconds he quickly picked the old lock, stepped inside, drawing his Hi-Power as he passed through, pulling and latching the door behind him as fast but as quietly as he could. He cautiously stepped in, pistol high, ready. The only sound was the distant burbling of the fountain. Down on the tile floor. A heavy smear of blood started halfway toward the arched entryway and around the corner. On one of the two small columns at the courtyard entrance was a large red handprint. He stared at it for a long second, going cold inside, in that mode again, in the moment, feeling nothing, allowing himself nothing, utterly focused on the Hi-Power and any target it might find.

Hawkins stepped into the archway, both hands now grasping the pistol, tensely peering around the columns. On the peak of the red-tile roof across the courtyard were another two vultures, waiting for something. There was a slight, sick, thick, rotting sweet smell, an odor that electrically struck violently at the nerves: the smell of death.

He carefully edged forward, scanning the courtyard and the colonnade. Stillness in the eerie silence. Moving slowly, carefully, he followed the smear of blood to an old paneled door. It was open a crack. He pushed it farther with one foot, sliding around the corner, watching carefully. It was one of the servant's rooms. The gardener-doorman was lying barely inside, arms flung wide, his head missing. He probably got hit the second he opened the door, no time to give the alarm.

Hawkins edged out, closing the door behind him, spinning around, scanning the colonnade, up, down, looking, looking. No one. He pressed his back against the wall, moving along to the kitchen, pushing open the door. The cook was lying on the floor in a large pool of blood. The ingredients of a half-cooked meal were scattered around the kitchen tables, pots on the stove with vegetables in them, waiting to be cooked.

Hawkins leaned over the counter and looked down. The woman had been neatly decapitated, too, the neck cut at a slightly downward angle, more like a piece of sausage than a human body. Whoever swung the sword or ax was a good foot taller.

*Eckhardt. It has to be Eckhardt,* Hawkins realized, *and he isn't using an ax or a sword. He's using the macuahuitl he made, the cut gleaming so unnaturally clean, it has to be an obsidian blade, a hungry blade, supremely, effortlessly sharp, like no metal blade on earth, a blade that would pass through like a breeze of death.*

Then he realized something else: *Where's the woman's head?* He carefully stepped back out into the courtyard, watching for Eckhardt, for anyone. Then he noticed flies buzzing around a pool of blood at one end of the courtyard. He slipped along the colonnade, checking, looking for another body. But there was no body. The blood was running out of the rainspout. He stepped out from under the colonnade, looked up and nearly gasped, his coolly controlled, careful mode of not feeling breaking for a split second, stomach abruptly heaving, a quick brush on the edge of vomiting before he went cold again. Several heads were lined up on the rain gutter at the edge of the roof: Herr Aust; Elise, her white hair now stained red with blood; a young man Hawkins instantly realized had to be their son at university, he so resembled his mother; the cook; the maid; and the gardener. The gardener's head had been slashed neatly down the center, a V-shaped gash nearly to the tip of his nose.

But that was not the worst part. Bobbing in the fountain below them, like apples at a Halloween party, were all six hearts, now washed clean, almost a pinkish white.

Increasingly confident no one was around, Hawkins began jogging from room to room. Inside the large living room he found the bodies of Elise and her son. Both had been bound and tied, hand and foot, with one of Elise's arms half severed. Their heads were missing, of course. The bodies were draped over the top of the Austs' baby grand. Both chests had been gashed from one side to the other, gaping wide, distended, giant mouths of baby birds, open, red and waiting. Blood poured off the piano, soaking the Persian carpet. There were sharp gashes in the top of the piano, by their necks. Eckhardt had taken their hearts first, then their heads.

*The terror they must've have known in those final moments ...* he thought, *tied over the piano ... watching the blade descend ... probably saw their own hearts, too ... after the other's ... who did he kill first? Did Elise have to watch her son die? Or him, his mother?*

It was too much for a moment. Hawkins closed his eyes and clenched his teeth, breathing hard, trying to control his reaction, to stay cool and keep his head, steady his stomach, despite every normal human instinct to recoil and flee. That, he realized, is what the Spanish must have felt when they first stood in the center of Tenochtitlan, at the foot of the Temple of Huitzilopochtli next to the Huey Tzompantli, the Great Skull Rack, and its many tens of thousands of heads. No doubt and no wonder hands tightened around their swords as they contemplated their next step.

Where were the other two bodies? Hawkins raced out again, away from that horror, searching for the next. In a bedroom, with the hem of a bloodstained sheet still grasped tightly in one hand, he found the headless maid. She'd been a big, husky woman, which might have prompted her fate: She'd not only been decapitated, but her body had been cut at a diagonal, from her shoulder several inches from the neck, through the torso and out the bottom of the rib cage on the opposite side. From the even, straight angle, it was clear it'd been done with a single clean blow, right through. The hollow lung gaped inside her ribs. At least it was quick for her.

Eckhardt had wanted to know, Hawkins remembered, could a macuahuitl really cut a horse's head off? The maid gave her life to settle that question, although it might have spared her from being bound and thrown on the piano with her employers, and the terror of that. The conquistadors hadn't needed to embellish anything at all, it seemed.

But where was Aust's body?

# -68-

Hawkins jogged back around the colonnade, gun still high, looking for more smears or spatters of blood. None to be found, the rest of the house was as slick clean and well kept as always, including the arched stairway to the second floor, except for the growing smell, of course. Aust's body had to be somewhere. But Eckhardt's and Falkenberg's rooms were up there, too. *Need to check*, Hawkins thought. He carefully edged up and down the corridor. It was spotless, too. He pushed open the door to Eckhardt's room with the muzzle of the Browning, looked in, then relaxed and walked around.

It was absolutely empty, all the drawers pulled out, the closet door open, only a few hangers and a thin layer of dust inside, the bedcovers thrown up to check underneath. Eckhardt had cleaned out his things and was long gone, not even a crumpled receipt or an old newspaper or magazine.

*Of course*, Hawkins thought. Either before or after, Eckhardt beat a path out. *Did he come to get his things after the chase at the airport? Kill them then? No, probably not*, he thought. Corrialles's soldiers had been at the Austs' for a day, but then left when neither Eckhardt nor Falkenberg had returned. Eckhardt had probably staked the place out and waited. Hawkins guessed the dead here were fresh, less than a day, the blood was still drying and sticky. But what about Falkenberg?

Next door, that room, too, had been stripped clean. Was Falkenberg here when Eckhardt did all this? Would he really stand by and watch? Hard to believe. Maybe.

Hawkins headed down the hall, checking each room. They were furnished and lived in, but that was all. At the end of the hall another door hung open. As he approached he felt an odd breeze. He looked in and up, following the draft.

There was a large hatch or skylight in the center of the ceiling. Through it stretched a mast extended by a large pulley and crank. At the top was a directional shortwave antenna that was flipped down into place with a cord, parallel to the earth. Another lever turned it, aiming it. A lone vulture sat on one of the rods warily looking down at him with mean little eyes. It decided it didn't like the company, slowly unfurled a pair of huge wings, scrunched down for a small jump and flapped off.

Against the wall across a long rough plywood bench was a large collection of radio sets and transmitters. They appeared to be American made: a National Radio Company HRO with a large round dial in the center, a Hallicrafters Super Skyrider, an HT-4 transmitter, a big linear amplifier with a vacuum tube the size of a coffee can, headphones and telegraph keys, several voltage regulators, a row of car batteries and chargers under the bench. On the floor, all around, broken vacuum tubes. Someone had pulled them out and smashed them.

The sight didn't sicken him like the spectacle downstairs, but nonetheless, another nasty, sobering surprise, Hawkins thought. Aust was hardly an amateur radio hobbyist, collecting continents and long-distance contacts, not with the hidden skylight and retractable antenna. No ham radio operator would bother with that. This was an Abwehr outpost, maybe even the nerve center of German intelligence in Mexico and possibly the rest of Central America. Top of the line gear, the latest, all bought on the open market. And why not? Easier to send the money over than cases of fragile gear and American companies made the best.

He carefully checked all around—no code machines or code books, only the empty spaces on the benches outlined by faint traces of dust. There were a few papers on the floor, including some scattered newspaper clippings. He began riffling through them. All were in German, some typed. A report on the 1940 Mexican national police budget. A report on Pemex production. One on the Mexican election. Unexceptional, all, and uninteresting. Nothing on Eckhardt, Falkenberg, their flight school, Corrialles. Whoever cleaned the place out—Hawkins now was guessing Falkenberg—undoubtedly took those away, too.

*My assumption Aust was a dupe or cutout couldn't have been more wrong,* Hawkins realized. *Should've followed my gut in the first place*, he thought, *and not talked myself out of listening to it. Fuck all … How did I miss it?* He mulled that a quick second. *Sure. I was taken in by his breezy and relaxed manner, falsely thinking he'd been assimilated into Mexico.* But Aust had to have been the head of the Abwehr in Mexico. *Long-term sleeper, most likely. Came over after the last war.*

Then another thought. *Where'd he get the money to create Seguro del Capitolio?* Of course, they'd advanced him the cash. Maybe when Hitler came in. The Nazis had owned Aust, in a sense. Hawkins remembered the banter between Wilhelm and Elise over their boys going back to Germany to join the army, how she said she'd disown him, his easygoing response. Berlin knew the risks of agents drifting off in a foreign country, losing interest, focus, commitment. Even if they were now half-Mexican, the Abwehr had Wilhelm and Elise Aust in its pocket, they'd have to go along. Smart. Aust probably got orders to put Eckhardt and Falkenberg up in his and Elise's house. And so they did, even if they didn't like them or want to. They couldn't escape the bargain they'd made.

He darted back down, checking the living room again. There, behind the piano, near the credenza, a small Walther automatic on the floor. He smelled it. It hadn't been fired, not in a long time. A drawer in the credenza was open, a splatter of blood across it down to the floor. Then he noticed a gold bracelet in the middle of the puddle of blood. *Damn, poor woman,* he thought, *a thoroughly decent sort. Didn't get to the gun in time.*

Hawkins pocketed the Walther and went back out into the courtyard, gazing up at the heads. *Where's the rest of Wilhelm Aust?* He did another quick run-through of the house. Not a trace. He came back into the courtyard and went into the living room again, searching. Then he saw it, a bloody empty sack. *Only Aust's head is here*, he realized. *The body must be somewhere else.*

When it happened was now clear, Hawkins realized. When Eckhardt was showing us his collection, Wilhelm had wanted to know how Eckhardt could afford such things: the mask, the obsidian skull. In truth, great treasures, pieces worthy of the world's top museums. Eckhardt gave a nervous answer. Of course. The three missing paintings Corrialles didn't get. Eckhardt had already diverted them, he was going private, at least partially, dipping into the goods to feed his obsession with the Aztecs.

The Austs had caught him. Reported it back. Taken together, the embezzling, the chaotic mess at the airport, it was too much. Berlin ordered Aust to kill Eckhardt. They were probably afraid to tell Falkenberg—or use the same channel for fear of tipping off Eckhardt—and so they ordered Aust to do it.

Only Herr Aust wasn't a trained agent. Or he was rusty and bungled it. Eckhardt killed Aust instead. Brought Aust's head with him, came back and slaughtered the whole household. Cleared out his things.

After that—and only after that—was when Falkenberg sent and received those telexes. The radios weren't working, that was key, the decisive clue—Eckhardt smashed them first to keep Falkenberg from reporting him. Falkenberg had no choice but to send back a telegram in the open, and another returning telegram from Berlin to Mexico City was the only way to send Falkenberg an order, at least temporarily. Falkenberg was probably hunting Eckhardt now. Or more likely they were hunting each other.

*No point in finding the rest of Aust now*, Hawkins decided. *Got to get the hell away from here.* He hurried out, locking the old door behind him. The watching vultures ruffled their wings, waiting for the August heat and the high sun to ready their feast.

# -69-

Hawkins set down the cardboard box with the burritos and cold bottles of Sidral Mundet. Riley was back working in her paint-splattered guayabera. It was hot out, late afternoon, the big door open on her garage studio. A slight breeze entered, cutting the reek of thinners used to hurry up the drying. The smell felt oddly good, cleansing the coppery odor of blood and the weighty reek of death from his throat.

"Here." He handed her one of the apple-flavored beverages. She was holding a photo in one hand, carefully signing Marc Chagall's name in the lower corner.

"There. Only a touch more," she said. Hawkins took the photo and compared it to the canvas. Having seen the original, he knew.

"An amazing copy, Riley."

"Muchos gracias."

There were two others drying against the wall: an elegantly simple Matisse and the blue period Picasso with green lips. He turned it over.

"Looks old now."

"I painted the frame and inside the canvas with acid. Turns the wood dark. Then you mix water and dust with a touch of water-based glue and spray it from a mister. The dust sticks that way, makes them appear to have been sitting for years." She sat and began rapidly eating. "It's good it's warm out. That helps with the drying." Hawkins took a burrito and began nibbling at it. It was very tasty.

"Also the thin air?"

"Maybe a little." Mouth full, she eyed him carefully. "Aren't you hungry?"

"Yes."

"You don't act like it." He was chewing slowly and swallowing hard.

"I am."

"I am an artist. I know how to look. Looking is my trade. I can see something is wrong with you."

"It's not something you'd want to paint."

"Remember the vase I did? The sacrifice?"

He answered hard and fast, rather dismissively, a nervous edge or agitation in his tone. "That was from a long time ago. Long time. Not now."

"I see. How—*ah*—"

"Very well. Yes, it was like that. Exactly like that. Vultures were waiting when I got to the Austs'. You can imagine the rest." They sat in silence for a moment. A truck rumbled by the entrance.

"I hate those birds," she said, "anything that waits for death."

A laugh burst out. It felt so inappropriate and disrespectful, and yet, at the same time, he was laughing. It all tumbled out, "And I am alive. We are all alive. We must *be* alive. Do you understand?"

"Yes—my art—"

He seized the side of her face with both hands, leaned forward and kissed her, hard, holding for a long moment.

He let go. She gazed at him for a moment, then reached down and whipped her shirt off. In seconds they were back on the bed, in their haste ignoring the open door, shielded from the street only by her art.

# -70-

The four days—or nights—were up, the street outside chaos. Diego, Frida and Riley's friends were dropping off their contributions, then standing in the road, noisily, eagerly talking. Hawkins uneasily watched. *Damn near like a convention*, he thought, *or the reunion of a very large family. No, a political rally is what it is*, he decided, *a gathering of the like-minded faithful, followers of the true cause. Crazy.*

"Riley, if these people don't shut up and get the hell out of here the whole city is going to know."

"These people already know."

"Yes, but they don't know who else knows. Word spreads." She looked at him for a second, half surprised, half leaning toward feeling put-upon. "You talk about looking? Seeing? See." He gestured out the door.

She gazed out, taking it in.

"Oh, damn." She put her scissors down, ran into the street, going from person to person, touching shoulders, whispering in ears, nudging along, *por favor?* Finally the crowd began dissipating, looking over their shoulders for one last glance at their fraudulent masterpieces.

One of Riley's friends, Emilio, a tall, dark, curly-headed man with a small Trotsky-style goatee and a beret, easily loped in carrying a canvas on his shoulder, setting it down with a cheerful *¡Hola!* and a little kiss on her cheek. Emilio had taken what was probably the toughest assignment:

quickly duplicating the Rousseau, with its dense foliage and waiting animals. He shook Hawkins's hand.

"Amazing job," Hawkins said. "Gracias."

"Por supuesto. Dé mis respetos a Diego y a Frida. And anything for Riley." Riley crossed it off the list, waving him away.

"¡Alejandro, ninguna hora!" *Exactly*, Hawkins thought, *no time for chat.* Emilio would be back later that night and there'd be plenty of time to talk. Of all of Riley's friends and artists, he was the one she said she trusted the most. As chance would have it, his day job was driving a truck delivering furniture. With Hawkins he would be one of the two drivers that night. Emilio made an ostentatious bow—"Your wish, my command"—smiled and left.

They'd set up a worktable with a large bolt of heavy brown paper at one end, rolling it out, setting the paintings down, hurriedly wrapping each canvas, wetting and slapping on fake gallery labels, sealing them with brown tape, stacking them against the walls.

Another woman came in from the opposite direction, soberly holding her contribution in front like the reliquary of a saint, her children in single file behind her, a miniature holy day procession. A small van on the opposite side of the street disgorged two more, both from Diego's friends. Riley's garage studio was rapidly filling, the paintings now several deep along the far wall.

Nightfall came, the last fake was wrapped. Riley and Hawkins sat on the edge of her bed, contemplating the scene.

"My god," Riley said, "all the paintings. We did it."

"Yes," Hawkins said. "The general has a surprise coming." Outside, in the dark street, the rumbling of a heavy truck. Hawkins leapt up. "There's Emilio." Since his services as a neophyte art faker were not desired, while Riley, Diego, Frida and their friends had been frantically working, Hawkins had been combing the city for trucks. In the north he'd found exactly what he was looking for: two fairly new, perfectly matched heavy rental trucks, identical in every respect except for the license plates. Now Emilio had arrived with the other truck.

Half an hour later, Emilio swung the door shut, latching and locking it. They had a simple plan: Hawkins would drive his empty truck to General Corrialles's army base and pick up the real paintings. He would then meet Emilio outside the city. They'd switch trucks and license plates. Emilio would come back to Riley's with the real paintings, where they'd hide them.

"Remember, it's not a synchromesh transmission like a car," Emilio said. "You have to clutch both up and down."

Hawkins nodded. "Righto. I go both ways. Thanks."

"Are you sure you don't want me to come and drive?"

"No. I have to go alone. Thanks, though. Meet you at the rendezvous in a few hours."

Hawkins geared up and rumbled out of town.

General Corrialles was waiting at the gatehouse. He came right out, big smile, wearing a full-dress military uniform for the occasion, heartily pumping Hawkins's hand, another hand on his elbow, congratulatory.

"An historic day. Hawkins, you are a real friend of Mexico."

"A friend of Mexico. That's all I ask. Well, and a commission." They both laughed. The general hopped in an open car and escorted Hawkins to the storeroom. Corrialles waved a hand and his men began a bucket brigade of paintings, all also wrapped in brown paper to save space and weight on the plane, ready for shipment. The truck quickly filled. Hawkins and the general watched.

"The plane will go into Teterboro Airport in New Jersey. The paintings will be in Manhattan before lunch tomorrow."

# -71-

Hawkins drove the truck around a bend in the dirt road and behind a small grove of trees. He smelled trouble before he saw it, a strange burning odor. He instantly snapped off his headlights, killed the engine and slowly lifted the Hi-Power from his shoulder holster, ready, letting the truck quietly roll to a stop on the side of the road, two or three dozen yards behind Emilio's truck. *Something's wrong*, Hawkins thought, *something's very badly wrong*. He tensed like a sprinter on the starting blocks, ready to leap, ready for whatever waited. *Oh no. Oh no, no, no … can't be*, he thought.

Ducking down, he swung out to the far side of his truck below the door, moving as quietly as he could, slowly, carefully stepping down, checking the trees. If it was an ambush, they'd be firing already, he thought, *knew*. He ran into the grove, darting from tree to tree, searching as best as he could see in the moonlight, up into the branches and behind the trunks, waiting for shots, listening for voices, looking for someone, anyone. After several tense minutes he decided there was no one around, at least as far as he could tell—no cars, no shots.

Around the back, a fair amount of smoke was pouring from the rear of the truck. Ignoring that, he ran forward, low across the road, and slipped underneath it, almost on his hands and knees, checking the other side. Overhead he could feel intense heat. But there was no one around to that side, either, nothing but a vacant field and the cropped stubble of harvested corn.

He slid out from underneath, stepping away, giving himself some room, holding the pistol straight out, swinging it back and forth, looking hard into the gloom. Where was Emilio? He decided not to call out, instinct dictated that, don't give yourself away.

He began circling the truck, looking, seeing nothing. Then a single thought struck him: *Betrayal. Riley said Emilio was a close friend. We could trust him. A good camarada, too. Must not be true. Could not be true. But then where was he?*

He reached the back, looking up and in. There was a strong smell of gasoline. Burning embers of wood and canvas covered the floor of the back, still glowing softly in the dark. Everything was destroyed, every last fake painting, suddenly gone. He edged up to the open door, watching the embers flicker as it all sank in, feeling the heat on his face.

*My god, all gone*, he thought. The whole plan, blown, all that incredible effort, destroyed, lost. All the canvases gone. And from the amount of ashes and burning embers of frames, all were here. Burned. No getting them back. A sickening sense of horror started to overcome him.

*Emilio must've torched it*, Hawkins thought. *But why? Makes no sense.* His own work was in there. He was an artist, an intellectual, whatever his day job was, not a man who would support a coup. *Makes no sense at all, no rhyme or reason to it.*

He came back around the front again and tripped over something, a soft object, and nearly fell. A body? Hard to see. He decided to risk it. He ran to the truck's cab, reached in and turned on the headlights.

In the dirt, a few yards from the truck, Emilio lay on his back. His head seemed turned around, facing down, one arm at an odd angle.

Hawkins instantly called out, "Emilio! Emilio!" running forward, couldn't help himself. He stumbled to a stop, almost falling over the other man in his haste. He started to lift him up, ready to check for a pulse. Emilio's head didn't follow. His neck was severed right through. Shuddering, he set the body down, and flinched back. Emilio's forearm had been severed several inches below the elbow. He'd instinctively raised his arm protectively. The first blow severed that. The next his head. Clean, fast cuts. Hawkins had one instantaneous thought:

*Eckhardt. He did this. Only him. Eckhardt was here. With his macuahuitl, putting it to use again, quick and silent, like with the Austs.*

*Can't stay,* Hawkins knew that instantly. *Dangerous. Get out of here!* he thought. *Eckhardt could come back. Or the policía. Could be a trap. Eckhardt could be lurking here. And no point in staying, now, anyway. It's gone. Nothing to salvage, including the truck.* He turned and ran back to his own truck, loaded with the real paintings, started up and lurched and rumbled between the trees, branches scraping the top of the vehicle, and roared down the main highway.

His mind raced the truck down the road, thoughts a feverish rush, one tumbling on another. *What happened? Someone talked. But who? Corrialles? No, he'd probably shoot Eckhardt on sight.*

*But … why would Eckhardt want them destroyed? He had control of them. Could've taken them. Emilio dead, drive off with them. He stole three others before. Why not make off with these? Instead, he burned them. What the bloody hell?*

*Falkenberg? No, he'd been ordered to kill Eckhardt, they were sick of his embezzling, his foul-ups.*

*Emilio.* The image of his dismembered body laying in the road sparked a queasy, sick feeling. *Am I responsible? All too obvious this was more dangerous than I anticipated. Should I have gone along, armed? But how? We needed to switch the trucks.* Emilio had volunteered, he wanted to stop Corrialles, too.

Would Eckhardt do this out of spite? *Maybe. He's a crazy bugger if there ever was one.*

*But …* back around again in his mind, to the big question, how did Eckhardt know? *One of that goddamn crowd in the street today? Maybe. Worry about that later,* he decided, *what now?*

There was a plane waiting, he knew.

One powerful thought now struck him, breaching the surface like a submerged U-boat, an instant obsession invading and filling all corners of his mind.

*What the hell is going on? I don't know. Not knowing, that's dangerous. Can't plan, can't react when you don't know,* he thought. Why did Eckhardt destroy the paintings? Crazy …

Then it struck him: the only chance to find out was to send the real ones through. *The money will come back. Get back on the money trail, that's it, trace the money … but if I do that, will there be a coup? What happens here, to these people, to leaders like Cárdenas? Lying in a pool of blood like the decent men and women of Spain? Another civil war? How could that not happen? And an American intervention? All too possible. Bloodshed in the streets? On my hands?*

Or is London still reconsidering? He mentally seized that thought. *Nothing is settled,* he told himself. *I have push on that end. They're listening. They will listen.*

*If I ditch the paintings, they'll know when they don't arrive,* Hawkins thought. *Corrialles is in contact with people abroad. He'll come looking for them—for me. And he has an army. How, where could I even hide them? Unless I destroy them.*

*But if I destroy them, how do I find out what's going on? No money to trace. No, no alternative to sending the shipment through now. They're reconsidering. It'll be all right.* He turned around and headed for the airfield.

# -72-

W and the staff in New York had made an excellent choice: a Western Air Express DC-3. WAE was an official US airmail carrier—a shield on the nose behind an Indian chief's head boasted that—so the plane came set up for cargo, with wider doors rather than the usual passenger ones. It made for a quick loading, fifteen minutes, no more.

Alice, one of the clerks with Lilly in Bermuda, had flown out to catch the plane and ride herd on the operation, handle paperwork, and the like. She was going to spend almost a full day in the air, but she seemed cheerful enough about it. She was breezily sorting through the last of the forms, waiting with Hawkins on the tarmac near the plane, puffing a cigarette, busily waving it in the air while the crew strapped their shipment down.

"Got to make this last," she said, deeply inhaling and holding the smoke, "won't get another smoke until we get to New Orleans."

"Any news of the war?"

"We bombed Berlin!"

"All right. 'Bout time."

"There. All done." She checked the plane. "Ready to go. Oh. Oops. Almost forgot. Supposed to give you this." She handed Hawkins an envelope. "Maybe it's a paycheck." She laughed. The copilot waved at her. They were done loading, the pilot starting the engines. She threw the butt down, "Bye!" sprinting in as the door shut behind her. The plane began rolling the instant it closed.

Hawkins watched, half absentmindedly, opening the letter with a thumb. A note was inside. From W. He stood in his headlights, reading.

*Roy—Brilliant job, all commendations to you, your service crucial. I have taken pains to ensure London is well aware of your achievements, which are considerable.*

*Your memo and the issues you raised were carefully considered. The risks of American involvement in potential Mexican civil war is recognized. However, war staff feels current Mexican situation different from previous Mexican civil war. Regular army forces are better equipped, and they have some light tanks now. It is their judgment that when brought to bear this will ensure control of urban centers, particularly Mexico City, and therefore eventual success of Corrialles likely. Therefore they have recommended proceeding. Awaiting final approval Whitehall. Be assured, your concerns are duly recognized and will be taken into consideration in future deliberations. See you soon in NYC.—W*

A minute later Hawkins watched the silver plane rise and hum into the night, a tourniquet momentarily tightening around his stomach.

*Bloody hell. They're going to go ahead … of course they're going to go ahead. Should've burned the other truck myself, driven it off a cliff, or something.*

But … was there a logical alternative? *No. There simply wasn't. I don't know what's going on,* he thought, *and there's only one way to find out. That is the simple, stark fact. Had to send them through. Find a way to make it work,* he thought. No alternative.

Next step, Lilly. He'd told her to wait on a side road near the airport. He quickly drove by, not stopping—that was the plan—flicking his high beams on and off three times. She flicked her high beams twice: all clear and message received. They both hurried off into the night, no waving, no contact, not now, a damn good thing. After what happened he was in no mood for the usual office chat over anything. She'd have a coded confirmation out within the hour.

As they both drove away the thought again rose: *What happened? How did Eckhardt know? Someone must've talked.* Then it suddenly struck Hawkins, a startling lightning bolt. No one told. Riley was keeping tabs on the galleries, going around regularly and checking them. He must've spotted her. *Damn! Of course.* He tailed her to her studio, saw Emilio. He was probably out there in the dark, in the crowd in the street. Then another lightning bolt hit him. *Goddamn it, Riley—that means he knows about her.* Hawkins stomped the accelerator to the floor, racing over the darkened streets back to Coyoacán and her studio.

# -73-

*Careful—careful,* Hawkins thought, *get the jump, this lumbering thing is damn noisy—he'll hear—if he's here.* He lurched to a stop at the near corner, one wheel over on the curb in haste, drew his Browning and raced up the street, holding the pistol high again in one hand, lightly tapping fingers on the walls, finding his way in the dark. The side door to Riley's garage studio was slightly open, lit from inside. He carefully edged up to it, peering through, hidden in the dark.

There he was, Eckhardt, inside, facing away from him in the dead center of the room, his feet spread wide, one hand easily resting on the hilt of his macuahuitl like a lethal cane, a cigar in the other. *Where's Riley?* Hawkins thought. *Can't see her.* Eckhardt said something in Spanish. From his tone it sounded vaguely complimentary or encouraging, gesturing with his cigar. Hawkins edged closer in. *Still can't see her,* he thought, *where is she?* Then he heard Riley's voice in the distance, very nervous.

"¡Necesito más tiempo, por favor! No esta hecho." *Tiempo* was "time," Hawkins knew. *She's asking for time. At least she's still alive. Thank god. Here in time.*

"Parece bueno. Trabajo más rápidamente." Eckhardt said. *Bueno* meant "good," the "rapid" part of *rápidamente* was obvious enough: "hurry up." He was getting impatient. Eckhardt moved out of sight. In the dark street Hawkins saw a form. He carefully slipped by the door, reaching out with his hand, feeling for it. Metal, a fender! Eckhardt had parked his car next to the wall, Hawkins realized. With a foot he found the bumper, holstered the Hi-Power and quietly, carefully stepped from the bumper to the fender to the hood to the roof of the car, feeling with both hands, moving slowly so not to fall. He reached up, grabbing the edge of the flat garage roof, pulling himself up. *Slowly, slowly,* he thought, *can't make any noise, the roof's old and half-assed built.* The ancient tar-covered metal crinkled slightly under his weight. Carefully moving on all fours, trying not to make a sound, he inched a few yards across, looking down from the open skylight.

Riley was slowly, meticulously painting on the blank far wall. Hawkins angled his head to see. It was huge, an image of a blue Aztec deity, vibrant colors, like the one Corrialles had excavated, caparisoned by a spiraling array of brilliant feathers, holding a fire-breathing serpent as a sword. It was a dazzling work, as surely executed as the ancient masterpiece Corrialles had in his church gallery.

*Huitzilopochtli,* Hawkins realized, *that's who Eckhardt would choose.* The hummingbird god of war and the sun, the ever-hungry deity that had to be fed human hearts without fail to guarantee the return of dawn and the life-giving sun, lest the world be plunged into perpetual darkness by a vengeful god. The hungry deity strode across the white wall, standing on the feathered serpent god Quetzalcoatl.

Eckhardt vaguely waved the cigar, then clamped it in his mouth. With one hand he dragged Riley's fake Chacmool across the floor toward Huitzilopochtli's feet, the vacant cavity in its stomach waiting to be filled with Riley's sacred heart. He was getting impatient. He was getting ready for another sacrifice, exactly as he had at the Austs'.

"¡No se hace!" Riley said. She was playing for time, buying time. *Smart,* Hawkins thought. *Very smart. And cool-headed. Amazing.* He watched for a few more moments, now feeling calm, on top of things.

*Could simply blow his brains out from up here,* Hawkins thought, *easy shot. But—that brain contains information I want, need to have. I know why he killed Emilio. Simple. He was in the way, the wrong place at the wrong time. But why did Eckhardt burn those damn fake paintings? And why does he want to kill Riley now? They did both know about the paintings ... Could Eckhardt think those were the real ones? Maybe.* He couldn't be in contact with Corrialles after the massacre at the airfield—the general would shoot him on sight. *No, Eckhardt probably doesn't know where the real ones are, or were. But if he thought the fakes were the real ones, why destroy them? Why not help himself? There has to be a greater reason than spite. He wouldn't take the chance. Eckhardt has to know something I don't,* Hawkins thought, *has to have something to hide, to cover up, something important enough he needs to take the chance to come out here and kill Riley.*

Another thought: *Can I be sure he's not in contact with Berlin in some way? No,* he suddenly realized, *it's possible he is.* They could be leading Eckhardt along while Falkenberg hunted him. If they found out where he was, they could feed that information back to Falkenberg, set Eckhardt up for the kill.

Eckhardt gestured again: *Put the brushes away.* That was clear. Riley shook her head, pointed at something in her painting, touching it up. Her paint strokes were still smooth and clear, but the other hand holding her palette was starting to shake and there was a quaver in her voice. Eckhardt shook his head, waved a hand. *Enough.*

*That's it, out of time,* Hawkins thought. *Shoot to wound. Always better to have a prisoner. Could we get him out, interrogate him? Maybe.* He lifted up and angled into a better position, got his arm and gun hand above the skylight, shoot through, aiming. Suddenly there was a light *snap*, the roof bounced slightly, then a slow, groaning, creaking sound, followed by a sinking sensation. *Damn it! Damn it! Oh, bloody hell not now,* Hawkins thought. The rickety roof beneath him was starting to give way, the corrugated sheets of tarred tin separating, nails popping. Hawkins fired a shot, quick, trying to hit Eckhardt anywhere now, the glass in the pane breaking and tinkling down as he fired through. Between the falling motion as the roof sank and his starting to roll to get out of the way and get off before it collapsed, he missed, hitting the Chacmool instead, shattering a corner, spraying pieces across the floor.

As he rolled away from the skylight Hawkins caught the briefest glimpse of Eckhardt dropping the cigar, turning, hand thrusting into his pocket, whipping out a pistol, flipping it toward the roof, looking to see where the shot came from. As Hawkins scrambled out of sight and away from the cave-in, Eckhardt fired a pair of shots at the roof, punching lighted holes in the tin. Hawkins kept rolling, Eckhardt fired again, a bullet caught the brim of Hawkins's hat, flipping it up into the air from the impact. *God!* Hawkins thought. *Actually felt the breeze as it whipped by,* his heart now racing.

Behind him he heard Riley in the street outside, a low shriek finally escaping, winding up into a siren of terror, running away. *Perfect,* Hawkins thought, *more than perfect.* Riley was outside, Eckhardt was in. *Not getting away,* he thought, *you're in the trap now.* He angled up on his knees and began firing into the roof, tracing the lighted bullet holes, guessing where Eckhardt was, trying to hit him. His new Hi-Power held thirteen rounds, the longest load of any gun in the world, more than twice what Eckhardt had in his revolver. Another shot up, Eckhardt was following him, too. *But I'm on top,* Hawkins thought. *I'll get you first.* He began blasting away, trying to catch him, laying down a circular pattern the other man couldn't escape, spraying the roof with bullets until he emptied the clip. A couple more rounds came up, punching out fresh new holes of light. *Oh, bugger it all! Missed him,* Hawkins thought. He ejected the clip, reached in his jacket, drew a spare, slapped it in and blasted off another six shots. He waited, listening. Nothing.

A thunderous crash. The old glass door in the skylight exploded in a rain of shards as a white object came flying through, flipping end over end. The heavy Chacmool slammed down on the rattling tin, shaking the whole roof, bouncing it up and down, the tilt of the roof's angle tipping sharply lower. *Eckhardt must be incredibly strong,* Hawkins thought. *Did he fling it up, trying to hit me? Or is he trying bring the roof down?* Hawkins guessed where he had to be from the angle, firing off more rounds. A small crack opened between two sheets of tin. Peering in, Hawkins saw a shadow flick by, followed by another huge shudder of the roof. He fired after the shadow. Another shudder of the roof, another heaving up and down, it tipped in more toward the skylight. *Eckhardt's trying to chop through the saplings holding up the roof with his macuahuitl, trying to bring the roof down!* Hawkins realized.

*Why? Of course, he thinks he'll be waiting at the bottom with that wicked black blade—slice me in half as I tumble down.*

*But fine!* Hawkins thought. *Stand there and wait if you will!* He swung around, kicking the Chacmool. It slid down the roof with a scraping sound, bending the tin underneath it, then plummeted through the open skylight with a loud crashing tumble. Hawkins fired around the falling stone, trying to hit Eckhardt as he waited to swing.

Another crash, another small quake, another blow against the sapling. *Damn! Missed again! He's moving too fast.* Hawkins swung back, hands against the tin, trying to hold on to the quivering mess of metal. The roof tipped more, a really dangerous angle now. He squinted through the cracks, watching and firing after the shadow, half guessing where Eckhardt was running back and forth below.

*Wait! No!* Hawkins thought. *Let it fall! Trap him underneath. Think you'll slaughter Riley like the Austs? Slice me in half as I plummet down? I think not, you bloody bastard. I'll bring it all down, stand on top of you, feel you struggle under the tin, maybe do a little dance, take my time and drill you good, wait for the blood to bubble up through the holes in the black tin …*

He stood, jumped up and landed hard on both feet. With a huge slow groan the roof ripped across through the skylight, tipping almost to the ground. A cry finally echoed up from below. Eckhardt hadn't expected that. *Must've hit him at last,* Hawkins thought. As it sagged he threw himself at the edge of the parapet to keep from going after it. He half missed in the dark, head flying out, upside down over the street. *Damn! Falling!* He caught himself with one arm, swinging around in a wild circle over the street, slamming against the outside wall, feet scrambling. He pulled himself up, got the other elbow over the edge of the parapet, then heaved with both arms, rolling back over, getting a knee up, then his butt, pulling both legs through, sitting on the edge, feet down.

There was a noise below. He instantly fired through the tin, waiting for Eckhardt to fire another shot, sliding sideways, crouching down, carefully watching the far side of the studio through the half-ripped roof. Another crash. He saw an object fly against the second sapling holding the roof. The Chacmool! Eckhardt had flung it against the sapling, breaking it. Hawkins fired down, gauging where Eckhardt had to be, holding on to the parapet with one hand as his half of the roof caved finally all the way down. Hawkins slid downward, holding with one hand.

Then he heard a slam. A car door. He rolled around on the edge of the roof, turning backward, feet scrambling on the wobbling, rattling tin, pulling himself up, racing back to the edge, reaching his gun arm over in time to catch the shadow of a car flying down the street, barely the glimmer of a chrome bumper, its lights out. He fired a pair of rounds. The car was too far, too fast, ducking back and forth from side to side. It screeched around the corner. *Too late*, Hawkins realized, *Eckhardt's escaped.*

Hawkins holstered his gun, then turned, holding on with one hand, and let go. He slipped down like a child on a playground slide, the old tin creaking and breaking, dropping the final two or three feet onto the ground, landing on his feet, ducking under the half-fallen tin on the other side. Several pieces of sheet metal fell behind him. He turned, pushing it, angrily kicking it out of the way. It took a second or two to catch his breath.

*Bloody hell, he got away! Goddamnit all! Fuck! Fuck!* He kicked the broken Chacmool hard, shattering it more. In a rage, he snatched a piece off the floor and almost threw it at Huitzilopochtli's open, heart-hungry mouth. A corner of his mind said, *That is awesome*, and he froze, gazing at it in wonder, and dropped the shard behind him instead. *No, it saved Riley*, he thought. If only for that reason, maybe it was truly sacred—it saved her life.

His foot touched something. He picked it up. It was an obsidian knife, a new one, the wood in the handle fresh and clean, ringed with gorgeous exotic feathers, a perfect copy of the priest's sacrificial knife in Eckhardt's collection. He collected the sheath laying on the floor, pocketed it and ran into the street.

"Riley! Riley!" But she was nowhere to be seen. He'd heard her screaming as she ran way. But where would she go? *Of course, I know*, he thought. In the distance Hawkins heard a siren. He began running.

# -74-

It was not quite dawn when Hawkins reached the Casa Azul, parking the truck across the way. The street, the house were dark. *No, Riley would not have gone to bed*, he thought. Who could, who wouldn't be intolerably wound up after that? Instead of knocking he simply stood in front of the door and in a normal voice said, "Riley. He's gone." Then he took his lighter, flicked it on and held it under his face. There was a sound, a light turned on inside, then the old door ground open. It was the maid, Juanita, holding a lantern. Her pinched face looked nervous and distressed too.

"Señor Hawkins. Señorita Echevarria most upset."

"I'm sure."

Riley emerged from the darkness behind the maid, her face tense and drawn. Holding Eckhardt at bay for several hours, the nervous tension, had drained her beyond measure, perhaps beyond repair.

"That man—" She stopped for a long moment, still breathing hard, gulping for air, trying to collect herself. "That man was going to slice me open like … like, a lamb, a clam, a melon, I don't know—"

"I know. That's what he does."

"Where were you?"

"At the field, coming back. Riley, what you did, on the wall, that was brilliant, you held him off, you did it—" She looked out, past Hawkins to a distant point, ignoring Hawkins's praise.

"Where's Emilio?"

Hawkins gulped. "Riley—"

"He had his cigar case! I made it for Emilio's birthday!" Tears started running, her words running freely, too, "My Emilio, what has happened to my Emilio? Is he dead? He is dead, isn't he? Did he butcher him with that knife?"

*My Emilio.* That instantly struck Hawkins. *My Emilio,* she said. *Oh no, oh dear god,* Hawkins thought, *they were lovers, at least at one time. Why didn't I see that? How awful, how sickeningly awful. Another god-awful mess. None of these people could really understand the danger of all this—the worst sort of neophytes, overeager, overconfident, and green as the spring grass. I shouldn't have involved them. But ... what then? What would've happened? No, there was no choice ... Sickening, so sickening, nothing to do now but admit the truth.*

"Yes, he's dead."

"Where is he?"

"At the rendezvous—"

"You left him!"

"I had to."

"How could you leave him! You bastard!"

"It was too dangerous to stay, and if I hadn't—Riley, my god, listen, your heart would be in that Chacmool—"

The commotion had woken up the rest of the household. Frida came limping in behind Riley, grasping her by the shoulders from behind, hugging her, a severe expression on her face.

"If Emilio is dead—why—what—" Riley was now starting to sob. "What happened? The paintings? Was that why—" Hawkins racked his mind for something to say—*What to say? What can I say?* Speechless for a moment. "Oh no, the paintings, what did that man do to the paintings! Did he take them?"

Hawkins shook his head no, still fumbling for something to say, words of comfort, words of sympathy—they helplessly tumbled out, "Riley, I'm so sorry."

"The real ones. Where are they?"

He hesitated. "There was no other way, I have to find out what's going on—"

"You bastard! You gave them to Corrialles! After everything! You bastard!"

"Riley, I understand how upset you are—"

"No! You do not know! You can leave, go back to New York, to whoever the hell you work for! Don't dare tell me you know!"

Frida started pulling her away, her expression tight and hard.

"Señor Hawkins. You must leave."

The maid quietly, slowly shut the door, nodding at Hawkins. From inside he heard a muffled shout.

"And you say you are a revolutionary! Bastard!"

# -75-

It was a bad, fitful sleep. With every sound from the Paseo below Hawkins would startle awake, expecting trucks of troops, militias, rioting crowds, shooting, shouting. But when he rose to see, expecting the worst, it was always deceptively normal, a calm before the storm. A bad dream. For the moment.

After several hours he simply gave up, sitting in his underwear next to the window, only occasionally and briefly nodding off, watching the people and the traffic. A horrible feeling that, overwhelmed by guilt, *what have I done, what have I done*, running over and over again and again in his mind, watching the people, wondering what he'd done to them. *I have to focus on finding Eckhardt*, he knew. *And Falkenberg. But how?*

A knock at the door. It was only seven thirty, eight o'clock. The bellhop held out a note. No perfume this time but he instantly recognized the handwriting. Lilly. *Damn*, he thought.

*Be careful here*, he thought. *I can't let on what happened last night, that I tried to switch the paintings … Lilly doesn't know that, Lilly mustn't know that—I can't put her in that position. That is mine alone.*

It was a thoroughly rotten feeling, having to deceive her, or at least holding out on her.

There was deviousness and deception every day in espionage. That was its nature. It could become a dangerous habit, and perhaps it had. But that duplicity was always aimed outward at the enemy. Lilly, W, and all those around them were not the enemy, even if the people behind Lilly and W wanted to do something terrible to Mexico, and also something deeply foolish. Who was the enemy here? *Perhaps, at this moment, we ourselves are our own enemy*, Hawkins thought.

A few minutes later he was down at the Reforma, nervously, uneasily waiting in a booth. His so-well-rehearsed professional demeanor, the coldness inside to control the outside, wasn't working very well at the moment.

When she turned in the aisle Lilly slowed, looking in his booth, an open-faced expression, eyes drifting the way they do when people are thinking hard over something. She sat in a booth across from him, paused a second, still thinking, then dialed. He waited, vaguely curious, on edge, reminding himself again—*don't let on about the fakes, two trucks, the ambush, the burning paintings, the gunfight*—but, but mostly he felt drained and tired. That realization made him even edgier. He waited for her to go first.

"Roy. Flash an hour and a quarter ago. Bizarre. No one knows what to make of this one, either."

His spirits began to rise, rousing him, from her tone he sensed change, or things in play.

"Have they reconsidered?"

"Ah, well—not exactly. No. It's just … Roy—those paintings are fakes."

"Excuse me? What'd you say?"

"The paintings you sent are fakes. When they got to Parke-Bernet, they were calling them out before half of them were unwrapped."

"That can't be. We saw them in Bermuda—the ship."

His mind began a mad, panicked scramble, a moment of terrifying doubt and indecision—*Did I screw up again, somehow? What the—did I somehow switch the real ones? Did I send the fakes by mistake? But … but—I picked up the paintings and went from Corrialles's base straight to the grove. Emilio went straight from Riley's to the rendezvous. No! Emilio had the fakes. They were burned before I got there. He was dead. If they were switched, it would've had to have happened beforehand—but … but—we didn't have the fakes then. The real ones were at the base. All along. Under guard. And the copies never left Riley's studio. Until Emilio picked them up. We didn't have them in hand to switch them first. No, no. Not me …*

*Then again, be careful—*

"Yes. We all saw them in Bermuda," Lilly said. "But Parke-Bernet did not. The real experts. W says they weren't looted, they are fakes, but the top experts there say they are very good ones, done by real pros, most people, even the gallery owners here in Mexico City, would never spot them. There were various things Parke-Bernet saw right away. Labels on some of the paintings were from the wrong galleries in Paris. The fakers probably got them mixed up. That's what started the alarm bells ringing. There was more when they started looking. The wood was treated. When they cut into the wood, below the surface? All new and white. Not old enough."

"My god. I—I—didn't … Ah—"

"Eh bien, Roy, no one is blaming you."

"I wanted to fly someone out from London, the National Gallery! You remember!"

"I know. I do remember. You were right. W knows. He feels responsible. We kept it too close, that's the problem. But there wasn't time. It's simply one of those things. Maybe General Houghton was right, too, maybe we should've seized them."

"No, there wasn't any choice on that, either." Hawkins instantly knew that. "We had to follow them to find out what was going on, what the Nazis were doing, to catch those two. Leave a pair of Nazi agents like that running around loose? Even if this scheme failed, what else could they do? No. Out of the question."

"Yes. I suppose that was just one of those things too."

A realization abruptly hit him, a little epiphany.

"That means no coup, then."

"No. The insurers are refusing to pay."

"Right. No money, no coup. That's—brilliant."

Hawkins's stomach settled a bit, but not his mind, the news had a dizzying quality as he tried to pick and think his way through.

"Why send fakes? At all?"

"That's the question," Lilly said.

"They can't have believed they could get all the way to a Fifty-Seventh Street sale with fakes."

"It is hard to believe, isn't it?"

"They made such a huge effort, the flight school, the command center, the sets of forged treaties—"

"But those things were fake, too, in a way, weren't they?"

"That's true, they only wanted to trick the Yanks." Then it struck him— "Wait! Maybe ... fakes for a fake operation? Lilly! Maybe they didn't think they needed real ones. General Corrialles caught Eckhardt and Falkenberg off guard. Maybe they weren't ready for whatever reason. After the massacre he had control of the paintings and they didn't. Then we stepped in with our offer to back a coup and he took over selling the paintings, assuming they were real."

"Righto, why would they tell the general the paintings were fakes?"

"They wouldn't, couldn't. I bet Eckhardt and Falkenberg were *always* planning to drop the plot on the FBI first, never had any intention to actually ship the paintings—why was there any need to? They'd tell Corrialles the paintings were on the way, he'd launch his coup thinking the money was coming. They needed to trigger an American intervention before Corrialles caught on he was being duped. The *whole thing* was an exercise in deception."

"Oh gawd, of course," she said. "It's all over, then."

"Pretty much. No paintings, no money, no coup. Anything else?"

"Yes, they intercepted another set of telexes." She checked her notepad. "The first said 'confirm again employment termination,' the next, 'imperative previous business must be concluded without delay,' the third had what they thought was an odd phrase, 'this diversion of our assets cannot be allowed to succeed.'"

"Diversion. That means they found out Eckhardt was pinching the paintings. That explains the initial order to kill him. It's not only Eckhardt, that's a warning to all their other agents out there: don't get any ideas."

"Ah, of course. What are you going to do now? Look for Eckhardt and Falkenberg?"

He thought that over a moment.

"Maybe not. That could take a long time. We'll probably need another intercept before we can pick up their trail. We'll see what W says. I need your car, I have to talk to General Corrialles first, tell him what happened. He's expecting a big check. He isn't going to be happy."

# -76-

The officer of the day hung up the phone and waved Hawkins through the gate. He drove to the base commander's house, another classic Spanish colonial–style building, red-tile roof, a low arched colonnade on wide Doric columns fronting a circular driveway. A valet had Hawkins wait on the veranda, offering a glass of lemonade. He'd barely taken a sip when Corrialles rode up on horseback. He'd been playing polo with the other officers. He handed off his mount and stick, accepted a towel and briskly skipped up the steps, wiping his face and hair, unbuckling his helmet, smiling at Hawkins.

"Hawkins, have you heard from New York?"

"Yes, I have," Hawkins said. He braced himself as Lilly had, to let the other man down gently. Only the news for Corrialles surely would be worse, Hawkins thought, because Corrialles was not the kind of man given to welcoming any thoughts that confirmed doubts about his actions. "I'm afraid I have troubling news."

There was very little reaction once Hawkins explained, certainly not concern, only a simple *uh-huh* or two. "The experts have been carefully examining the paintings." *Uh-huh.* Unconcerned. Hawkins began to sense something peculiar, his mental guard dog quietly rising again to watch the door as a stranger approached. "Something has gone wrong." Still no reaction. The general snapped his fingers and ordered a drink. Hawkins restarted, waiting for attention, or a reaction. "The experts have been going over the paintings. The sales have been called off. The paintings are fakes."

"Yes?" Corrialles seemed to be distracted, waiting for his drink.

"Yes. They're all copies." Corrialles finally began paying attention. "Very good copies, done by professionals, but still copies. Parke-Bernet will not accept them, of course. And the insurance companies will not pay, of course."

"I see." The drink arrived. A long sip. A bland response. "That is very disappointing."

"Yes. It's quite embarrassing. General—"

"Yes, yes." Corrialles almost seemed to be waving it off. "I understand." Hawkins pressed on, hurriedly and instinctively trying to stay ahead of a dismissal, probing the way you'd feel your path in a dark room.

"Eckhardt and Falkenberg, did they—is there—was there—do you think—there was a sort of strange scheme going on? I know they—well, for the lack of a better phrase, originally said they wanted to assist your political ambitions, even though—I am thinking of that treaty they forged—"

"Hawkins, after the … *incident* at the airfield, you said you still wanted to do business. Do you still want to do business?"

Hawkins's mental guard dog was now hackles-up, barking loudly at the door. Something weirdly wrong, something inexplicable, was rattling with a ghostly clamor on the other side.

"I guess so. I'm a little confused, though."

"Don't be. Wait a few days. I think we can still do business. In fact, I'm sure."

"Oh. Very well. Fine, actually. These would be some things from your collection?"

"No. A large collection, like before, forty pieces, major works."

"I see—ancient ones? Like the warrior in your gallery?"

"No. Modern works only."

"Oh, very well—rather, very good! They'll be excited in New York. Time is an issue. They'll want new pieces for the fall season. That should bring in a great sum, enough—"

"I know. And, yes, time does matter."

"But I am a little surprised. Aren't you concerned about Eckhardt and Falkenberg? You did try to shoot them after they tried to dupe you and entangle you in a war with the Americans."

"Yes. And I would do so again."

"You're not worried about that, then."

"No."

"Were fake paintings part of that?"

"I don't think so. But opportunities may present themselves again. Do not worry." He got up and offered his hand. "I have a scheduled meeting with my officers. Very sorry. As I say, let us wait and see."

As an agent of the SIS Hawkins always kept an eye out for things large and small: one did not always know what might prove to be significant. Over there—what's that column of trucks? Overhead—what plane is that? Are those people behaving oddly? One never knew what could be important, if properly put together. But Hawkins quickly drove out, noticing and assessing nothing, oblivious to the army camp, the number of men, the equipment, disposition, training regimen, nothing. Instead his eye turned inward, his mental guard dog trying to visualize the specter on the other side of the door.

His rumination popped like a soap bubble at the outside gate, leaving not a trace of mental residue behind. A car had paused at the guardhouse.

# -77-

A royal blue Packard 180 convertible coupe, the latest model, showroom fresh, geared up and drove past Hawkins as he slowed at the guardhouse, a remarkable sight, such an expensive luxury car here in Mexico City, not the least at a base full of underpaid soldiers and civil servants. Sleek, no running boards; bulbous, streamlined fenders; a solid low purr and then a growl from the motor. Atop the high tombstone radiator gleaming with chrome was another remarkable sight: as if the usual swan with raised wings wasn't flamboyant enough, the owner had ordered a custom hood ornament, a large chrome bull's head with frosted glass horns tipped up at the ends, at least as wide as the big radiator. Easy guess the horns were lighted at night. *A friend or colleague from the bullfighting world?* Hawkins wondered. He glanced back as it passed and caught the license plate. *No. Not at all.* Instead of the light-blue Mexican plates with clipped corners was an all-white plate with a star in the center: 281 ✯ 387 ... Texas.

The top was down revealing a man behind the wheel wearing a large cream-colored cowboy hat with a cigar burned down to the corner of his mouth. It wasn't the sort of cowboy hat you saw in movies now, but from the old silent stars of the 1920s like Tom Mix, an extra-wide brim slightly turned up with a high pointed peak that tipped far to the back. The Packard disappeared around the corner of the company street. *Check*, Hawkins thought. *He's heading to Corrialles's villa.*

Hawkins didn't think it over, watch curiously, wonder why or what, or need to, only felt a quiet sense of intense focus. He drove across the road and down a hundred yards heading back into the city, rolled to a stop by a taqueria and slowly got out, leaning on the stand. The woman was opening up, it was still late morning. Barely drawing his eyes from the gate, with a few gestures he bought a taco de birria, waiting as she prepared it, then took it back to the car with a bottle of *agua mineral*. He ate very slowly.

Two barefoot children dressed in rags, an older girl with a smaller boy clutching the hem of her skirt, uneasily approached the side of the car, soberly watching him with large brown eyes, silently holding up a cupped hand. Lacking any centavos, he absentmindedly dug a one-peso coin from his pocket—a few cents—and dropped it in her hand. The children's faces exploded in wide-eyed glee, and they ran off squealing.

An hour and ten minutes later the Packard reemerged from the gate and sped by. Hawkins tailed it back to town, half an hour, around Chapultepec Park, through Polanco and up the Paseo de la Reforma. The man pulled in front of the Hotel Reforma, spoke with the doorman for a moment, gesturing slightly at his car, gave him—judging from the man's smile—a big tip, then went inside. Hawkins found an empty parking spot and raced after him. Nowhere in sight. The man must've headed upstairs. But he couldn't be gone for long—the doorman was holding the car out front for him. The desk clerk rang Lilly's room. Hawkins watched the elevators, nervously drumming his fingers on the counter. The phone kept ringing. Nothing. The man shook his head, *Lo siento. Sin respuesta.* Not in.

Hawkins headed for a chair, started to sit, watching the Packard still waiting outside. *Damn, where is she?* he thought. Then a minor miracle. Lilly sauntered through the door carrying a big pink hatbox, huge smile on her face. Of course, mission over, she'd gotten some shopping in before they broke camp. Hawkins intercepted her with a slight hug, then a little kiss, whispering, "Keep smiling. We have to follow that blue Packard in front. Go out and wait, I need to tail him, stick with him in case he goes to the bar or someone comes. The car's four or five cars down, nod like we're going for a drive. Be ready to move fast, we can't lose him." He handed her the keys, she carefully smiled, waved with her fingers and sauntered back out, easily swinging the hat box.

Church bells had barely begun their noon toll when the cowboy exited the elevator carrying a single suitcase, setting it down in front of the desk. Hawkins finally got a close look at him. He was a huge man, easily six-four or six-five, not merely tall, but big and powerful all over, lean, not an ounce of fat, with massive, calloused hands stained dark yellow from years of pickling in tobacco smoke. A new cigar was now lit, the gray smoke exaggerating his deep five-o'clock shadow. His size was magnified by the huge hat and a pair of elaborately tooled cowboy boots. One might guess he was an entertainer, but the dark suit was very subdued, only a touch of Western embroidery on the jacket pocket. The man set his hat on the counter, revealing a full head of steel-gray hair and asked for a telegraph form in what sounded like good Spanish—"Quiero enviar un telégrafo, por favor"—his booming voice filling the lobby. While the man jotted a quick note on the form, Hawkins ambled over, bought a paper from a case by the desk and bent down to retie his shoes. Hawkins could barely make out REEMER monogrammed on the side of the expensive alligator suitcase in small gold letters. His name? The man finished his note, handed the form back to the concierge and settled the bill in US dollars, drawing a large wad of cash from his pocket.

The concierge smiled and bowed ever so slightly.

"¡Gracias por elegir el Hotel Imperial, Señor Reemer!" And then Reemer left.

# -78-

She started driving the minute Hawkins swung into the car, pulling into traffic, catching the Packard at the light. Hawkins might have ordinarily grabbed the wheel away, but they'd risk losing sight of him by changing drivers. Lilly seemed quick to learn to do a proper tail, however.

"Roy!" she said, eyes darting side to side, mischievously smiling. "Is this a drill, some training?"

"Sorry, it's not."

"What's going on?"

"I don't know."

"That's not much of an answer. Why are we following this man?"

"Because I don't know who he is or anything about him except an hour ago he was meeting with General Corrialles. Oh, and he's from Texas and has enough money for that very expensive car," jabbing a finger at it. "His name is Reemer. That I know."

"Ah." She stretched up, looking at it over the steering wheel, puzzled, while Hawkins slouched down, hat half over his eyes. They were close enough to hear music on the Packard's radio, a thrumming guitar piece. A waft of gray cigar smoke floated up. "I guess—so what? The paintings are fakes, the plot's over. No coup. The Germans are trying to kill each other. Isn't our mission over, too? What difference could anything possibly make now?"

"Corrialles wasn't upset," he said.

"No?"

"No."

It took a minute to digest that, her smile slowly collapsing into a frown.

"Why? He lost. I'd be upset. Or angry or disappointed. That makes no sense at all."

"When I told him millions of dollars' worth of paintings were fakes he almost shrugged. *Then* he asked if I still wanted to do business. Felt like asking, 'Oh—and with what?'"

"Could he have other ones? Your report said he was illegally looting his lands."

"At first I thought that, too, that he meant things from his personal collection. Then he corrected me: another forty or so—that's the number he used—modern works, like before. But I don't think he has them now, otherwise, he'd give them to me right away. The autumn sales in Manhattan are bearing down on us. We're running out of time. He knows that."

"I don't get it, why the fakes, why bother—"

The Packard turned off the Paseo at the Cuauhtémoc monument, heading north on the Via del Centenario. Lilly easily followed around in the far lane on the wide avenue. Within moments the big blue convertible blew past the train station with them a few car lengths back.

"I don't know. The only thing we can do now is follow him, see where he's going—don't get too close, give him a lead." He glanced over at the station. "At least he's not taking a train."

"Righto. Don't make it obvious."

Twenty minutes later they were leaving the city, passing the usual shantytowns, the traffic thinning. They picked up speed.

"This is the route I took coming in. Is that good or bad?"

"You came in from the north?"

"Yes, through Monterrey. This is the best road, the Inter-American Highway."

"That's good. If he stays on this route he's not going east to Corrialles's little finca, as he likes to call it, in Tlaxcala."

They hit the open highway and the Packard's driver opened it up, going fast now through the open countryside, quickly passing trucks and cars.

"Pretend you're chewing one of those Benzedrine inhalers," Hawkins said.

"I don't need that, I like driving fast. We drive fast in Canada! It's a big country."

"Good. I like fast women—"

She burst out laughing. "Oh, you do, do you!"

"Ah, well, what can I say? The whole world is running out of time."

They began climbing out of the Valle de México heading toward the mountains ringing the valley. Lilly kept her foot hard on the gas, right to the floor, still barely keeping the Packard in sight. The Ford's engine began badly overheating from the speed and altitude—about 8,300 feet. When they rolled into the intermittent stops the radiator hissed and steamed in complaint. Finally about ninety kilometers out, at Pachuca, the road bent to the west on the broad plateau through the mountains.

"That's it. He's going home," Hawkins said. "Pull over and let it cool before we blow the head off. This thing's no match for a new Packard." She braked to the side in a cloud of white dust, quickly switching it off. They got out and Hawkins opened the hood, releasing waves of heat before walking along a line of dry trees, both of them stretching and squinting in the haze of intense high sunlight.

"Well, what now? Is our mission over or not?" Lilly said.

Hawkins sighed in exasperation.

"I don't know. I mean, what the hell? I hate that feeling."

"What?"

"Not knowing."

"Maybe it's nothing, Roy, maybe he has nothing to do with anything."

"It's possible. He could be a cattle rancher buying bulls. Did you see that god-awful hood ornament?" She giggled. "We have to be careful. But I don't believe in coincidences. When you get back, contact W and General Houghton immediately. Don't wait for Western Union. By radio. Tag it most urgent. Scratch that. Extremely urgent, emergency urgent. See if they can trace that license plate, find out who Reemer is."

"What about Corrialles?"

"Right. Then a follow-on report about him, that weird conversation I had."

"Do you think he really has more?"

Hawkins mulled that a second.

"There's no guarantee of it. He could be lying in all kinds of ways. Maybe he's trying to save face."

"Eckhardt was stealing. Maybe Corrialles is stealing."

"Holding out on them?" *Careful here*, Hawkins thought. "I wouldn't tempt him. But where'd the fakes at Parke-Bernet come from?"

"Oh. Right. That's crazy," she said. *Not as crazy as you think*, Hawkins thought. "Could more paintings be coming from Europe?"

"I suppose anything's possible at this point."

"But why would there be two sets, one fake and one real? Why bother! It doesn't make any sense." They sat down on a pair of painted boulders by the side of the road.

"Maybe …" He began turning it around in his mind, thinking aloud. "The whole scheme was a deception. Deceive Washington, start a war. Deceive General Corrialles, set him up with fake treaties, make him the fall guy. Maybe this was another deception?"

"Of whom?"

*Who were they trying to trick—that's the question*, Hawkins realized. *Seeing*, he thought. *What am I not seeing?* Then in his mind's eye he saw the *Santa Lopez*. The secret compartment. Commander Blake and the HMS *Dendrobium*. General Houghton shouting at Perez that the ocean was a war zone. The pieces mentally clicked together. Ships, the ocean, the navy. *That open ocean is a war zone!*

He snapped his fingers, leaping up, whipping his hat off and waving it.

"Us! Of course! Us!"

"I don't—"

"They knew they had to fool us. Lilly, it's like a magician's trick. Misdirection! Or a decoy. They must know full well the Royal Navy's out there on the ocean, keeping tabs on whatever goes by. They might have guessed we were intercepting their messages, like those telexes, or that it might leak somewhere along the line. That's a real possibility on this end, the people they're dealing with, people they don't control. And if we didn't know, there was a real danger anyway that we would stop and search *all* the ships going by, law of the sea be damned, and find them. Lilly! My guess is they did this to throw us off the trail. They want to make us think the whole thing has fallen through, give the Allies a sense of false confidence, get complacent, stop looking, when it's really only a feint. Maybe the real ones are out there, somewhere, right now."

"If they're real."

"Maybe I can check on that." He leaned in the engine compartment, sniffing the radiator, then slammed the hood down. "Let's get back."

"Want to drive?" she said.

"You do just fine!"

# -79-

Hawkins parked at the corner and sat in the car for several minutes, going over the photos of the paintings again. *What am I actually looking at?* he thought. *Or looking for? Looking. That was the thing,* he thought. *No one looked, or knew how to look or, perhaps, knew enough to make sense of what they saw.*

He got out and walked up the street to the garage, holding the prints out slightly in hand, not quite an offering, but to show. Riley was inside with a pair of men, propping her caved-in roof back up with poles, pulling down the tin sheets filled with bullet holes, replacing them. She glared out at him.

"The paintings we copied are fakes," he said. She still glared. "When they got to New York, they spotted it right away. We made fakes of fakes." He held the photos farther out, gave them a shake. "There was something we didn't see. Look." No change in her expression, but she silently came out and took the photos, thumbing through them. "We missed something," he said.

After looking at the fronts, she began flipping those away, keeping only the photos of the backs. To save time and money—the color prints were expensive—Hawkins had the photos of the backs mostly printed in black and white, mainly to get the labels and any writing. But the lab did do a couple in color. She riffled through until she came to those, then stopped, holding first one, then the other to her nose.

"Yes. I did not see this. And I probably wouldn't have noticed, we were in such a hurry. The color is wrong. They used acid, like I did, to age the frames. The color is distinctive, too much yellow in the brown, once you're used to seeing it." She sat down on the doorstep, wiping the tears welling again in her eyes. "If the paintings are fakes, Emilio died for nothing?" Tears began streaming down her face, her voice rising, warbling on the edge of a cry. He struggled for an answer, one he himself felt right with.

"No. It was for everything that matters. He was like a soldier who gives his life in a war, to stop a coup against Mexico, it's revolution. If one is truly a revolutionary, then it's one's duty to sacrifice."

She began nodding her head, still wiping tears.

"Yes. We must make sacrifices. All artists make sacrifices for their art."

"And if we see—if art, if seeing itself is a revolutionary act …"

"Yes, then we must sacrifice for that, too." After a moment, "Why are you showing me these things?"

He sat next to her.

"I need to make absolutely sure. Could they have made these fakes here? In Mexico? Maybe not La Capital but elsewhere?"

"No. There are artists outside Ciudad México, yes, but they are folklorists, very good, very authentic artists, but they could not duplicate such works. All the artists who could do something like that are here. And we would know. What we did, it was a huge project. You saw it. There are many artists here, but not that many. What does it matter now?"

"General Corrialles says he has more paintings. I was worried he was stealing the real ones, two-timing us somehow, trying to do to us what we did to the Nazis. You see? I needed to make sure he didn't make the fakes that went to New York, and switch them here. But if what you're saying is true—and I'm sure it is—"

"More? Another set?"

"Yes."

"From where?"

"I have to find out. The real ones, the ones he expects to get, are out there somewhere."

"And what will you do then? Send them to New York City as your greedy employers demand? Finance another coup?"

*Another coup*, he thought. *Yes, I have to face that danger again now. If there are more paintings, real ones, the coup is back on track. If Berlin can't back one—Corrialles said he would shoot Eckhardt and Falkenberg again—New York and London would surely put their foot forward and sponsor a "friendly" coup. Corrialles would give back the assets President Cárdenas nationalized.* Yes, someone, somewhere would be willing to go along. Finally he answered, in a low, quiet voice, almost a whisper.

"No."

"You betrayed us once."

"I didn't know what was going on. I can't help anyone if I don't know what's going on."

"You left Emilio!"

"And you'd be dead if I hadn't!"

"You will leave us! Go to El Norte!"

"No. I won't. I would help with your roof, but I have work to do." He rose.

"What—your duty?"

*Duty. What is that exactly?* Hawkins thought.

"Perhaps sometimes rebellion is our duty."

# -80-

When she came around the corner Hawkins was sitting half in and half out of the phone booth. It was late afternoon, almost dinnertime.

"Lilly. I'm sick of this routine. Go to the ladies room, take four or five minutes. I'll come and wait for you outside. Make it look natural. We'll go eat."

"Right."

Five minutes later he casually strolled through the sleek, modern lobby at the Reforma and loitered outside the ladies room like he was expecting her, a regular couple, swinging his keys impatiently on a finger.

Lilly emerged.

"The restaurant. This way," Hawkins said, escorting her in on his arm, the maître d' seating them in a circular leather booth at an angle to each other. At the far end a small combo was tuning up.

"Start with a cocktail?" she said.

"I should think so." They ordered a pair of margaritas. There was excitement in her face.

"Well?" he said, eager. "Anything?"

"His name is Benedict Reemer. And, yes, they know who he is! The request did the circuit in a flash. Because it was daylight I had to use the twenty-one meter shortwave bands, could barely reach Jamaica. They relayed it to Bermuda and it went by cable from there. The Mounties in Ottawa put a standard police request for the license plate on the wire to the Yanks, they got it back in an hour. He lives in Houston. Then Stephanie at BSC in New York remembered an article a year or two ago in *Life* magazine about oil wildcatters. They ran down to the Forty-Second Street library to check. There was a picture of him wearing a tin hat, covered head to toe with crude oil. There'd been a blowout and he saved several of his men by catching a flying drill pipe in midair."

"So he's not a cattleman."

"Nooo. They call him Bull Reemer. He used to settle claims disputes with his fists and a six-shooter. He owns Pan-Texas Petroleum."

"Good lord. Pan-Texas? Their gas stations are all over."

"They are? We don't have them in Canada."

"Can't miss them in the States." The waiter brought the cocktails and they clinked glasses. "It just struck me. Their signs are a red square with a white star—the Lone Star of Texas—crossed by a black bull's head. It looks like the swastika flag."

"Oh my … Then here's the big part. London says they are now reasonably sure he was illegally selling oil to Franco and the Fascists in Spain during the civil war. Several million tons, oiled the coup. Did it through subsidiaries in Latin America, probably Argentina. All in violation of the American Neutrality Laws, of course. Franco probably would've been crushed without him. Bull Reemer helped destroy the Spanish Republic."

"And Washington didn't know."

"I guess not."

Hawkins thought that over a second.

"No, of course. They don't have an intelligence service. How would you know if your own companies are breaking the law once they pass the three-mile limit? So—who's Reemer working with? The Nazis? Or is he one of the American companies London connected with that wanted their properties here back, wanted that … *friendly* coup? Did they say?"

"No, they didn't."

"Damn. Could be either one. Or he could be talking to both."

"Easily. He must've lost oil fields, too, when the government nationalized them. Shall I ask?"

"No! Let's not give them any ideas." The little orchestra started playing, a lively *Son jarocho* tune. "Wanna dance while we wait for dinner?"

"Sure!" Big smile. He took her hand and they began a quick-step alone on the floor.

"You dance well. And fast!"

"Thanks. We do that in Canada too."

"And after ten."

"Oh, tard dans la nuit, joyeux Montréal."

"Ah, la joie de vivre."

"Oui. Les peintures, bien que? Could Reemer have the paintings?"

"No. Not with the US Neutrality Laws. And the Continent is almost completely cut off. The Royal Navy is blockading Europe. Germany has a submarine war against Britain. Italy has now entered the war. France and most of Western Europe are under German Occupation. There are only a handful of neutral countries left where the paintings might transit. When I was in New York, W told me that there are now only two DC-3 flights a week in and out of Switzerland, and the outgoing plane is completely filled with mail and watch parts to be put in cases elsewhere. There are only a couple dozen long-range planes that can fly the Atlantic, and they all belong to Pan Am and TWA. They'd have to go by sea straight here to Mexico."

The waiter came pushing a cart with a pair of plates covered with chrome domes. They half danced back. They'd hurriedly ordered off the menu: a chop for Hawkins, a roast squab for her that was obviously not an iguana. After a couple of mouthfuls of the "international" food he glanced at her and shrugged.

"I had a taco earlier."

"Um. A little boring, isn't it? This could stand some mole sauce."

"Yes. I've mainly been on the run since I got here, grabbing food from stands or small cafés. The street taquerias are more tasty and interesting."

"I've been doing that, too! Go down, bring it back to the room, save on my per diem. Is that chiseling?"

"Naw, we all do it. You have to."

"So now what?"

"Get back to W and General Houghton right away. Tell them to look for another ship. And tell them to send the *Dendrobium* back to Veracruz. Fast. I may need Blake and his men."

"Will do. Our mission goes on."

"So it does." Then a fact suddenly struck Hawkins—*Eckhardt and Falkenberg are still out there. Let's not take a chance on anything else going wrong.* He reached into his pocket and loosely dropped Elise Aust's unused Walther into Lilly's lap, keeping it under the tablecloth, out of sight. She felt it out with one hand and made a slight humming noise.

"I gather things have gotten more … hairy?"

"Maybe. Have you ever fired one?"

"Sort of. They gave us a half-hour training. Everyone got it."

"Half an hour? Better than nothing, I guess. Do you have strong hands?"

"I think so."

"Then leave the hammer down. You can cock it by pulling the trigger through. Make sure the safety is off. You don't actually have to use that if the hammer is down. I would buy some more bullets. It's a .32."

"Am I a real secret agent now?"

"You've been that since you crossed the border."

# -81-

It was a short walk up the road in Chapultepec Park to the large white stucco house. Hawkins presented a letter of introduction he'd gotten from Diego Rivera, asking El Presidente to see him right away, as a favor, then added the letter from Trotsky he'd retrieved from Kahlo—she'd hated to part with it, it was Trotsky's last letter. He was escorted from one secretary to another staff officer, who looked over the two letters with some surprise and curiosity, then told Hawkins he could sit and wait in an anteroom. *El Presidente is a very busy man, we will try to get you a moment*, he was told.

Three hours later the aide came to the door and gestured for Hawkins to follow. He led him down the hall to a surprisingly simple office, not much on the white walls, a plain mahogany office desk and chairs, the only color a silk Mexican flag. Compared to the Salon Doré in the Élysée or the Oval Office of the American White House, jammed, as news photos revealed, with Roosevelt's ship models, it had an almost monastic quality. But it was brilliantly lit by large picture windows overlooking the verdant Chapultepec Park, bringing in greenery and Mexico City's high, brilliant sun intensified by the white walls and the president's white suit, an almost blinding haze of light.

Cárdenas rose from behind the desk, suit buttoned up all the way, hiding a heavy frame, extending one hand, the other holding the letters, a simple *Hola.* He looked tired, but curious and relaxed. He spoke English quite well, as Rivera had said.

"Mr. Hawkins, welcome. I have not heard from my friend Mr. Rivera lately. Did you know Leon Trotsky? My condolences if you were friends."

"No, I only met him once."

"I see. Is this about artistic matters? I find Diego's letter mysterious."

"No. It isn't." Hawkins took a deep breath. "Mr. President. I'm an officer of the Secret Intelligence Service of the United Kingdom. I hold the reserve rank of group captain in the Royal Air Force—a colonel. I am here because I am in possession of information critical to the safety of this country."

Cárdenas rocked back in his chair, contemplating him with some interest and amusement, hands flat on his desk, eyebrows raised.

"I am not surprised England has spies here. Most big nations have spies. I am surprised you have come to me. Why would you trust me? I could have you thrown in jail for what you have told me."

"Because I know you want to do the right thing, too. Trotsky told me you were the most honest politician in the world. I thought that was a joke. But I now know he was right. Since coming to Mexico I have seen that, again and again."

"I'm flattered. You are young for a colonel."

"The uniform fit. We were in a hurry."

"Truly?"

"Yes."

"What is this information?"

"Under the direction of the SS, the new Nazi German governments for the territories they have occupied are seizing prominent art collections, particularly those belonging to Jewish collectors. Objects of very great value, including works by major modern artists." At that Cárdenas's mien totally shifted, back to the serious expression of his official appearances and portraits, leaning forward, picking up a pen, a mental readiness, then frowning.

"That kind of looting is prohibited by the Geneva and Hague Conventions."

"Exactly."

"I suppose that is not surprising. Go on. How does this concern Mexico?"

"They are trying to bring a collection of these art objects here, modern art they don't want."

"Why?"

"At first we thought they wanted to finance espionage activities against Britain, Canada and the United States. We assumed they were shipping them through Mexico to New York to evade the American Neutrality Laws. That was my original mission, to stop that. But we have now learned they are attempting to finance the overthrow of the government of this country, very much the way they did to the republic in Spain, and—"

"Who are their accomplices?" Crisp, right to the essential point.

"General Miguel Corrialles. There are others involved. But he is the leader, or is to be the leader."

"Ah, of course. Stolen artworks." The president paused, thinking. "And he recently opened a gallery. These are very serious charges. Can you prove them?" Hawkins drew one of the Spanish-language copies of the treaty from his coat, flipped to the signatory page and pointed.

"Yes, Mr. President. Please look closely at this first. That actually is Adolf Hitler's signature."

The president reached for glasses, squinted hard at the signatures, holding the paper against a desk lamp, then carefully flattened the treaty out and read from beginning to end. After several minutes he flipped the glasses aside. Apparently it was all so obvious no questions were required.

"Where are these artworks?"

"I—we, are attempting to find that out. Only days ago they sent a decoy shipment through, to throw us off the trail. The real ones could be here already, probably through the Port of Veracruz."

Cárdenas's expression toughened, mouth tightening first.

"We are aware of elements who would seek to block the coming peaceful transition to my friend Manuel Camacho. I am saddened to learn this about my old compatriot in arms Miguel. We fought many battles together in the old days, during the civil war, but he has changed. We cannot go backward. Mexico has a great destiny and we must seize it, but only if we have justice. Why are you doing this?"

"I can't live with it."

"That is an opinion, not an explanation."

"I came here to fight the Nazis. I only wanted to beat them. That is no longer enough."

"Ah, I understand." He intensely, rather uncomfortably studied Hawkins for a long moment, as if he could see through to his bones. "Yes. A man must fight for things, not against them. That always has been my ambition, to be for the people, and why I have been successful. When you are in the position of being against, you are always reacting to the actions of others. In a way, they control you because you give them the initiative, and you can never catch up. Only when you are for something can you control events and not be at their mercy. To stand for something is the essential thing in life. There are no great men without great ideals."

"It's more than that. I have learned—no, I *see* now that if you don't know what you are for, if you only know what you are against, you can end up doing things that horrify you. You wake up one morning and wonder how you got to where you are, how you went in a circle and became like the people you're fighting."

"Yes. I sense a missing element, though. What horrified you so that you had to come to me?"

"There are some people who thought a coup a good idea."

"And?"

"Mr. President, I'd rather not get into all the details and we may not have time. But they are lost in this dilemma. They are against the Nazis. And they are for Britain's survival, which is right. But I am—and I believe all of us are, ultimately—for the rule of law, democracy, civilian rule, freedom … and, I suppose, also, at least for me, the success of the Mexican Revolution."

"Ah. I see." Another long, penetrating pause, then Cárdenas's head rose with a quiet *uh-huh*. No illusions what *that* meant. "I will not press further. When you are done, will you be leaving my country? I respect and appreciate your concern for Mexico, but your presence is ultimately unacceptable."

"Of course. And I agree."

"What do you expect of me?"

"Do you have regiments loyal to you?"

His head lowered, an eyebrow raised. "You mean loyal to the Constitution—"

"Excuse me, sir, right."

He smiled. "There are."

"I can't do this alone. I need help. I want these artworks to go into your hands. They need to stand ready."

"Because you think I am honest?"

"In part. You must seize them, to be sure they cannot be misused. Of course, they should be returned to their rightful owners when the war is over."

"I will be gone by then, but Camacho is an honest man, too. He will do his best. You seem certain you are going to win."

"I met a German agent here, an air force officer. He's slightly conflicted over what they are doing, but the interesting thing is that he's very worried the air battle over Britain is taking longer than expected. He senses something is wrong. He's right. The Royal Air Force will prevail."

"Only men and women who have conviction, who love their country, their people, will have the heart to make the sacrifices needed for victory." He made a small, happy grunting noise. "That is good news. Like you, I am relieved."

# -82-

When the elevator opened Lilly was leaning out her hotel room door, an excited, slightly flushed expression on her face. She must've been ready to leave. She had her latest hat on, an elegant confection of fine black palm, with big silk ribbons and a very long orange feather on a stem, dancing and waving. Her note he'd found waiting at the Imperial had said *Urgent— come up at once.* She grabbed his sleeve, pulling him inside, closing the door quickly, feather caressing his face. Her words tumbled out in a rush.

"Falkenberg has reestablished contact with General Corrialles."

"What? How—"

"Bermuda intercepted another burst of telegrams. Like before, they're piecing together several different telexes to a couple of different addresses to get this intel. They say it's quite confusing, some of them almost seem to contradict each other."

"How so?"

"Berlin's redoubled their orders to kill Eckhardt. Mentioned him by name this time." She checked her pad. "Demanded to know, 'Why no progress on Horst Street property closing …'"

"They must badly want him dead."

"Yes. Also 'Second installment payment on way.'"

"The paintings. Same message?"

"Yes."

"Any mention where they are?"

"No. And another one, after some filler about fertilizer sales—"

"Bullshit!"

She laughed. "Yes. Someone said put in some BS so they did. Anyway, 'Remit Banco National de Cuba to Credit Suisse.' Yet another says, 'Congratulations on successful meeting with General Cor.'"

"That's Corrialles."

"Right. We don't have the ones going out from here, only the ones coming in, we can't see the full conversation."

"That's it, then. The general's back in with the Nazis."

"Right."

"What the hell's all that stuff about banks in Cuba and Switzerland?"

"Unknown. Could be more filler."

"Any mention of Bull Reemer or Pan-Texas?"

"No."

"If he was illegally selling oil to the Fascists in Spain it's a safe bet Berlin contacted Reemer and sent him in to patch it up with Corrialles, get the train back on the tracks, get him working with Falkenberg. And these orders to kill Eckhardt, that means those two aren't working together. The paintings must be going to Falkenberg."

"Yes. And you were right. That means the first set had to be a decoy. W, General Houghton, the staffs, they agree, too—what else could it be?"

"I guess. That stuff about banks is bothering me."

"How so?"

"I don't know. It just does, a gut feeling. It's like someone's expecting money back. But Corrialles needs all the money from the sale in New York and the proceeds of the sale will come back to him here. Why would he give any money back?"

"It must be more filler."

"Must be." He settled back, thinking. "So there's to be a coup."

"I would guess."

"Send them a priority flash." He looked around the modern, airy room. It was his first time there. The cypher machine was set up on a desk next to the bed, crank at ready, a roll of tape spooling out filling a waste basket. A suitcase radio like his was open next to it, at ready, headphones dangling from the chair, hissing slightly.

"Tell them no more flirting with Corrialles, angling for a friendly coup. Tell them I said that explicitly!" Hawkins vehemently punched a finger at the code machine. "Tell them I am *not* going along with any damn fool scheme to divert those paintings from Falkenberg and overthrow this government and put Corrialles or anyone like him in power here. They can go suck a lemon, or an egg, or whatever it is you tell people to go suck on."

She lightly laughed. "No need." She plucked up a piece of tape and waved it. "Not that they don't deserve to hear that. But they've done a complete about-face. No coup. Absolutely not! No-no!"

"They have? Really?"

"Righto. They instantly realized Corrialles can't be trusted when they intercepted Falkenberg's messages. Roy! It's thrilling! You won! No civil war, no shooting in the streets, only"—she waved the tape at the window—"more traffic."

She took his hat, then sat on the bed with it, setting it aside, neatly arranging it on the corner, as if that was where guests' hats always went, gesturing for him to sit at the desk. He plunked down, curiously eyeing the cypher machine.

*Incredible*, he thought. *In the space of twenty-four hours I went from waiting for tragedy to unfold on the Paseo, to tailing a Texan, to conspiring to commit gross insubordination and rebellion with the president of Mexico and back again to being a good servant of King and Country.* The sudden succession of images had the dazzling effect of a rapid series of camera flashes firing off, it took a second to see anything.

"I'll be damned." He looked over at the cypher machine again. "This thing looks complicated." Then at the radio, then her.

"It is," she said.

"No troops in the streets."

"Not if we can help it."

Then he started to laugh, several days' worth of tension bubbling off.

"Are they embarrassed?"

"You know better than that!"

"Ah, well, right. Anything else?"

"Yes. You are to destroy the paintings if necessary. Very firm on that. Take no chances. Those are the orders."

"If …" he said. She raised her shoulders slightly, as if to say, *Well, what else?*

"Not if I can help it."

"No chances, they said." She raised her head, shaking it, feather flying, tightening her lips, then sighed. "But … can you find a way? Roy, you must find a way not to do that. We have our orders, but—"

"I will," he said.

She smiled. "Good. I know you will."

*Duty has its limits, even for Lilly*, Hawkins thought. An interesting act of rebellion.

"Have to know where they are first."

"Ah, oui—they've identified several suspicious ships. There's a mad scramble to catch up, I suspect. HMS *Dendrobium* is rushing to Veracruz as fast as possible, and they'll try to intercept if they can identify one. Unfortunately, *Dendrobium*'s about fifty miles north-northwest of Great Abaco in the Bahamas. The Royal Navy's a little thin on this side of the Atlantic right now."

"Do you always wear a hat inside?"

# -83-

Both her eyes rolled up at it.

"Oh, my goodness, I was thinking of going down, I forgot all about it." She pulled a big hat pin out, waving it merrily at Hawkins. "I was already armed and dangerous, you see."

"Truth be told, that'll do the trick." She lifted the hat off and set it on the bed next to Hawkins. They both looked at the two hats sitting side by side on the bed for a moment. She made a little giggling *oop* sound.

"We should do something to celebrate," Hawkins said.

"Yes," she said. There was another long awkward moment. She smiled. "We *need* to celebrate. We've been working hard."

"Wonderful working with you, Lilly."

"Yes. This has been a thrill." She gazed at him a long moment. "Doing things I never dreamed of doing," in a breathy voice.

He reached over and picked up his hat, tossing it aside. She watched it sail to another chair, then looked at her hat on the bed for a long moment. She sighed slightly, tipped her head, gazing up at him again, smiling.

"What shall we do?"

She looked down, out the window, then over at the dresser, rolling her head. Inside a silver frame on the dresser was a heavily retouched photo of a young man in battle dress uniform, the three stripes of a sergeant and the Canada patch barely visible. She smiled slightly, raising one shoulder, as if to say, *Oh.* She took her hat and set it on the cypher machine, then leaned over, one hand flat where the hat was. Hawkins moved over and sat next to her. He put his hand over hers. She put her other hand over his, fingers lightly caressing the back.

They both leaned over, lips meeting for a soft kiss, then a long hard one as they embraced each other. He ran his hand up her back, feeling the buttons, ready to slip a finger under and pop them out.

A faint, regular beep came from the headphones. He could feel her tense and freeze, waiting. The regular beep repeated itself. One long beat held, then three short, a perfect "Rule Britannia" rhythm. He quickly dropped his hand. They both drew back slightly, turning. It repeated a third time.

"The call signal!" Lilly said. "Stand by."

She leapt up, all else forgotten, plucking her hat from the cypher machine. Uncertain where to set it, in a hurry, she put it back on, sailing the pin through with a scary finesse. She grabbed the key and clicked back the response code. A few seconds later she began transcribing the transmission, one headphone held to her left ear, head nodding slightly as she listened, the feather dancing in the air in time with her head.

*Yes. Duty calls,* Hawkins thought. Riley would've ignored it. But Lilly was not *quite* the rebel Riley was. Still, not wanting to destroy a shipment of stolen art treasures was something. And all the wild hats, don't miss that, he thought, a touch of nonconformity, an act of self-assertion, perhaps an upraised finger, her way of saying *so there.* But that was as far as she was willing to go. *Or perhaps now, myself.* Or at least until the signal had come. Lilly would do her duty.

*For me,* he thought, *this is a golden moment between duty and rebellion where there's no contradiction, they've become one and the same.*

He studied the picture on the dresser, the man's face, his uniform, thinking of him over on the other side of the ocean, gazing out across the Channel at the Nazis, boredom and anxiety whipped together in a nasty stew, always bubbling away. Then he thought of Daisy, back in the States. She must be waiting and anxious all the time, too. *Perhaps we have pushed rebellion and revolution far enough for the moment,* he thought. *Rule Britannia.*

She finished the transcription and shifted to the cypher machine, laboriously tapping in the columns of numbers on its keys, cranking it like an adding machine, advancing the tape and the decrypted message. He leaned over her shoulder, holding the feather out of his face with one finger, and saw the characters: *RNI identifies SS* Betelgeuse ... "When you're done I'll have to go," he said. She stopped and looked up, still brightly smiling. For a second he thought, *Maybe not* ... But then her head went right back down.

Moments earlier he was as ready to sleep with her as he had been with Riley, and she seemed set on adultery, too, at least for a brief instant. But now Lilly was humming, happily working on the transcription, and it abruptly struck Hawkins he wasn't disappointed at all. *I am truly in love with Daisy*, he realized, a real, personal epiphany. *How interesting. Had to come to Mexico to see that. Many lessons in seeing here*, he thought.

"We'll have to have a drink first," she said.

"Champagne cocktails in the bar, I should think."

"Ooh! Champagne, yes!" she said, busily clicking away. "We'll toast Empire and Commonwealth."

"And Estados Unidos de México," he said.

"Yes, Mexico and revolution!"

# -84-

SS *Betelgeuse* shimmered in the Caribbean heat as the tug slowly nudged it into a slip in Veracruz harbor.

Despite the heavy heat, Hawkins kept his jacket carefully buttoned. Underneath each arm and below his Hi-Power on his left he'd hidden a pair of leather wine sacks hanging from his shoulders. Each sack contained two liters of gasoline mixed with a dash of pure liquid soap to make it stick and not run. Worse comes to worst, spray, light and run.

And it might. The Royal Navy hadn't been able catch the SS *Betelgeuse* in time—*Dendrobium* was a full twenty-four hours behind. *A bad break*, Hawkins thought. *Meanwhile, the odds are Falkenberg is somewhere out there, in this sprawling city of a million and a half people.* And he could clearly see the ship itself was much larger than the *Santa Lopez*, probably half again bigger, at least, and newer. Not a good break, either. And finally, if all that was not enough, the troops President Cárdenas was sending wouldn't arrive for hours, maybe another day.

*No choice but to stake it out as best I can*, Hawkins thought. The *Betelgeuse* berthed at a different quay than the *Santa Lopez*. As the ship tied up Hawkins began walking along the docks, getting a feel for the locale, what was there, the possibilities. *Was Raul around with his cab?* he wondered. That had worked well the first time. But this section of the harbor was laid out differently, more open. Parking for hours would be a problem. Standing around on the sidewalk all day watching wouldn't do, either. *Dangerous, actually. Too obvious. And too damn hot in the sun,* he thought. *Need some shade.*

Then he spotted his opportunity. A seedy-looking harborside building, masonry or stucco painted bright red, HOTEL in crude white letters, no name apparently. An overlooking room would do the trick.

At the door he instantly got a rather different impression. An older woman with white hair in a tight bun pulling her face back in a near grimace sat on a stool behind a high desk. Six younger women sprawled on a pair of sofas covered with worn brocade upholstery, heavy makeup masking exhaustion and depression in their eyes. All smiled a little too brightly as he passed through the door.

*Ah, no, not a hotel,* Hawkins thought. *Still, these are businesswomen. One thing I already know: They have a price.* He pulled out his pocket phrase book. The women all stood, smiling even harder, fluttering their eyelashes and the fronts of their robes back and forth suggestively.

After sitting on a bed in the ultramodern and immaculate Hotel Reforma with the ever soignée Lilly Billedoux, and, in effect, *seeing* he was in love with someone else, Hawkins did not find this display particularly enticing, although it admittedly had a certain morbid fascination. What would they do? Or be capable of?

Still, there was an opportunity. And he had cash.

"¿Hablas inglés?" he said.

The madam smiled. Enough for her purposes.

"Yes. Two dollar." She held up two fingers.

After a hurried thumbing through the phrase book he asked, "¿Vea el puerto?" *See the harbor?* He pointed up. "¿Sitio? ¿Vea?"

Their eyes flicked back and forth. This gringo did not seem to be the usual sort of freak. What did he want, exactly? The madam frowned, shook her head and pointed downward with one finger.

"No. Aquí." He checked *aquí.* "Here." *Do it here,* she meant.

"Si," he said, nodding and smiling in agreement. "Barco. Visión. The ship. I want to see the ship." He began a hurried pantomime, pointing at his eyes, upstairs, out at the harbor, the outlines of the SS *Betelgeuse.* The madam shook her head no. Then firmly pointed her finger down.

"Aquí." *Not getting through*, he realized. *They think I want to do it out there.* He got his pen and drew a sketch in the flyleaf of the phrase book, the hotel, a stick figure in the window, a dotted line to the ship, holding it so she could see. She still didn't get it, shaking her head.

"Aquí." She pushed lightly on his sleeve, pointing to the door. Fumbling in the phrase book, he couldn't find the right word, then realized it wasn't there.

"No sex," he said. She got that. "Ver. Por favor." Then he held up an American twenty-dollar bill. Her expression totally changed. It was obvious what she was thinking, the girls started to giggle a bit, too. *Gringos! Strange people. A voyeur? Wants to sit in a bordello? Watch? Whatever.* Moments later he was given a tour and made his selection: a corner room with a perfect view. He could loiter all night without suspicion. The women followed him up to watch, curious, expecting *something*. What exactly was he going to do with himself in there? He forsook the questionable bed—no doubt crawling—and sat on a wood-and-cane chair in the blessed shade by the window—a slight breeze and a perfect view.

Longshoremen bustled around the ship, unloading it. No tires this time, the cargo seemed to be a mixed lot of industrial goods: plumbing fixtures, Spanish wine, bolts of Italian textiles. Nothing very interesting or particularly subversive. No evidence of arms, for instance, or crated airplanes.

Given that the Germans couldn't rule out the possibility that the ship—any ship—could be stopped and boarded by the Royal Navy, the odds were high they were using the previous tactic, hiding the contraband *in* the ship rather than *on* it. Keeping track of the people, the patterns of how they came and went, that was the job now.

Several hours passed. Two of the younger girls, who with gestures introduced themselves as Dolores and Estrella, came by, peeking in, giggling, expecting a self-absorbed and onanistic indulgence, making double sure—*Ho-la señor!*—that he really, surely didn't want some *help*. They settled back in a convivial way on the bed, arms around each other, flipping a high heel from the toes, watching him watch the wharf.

After a couple of visits they realized something was in this gringo's coat. That only added to the mystery and challenge. Every little while they'd hear the madam call and run downstairs, then Hawkins would hear the clicking of heels and the heavy thud of male shoes going down the hall. There was always a low din of odd noises, music, laughter and shouts, a tumultuous quality, a carnival in progress, including a porter selling colas.

It was quiet along the quay—most of the longshoremen had quit work, only a few were left—until shortly after eight when he heard a rumbling noise up the street, then distant shouting and chanting. Down the esplanade a procession of men carrying torches and signs came around a corner, singing something and marching to the beat of drums.

Hawkins bolted down the stairs, calling a hurried phrase book *¡Bien conocerte!*—"nice meeting you"—to Dolores and Estrella, who were coming up with a pair of confused-looking sailors. Estrella and Dolores paused on the staircase, calling for the porter. Estrella whispered something in his ear, and Hawkins raced out and up the street.

# -85-

Two or three blocks away a solid rank of men, at least two or three hundred, was proceeding up the esplanade heading toward the SS *Betelgeuse* and a row of other ships. Half were carrying torches, the others waving flags, banners and placards. A solid beat of drums echoed the heavy tread of marching feet. Behind him he heard the slam of doors and shutters, bolts being thrown. When they got closer Hawkins could see Gold Shirts, the Camisas Doradas. Most of the men were carrying clubs or truncheons, ready, spoiling for a fight, the same spectacle he and Riley had seen after the demonstration in Mexico City. Same flags, red Nazi banners, only with a green outline of Mexico in the center.

*Eckhardt was at that demonstration in the Zocalo*, Hawkins thought. *Is he here now? Or Falkenberg?*

Hawkins stepped back into the doorway, smiling and nodding, letting them pass by. They ignored him. Unlike the dockworkers, he was wearing a suit. Probably not a target. On the opposite side of the esplanade a scattering of dockworkers began jeering, running off the ships and docks, out of the quayside bars, confronting the marchers. A bottle sailed through the air. Two more followed. A roar of curses answered back, fists shaking. Safe assumption the longshoremen were all union men, generally on the left, angry at the banners and placards calling their unions Communist fronts. More men began gathering.

As the marchers passed, Hawkins scanned the faces for Eckhardt's, trying to remember the other faces from the riot. But none registered. *Most of these men are probably local,* he decided. Hawkins stepped out onto the end of the procession, close behind, hiding, in a way, using them as a screen, quickly skipping sideways across the street, closer to the ship.

More bottles were thrown, breaking and crackling on the pavement. With a roar the Gold Shirts began chasing some dockworkers. In seconds a full-blown riot broke out, hundreds of men fighting in the street, throwing whatever they could get their hands on. Some of the longshoremen appeared waving iron pry bars, swinging them like swords, hitting the Camisas Doradas on their heads, shoulders, breaking a few upheld arms with definitive cracks.

Both crowds of men began swirling in circles, pursuing and chasing at the same time, grabbing and tearing clothes, knocking and tripping men down, fists swinging, deafening screams, curses and taunts rending the air. The volume rose and rose over the vicious chaos, clubs, pry bars, fists and kicks flying.

Hawkins ran around the outside of the melee, hand in his jacket, gripping his Browning, ready if he needed it, but not showing it, either, carefully holding his arms in against the wine sacks, protecting them— and himself. Not a brilliant thing to be loaded with gasoline in the middle of a riot.

*Eckhardt has to be here*, Hawkins thought, *or had to be behind this.* Falkenberg? Not him, not the Prussian aristocrat. No, this was the style of a dockworker. Violence in the street, that'd be Eckhardt's style, the old Sturmabteilung way that got Hitler to where he was. Although the question there was why? But the escalating fight blotted that thought out.

The Camisas Doradas began suddenly stepping back, aiming the sticks and throwing them like spears, arcing in at the dockworkers, and him. *Damn! Watch out!* Hawkins thought, there were spikes or nails on the ends. The longshoremen began picking the sticks up and throwing them back. In seconds the air was filled with lethal spears flying in both directions. Hawkins began dodging from side to side, watching the sky, spotting the pale poles arcing in, ducking. One landed a foot away, embedding itself in the asphalt, waving like a flower in the wind, twanging and vibrating. A Gold Shirt darted back, yanked it out and threw it again. More flew back, Hawkins kept ducking and running.

Now whistles and sirens began joining the uproar. A few badly outnumbered police officers arrived, firing guns in the air, shouting orders to disperse. Instead of stopping the fray it revved it up. More shots rang out.

Hawkins reached the edge of the quay. The SS *Betelgeuse*'s gangway was empty, the castle dark, no one going on or off. He ran back a few yards, squinting alongside the ship in the semidarkness.

He saw a motion. There, by the accommodation ladder, a pair of men were coming down carrying a wooden case, identical to the ones hidden in the *Santa Lopez*. At the bottom a barge or lighter was already mostly filled.

A rumbling of trucks, the blasting of horns. At the far end of the esplanade an army unit was rolling into place. Hawkins climbed a stack of bales to see. The trucks began unloading soldiers, lining up in a formation spanning the street, the men fixing bayonets, starting a slow march forward. These were the trustworthy units President Cárdenas was sending from La Capital. In a few minutes they would be sweeping the street.

Hawkins climbed back down, running to the edge of the wharf. The men on the accommodation ladder must've gotten all the cases, they were casting off lines and pushing off. Seconds later they were chugging around the edge of the pier, heading away from the riot and the soldiers pushing along the street.

Hawkins ran along the esplanade, following the barge. *Can't be going very far*, he thought. *It's small, certainly not seagoing, and loaded.* Behind him the riot began breaking up, the Camisas Doradas retreating up the side streets, the longshoremen cheering for defending their ground. As they moved along, the troops began setting sentries on each dock, guarding the ships, blocking access. But they were too late for the *Betelgeuse*.

*That lighter's heading somewhere near*, Hawkins thought. As he ran by he heard a whistle and shout and glanced up at the "hotel." The women were all hanging out the upstairs windows watching the show. Dolores and Estella saw him and waved. He waved back and kept jogging.

# -86-

A quarter-mile down the barge turned into another slip beside a long dock capped by a large dark warehouse. The tide was flowing in now, close to the shiny high-water marks on the pilings, the lighter almost level with the deck.

There were three of the Camisas Doradas on the barge and one on the dock waving them in with a small kerosene lantern. One man clambered ashore. The two left aboard began quickly pushing the cases up to the two men on the wharf. When they were through a third man climbed on the dock. They cast off the lines. The one man on the barge backed it out into the harbor and disappeared into the dark. The three quickly hustled the cases inside.

Hawkins began edging along the catwalk beside the warehouse. He reached a window, peering in at a careful angle. The three men were sitting on the carelessly piled up cases, smoking cigarettes, casually talking in Spanish. *Do they realize how valuable that cargo is?* Hawkins wondered. *Probably not. Would I tell them? No. Probably not. No need for them to know.*

But there was no trace of Eckhardt or Falkenberg, or General Corrialles, either. Had the unexpected arrival of the Mexican Army scorched their plans? *Could be, must be*, Hawkins decided. *But I have what I need now*, he thought: the location of the contraband. Even better, no need to destroy them, now that the army was on the street. Time to find the commander of that detachment. Have him arrest those men inside, slap a guard on this place and put an end to this. The rest was up to President Cárdenas and the Policía Judicial Federal.

Hawkins began edging backward in the dark, thinking about finding the major, watching the window to be sure the three men weren't about to interrupt their smoke. Several feet away he briskly turned around and walked hard into a cold object poking him in the forehead with a neck-snapping start. Hawkins froze, mind stilled. One thought: *Oh god … barrel of a gun …*

"Zurückgehen!" It was Eckhardt. Saying *move back.* "Langsam!" *Slowly.*

"Ja, ja …" Hawkins stepped back a pace, Eckhardt following.

"Rückwärts gehen! Hände oben!" Eckhardt said. Hawkins raised his hands as ordered and stepped back another couple of paces. "¡Oye! ¡Muchachos! ¡Muchachos! ¡Él está aquí!" Eckhardt shouted. The men inside came running out. They instantly grabbed Hawkins's arms, turned and roughly pushed him into the warehouse, Eckhardt right behind them.

"¿Hicimos bueno?" one eagerly said to Eckhardt, all three smiling and grinning, looking for praise, crowing, asking if they'd done good. They'd obviously been waiting for Eckhardt. *Why? They're not with Falkenberg? How does Eckhardt even know about the paintings?* Hawkins choked down a brief flicker of panic. *Did I walk into a trap?* Hawkins wondered. *But— Eckhardt spoke German to me. Why? No—wait. Wait! Not me. He's gunning for Falkenberg.* Eckhardt easily waved his pistol, congratulating them.

"¡Sí, sí, gran demostración!" Eckhardt gestured out toward the street and the riot. "¡Bien hecho, hombres!"

Hawkins slowly turned. Eckhardt saw his face for the first time. He looked surprised, half smiling. *No, right! Exactly, he wasn't expecting me,* Hawkins instantly realized. *He's waiting for Falkenberg. That's why he's speaking German. Keep talking, keep him talking—*

"Herr Hawkins!" Eckhardt said in German. "What are you doing here?" He scowled. "Not working for Falkenberg?" *Doing here?* Hawkins thought. That brought on another furious, fast mental scramble. Then Hawkins caught up. *Eckhardt doesn't realize I was on the roof at Riley's, he must think it was Falkenberg.* That's why he was surprised just now. No, he definitely wasn't setting a trap for me. Hawkins switched to German, as well.

"No. I was in touch with General Corrialles. We were ambushed, we thought the paintings were destroyed. Did you know?"

"Yes. I knew that."

"You did?"

"Yes. That was part of our plan."

"Oh. I see, I guess. Whatever the case, the general knows, too, now. He told me to stand by. And not worry. Said he intended to go ahead. Wanted to know if I still wanted to do business. I said yes, of course." Hawkins forced up a big smile, trying to act happy. "This is good news. You want to restart—"

"Perhaps. We started to make other plans. But, maybe—but—how did you know to come here?" Eckhardt said.

"The general told me the paintings were coming in by ship, soon, and to come and wait. When I saw the riot I guessed something was up. Then I saw these three bringing the cases off."

"I see."

"I assume you now want to sell these and get the funds to the general?"

# -87-

"No. Don't need him."

"I thought you—"

"No, no. I'm not interested in him!"

"But the takeover—"

"Oh, that's Falkenberg! Him and those twits at the General Staff. Afraid of their own shadows. Worried we could lose. Want to play it safe. I—my bosses—we don't need any damn fool scheme here. All this bull about duping the Americans, getting them to invade. They'll be with us before you know it, especially when they see us marching through London. We have powerful friends in America. They'll be in charge soon. Then we'll set things right. Here, too."

*My god, of course*, Hawkins thought. *That's the missing piece. Eckhardt— or his Nazi buddies—they're embezzling all of the paintings.* Ambitious, in a way. When Eckhardt took the three paintings, he was aping the big plan, following his superiors' inspiration, a thief stealing from the thieves to feed his obsession with the Aztecs. Stunning. The Nazi elite only saw—or cared about—a chance to line their own pockets. And the same with Eckhardt.

Apparently at least one of the Camisas Doradas spoke some German. He looked confused.

"Herr Eckhardt?"

Eckhardt's expression completely changed in an instant, as if a mask had fallen, or perhaps a mask assumed, a cold look, death or deadness in his eyes, an uncaring glare devoid of empathy or any human connection or feeling for them, any more than you'd feel for a chair you tripped over.

"Don't need you, either," Eckhardt said, in a detached, totally conversational tone.

He turned the long, silenced pistol on the three young men, stricken expressions barely beginning to flicker across their faces. With quick soft pops he put one bullet right between the eyes of the nearest one, the one who said Herr Eckhardt. The man fell straight back, hands still out raised. The other two barely managed a quick, "¡No! ¡Por favor! ¡Usted no puede! Para dios!" Eckhardt caught the second in the temple as he turned to run and popped the third in the back of the head as he got one step away. The first man landed flat like a logged tree, eyes and mouth open wide in surprise. The second spiraled away in the direction of the hand slapping the side of his head, his face a tight grimace, and the third fell straight forward on his face and knees, then slowly tipped over sideways, head running blood.

Hawkins froze, raising his hands slightly, chest high, fingers as near the flap of his jacket as he dared. *Can I get to my gun in time?* he thought. *Damn … only a few inches … what's this crazy bastard doing?*

Eckhardt stepped over checking the three bodies, one eye on Hawkins, gun at ready, covering him. After a few little kicks he shook his head, disgusted and disappointed.

"What a wasted opportunity."

He sat on an overturned case facing Hawkins, watching him for a moment, lightly holding the pistol with one hand, the other around the barrel. Hawkins slowly turned, too, hardly daring to move.

"Horst—what the hell? What'd they do?"

Eckhardt's expression changed again, a curious, penetrating gaze, looking Hawkins directly, deeply in the eyes, the way you might a lover.

"Nothing. You're a cool one, Hawkins, you're used to death and dying, you can't hide that."

"I don't know what you're talking about—"

"How many men have you killed?"

"I've never killed anyone."

"I can tell. I know how men react when they see death. And when they don't expect to see it. The shock, the horror, the way they can't help flinching."

"I am shocked—"

"Not in the same way, there was calculation. You were thinking. A real art dealer would only react, jump to the roof. You gave yourself away." He pointed the gun directly at Hawkins. "I think you are carrying a gun. Are you?"

"Yes. Horst, this is a dangerous place—"

"Reach in, slowly." A little wiggle with the barrel of his gun. "Take it out with two fingers."

*Aiming directly at my head*, Hawkins thought, *never get a shot off in time.* He did as ordered, like most men or women facing the muzzle of a gun, playing for time, hoping for *something*, pulling the Hi-Power out, dangling it between right thumb and forefinger. "Throw it over on the other side of the cases." Hawkins did. "Interesting. You have something else in there. Open your coat, slowly."

Hawkins pulled one flap back, then the other, exposing the two wine sacks. Eckhardt looked slightly puzzled, then reached into his coat pocket for his small leather folder of obsidian knives. He set it on top of a case, still holding a bead on Hawkins, and plucked one out. Leaning forward carefully, holding out the blade, he flicked it through the two leather straps holding up the wine sacks, then the ones to Hawkins's shoulder holster. They all fell to the floor. Eckhardt carefully pocketed the knife in the breast pocket of his jacket.

"Step back—back! Against the wall!" Eckhardt said. Hawkins did as told. Eckhardt drew one sack toward him with his right foot, then carefully picked it up. He clicked it open for a quick sniff, then threw it several feet away, quickly picking up the other, throwing that aside, too.

"Gas," Eckhardt said.

Hawkins mentally scrambled for something to say, "If there were more fakes, I—the general—"

"I could understand a gun, but together this is too much. Impressive cover, Hawkins, my compliments."

"Am I supposed to say thanks?"

"If you want." Keeping the pistol carefully on Hawkins, Eckhardt sidestepped over to the first man he'd shot. "Don't move," crouching down, feeling the man's pocket, then hooking out a pair of handcuffs with his pinkie. "Stick your arm out." Hawkins did. Eckhardt snapped one end around Hawkins's left hand then pulled him several feet by it, snapping the other end through a steel handle on the biggest of the cases. Then he slowly patted Hawkins up and down, looking for another gun.

The curious mask fell again, revealing the same face that shot the three men.

"I won't be wasting this opportunity."

# -88-

Hawkins instantly had one thought: *He missed my lockpick set. In my pants. He missed it. Only looking for a gun or knife. Big mistake, you crazy bugger. Steady, steady . . .*

Pressing the muzzle of the gun to Hawkins's temple, pushing his head aside slightly, Eckhardt plucked the obsidian knife from his breast pocket. With a single deft movement he slid it under the cuff of Hawkins's shackled hand and effortlessly sliced through shirt and jacket to his other armpit. Another stroke cut the shirt from neck to gut. A final one severed jacket and shirt from his other arm. Breathing hard, gritting teeth, Hawkins tried to stay motionless as the wicked sharp knife flew by, only nicking him slightly in a couple of places. Hawkins's shirt and jacket loosely fell to the floor, leaving him standing bare chested, still handcuffed to the case.

Eckhardt stepped back, gun still pointed, sliding the little knife back in the case.

"If you call out I'll come back and shoot you." An excited expression of wonder and excitement began dawning on Eckhardt's face, his whole body seeming to follow. It wasn't a sexual charge, the rush of blood behind a man's eyes that darkens them with lust. Instead he showed a relaxed sense of exaltation, of transport, of communion with another world, the cold expression of death in his eyes gone. "Going to get this one right," he said.

Eckhardt breezily walked off into a side office, looking for something.

Hawkins could see his shadow through a long row of frosted glass windows, the exchange moments ago still ricocheting in his head. The first set of paintings hadn't been a decoy at all. No, they were fakes. That was why Eckhardt burned them—his Nazi Party bosses had sent fakes so that they could embezzle the real ones. *No wonder the Abwehr ordered Falkenberg to kill him.*

The minute Eckhardt crossed the door Hawkins began fumbling for the lockpick set in his pants, checking the handcuff at the same time. *Good*, he thought. Peerless, the standard American-made brand. Not terribly difficult to jimmy open. Eyes darting back and forth between the frosted glass windows and the picks, he began working it almost by feel.

There was a noise. Hawkins hid the picks. Eckhardt came through the door holding a metal waste basket. He set it down next to Hawkins then went back in. As Hawkins watched his shadow move around in the office, he picked the last little tumbler. The cuff gave. Hawkins opened it enough to get his hand out quickly, but not all the way, just enough that Eckhardt probably wouldn't notice.

Hawkins barely got the set back in his pocket. Eckhardt came out with another metal waste basket filled with rags. He looked around the warehouse, then spotted a large wooden crate. With a grinding noise he pushed it in front of Hawkins, then walked over and picked up one of Hawkins's wine sacks. Eckhardt squirted the gas over the rags in the two baskets, then took a lighter and lit both of them, creating a pair of smoky torches for his improvised altar. He sighed with a sort of happy satisfaction.

"Almost ready," Eckhardt said. He disappeared back into the office. Hawkins tensed himself, ready to hoist and throw one of the cases. *Catch him off guard*, Hawkins thought, *knock him down, get past him and out that door before he can get up.*

A moment later Eckhardt reemerged. It took all his self-control for Hawkins not to gasp.

Eckhardt was wearing the jade Aztec priest's mask he'd displayed at the Austs'. In one hand he held a sacrificial knife, its obsidian blade gleaming and ready. In the other, he raised his copy of the ancient macuahuitl.

Eckhardt stood for a long moment, gazing at Hawkins, savoring the coming moment.

"If only I knew the ancient hymns," he said, then began loudly humming, feet dancing very slightly, up and down, up and down in place, head and mask swaying slightly from side to side. Raising the knife out, he walked forward, gesturing to Hawkins. "Lay down. It'll be easier for you, too, that way."

Hawkins shifted his position slightly, waiting for Eckhardt to get close enough, ready to yank his hand free and throw the case.

A shot rang out. Eckhardt doubled over, turning toward the sound. Two more shots, then another, all in quick succession. Each time he was struck Eckhardt shuddered, staggering backward very slightly. He rested the tip of the macuahuitl on the crate he intended to use as an altar, bracing himself, his eyes invisible. With a sharp sound he gasped or coughed. Blood flew out the mouth of the mask, running down in a small tide over the red jade that flowed from Huitzilopochtli's mouth, dripping to the ground.

"As it should be," Eckhardt said. "Death and the gods must be honored." Then he pivoted on the macuahuitl and fell backward on the crate.

# -89-

"It's really you? Roy?" Falkenberg emerged from behind a stack of bales in the dark at the far end of the warehouse. He looked surprised, face, eyes and mouth opening, the pistol wavering down slightly. Then he snapped it up sharply on Hawkins.

"How long have you been there?" Hawkins said, after a slight gasp, then a deep breath, easing slightly. *He didn't see me loosen the cuff*, Hawkins realized, not down there behind those bales. *Careful, keep the hand in the cuff, keep that surprise—*

"About ten minutes."

"My god, thank you!"

Falkenberg laughed slightly. "No, I should thank you, Roy."

"Why?"

"Without you I would never have found Eckhardt, or all this." He briefly waved the gun at the cases. "Eckhardt was right. We always assumed there were British agents here. But I never suspected it was you."

"You didn't know where the paintings were, the ship?"

"No. I only knew the paintings had to come through Veracruz. I had to get them back."

"What the hell—you aren't working together?"

"No—or I thought we were, at first."

"But Eckhardt did know, that the originals were coming, I mean?"

"That's right. I was guessing you—or the agent we suspected was here, would be able to trace them. I had people watching along the harbor."

"You were using me—us—as bait, to catch Eckhardt?"

"Exactly. Never would've found him otherwise, or the paintings. I needed you to lead me to him. Only he—they—knew where and when they were coming."

"What he said—about the army, afraid of their own shadows. That Germany didn't need any scheme here—"

"Yes. Crazy overconfidence, isn't it? Ah, well, look at that, though." He gestured down at Eckhardt and the mask, shaking his head. "All his cups are out of the cupboard. No professional soldier would think that way. Sheer arrogance thinking victory is inevitable."

"But he used the word 'we'—that's not you?"

"No. Someone big in the Nazi Party hierarchy decided to use our operation as a ploy to get rich quick. They enlisted Eckhardt to create an operation inside our operation. We're trying to find out who. Maybe in the Sicherheitsdienst. We're not sure."

"They made the fakes and switched them in Europe?"

"Yes. We didn't realize at first what was going on."

"You—the Abwehr, still want to help General Corrialles overthrow the government?"

"Yes. We won't draw the Americans into a war, but Germany still needs friends. The more governments like ours, the closer we are to a final victory. And if the war with Britain ends soon, Mexico will probably sell us oil—it's a poor country, they have to—but the United States is a rich nation, it doesn't have to, and may not. That's the kind of deep strategic planning those idiots in the Party don't think about. I am sorry, Hawkins. We could have been friends, too, under different circumstances, but I—" A long pause, a hard gulp, "I have to kill you too. I am so very sorry."

"Werner, you're not going to be able to escape this country. The Mexican Army's out there now—"

"I have to chance it. General Corrialles is coming."

"Werner, I've seen you, you're not Eckhardt, you don't want to be like him, to become him, to be crazy like him."

"I must do my duty to my country."

"Duty? Look what duty did to him. Corrialles told me Eckhardt was an executioner in Spain, murdered wounded soldiers in the hospitals, that's why he lost his mind. Duty is very overrated sometimes."

"I have my orders."

"Werner, have you ever shot a man, not armed and dangerous like Eckhardt, but like this? A prisoner? Cold?" Falkenberg nervously started to raise the gun. "Think for yourself, no—think *of* yourself—" Falkenberg took aim, a deep breath, slowly steeling himself, then pursed his lips, slowly exhaling.

*Oh god*, Hawkins thought, *oh god*. He blinked his eyes closed, waiting. *This is it …* A shot rang out. A banging noise in the near distance, to his right. The sound of broken glass. *I'm here*, he knew. His eyes instantly blinked open. Falkenberg's head was turning to Hawkins's left, looking at something.

# -90-

*There, at the end. Is that Lilly?*

She was taking aim again, holding the Walther high with both hands in front of her face, carefully squinting through the sights. She'd fired and missed—way too far away with a pistol like the Walther. Hawkins glanced down. Another shot. She missed again. The macuahuitl lay across Eckhardt's chest. Hawkins pulled his hand from the handcuff, reached down, grabbed the macuahuitl, took a dive and wildly swung it. The hungry blade sailed through the air.

Falkenberg's eyes were locked on Lilly. She was starting to duck behind the door, hand bobbing, still trying to aim. The macuahuitl caught Falkenberg's gun hand two inches above the wrist, instantly, effortlessly slicing through skin, bone and tendons. It fell free, spinning end over end in the air from the weight of the pistol still tightly clutched in the fingers, blood squirting from the stump. Falkenberg's hand tumbled with a loud *thunk* on top of one of the cases. The cut was so swift and sudden Falkenberg didn't feel it, didn't realize anything was wrong until he tried to fire. Hawkins could see Falkenberg's eyes flicking down to the stump spurting blood in a long arc. He gasped in shock and horror, stepping back, then starting forward as he saw his hand and the pistol land on the case. Hawkins stepped forward, too, but Falkenberg was closer.

"Werner! No! You have a choice," Hawkins shouted. "You can pick up the gun and shoot me or you can grab your arm before you bleed to death. You can't do both! Think, man, think!"

Softly crying *Uh! Uh! Uh!* Too stricken to shout in horror, now raising his arm, his eyes locked on the ring of pink bone, red muscle, white tendon and skin. Blood fired hard out of the artery, spraying him in the face, covering it with blood. Falkenberg blinked hard, trying to see, stumbled back and seized the stump of his arm, holding it tightly. The spurting blood stopped. He half fell, half tripped, landing hard against another case, sliding down, sitting against the case, now starting to gasp and cry in pain.

Hawkins stepped over him and picked up Falkenberg's gun by the barrel, prying the warm, resisting fingers away one by one. Not knowing what to do with it, not wanting to return the hand to its owner, he gently set it back on the case, its fingers still twitching.

Hawkins pocketed the pistol, then stepped around the cases and collected his Hi-Power.

Lilly briskly walked up, still aiming her Walther at Falkenberg with both hands. He now seemed utterly distraught, moaning in German.

"My hand, my hand, Oh no! *Oh noooo! Oh gawd!* I'll never fly again …"

Hawkins threw his arms around Lilly in a huge hug, slightly lifting her off her feet, her gun hand held under his arm, still pointing at Falkenberg.

"Lilly, how in hell—what? How did you get here?"

He set her back down, holding both shoulders, grinning the grin of the reprieved, then gave in to impulse and planted a big kiss square on her lips.

"I took a cab."

"You took a cab. You took … a … *cab?*"

"Yes."

"From where?"

"The train station. I caught the Jarocho Express."

Hawkins could still hardly believe it.

"You took the train and caught a cab."

"That's right."

"But how did you know where we were?"

"Eckhardt—" She looked down at the jade-masked body at their feet. "Is that him?" Hawkins nodded.

"Dear god. What's that on his face—never mind. He contacted Parke-Bernet in Manhattan looking to set up a sale. W's contact there phoned him right away. W had his contact telex back to Corrialles that he would fly down and asked where he should go. Eckhardt told him to meet him at dock ten. We instantly realized Bermuda was confusing two different sets of messages, one to Falkenberg from the Abwehr and one to Eckhardt from some unknown person or persons in Germany—"

"Falkenberg said they—the Abwehr and the military—wanted to find that out, although they knew it was high up in the Nazi Party, maybe the SD."

"Ah. Of course. Someone had to find you and tell you. So … I took a cab from the station. The driver's still outside. Nice man, named Raul."

Falkenberg's moaning was getting louder, the pain hitting him.

"Keep that gun on him," Hawkins said. He unbuckled and yanked off his belt, wrapping it around Falkenberg's wrist, tightening it into a tourniquet. "Did you bring your radio? And the cypher machine?"

"Didn't dare leave it unguarded in the room."

Hawkins pulled his lockpick set back out and quickly unlocked the handcuff from the case, snapping it to Falkenberg's good hand and his arm above the other elbow.

"Go get it, I'll watch him."

Falkenberg looked up at Lilly, panting slightly, face contorted from the pain. "Who are you?"

She raised her head, looking down at him, holding her pistol up and out, smiling, the big feather on her hat waving back at him.

"Lieutenant Lilly Billedoux, secret agent."

# -91-

One long flash of the headlights, three quick and short—*Rule Britannia.* Out to sea, in the distance, a ship's blinker flashed one long back, then two short. The outline of HMS *Dendrobium* could barely be made out against the western horizon. A few minutes later came the gentle splashing of oars over the cresting waves as the white-hulled launch, rowed by eight sailors, emerged from the dark. Two sailors leapt out, holding the gunnels, pulling it in by the bowline, steadying it. Lieutenant Commander Blake rolled up his trousers, jumped over the side and waded ashore, hand extended.

"Hawkins! Damn good to see you!" Then he saw Lilly, gaping for a second. She still had her gun dutifully pointing in the direction of Falkenberg. He was sitting on the sand, rocking back and forth slightly from the pain.

"Skipper, meet Reserve Lieutenant Lilly Billedoux." Hawkins looked at her, leaning over in the light of Blake's flashlight, smiling, and added, "Secret agent." A big flash of her white teeth and red lips came smiling back, now delighted at the rank.

"Oh, I see," Blake said. He lightly saluted and extended his hand. "My pleasure, *lef-tenant*—" Lilly clicked the safety on, put the gun back in her purse, returning a firm handshake. Blake turned to his men. "Get the lieutenant's luggage, too."

The pharmacist's mate had already hurried by them, checking

Falkenberg. The medic opened his case, took out a small ampule and gave him a shot of morphine. Three more sailors came ashore, carrying a stretcher. They gently hoisted Falkenberg on it and began carrying him to the boat. The morphine seemed to be working quickly, Falkenberg's groans increasingly easing into sighs of relief. As they passed by he looked at Hawkins.

"Why didn't you kill me?" he said. "Why don't you kill me now, instead of waiting?"

"We're not going to do that," Blake said.

"We're on neutral soil. But you are an enemy combatant, so you're our prisoner of war now. Besides, you're more valuable alive than dead," Hawkins said.

"Why? Where are you taking me?" Falkenberg said.

"You're on your way to Canada," Blake said.

"Werner, I know you've had your doubts. Think about it. Maybe we will be friends after all, someday."

"Ja, maybe friends."

"What's your name, soldier?" Blake said.

"Ah, of course. Werner Frederick Maria Graf von Falkenberg, Hauptmann," then added weakly, his voice fading, "Luftwaffe 86079091."

*A graf, a count? No wonder he and Eckhardt didn't get along,* Hawkins thought. Falkenberg nodded off from the rush of morphine. The sailors waded into the surf, loading him and the luggage, including a pile of hatboxes, into the boat.

"Lieutenant, we have to hurry before we're spotted," Blake said.

"Be right there."

She grasped Hawkins's sleeve. "Roy, how can we go back?"

"Home?"

"No! Not that!" She paused, obviously thinking hard, biting a lip, gazing off, then back, one emotion or reflection after another dancing in the expression in her face. "How to explain it? I don't know how to go back to the plow, so to speak, after all this. We've been living life on such a different, higher level—how can we go back to what we were?"

"We cannot," Hawkins said. "Nothing will be the same, for any of us, after this is all over, after the war. You can't go back into the cocoon. You have to fly away."

"Lieutenant!" Blake shouting from the boat.

"Right! Flying away! Thank you, Hawkins!"

"Lilly, *you* saved my life."

"I did, didn't I? Think of that." Another big smile exploded, an expression of sheer delight.

"Goodbye, Lieutenant."

"Goodbye, Group Captain!" She gave him a long, powerful kiss on the lips and ran to the boat. She turned back and saluted, then climbed aboard. In seconds the boat vanished into the darkness.

# -92-

General Corrialles was wearing his full-dress uniform. He actually marched into the warehouse, swinging his arms, six men following behind, in step, swinging their arms, too.

"Werner," he called.

"Coming," Hawkins said. He stepped from behind a stack of cases. Corrialles looked surprised, although not particularly worried.

"You're working with Falkenberg now?"

"You could say that. Still going ahead with the coup?"

"Of course."

Off to one side, by the office, a voice, "Luces."

Around the perimeter of the room, behind rows of carefully arranged bales and crates, fifty soldiers trained their rifles on the general and his little detachment. An officer stepped forward, pistol trained on the general. Corrialles looked surprised, then vaguely shocked, trying to keep his face from falling.

"Major Ortiz—"

Major Ortiz reached for Corrialles's Colt, ripping it from its holster. The other men held their hands up, confused, looking around, checking for an escape, or unsure if they should, but Major Ortiz's men had all the exits covered.

"General Corrialles, I have orders from the president of the Republic to place you under arrest."

"On what grounds!"

"I think you've incriminated yourself well enough. If you agree to his terms, which is your resignation and permanent silence, the president is willing to have you flown tonight to exile in Texas."

"I demand—"

"I would not if I were you. Yes or no."

He hesitated, calculating, then he sensed something. "I smell blood."

"You do," Hawkins said. He pulled back a sheet, exposing Eckhardt's body sprawled across the altar. Corrialles stared at it for a long minute, calculation dancing in his eyes, then his face caved in, and he gave in, his voice quiet.

"Yes."

"The papers are over here."

# -93-

Hawkins carefully untied the end of the flannel sleeve and carefully drew out the ancient macuahuitl, Eckhardt's original one. He held it up a second, turning it slightly, letting the light play along the eerie black blades, then laid it across the front of President Cárdenas's desk. He stood and leaned over on both hands, gazing at it.

"How astonishing. And he found this in Spain?" the president said.

"Yes. In the castle of the Conde de la Altavista. He claimed the castle was overrun and looted during the Spanish civil war. Said he took it to save it, that he knew it would be lost."

"Perhaps, those were terrible times in the old country, but self-serving." The president sat down, sighing slightly. "I know of this family. They still own silver mines here."

"For four hundred years?"

"Yes. From the days of the conquistadors. Very old family. What about the other things, the blades, the mask and skull?"

"I have no idea. But Eckhardt was embezzling, he probably found them here. Perhaps General Corrialles dug them up."

"Then they belong to the Mexican people. We will send those to the anthropological museum. They are a great gift. However, it pains me to say, this we must return to the Conde."

"Perhaps you should expropriate it in the name of the nation, like the oil fields."

"It's a national treasure, on that I agree. It is unique. To my knowledge no other original macuahuitls have survived. We have masks, knives, skulls, although his were of extraordinary quality. I must say, he may have been a Nazi barbarian, but he had a great eye for art, a deep understanding. Perhaps it stemmed from sharing that barbarism in some way." Cárdenas picked the macuahuitl up, studying it. "And yet, this is still personal property, like the paintings, not an asset like an oil well. It has to go back. It's been in the Conde's family since the conquistadors. We will hold the paintings in trust. Hopefully President Camacho will be able to return them someday."

"Mr. President, I'm curious. I am told Manuel Camacho is more conservative than you—that's why you're rushing these reforms. Why did you endorse him if that's the case?"

"Exactly the point, Mr. Hawkins! The way to dig the Revolution's reforms in for eternity is to maneuver a conservative into defending them as part of the established order. With the army reformed also, the Revolution is now safe. We will never go back. Besides, he's not that conservative. People say that because he's a man of faith, and yes, he'll make peace with the Church. But that is part of the same project, protecting the Revolution, giving them a stake in it, too."

"I see. Of course! In my line of work, I think from one week to the next. You are thinking in terms of years."

"Centuries."

"Right. Centuries. Thank you."

"We are in your debt. And I assume you are quitting our country now?" Hawkins laughed.

"Very shortly." Cárdenas rose and shook Hawkins's hand.

"You are an uncommonly decent man, Mr. Hawkins. You will always be welcome as a guest."

"Perhaps I was inspired."

"I remember our conversation. Go fight for great things."

"Yes, for Britain, but for freedom and democracy, too."

"That is as it should be. That way you will truly win."

As Hawkins left he looked back. Cárdenas was studying the macuahuitl, a pensive expression on his face, a touch of resignation. He picked up the Dictaphone and began a memo.

"To the Conde de la Altavista—"

*Yes*, Hawkins thought. *The most honest politician in the world.*

# -94-

Late in the afternoon the sky over Coyoacán was as blue and deep as sapphire. *I'll miss that incredible high sky, this city*, Hawkins thought. He turned into the alleyway eyeing Riley's garage studio partway down. *I'll miss the art, too*, he thought. When he reached it he found a pile of mangled, corrugated tin stacked on the street. The roof had been repaired, pushed back up in place, new pieces replacing the ones he and Eckhardt had holed. The big door on the street was closed. He was about to rap on the side door when he noticed artful letters painted next to it on the white stucco: *H—at Casa Azul.*

A few minutes later he was knocking at Kahlo's door. The maid opened it.

"Juanita, buenas tardes. Senorita Echevarria?"

"Señor Hawkins. Por favor." She gestured inside and handed him a note on a side table.

He quickly opened it, not sure what to expect.

*Hawkins. I am sorry I will not see you. I have not properly thanked you. But Frida has asked me to go to San Francisco with her to see a new doctor. She will also introduce me to gallery owners. I know you will understand how important that is to me. I forgive you. I know you cannot help with that. The large box is for you. Be safe, Mr. Spy.*

*Perhaps you will come this way again.*

*With my love,*
*Riley*

*PS And thank you again for the suit. I will wear it north.*

He finished reading. *At least we part well,* he thought. *No hard feelings. It is at once too bad and for the best.*

Juanita pointed at a large package sealed in canvas.

"Para usted."

# -95-

Hawkins unlocked the door and rushed to the window, opening it, the Manhattan air stale and hot in his short-term rental on Tenth Street.

*So, back "home,"* he thought. *I suppose everyone needs a base, a place you return to, regardless of how little time you actually spend there. And yet, it doesn't seem very homelike. But I can change that.*

After a two-day train trip from Mexico City he'd spent the afternoon being debriefed by W at British Security Coordination's office in Rockefeller Center. He'd been very worried going in. But it went well, ending with the usual icy martini. Their own mortifying realization of how badly they'd misjudged Corrialles chilled any complaints. And at the end of the debrief W casually revealed a final tidbit, so to speak. He leaned back, put his feet up on the desk, drink in hand, then added, "By the way, Roy, when it reached the PM's office for the final go-ahead, it seems he agreed with you."

"'Bout what?"

"Churchill repudiated the whole notion of backing a coup: No distracting the Americans was his word! And a reminder, Empire we may be, we are still in the business of defending everyone's freedom." *Good to know, even if it was too late to matter,* Hawkins thought.

Hawkins went back into the hall and brought his bags into the apartment, then several paintings. The fakes Parke-Bernet sent back were stacked in W's office. W told him to help himself. He did. He began arranging them around the walls, then hung up the macuahuitl Eckhardt had made. He'd carefully washed off the blood, but it still had a line of brownish red stain. Riley's vase went on the tabletop by the obsidian knife.

He stopped, made himself a gin and tonic and sat down, contemplating it all. *It's rather appropriate*, he thought. *My job—my calling—requires deception, fake identities. My new art collection is an exercise in deception too.* And they were, in fact, very nice decorations.

That left Riley's box. He cut away the protective cardboard and cloth with Eckhardt's knife. Inside were the mask and Riley's canvas. One mask was a skull, the mask of death. Another, a woman—Riley. Another, clearly him. He lifted the painting up, moving some others, putting it in a central place of honor. He went and got a drink, then sat down to contemplate it.

It was a modernist Mexican work in the muralist style, heavily influenced by Rivera, but personal, like Kahlo. Similar to Riley's self-portrait, there were several images of Hawkins superimposed on each other: him as a ghost—was that as a spy? A specter? Another holding the very painting he was holding, cleverly mirroring itself—the connoisseur? Yet another as a … what was it? One of the conquistadors? No, that wasn't it, a knight in armor, shining, perhaps, but the armor was bluish-black and he was holding a raised Hi-Power in hand. Towering behind that, a large man in a guayabera with a sombrero masking his face, a machete raised in a militant fist, ready to strike in a swirling motion. A revolutionary, after all. It was a vibrant, dazzling image, bursting with color, life, and energy.

*Yes*, he thought, *Riley intuitively saw me as a man between many worlds, a man with many faces.* Then he noticed something he'd missed, an inscription on a banner winding through the figures: GRACIAS, SEÑOR ESPÍA.

# THE END

# AUTHOR'S NOTE

The closing days of President Lázaro Cárdenas's administration and the Mexican Revolution as described in this story are factual, including one of the most astonishing episodes of the twentieth century, the mass movement of ordinary Mexicans voluntarily handing in wedding rings and other valuables to finance Mexico's oil nationalization. Nazi espionage and subversion in the hemisphere are also based on fact.

Few in the United States have heard of him, but Cárdenas is the forgotten great man of the twentieth century, truly equal in stature and impact to Roosevelt, Churchill and de Gaulle. As president of Mexico it was Cárdenas who started the revolution of the Third World when he nationalized Mexico's oil industry and railroads in 1938. Cárdenas saw it was possible for a nation to be an independent country and still be just as exploited as any colony.

Highly innovative in nationalizing oil and creating Pemex—Mexico's national petroleum company—Cárdenas laid down a template that dozens of other nations followed after WWII, showing the way for generations of peaceful change and development. Cárdenas redistributed 180,000 square kilometers of land to poor, landless campesinos, built roads, secularized and expanded the schools, promoted labor unions and the rights of the indigenous peoples, and abolished the death penalty. Thanks to his sponsorship, Mexico's arts and culture blossomed as never before.

As a measure of how far ahead of his time he was, in 1940, Mexico instituted a drug-reform program that moved addiction out of the criminal justice system, creating a network of clinics that provided drugs under medical supervision to addicts. It was a brilliant success. Crime and violence fell, police and official corruption were foiled and drug dealers and their gangs all but vanished. So what happened? Under pressure from US Drug Administration Chief Henry Anslinger, American pharmaceutical companies cut off the supply of drugs, forcing Mexico to retreat. (There were some forms of imperialism beyond Cárdenas's reach.)

When Hawkins encounters this revolution and its leader, he refuses to be a destroyer and finds himself forever changed by the vitality of that people's revolution, to which the world still owes so much.

The Nazis exploiting looted artworks is also based on fact. After the German occupation of the Continent the Nazi leadership began what can best be described as an industrial program to strip conquered countries of their art treasures and ship them back to Germany. These seizures initially focused on Jewish collections but quickly branched out into a wild free-for-all of looting. In Paris the Galerie nationale du Jeu de Paume was taken over by the Reichsleiter Rosenberg Taskforce of the Nazi Party and used as a central storage and processing depot for tens of thousands of looted artworks, much of which wound up in the hands of top Nazi leaders like Reichsmarschall Hermann Göring, who between 1940 and 1942 made twenty trips to Paris alone to select artworks for his collection. The first shipment of looted works from the Jeu de Paume was large enough to fill thirty boxcars. Undesirable artworks, i.e. modern art, were often sold abroad to finance the Nazi war effort. Looted artworks went all over the world and many have not been recovered to this day.

The US and Royal Army's extraordinary effort to retrieve these works and return them to their rightful owners was featured in the 2014 film *The Monuments Men*. Europe's treasures were safe in the hands of the Allied Monuments, Fine Art and Archives unit, and they certainly would've been safe in the hands of Lázaro Cárdenas, whom Leon Trotsky rightfully described as the most honest politician in the world.